P9-BZG-376

continued . . .

"If you simply want a book where a female character sinks and swims based on her own insights and courage as well as precognitive powers all the while knowing that the fate of a galaxy will be determined by her actions, this is the book for you."
—*CSI: Librarian*

PRAISE FOR JEAN JOHNSON AND THE SONS OF DESTINY NOVELS

"Jean Johnson's writing is fabulously fresh, thoroughly romantic, and wildly entertaining. Terrific—fast, sexy, charming, and utterly engaging. I loved it!"
—Jayne Ann Krentz, *New York Times* bestselling author

"Cursed brothers, fated mates, prophecies, yum! A fresh new voice in fantasy romance, Jean Johnson spins an intriguing tale of destiny and magic."
—Robin D. Owens, RITA Award–winning author

"A must-read for those who enjoy fantasy and romance. I . . . eagerly look forward to each of the other brothers' stories. Jean Johnson can't write them fast enough for me!"
—*The Best Reviews*

"[It] has everything—love, humor, danger, excitement, trickery, hope, and even sizzling-hot . . . sex."
—*Errant Dreams Reviews*

"Enchantments, amusement, and eight hunks and one bewitching woman make for a fun romantic fantasy . . . Humorous and magical . . . A delightful charmer."
—*Midwest Book Review*

"A paranormal adventure series that will appeal to fantasy and historical fans, plus time-travel lovers as well . . . Delightful entertainment."
—*Romance Junkies*

THEIRS NOT TO REASON WHY

HARDSHIP

JEAN JOHNSON

ACE BOOKS, NEW YORK

THE BERKLEY PUBLISHING GROUP
Published by the Penguin Group
Penguin Group (USA) LLC
375 Hudson Street, New York, New York 10014

USA • Canada • UK • Ireland • Australia • New Zealand • India • South Africa • China

penguin.com

A Penguin Random House Company

HARDSHIP

An Ace Book / published by arrangement with the author

Ace Books are published by The Berkley Publishing Group.
ACE and the "A" design are trademarks of Penguin Group (USA) LLC.

For information, address: The Berkley Publishing Group,
a division of Penguin Group (USA) LLC,
375 Hudson Street, New York, New York 10014.

ISBN: 978-0-425-25649-7

PUBLISHING HISTORY
Ace mass-market edition / August 2014

PRINTED IN THE UNITED STATES OF AMERICA

10 9 8 7 6 5 4 3 2

Cover art by Gene Mollica.
Interior text design by Laura K. Corless.

ACKNOWLEDGMENTS

My thanks to my beta team for this book, Breimh, Buzzy, NotSo-Saintly, and Stormi, and to my editor, Cindy, and the others at Ace/Berkley, particularly for being gracious about several health-caused and other scheduling delays in finishing this story. My thanks to Ace Books for being willing to take a series-sized chance on an author who got her foot firmly in the door in the romance genre first. Since these books have been bestsellers with an award nomination, I think I can safely say their faith in me has been justified.

Additional thanks go to my dear friend Eoin for loaning me his books on small-team tactics and for serving in Vietnam. I was born toward the end of the war, too young to understand what was going on until I was much older, but I do understand now. You and your companions, your brothers- and sisters-in-arms, should have come home to welcoming cheers and helping hands. I'm sorry it took so long for most of you to be welcomed home. I'm sorry it took so long to get your companions the help so many veterans have needed, and so long for everyone else to understand what you all went through, both during and after the war. I do think we have learned from those mistakes, though.

A bit of trivia for everyone: A lot of the ship names throughout this series have been selected from real-life heroes, military and otherwise. I selected them from the past and present, and from locations around the world, ranging from Liu Ji to Simo Häyhä, Max

Hardberger to Nadezhda Popova, and beyond. Please feel free to look them up; their courage and skill, knowledge and effort deserve recognition, among many, many other heroes I had no room to include in this series. Perhaps in the next one, I'll be able to squeeze in a few more.

As ever, this series is dedicated to the men and women who serve in the armed forces, all the way around the world. This isn't about politics or governmental decisions; this is about being willing to put one's life on the line for a fellow human being . . . so those who work in the emergency services, police, firemen, medics, so on and so forth, you all count, too. Your love for your fellow beings is noted, appreciated, and admired more than you know.

The next time you see someone in uniform, please take the time to thank them for the work they do, for being willing to put their lives on the line in exchange for yours. If I have done nothing else with this series, I hope I have helped at least a few of you develop the deep respect these people deserve. Stop and give them your thanks, buy them a cup of coffee, whatever you like and whatever they'll accept. Just let them know that you care, that— hopefully—you now understand at least a little of why they're in that uniform, doing what they do, with all the risks and dangers and insanities they may have to face in the course of their day.

Let them know that you'll always remember to welcome them home, regardless of the areas they served in or the outcomes of any wars.

Enjoy,
Jean

CHAPTER 1

Yet another joy-filled delay . . . Thank you again for being willing to pause this interview so I could take care of certain shipboard details. We're getting close to bringing everything up to date, though, so I trust you'll find this last leg worth the wait. And I thank you for allowing me to address everything chronologically, since I know some of what's coming up contains some of the biggest questions people have held about me, my plans, and, well, everything. At least this way, you and your viewers will have a reasonably solid understanding of everything that led up to these things.

Now, if I remember correctly, we'd reached the point where I had destroyed my previous ship, the TUPSF Hellfire, to keep it out of enemy hands—which enemy? The Feyori, of course. The undergalaxy isn't my concern. There's no way a Salik or a Choya or even a Grey could get onto my ship without my permission, let alone a Human impostor . . . but the Meddlers are another matter. Unfor-

tunately, there was only one way to keep the Hellfire *out of their hands and, at the same time, force them into faction with me—and yes, I had the Admiral-General's permission. Extremely reluctant permission, but it wasn't as if I could pilot two starships at once, so* Hellfire *had to make way for* Damnation . . . *which is ironically apropos, given the hardship that followed.*

I can't go into all the details of that incident, since most of it is still classified, but I can pick up the thread with my arrival on Dabin—if you've never been to Dabin and can tolerate the gravity, I can recommend going there for a vacation once the war ends. Gorgeous world, even if it's still recovering. I can honestly say I would love to go there again, once the war is over . . . Actually, a lot of places are like that.

But that's a thought for the future, and we're here to talk about the past, aren't we?

~Ia

JUNE 3, 2498 TERRAN STANDARD
OUTSKIRTS OF ELTEGAR CITY
JOINT COLONYWORLD DABIN, DABINAE SYSTEM

Three silvery, interclinging soap bubbles slipped their way down past the ugly, ceristeel-coated Salik vessels in orbit. Descending through the layers of Dabin's atmosphere, they ignored the heat of reentry because there was no matter for the air to rub against for the necessary friction. A slight course correction brought them down through the night toward a particular scattering of lights; otherwise, their descent was steady.

At the edge of those lights, they swerved again, detouring

toward the hydroplant powering the town. Drifting to a stop just in front of the step-down station, the silvery soap bubbles dipped down into the faintly humming cables. The town lights in the distance dimmed slightly, then blinked out for a few seconds.

All three surfaces darkened until one of the bubbles popped. The lights in the distance flicked back on. A new figure dropped toward the ground, falling from the middle position. At nearly twice Terran Standard Gravity, the pull of the planet made the female Human drop fast . . . except she slowed at the last moment. Telekinesis cushioned her landing, burning off the excess energy left over from her transformation.

Ia touched down with a sigh. The gravity was the same one she and her crew had slowly gotten used to over the last two years, though not nearly as strong as the pull of the planet she'd grown up on. Raking her chin-length white locks back from her face, she looked up at the other two bubbles, who were now merely sipping on the energies contained in the power lines overhead.

She still wore the same rumpled clothing from just a few days before: gray shirt and slacks with black stripes down the legs and sleeves; gray underthings and black ship boots; a gray plexi officer's bracer clasped over her shirtsleeve on her left forearm; and a crystalline bracer tucked under the sleeve of her right arm, its faint glow barely visible at the cuff opening. Her companions still looked like two dark, silvery soap bubbles roughly half the size of hovercars.

(*Thank you for the lift,*) she sent telepathically. It wasn't a strong psychic gift—one of her weakest, in fact—but she managed to make herself heard. Not that they couldn't have read her mind directly, but that wouldn't be polite . . . and they were now more or less equals. Or rather, she was now a fellow Player in the Feyori's great Game. (*I'm still not very good at that whole interstellar-travel thing, and I won't get a lot of chances to practice anytime soon.*)

(*The principle is the exact same as your faster-than-light technology: projecting a field of energy that neutralizes the Higgs Field, a bubble that "greases" you through space, and make one side slippery enough to squirt you past the speed of light,*) Belini replied. She was the silvery soap bubble on the left. (*You just haven't learned yet how to regurgitate and reshape your food on demand. It's all about projectile vomiting,*) she giggled mentally.

Ia rolled her eyes. Belini had a strange sense of humor at times. (*Like I said, I won't get a chance to practice much, so thank you for the lift. But it was worth it,*) Ia added. (*I'm glad so many of you were swayed to my cause.*)

(*I don't think you've convinced all of 'em, kid,*) Kierfando warned her. He was the soap bubble on her right as she looked up at the two aliens. (*Not one hundred percent.*)

(*I know I haven't. It'll be an uphill struggle to get enough of your people on my side in time to do the most good,*) Ia agreed. (*But they'll see how determined I am to help them when they do faction with me, now that they're all watching me.*)

(*I know Miklinn will be furious when he finds out. He will continue to counterfaction you,*) Belini warned Ia. (*A pity you didn't pull him in. But you did pull in and receive ten times the quorum you needed for formal recognition, so you're not the least-ranked among us . . . which is bound to upset a few of the others. Hopefully, they'll be smart enough to faction with you.*) A touch of smugness colored her sending. (*As for myself, I've just made up all the ground you made me lose, and plenty more. I'm now almost three times higher-ranked than I was before.*)

(*I told you I'd repay your faith in me,*) Ia told the sphere on the left, giving her sponsor a brief, theatrical bow.

She shifted her attention back to the one on her right. To her Human eyes, they looked the same, virtually identical silvery soap bubbles. To her inner senses, they were distinct individuals. To the needs of the future . . . well, their species tried to make the matter-based races their pawns. Ia had to use them the same way. At least her reasons and needs were aimed for the good of all and not some sort of Game-based whim.

(*Thank you for* your *help and support, Kierfando,*) she told him, though "he" was only a male by choice in this era. His long-lived species didn't exactly correspond to Human analogs in their native state. (*You'd better get back to V'Dan, though. You have a couple of the younger ones jockeying for power in your absence. Both of you need to get going within two minutes, or you'll lose momentum back in your home territories.*)

(*You'll be fine out here?*) he asked her, sounding a bit like a fond uncle fussing over his niece. In the sense that her father was a fellow Feyori, he probably was. (*We could move you closer if you like, but all of us needed a good meal, first.*)

Ia shook her head. (*I'll be fine. I'm about to call up my Company and let them know I've arrived. They'll make sure I get to where I need to go in time to start doing some good.*) Something cold and wet smacked into the tip of her nose. Squinting, Ia looked up, then sighed as another droplet hit her chin and her cheek. A fourth stung her forehead. She wrinkled her nose. (*Lovely, it's starting to rain. Lucky you. Energy beings aren't affected by things like rain, unlike us matter-based ones. Well, maybe by the thermal chill of the water . . .*)

(*That's because you limit yourself to matter-based*

concerns,) Kier sent, a mild scolding and a dry quip rolled into one. (*You have a very compelling reason from a matter-based perspective, but it's still a limiting one. We'll see you soon. Pluck our strings in the way I showed you if you wish to talk. But beware that we ourselves are not in faction to the Dabin contingent, on either side of the war. You will be hard-pressed to convince them without another massive squandering of energy.*)

(*Remember also that plucking our strings for a summoning costs energy as well, and stock up before you call again. You don't want to drain yourself. Starvation in a Feyori can be deadly if you don't conserve your reserves carefully,*) Belini cautioned her. (*At least we could come back to rescue you, this time. Do also take into account that we may be busy with our own concerns since we now have some serious realigning to do following your little shake-up. You're lucky I'm inclined to think this'll be fun instead of a stellar-sized headache.*) Sucking one last time on the power cables, she swirled and lifted into the sky.

Kier did the same, dipping into the electrical current before following her. (*Take care, half-breed. As you fleshies put it, straddling the fence between two worlds may give you a foot in each world, but it also gives you a hell of a wedgie if you're not careful.*)

Caught off guard by his quip, Ia chuckled. She watched for as long as she could detect movement in the sky as he left, following Belini up to where they could feast on the local solar winds for a bit more energy, then sighed. Alone in the late-evening drizzle, she flipped open the lid of her command unit.

The buttons of the interior had no symbols on them, in order to prevent outsiders from accessing their functions; instead, every soldier in the Terran Space Force had to memorize which rounded square did what. Punching in the contact codes for her second-in-command's unit, Ia started walking toward the town.

It took him twenty seconds to answer. When he did, Meyun Harper's voice was both startled and relieved. And sleepy-sounding. *"—Captain? Ia, is that you? I, uh . . . time, time . . . You're almost half a day late!"*

"And a good evening to you, too," Ia replied, smiling. *"Turns out I didn't have a knack for mastering the trick of interstellar flight without a ship. I had to get a lift from some friends. Any chance you could send me some matter-based transport? All I have at the moment are my clothes, ship boots, and arm unit."*

She heard a fumbling sound, followed by a loud clatter and a crude epithet. *"—Sorry, dropped the arm unit. Uh . . . ground car, we can do. I think. The Army hasn't been entirely cooperative about our presence here, mostly because of the higher-ups. Captain Roghetti has been fairly good about it. But it'll take time. Unless you can come up with something better I can commandeer?"*

"I am aware of the difficulties of our situation, Commander," Ia admitted. *"Give me a moment to check the timestreams."*

Aside from the pattering of the rain and the crunching of her boots as she walked along the gravel-paved access road leading away from the substation, there was nothing but her voice and his to break the quiet of the night. Off in the far distance, small flashes of orange and reddish light lit up pockets of the horizon, a reminder that this colony world was busy battling a ruthless, hungry enemy. But that was dozens of kilometers away. Turning most of her attention inward, down and around, she flipped her attention onto the timeplains.

Telepathy wasn't her strongest psychic gift. Precognition was. The local timestreams were just that: a visualization of rivulets and creeks crossing a vast, grassy prairie. Each stream represented a life, and wherever they touched and crossed lay a nexus of interactions rich with possibilities and rife with probabilities.

Dabin—or at least the local corner of this world—was a particularly muddy world, both literally and temporally. There were many things the enemy could do to block them from leaving, and many things they could do to counteract their foe. But there were other enemies, too: arrogance, fear, and apathy among them. Those were doing their own work, clouding the waters, fogging the probabilities. Such factors weakened the overall war effort by eating away at the hearts of the men and women struggling to fight back a strong enemy presence on this heavy-gravitied world.

"*. . . Contact Lieutenant Frederich. He has a ground car that can come pick me up. Tell him we'll swing by the liquor store, my treat, so he can call it an official beer run if his commander asks,*" Ia added.

Meyun chuckled. "*This from a woman who doesn't drink.*"

"*Alcohol ruins my self-control faster than sex,*" she quipped back. "*But that doesn't mean I'll stop others from having fun.*"

"*Sex and alcohol? Does this mean I get to call it a date when I come pick you up?*" he asked, humor still warming his tone.

"*He'll insist on driving the car himself,*" Ia warned her second-in-command. "*So unless you want the lieutenant to watch . . . ?*"

"Shakk *that. But I will take a rain check.*"

Squinting up at the clouds as the droplets started coming

down in greater numbers, Ia sighed. *"You would have to mention the 'R' word . . . Bring a thermal blanket and some towels so I can dry off on the ride back. I'll keep my unit active, so you can trace my position. And don't dawdle, Commander."*

"Aye aye, sir. Harper out."

Tapping the buttons that would keep a subchannel linked between their units, Ia closed the lid. She kept walking, not having anything better to do. Examining the timestreams as she headed west, Ia peered both upstream into the past as well as downstream into the future. Her stomach rumbled with hunger, threatening to distract her, and the rain only made her thirsty. Electricity from the town's power grid had fed her in her other form, but it did nothing for her as a matter-based Human.

Ia did her best to ignore those discomforts as there was nothing she could do about them just yet. She had bigger worries than where her next meal was coming from, or when. The Salik had landed here in force, and in person.

Nobody expected a race of flipper-footed aliens from a lightly gravitied planet to want to invade a heavyworld. But Dabin was a mostly warm, M-class planet without too many inimical native life-forms, and none of them sentient beyond the Humans who had claimed it. Dabin was ideal for most oxygen-breathing, carbon-based life-forms to colonize and inhabit once the gravity problem was overcome.

Normally, that took a couple generations of adaptation as people moved from one world to the next, increasing their gravitational endurance generation by generation. The Humans back on her own homeworld, Sanctuary, were still struggling to adapt to its exceptionally high gravity, but Humans had evolved as fairly sturdy creatures. Only the Solaricans and the K'Kattans could match them. The

K'Kattans themselves were natural heavyworlders, evolved with a dual endo-exo skeletal system, but even they had to spend a few generations adapting to planets outside their comfort zone.

The Salik had done something similar via the gradually increasing tug of artificial gravity, slowly breeding several generations of their kind in crèches hidden in the black depths of interstitial space. They still couldn't invade truly heavy-gravitied worlds, but then not every M-class world was as water-rich a prize as Dabin. With low mountains, shallow oceans, and mild winters, the planet was nearly ideal for their amphibious species, very much like their Motherworld, Sallha.

Ia knew through the timestreams of the past that this invasion had been carefully planned for almost 150 Terran years. She also knew through the streams stretching into the future that if the Salik gained the upper hand on this world here, it would take far too long to dislodge them. She needed them pushed off this planet, and pushed off soon, before the worst of the war unfolded.

The colonists did have a few advantages on this planet. Elsewhere, the Salik were using robots to augment their troops in combat. Mostly they were used on various dome-worlds, where the vacuum of space or the thin atmospheres outside those self-contained biospheres wouldn't slow them down for long. But robots, however cleverly programmed, had three weaknesses.

One, they were mechanical, so they were vulnerable to water, weather, and the sucking muds of the wilderness, however well sealed they might be made. Two, destroying them outright or turning them off was far less of an ethical problem for troops than slaying living sentients; colonists rarely hesitated to shoot robots when the two forces were even vaguely close to being equal. And three, they were reprogrammable, either to shut them off *en masse*, or turn them against their masters.

Humans didn't use artificially intelligent robots anymore. Not after the mistakes of the AI War . . . and the Salik were beginning to relearn the cost of those mistakes thanks to the Alliance's counterprogramming efforts. But that was on other worlds. This fight was on Dabin.

For this world, the Salik had bred organic weapons. They liked the thrill of the hunt—needed to hunt, psychologically— and had maintained many of their wilderness areas on their Motherworld with a near-fanatic zeal. The Salik had brought in fast-growing carnivorous vines, hunting beasts that would herd the colonists into easily contained zones . . . even nuisance pests. Those were supposed to inject a narcotic into their victim's blood to make each colonist and planetary defender sleepy.

They hadn't worked all that well once the bugs had been released into the field. Apparently, the local leathery-winged avians were thoroughly enjoying them as a special snack, snapping them up faster than they could infect and breed. It was a modest break for the colonists. Ia smiled to herself as she checked a report on that fact in the life-stream of a local xenobiologist. She only skimmed the waters of the man's life, though, before moving on to the next key checkpoint.

The colonists knew the terrain and were used to dealing with potentially dangerous wildlife. They had various weapons, plenty of ingenuity, and a certain tough, survivalist mind-set on their side. They even had almost four hundred thousand soldiers from the Space Force Army on their side, culled either from Dabin's own recruits or from colonists from similar heavyworlds. Those troops had been dropped off to protect the planet before the blockade had gone up, preventing the Space Force from bringing in any more.

Unfortunately, four hundred thousand wasn't nearly enough since those forces were scattered across a colony-world one and a half times the size of Earth. The Salik had more than twice as many troops, top-quality arms and armaments for all their soldiers, and ships in orbit blockading most sources of outside help. Beyond their systematic pogrom of destroying anything mechanical that took to the skies above a thousand meters, the frogtopus-like aliens had plenty of psychological horror on their side, too. They ate their captives, after all, preferably while still kicking and screaming.

The Humans and handful of other races who had settled on this world for more than a century and a half had the superior numbers, true. Before the war started, Dabin had boasted a population of over 300 million Humans. But this was a Joint Colonyworld, neither fully Terran nor fully V'Dan, one that was still a few decades away from true independence. They were still trying to build up their local military and defense forces, which meant relying upon whatever the Terrans and the V'Dan could spare . . . which wasn't much, at the moment. The Salik had the superior force multipliers, and were slowly winning the war on this world.

That was why the Damned were here. Something which Ia and her Company would do in the next two months would tip the scales in the Alliance's favor, but Ia didn't know what, yet. She had battle plans that would work, but it was something else, something more. Something that required her to personally be here to pull it off. Most days, the timestreams were fairly easy for her to see. Do X, and Y would happen, or do G, and H would follow, depending on which outcome she wanted. Dabin, however, was a nexus. Too many possibilities, with too many tiny little butterfly effects tipping the scales wildly out of balance one way or another. Mainly because there were two Feyori at work here, neither of them yet in faction to—

Ia stopped. Something wasn't right. She'd turned the correct way when her boots reached the paved road, heading away from the town. She knew she had. Her forces were bivouacked with one of the Companies from the 1st Division 6th Cordon Army, camped halfway to the nearest battle line somewhere several kilometers ahead of her. Salik scouts, if they slipped through the 1st's lines, would be approaching most likely from ahead. The sense of danger came from behind her.

The road had solar lights embedded in the slightly bouncy plexcrete, forming three parallel, dotted lines that stretched off in either direction. They delineated the driving lanes for ground cars and gave aircars a point of reference for night flying. One of those pale yellow lights a couple hundred meters away winked out for a brief moment. Trailing mental fingers through the waters of her immediate future, Ia bit back a curse. She was being hunted by a not-cat.

That was the best way to describe the beast: *not* a cat. Not a typical cat by three meters long, with a prehensile, poison-barbed tail, armor-tough scales, long claws, and overly sharp teeth on a jaw that could unhinge itself on a frighteningly wide scale, much like a cobra's. The only weapons she had with her were her psychic abilities and the crystal bracer encircling her right wrist. The psychic ones were a little underpowered at the moment. It was cold out, she was wet, and she had a long way to go before she could rest, which meant conserving her energy.

Though she had eaten energy in the last couple of days, she hadn't eaten physically. That made a difference. There were little things she could do. Telepathy, a short spot of telekinesis in a pinch, even a little electrokinetic manipulation. Not much more than that, though. Not until she ate and slept. The attempt at flying through the depths of space Feyori-style had exhausted her, forcing her to call on two of her faction-allies for a lift, which had drained her even more.

She did what she could do, though. Drawing energy from the crysium bracelet, she molded it down out of her sleeve, reshaping it with a couple of practiced thoughts. The biokinetic mineral glowed faintly, forming the slender lines of a swept-hilt schlager. A touch of electrokinesis rehardened the tough mineral, making it radiate a slightly brighter shade of peach-gold. It might have been a few years since she last served in the Marines, but Ia hadn't neglected her combat training. That included wielding a sword as well as a laser rifle.

That ambient, crystalline glow blurred when she slashed the weapon up, ducking down and to her left at the same moment. She hadn't seen the not-cat pounce with her eyes, but she wasn't looking at this battle physically. Her psychic abilities, her battlecognition, had been honed in hand-to-hand combat years ago even if this fight was technically sword-to-claws.

The blade smacked through something, evoking a howling hiss. It was probably expecting a tasty civilian. A soft, frightened colonist. What it got was a Terran Marine who had not stopped her daily weapons drills just because she'd moved on to serve in the Navy as an officer, then into the Special Forces as the captain of her own ship.

It pounced and lashed again. Droplets of rain sprayed outward from the whipping tail. She swirled, swiped, then stabbed, catching it in the shoulder. Her reflexes were dulled a little from exhaustion and hunger. The not-cat's were slowing from its injuries. Lights appeared in the distance, coming from a trio of ground cars. It wasn't Harper and Frederich, though; these lights were coming from the direction of the town.

The not-cat attacked again, trying to take advantage of her distraction. Bred for high gravity, it was fast, and slashed at her thigh. Bred for even higher gravity, Ia lopped off its right forepaw. Crysium was not only tough, it was a mono-crystal shaped to a monofractally flawless edge. Biological armor wasn't nearly strong enough to slow the blade down, let alone stop its attack.

Yowl-screeching, the cat hopped back. Its long tail lifted and whipped toward her, barely visible in the night. Ia slashed again, severing the lashing limb based on the prob-abilities of its incoming position, not on pure sight. The stinger hit her, but not point-first; chopped off, it tumbled, struck her shirt with a splat of warm blood, and fell to the pavement. Torn between the instinct to fight and the sheer instinct for survival as its leg and its now stump of a tail bled, the not-cat hesitated.

The poor thing never had a chance. Ia lunged hard, stab-bing it deep in the side, piercing its circulatory organ. Hot breath and angry teeth snapped shut centimeters from her face. Her arm jolted, hilt cracking the creature's ribs. A touch of overkill, maybe, but she still had to yank the blade out and scramble backwards while it thrashed and snarled and tried to deny it was dead.

Dark blood pooled on the road and coated her blade in a translucent crimson smear. The scaly hide of the shuddering creature glistened in a damp shade of bluish green smeared with deep red when the approaching lead car activated a spotlight, flooding the road with bright white light. Like many of the living creatures found on various worlds, its blood was hemoglobin-based; the floodlight picked out the puddle of it now spreading across the damp road.

Squinting against that bright glow, Ia raised her left arm to protect her eyes from the light and waited. The not-cat slumped, twitched, and lay still. All three cars—trucks— rolled to a stop a few meters from the beast's body, their engines whisper-quiet. The floodlight cut off, and a voice called out, ". . . Meioa-e, are you alright?"

With her clothes half-plastered to her body from the rain, it wasn't difficult to guess her gender, hence the feminine suffix on the honorific. Ia nodded, lowering her arm since she didn't have to protect her eyesight. She couldn't see the speaker, but she could hear him. "I'm fine, meioa-o. Just one less not-cat for you to have to deal with."

"What are you doing all the way out here? And who are you, anyway?" the man challenged her, opening the passenger-side door. She could see his silhouette in the light of the other two vehicles as he jumped down. "I don't recognize you."

"That's because I'm not a local. Ship's Captain Ia, A Company, 9th Cordon Terran Special Forces," Ia stated, giving the abbreviated introduction. "I just made planetfall, and I'm on my way to connect with my Company. My first officer is trying to scrounge up a ground car to come pick me up, but it's several klicks to their camp, so I thought I'd start walking. Of course, if you meioas wanted to give me a ride out that way, I'd appreciate it," she added, gesturing behind her with her free hand.

"You just made planetfall? In shirt and slacks, no kitbag, no sign of a vehicle, or any other means of getting here?" the man asked her skeptically.

He finally moved close enough, she could see his features in the faint glow from the embedded lights in the road: Asiatic like Harper, but with darker brown skin. Like Harper, his ancestors had lived just long enough on Dabin for the generations to breed their way back to a more normal sense of height, leaving his head level with hers. He lifted his chin at her.

"Pull the other leg, meioa. We checked the scanner records," the colonist added. "Nothing dropped into local airspace but a couple of damned frog ships looking for airborne targets."

"That's because I arrived via stealth tech—I'd tell you about it, but I'm under the standard 'but then I'd have to kill you' clause, and I'd rather be out killing Salik. Or not-cats, as the case may be." She started to say more, but her arm unit beeped. ". . . Excuse me, I have to take this."

Flipping it open, she heard Harper's voice the moment the link was established. *"Captain, we have the vehicle and are on our way, sir. ETA twenty minutes."*

"Acknowledged, Commander. Ia out."

"What's a Ship's Captain doing planet-side?" the colonist asked her next.

"My Company and I specialize in a lot more than just ship-to-ship combat, meioa. We're here to help break the blockade. With luck, it'll take a couple weeks. If not, two months tops." She peered past him at the vehicles. "The energy dip was related to my arrival; I apologize for any inconvenience it may have caused, Meioa Quan. My transport has left the area now, so it won't happen again."

He narrowed his eyes, hands going to his hips. "How did you know my name?"

"I'm Special Forces?" she retorted blandly, biting her lower lip subtly to keep from laughing. Civilians would believe just about anything. Saying she was some sort of intelligence guru was easier than explaining she was a precognitive. At least, at this moment in time.

". . . Right. So, you're here to beat back the enemy? With

you and what army?" he challenged her. "And don't tell me the *Terran* Army. They dropped a whole Division on us and haven't been able to do *shova v'shakk* against the frogto-pods," he added, spitting on the ground.

"Just myself, and the 160 members of my Special Forces Company. But, then, that's all I'll need." Lifting her sword, she showed him the hemoglobin smeared on the blade. "The V'Dan know me as the Prophet of a Thousand Years. The Ter-rans call me Bloody Mary. The Salik tried to call me *lunch*, and I slaughtered them for it single-handedly, in the heart of their own stronghold on Sallha. A little dustup on Dabin with a full Company of the Space Force's finest versus the Salik isn't going to be that much harder.

"Now, the faster I meet up with my crew, the faster I'll get around to getting rid of your little invasion problem. Are you going to give me a lift westward, or not?" she asked.

He snorted, hands going to his hips. "Hardly. Anyone who thinks a mere 160 idiots will be enough to turn the tide of this war is a gods-be-damned fool."

That was the majority percentile for this encounter, and what Ia expected him to say. Shrugging, she turned back to the west. "Then I guess I'll have to go for a little walk and prove you wrong in the days to come. Good night, meioas. Drive safely."

Turning away, she started walking, following the road outlined by the lights of the three vehicles. Someone else called out behind her, "Hey, we just gonna leave 'er here?"

"She's insane," their spokesman stated, his words reach-ing her through the patter of droplets. "Start up the trucks. Let the night and the not-cats have 'er."

Lights lit up behind her, illuminating the road ahead. Ia turned and squinted, walking backwards in time to see him waiting for the door of the ground truck to slide down out

of his way. She could have said more, but Ia decided not to
bother. She watched the door rise back up into place, cutting off whatever else he or his companions might have
said. Raising her sword in salute as they left, Ia slashed it
down, flicking off the not-cat's blood even as she gave a
little bow. The trio of vehicles rolled out and around, pointing back the way they had come. Leaving her in the rain.

Now that those beams weren't aimed in her direction,
her eyes were beginning to readapt to the darkness beyond
the trucks' headlights. Re-forming her sword into a thick
bracelet on her right wrist, Ia faced west and picked up into
a steady jog, the kind that would eat away at the kilometers
between her and Harper's oncoming car. The kind that would
keep her warm, too, as the rain started to fall in earnest now.

At least the local gravity wouldn't be a problem while
she ran; she was used to jogging on a treadmill in her native
pull of 3.21Gs, not this modest 1.85.

The torrent of drops falling from the sky splattered down
onto the spark-snapping dome of the camp shield. Ia felt a
little sorry for the sentries standing duty beyond the innermost perimeter since just opening the shield long enough to
hard-scan their wrist idents had let in more than enough
cold, damp air and splatting rain for her tastes. Sentries had
ponchos, and the generator kept the rain out of the camp,
but it did nothing for the constant, damp chill in the air.

What she wanted was to be warm and dry, preferably
clad in clean clothes after a hot shower. What she got was
a chilly dash when Harper shooed her out of the car and
into the nexus of tents and portable, expandable facility pods
that formed the command center for the two joint Companies. The outer two tents they passed through were storage

and prep facilities, with gear suited for the mud and the forest around them, but the command center was more electronic than pragmatic at its heart.

That heart was filled with tables, machines, boxes, and bodies. On one side—technically occupying almost three-quarters of the tent—sat the unfamiliar clerks and scanner techs of Captain Luca Roghetti's Roughriders of the TUPSF Army, clad in russet camouflage colors that were well suited for the local terrain. On the other side, tucked into their allotted little corner, sat a handful of familiar faces from Ia's bridge-crew rotations.

"Captain on deck!" Harper called out as soon as he wiped the rainwater from his eyes. He grinned at the puzzled looks from Roghetti's soldiers and chuckled. "Not your captain, meioas. *Our* captain."

It wasn't just the humorous way her first officer announced her presence that warmed Ia down to her bones, it was the widened eyes and broad smiles of relief from the three members of Ia's Damned as they looked up from their workstations. They didn't move to greet her since they were technically on duty, but they did flash her smiles and grins. She found herself grinning back as well, an unusual thing for her.

"Sharpe, York, Douglas," she greeted the trio. "I'm glad to see you made it here alright."

"I'm glad to see *you* made it, sir," Private York offered, relief in his light brown eyes. "We were expecting you hours ago."

"I had a slight transportation problem," she dismissed. "Nothing a couple friends couldn't take care of."

"The ship, sir?" Private Douglas asked, her gaze flicking to the other side of the room and back.

Equally mindful of the others, Ia touched the fingers of

both hands together, then flicked them up and outward, mimicking a silent explosion. Out loud, she said, "Everything went according to plan and on schedule . . . except for my little post-party transportation snafu. But I'm here now, and here in time to do some good. As you were, gentlemeioas. Eyes to your boards, thoughts on your tasks."

"Aye aye, sir." Douglas nodded, returning her gaze to her screens. She wasn't monitoring ship functions since they had no more ship. From the looks of things, she was instead monitoring the battlefront perimeter, located about twenty kilometers to the north and west.

Ia looked back over at the comm tech. "Private York, how soon can you get me Admiral Genibes?"

"Ahh . . . it might take a while. And this comm system is not secure, sir. Not like it was on the ship," he warned her. "We're on a portable lightwave relay here at the camp. It links to the main hyperrelay hub in Gonzalah, which is the nearest big city. From there . . . it's three, four hub jumps before it gets anywhere near Earth. If the Salik take out another of those hubs between here and Earth, or if they find and smash through the local one planet-side, it'll be five or six links, assuming they can retune the transmitters well enough to get a signal picked up by one of the other relay centers. I'm sorry about that, sir," he apologized, "but there is no way we can get a direct secured line from here."

"Understood. We'll have that fixed soon enough. Raise the Admiral anyway," she ordered. "Use the gamma-level code from the Company bible so Genibes knows it's not secure."

"Aye, sir."

A new figure stepped through the drapes covering one of the doorways into the command hub. Apparently, Roghetti's crew had summoned their CO, given the twin silver bars gleaming on his collar points and the front of his soft cap. He didn't waste any time in spotting and approaching her. "You must be Ship's Captain Ia."

"That I am, Captain Roghetti," Ia greeted him, turning away from her crew. He saluted her first, since she technically outranked him even if they weren't in the same Service Branch. Returning it, Ia dropped her arm, then flicked her fingers at her rumpled clothes. "I just arrived the hard way, so you'll have to forgive me for my lack of formal Dress Grays."

"This is a combat command. We don't 'do' formality," he dismissed, and gestured at her solid gray dress shirt and black-striped gray pants, a plain contrast to his mottled camouflage, dyed in reddish, brownish, and yellowish hues that matched the local foliage. "That outfit's more formal than things will ever get around here, unless and until we can get the damned frogtopi off-planet.

"Speaking of which," Roghetti added, glancing at his comm techs briefly, "we heard down the line about an hour ago that the frogs shot up two more ships poking their noses into this system in the last twenty hours Standard, but that was about a thousand klicks from here. Blew them to bits, too, according to the passive lightwave scans. Your lieutenant commander, here, swore you'd make it through," he added, lifting his chin at the Asiatic man at her side. "He even tried to bet on it. I'll admit I had my doubts. I'm pleased to see I was wrong."

Harper smirked. "If you'd taken me up on that bet, you'd owe me a hundred creds since she clearly made it."

"Good thing I'm not into gambling, then, or I'd be out of Leave money. Or rather, bail money. Brigadier General Mattox doesn't have a sense of humor when it comes to Fatality Forty-Nine and 'Fraternizing' by laying bets," he quipped darkly. Then muttered, "Or so-called 'rash' battle plans, or using vehicles for 'unauthorized activities' or other *shakk* like that."

"I'm already aware of the general's . . . viewpoints," Ia replied dryly. Diplomatically.

"I take it Harper's been giving you an earful since his arrival?" Roghetti asked, lifting his brows. "I wasn't aware of any extra calls going out."

"No, Captain Roghetti, I wasn't in contact with her," Harper said, hands clasped behind his back. "As I explained, Ship's Captain Ia is a high-ranked precognitive, among other things. I'm confident she has already foreseen the many difficulties of our current situation."

"Such as the fact that the Salik are thoroughly enjoying the heavy rain out there, if not the cold. They'll be attacking within the hour," Ia told him. "It'll be mostly potshots in our direction, but you should pass word down to D and C Companies in your Legion to evacuate their biggest tents and get all their vehicles moved to rearward cover. The more their people scatter, the fewer casualties they'll take. Suggest moving things around."

Roghetti narrowed his eyes. He studied her a long moment, then turned his head slightly. ". . . Corporal Sung, send word down the line to D and C to watch for an air raid on all vehicles and large structures."

"Sir, yes, sir," the corporal replied, bending to that task.

Lifting his chin at Harper, Roghetti addressed Ia. "Your second-in-command, there, isn't the only one who's mentioned your precognitive abilities, Captain. Your Company has been giving mine an earful while they've been waiting. I didn't know what to make of being asked to set up extra barracks tents, stockpile extra weapons, ammunitions, various supplies . . . or the hundred mechsuits your people showed up wearing. Mechsuits don't work well on this mudball; they sink in with every step. And I don't know what to make of them claiming you're some long-foretold V'Dan prophet."

He shook his head. Ia stayed silent, waiting for him to finish what he had to say. Eyes unfocused as he stared across the command tent, he thought a moment, then spoke.

"But to have 160 soldiers show up and know exactly where everything is in the camp, to hear your officers address my men and women by name when we've never met, to advise my scouts where to catch Salik infiltrations and what to look out for when on patrol, and then they simply tell me it's because you knew all of that in advance and told them what to do? That's earned a little leeway in my trust . . . but only a little," he allowed, meeting her gaze. "Don't abuse it, sir."

"I'll try not to, Captain," Ia said. "I make no promises, other than that I'm here to help you kick the Salik off-world."

Someone else entered the tent, bringing a gust of cold, damp air. The man approached Captain Roghetti and started discussing some matter concerning the camp with him. Shivering, Ia reviewed the immediate future. She pinched the bridge of her nose and focused through her exhaustion and hunger. Finally, she nodded. "Harper, get me your arm unit."

He held out his left arm to her. Touching it, she sent it a jolt of electrokinetic programming. He lowered his arm when she was done, giving her a curious look. "I take it these are my orders, sir?"

"Carry 'em out, Commander. I'm going to go have a hot shower, a change of clothes, and a meal before those potshots come *our* way. Right after I speak with—" Ia broke off as York called out her name. She smiled wryly at Harper. "With my superiors. On an empty stomach and low reserves."

Harper clasped her shoulder, his hand sharing its warmth through the damp fabric of her dress shirt. He didn't let it linger, though; he knew all too well why she didn't like people touching her for long. Squeezing and releasing, he nodded at Private York's workstation. "Go get 'em, sir."

Returning to York's side, she braced her hands on the back of his folding chair and leaned over his shoulder, gazing into the pickups. "Patch me through, Private."

He nodded at the commscreen on his left as well as the center one. "We're receiving two pings, sir. The first one's from Admiral Genibes, but the Admiral-General's also on the line. Either way, it's an eight-second delay one way, sixteen seconds round-trip, thanks to all the rerouting. Who do you want first, sir?"

"Patch it for a three-way conference," Ia ordered.

". . . Did you just say 'Admiral-General'?" Roghetti asked, moving closer to the two of them. He straightened abruptly into Attention at the sight of the graying-haired, Asiatic Human on the left side of York's primary screen, her brown eyes sharp and searching. On the right side, the less-well-known, mostly brown-haired and hazel-eyed face of Admiral John Genibes appeared, his nose long and sharp compared to her flatter one, his skin a few shades lighter, his face more rectangular than hers.

"Admiral-General Myang, Admiral Genibes," Ia greeted them, speaking right away. "I apologize for my delay in reporting in, but I had some transportation difficulties following the destruction of TUPSF *Hellfire*. Suffice to say, my—" She cut herself off as the link from Earth caught up with her.

"Captain Ia, I gave you that ship in the understanding that you would *use* it continually to fight our enemies," Admiral-General Myang stated. "While I understand the need for you to keep it out of enemy hands, and to—*shova v'shakking* damned time lags," Myang muttered, just as Genibes spoke.

"I'm glad to see you made it out alive—Sorry, sir," he added, shifting his gaze slightly to one side and nodding. "You first, Admiral-General."

"It's an eight-second delay," Ia warned both of them. "I'll remind you the Salik are determined to take over Dabin as a new colonyworld. I need to kick every last one of them off-planet. They want to establish a foothold, and as I told you, this must not happen."

Myang frowned. She looked older than when Ia had first met her in person, bartering to gain the *Hellfire* as her ship. Back then, her hair had been mostly black, with a few streaks of gray. Now it was mostly gray, with a bit of lingering black. The Admiral-General had 2 billion soldiers to keep track of in a nasty war against a well-prepared foe, and it showed.

"I gave you that ship, *Captain*, in the understanding that you would use it to our best possible advantage," she stated sternly. "You did warn me it would need to be destroyed when you switched helms, and I agreed that it was too great a danger to let it fall into anyone else's hands, but I was *hoping* we could actually mothball it. As it is, the *Damnation* is still not yet ready for service, and I need you at its helm.

"Or rather, I need you at the helm of the *Hellfire* right now. You proved that with your adroit management of the *Hellfire*'s weaponry, and its little 'overshoot' problem. You *owe* me the fighting power you've squandered with the premature loss of that ship, Captain," she told Ia. "I was hoping you'd use it right up to the point where you'd transfer to the upgrade."

"I am aware of that, sir. The timing demanded otherwise . . . which is why my crew and I are here on Dabin," Ia replied, dipping her head in acknowledgment. "The war isn't going well on this battlefront. It's . . . cloudy . . . but something isn't going well, and it's going to get worse. I have less than two months to turn it all around and save these people. The things my crew and I can do will turn the tide for this world and save the majority of these colonists' lives. You need that a lot more than you need our firepower out there right now. My Prophetic Stamp on that.

"As for the destruction of my ship, I may have lost you the main cannon when it was destroyed," she acknowledged, "but in the same move, I *gained* us 1,658 Feyori factioned to *my* side, which means they'll be on *our* side when the Alliance needs them most. I trust you'll count that as a bonus on that long ledger of all the things I owe you, sir?"

Behind her, Roghetti choked. Ia didn't even glance at him. He wasn't a security concern in her eyes, nor were the on-duty members of his surveillance crew. This wasn't a secured channel—by its very nature, lightwave couldn't ever be completely secure, however heavily encrypted—but neither was it being monitored by the Salik. At least, not immediately. She knew they'd send ships outsystem to look for lightwave records of her arrival, once the Salik realized she was now on Dabin.

Ia continued lightly, letting her tone speak silent volumes on Roghetti's trustworthiness in the way she ignored him for the moment. "Of course, I will also need to multiply that number by a factor of fifteen to twenty. Their help will be necessary when it comes time to save the rest of the Alliance from the Salik's worst attack, which is yet to come. But as much as I want to tell you more about that, sirs, this is *not* a secure line or location," Ia stated. "I'll happily explain in more detail once we're aboard the *Damnation* and can lock on with a direct link through hyperspace. Until then, I'll do my best to win back Dabin for you."

"And, what, I'm supposed to just sit here for the next two months?" Myang retorted.

"Well, I don't expect the Admiral-General of the Terran

Space Force to just twiddle her thumbs," Ia returned lightly. "You have all those other battles to plan for. My crew and I will catch up in due time, as I outlined on the last set of data files I sent to you."

Apparently thinking it would be a good moment to distract both strong-willed women, Genibes lifted his chin. "Captain Ia, who's that behind you?"

"Admiral-General Christine Myang, Admiral John Genibes, meet Captain Luca Roghetti, 1st Division 6th Cordon Army," Ia introduced, giving them the short version. "Admiral Genibes knows I arranged to have his Company babysit mine while I was still *en route* this world."

Roghetti nodded, still standing At Attention behind her. "Sirs! It is an honor to meet you, sirs."

Ia didn't bother to straighten up since that would have blocked their view of him. "They're honorable, reliable, and trustworthy, which is why I didn't bother to ask for a private comm somewhere else. Not that I'd get one, as we're currently on lightwave to the local hub."

"I'm glad to hear that, Captain Roghetti," Admiral-General Myang stated after eight seconds of lag had passed. "I sincerely hope Ship's Captain Ia is right about breaking the bad stalemate your Division is in. Brigadier General Mattox has been assuring me the tide will turn in our favor, but then he's been reassuring me of that for months. Ship's Captain Ia, at least, can give me a much more exact date than that. When you *can* give it to me."

"Admiral-General, I would love to give you an exact date beyond some point within the next two months," Ia promised, "but at the moment, I have forty minutes to shower, change, and eat something before the next attack hits this camp, and I'm still in the same uniform from three days ago, which was the last time I had any chance to sleep. Until then, what I can safely say is that I've met my last mission's objective, and I'm now working on the next one. May I go about doing so, sir?"

Myang studied her for more than the eight seconds of delay between them. On the other half of the screen, Admiral Genibes waited for her to speak. When she did, her tone was colored with a mix of aggravation, resignation, and admiration. "You are a royal pain in the rogue asteroid belt, Captain . . . but you do get the job done. Get it done. That's an order. And keep me updated to the best of your ability. Try to find a more secure channel than this while you're at it."

"Aye, sir," Ia agreed, thinking of the hyperrelay she had asked the Afaso Order of civilian monks to purchase and hide for her on this world. Now that she was actually here, she could get it shipped out to her. "If I can do something that'll help this mess, you know I will. And when I do, you will hear from me about it, sir."

"Yes," Myang drawled wryly. "I have all those tons of paperwork and recordings you've sent to prove your sense of ethics, plus the black-box recordings you dumped in our laps . . . Just get it *done*, Captain. Admiral-General out," Myang stated, before reaching forward and ending the link.

Her image vanished. At a tap from York's hand on the controls, Admiral Genibes's face filled the whole of his primary screen.

"Not to delay your orders or intentions, Captain, but I do have some good news, which has been waiting for you to check in so I could release it. The DoI and I have agreed to promote Lieutenant Commander Meyun Harper to the rank and pay of Commander. He's been keeping me up to date on your Company's movements for the last few days, including that harrowing drop through enemy-controlled airspace you—they—had. Between that and his other displays of leadership, he's earned it. As per your request, he will continue to work with you for the time being, but the promotion is to take place immediately."

"Thank you, sir. I couldn't have done more than half of it without Commander Harper's genius keeping my ship and crew alive," Ia told her immediate superior. Like with Roghetti, she didn't bother glancing over her shoulder; she knew Harper had gone elsewhere already with her orders. "He's not here right now to hear it from you directly, but I'll pin his oak leaves on myself as soon as I can scrounge up a set. Speaking of which, I'll need to work on getting a local hyperrelay hub put together for a more direct link. Or at least to cut out the lightwave portion of the signal."

"Like the Admiral-General said, get it done. Which means that, now that you are where you're supposed to be," Genibes added as the eight seconds of delay ticked away between them, "we need you to break this stalemate. If you haven't noticed it in those timestreams of yours, Captain, the Dabin situation has been slipping down over the last few weeks to the wrong side of that stalemate line. Since you're so insistent on needing to be there, I trust you do have a plan on how to break the Salik attack?"

"I should have several battle plans ready for Brigadier General Mattox's perusal by midmorning local, tomorrow," she promised. "If you'd call ahead and let him know those plans will be headed his way, Admiral, that would help expedite matters. I am technically outside his Branch, so he may not otherwise listen to me."

"I'll do that as soon as I sign off. Captain Roghetti," Genibes stated, catching the Army officer's attention, "you've been babysitting the finest Company in the Space Force. For that, I thank you. Now that their CO has rejoined them, I recommend you heed Ship's Captain Ia's suggestions as if they were coming from a superior in the Army."

"Heed them as orders, Admiral?" Roghetti asked, glancing at Ia.

"As very smart suggestions, soldier. She's technically not in the Army's chain of command, but she'll do her best to keep you and yours alive," Genibes promised. "If, in *your* best estimation of a situation, her suggestions make more sense than your other orders, then I suggest you heed them.

"The Space Force relies heavily upon the cognizance and flexibility of the many meioas serving out there in the trenches," John Genibes added formally, clasping his hands in front of him on his desk. "Particularly when the higher-ups are too far from the actual needs of combat to design and plan effective tactics. We'll give you the objectives, but it's up to you to carry them out. I served in the Army as a grunt for two years, Captain, before my transfer to the Navy as a petty officer, and my eventual Field Commission. I know what it's like, and what it's *supposed* to be like. Don't let me down."

Roghetti nodded. "Sir, yes, sir. We'll do our best, Admiral."

"That's why I picked this Company, sir," Ia added. "Roghetti's got the best head for improvisation in this muddy mess."

"I'll let the Department of Innovations know you recommend him, then," he quipped. "It's good to see you alive, Ia, given what you did to your ship. *Stay* alive, and keep me updated. Genibes out," he said, ending the call with a shift of his hand.

". . . Thank you for the link, York," Ia praised, briefly squeezing the private's shoulder. "That's exactly what I hoped would happen."

He nodded and resumed the task of monitoring for Salik transmissions. "My pleasure, sir."

Straightening, she turned and found Roghetti eyeing her.
". . . What?"

"Should I order everyone in this tent to completely forget
we heard you mention the 'F' word?" he asked.

"What, Feyori?" Ia looked over at the other occupants,
seated at various screen-cluttered tables. "Everyone in this
tent is reliable, trustworthy, and discreet. They know their
reputations are already on the line regarding their discretion
while working in a command tent, and they know that the
'F' word, as you called it, is being monitored by the Admiral-
General herself. Anyone chatting about it outside this tent
would be betraying the high level of trust which you, I, and
the Admiral-General herself has just placed in them . . .
and everyone in this tent also knows that's not going to
happen."

Roghetti's soldiers sat up a little at her words, though
they didn't look up from their posts for more than a brief
moment at most. The subtle shifting in postures let their CO
know they'd overheard her words.

"Not to mention the Department of Innovations would
end up hearing about it, sirs, and put it down as the black
mark of a blabbermouth," her comm-tech private stated. He
offered Captain Roghetti a wry smile of his own, looking up
briefly from his boards. "I may be content to remain a private
the rest of my career, so long as I can work for Captain Ia,
here, but not everyone else is."

"The DoI doesn't recommend loose lips for promotions
when they spout off and sink ships, no," Roghetti agreed.
He looked around the tent and nodded in affirmation. "I do
trust my people . . . and I thank you on their behalf for your
trust as well. Mind you, we're not used to being under the
direct scrutiny of the Admiral-General. Is that a . . . a *normal*
thing with you?"

"Captain Roghetti, my Company and I—all 161 of us—are the *entire* 9th Cordon of the Special Forces," Ia told him. She gestured toward the others with one hand. "We stand or fall entirely on our own, and we have not only stood, we have run . . . with exactly one stumble along the way, so far. We have hit every single corner of this war from the far side of Tlassian territories to the far side of the known Solarican worlds, from the Choya colonies all the way to my own homeworld on the edge of Grey space, and all throughout the depth of the known galactic plane.

"You want to know if I have to deal with her on a near-daily basis? I have operated my missions with full *carte blanche* over the last two years, so that I may plan exactly where my crew goes and what my crew does," she said, watching his brows rise at that little revelation. "And in the face of all of that authority, leeway, and outstanding performance, you just heard the Admiral-General herself telling me I am a pain in the rogue asteroid belt to my face, *without* demoting me or stripping me of my command." Hand resting lightly on her hips, she asked sardonically, "What do *you* think?"

"If I were you . . . I think I'd need a drink," Roghetti finally quipped. "Maybe two or three. Given the help your Company's given mine over the last few days, I'd be happy to spot you the first one. Dabin's a muddy world, but the locals have come up with some rather potable brews."

"Unfortunately, strong psis don't have that luxury," she muttered. "Unless you make it a hot cup of caf'; that's a drink I could actually use." Sighing, Ia raked a hand through her damp hair, then grimaced at the moisture and loose hairs clinging to her fingers. Loose, greasy hair. Shifting to Feyori form and back hadn't rid her very matter-based sense of self of the need to bathe. Looking around, she oriented herself in the tent and pointed at one of the doors. "I will take a hot shower, though. My things are . . . that way, three tents down, hang a left, and one more down the side spoke, yes?"

York and Roghetti both nodded. Private Douglas spoke up from her duty station. "Yes, sir. I overheard Chaplain Bennie saying she'd put them there herself since that's where our officers are bivouacked. The nearest showering box is two tents down the chain from that, sir. There are signs, so you can't miss it."

"Thank you, Douglas," Ia told the other woman. She looked at Sharpe, who hadn't moved his eyes from his screens, watching the current combat in the distance via hovercam drones. "If you meioas need me, you'll know where I'll be for the next fifteen minutes. After that, I'll be in the mess tent set aside for our Company."

"We should be fine, sir," York reassured her. "At least until those potshots come our way."

Unfocusing her eyes, Ia checked the timestreams for a moment, then nodded.

"Harper's off making sure the appropriate tents will be evacuated by the time the Salik start shooting at us—the one *good* thing in their invasion is that they'd like this planet and its infrastructure left intact, so at least they're not dropping hydrobombs on the cities, or lobbing asteroids from afar." Ia sighed, rubbing her forehead. Part of the fog in her mind was from fatigue. "This is not going to be an easy fight, but it will be a worthwhile one. Call me if a low probability crops up, but we should be fine for now."

"Aye, sir," her crew members agreed in ragged chorus.

Roghetti joined her as she headed for the correct spoke in the interconnected tent complex. "Just one more question, Captain—and you can shoot me down if this is above my security clearance, but I'd like to ask it, if I may."

"Yes, we need the Feyori on our side," Ia stated as they moved down the canvas and plexsteel tunnel. "No, it has nothing to do with the Dabin engagement, other than that I need the Salik pried off this planet and shot back into space, and there are some Feyori influences I will have to deal with along the way. No, I cannot tell you why we need them. If word gets out what they'll be used for, nearly everyone in the Alliance will wind up dead.

"No, that is *not* hyperbole," she continued, answering his questions before he could even draw breath to ask them. "Yes, this is so far above your pay grade, not even the Admiral-General knows one hundred percent of what is coming. And yes, I can get away with keeping quiet about what's coming under the umbrella of the old 'Vladistad, *salut*' and the precognitive-protective statutes governing Johns & Mishka versus the United Nations, because it *does* involve the safety of the Alliance as a whole. Any other questions?" Ia offered lightly.

Roghetti narrowed his eyes warily. "Were you reading my mind just now?"

"Nope. Just reading the future in all its infinite variety," Ia replied, hands clasped behind her back as they walked. The rain started drumming harder on the force-field dome, sizzling as well as spattering somewhere overhead. "Telepathy is actually one of my weakest skills, being the least liked and least utilized. I truly dislike touching other people's thoughts. It is rude, it is invasive, and it is quite frankly unnecessary for all that I have to do. I also have far too many things going on in my own head to *want* to go rummaging around in anyone else's thoughts needlessly. I'll see you in the mess tent in about twenty, twenty-five minutes."

"I don't intend . . ." Breaking off, he frowned at her, then shook his head. "Have a nice shower, Captain. There's plenty of hot water at this time of night. Enjoy it while it lasts."

Nodding in farewell, Ia headed for the tent spur that contained her kitbag, packed and shipped along with Harper and the others when they had left the *Hellfire* four days before. Nobody in her crew had more than a kitbag's worth of gear and their mechsuits on hand; the majority of their personal belongings had already been packed off to the new ship to await their arrival.

Even her mechsuit had been shipped out with her Company, air-dropped with the others in a bulky packing crate two days ago and salvaged out of the swamp by her crew, since Ia herself hadn't been in a position to wear it off her ship. Not when she had been forced by layers of circumstances to blow up that ship. Clothing, she could re-create from the constant familiarity of wearing it. Even the complexity of her officer's arm unit was within her grasp. But the intricate mesh of machinery and electronics in a mechsuit was beyond her personal comprehension level.

Wearing it wasn't on the schedule for the next few days. Bathing, sleeping, digging up a certain prepurchased-and-stashed hyperrelay unit and transmitting several battle plans to the general in charge of the 1st Division were. Between then and now, Ia had to figure out why things were going wrong here on Dabin, why they were going to get a lot worse over the next few weeks, and fix them firmly enough that the colonists would be able to drive the Salik fully off-world.

First, though, she desperately needed a hot shower. After her long, cold jog, a barely warm enough ground-car ride, and standing around in damp clothes in an unheated camp, her flesh-and-blood body needed to feel warm again as well as clean. At least she had the time to spare for it.

————————

Her first battle came in training, in the mud when it was
  raining,
Of the other soldiers, one did go berserk.
He attacked the recruits' teachers, bloody madness in his
  features,
But our Mary faced him down with just a smirk.
"I'll kill 'em all!" he screamed, and success was near, it
  seemed,
'Til he faced the girl with hair as white as snow;
Now he's praying for some ice while his balls are used for dice,
For she's sent him down to live in Hell below!

Ia laughed under her breath at Clairmont's choice of lyrics. "That is *so* not how it went! The storm hadn't even begun yet, for one."

"Hush, you," Helstead admonished her. The petite lieutenant commander's duty shift was scheduled to start in the next hour and a half. She gave her CO a mock-dirty look. "I'm trying to enjoy the song."

Warm and dry—mostly dry; she'd had to don a poncho to get through the mist seeping through the force fields to this tent—and with her boots propped up on a spare bench across from hers, Ia lounged with her back to the mess table. She clasped the remains of a sandwich in one hand and a mug of caf' in the other, listening to the singer. After being enthusiastically greeted and quickly supplied with steaming-hot food, she had settled in to enjoy the entertainments offered by her off-duty crewmates.

Some of it was quite good, including Private Clairmont's recently written song about his commanding officer—even if he kept getting the details wrong. The storm hadn't broken until *after* Recruit Wong Ta Kaimong had been captured back in Basic. Ia remembered that day all too well. The chorus was catchy, though. Ia found herself humming along as she finished her sandwich.

> *Bloody Mary! Of her skills you should be wary;*
> *When she goes into Hell, the devil knows well*
> *He doesn't want to be her foe.*
> *Bloody Mary! Of her enemies left, there's nary;*
> *For their blood runs red from her toes to her head,*
> *And it drips down her locks of snow!*

A gust of cold wind entered the tent, along with the poncho-draped figure of Captain Roghetti. Clairmont hesitated a couple beats, in case it was for some sort of an announcement, or someone demanding he get back to serving food, since that was his cross-duty task for this hour. He continued with his song when the Army captain merely looked around, spotted Ia, and headed her way.

Dropping onto the bench next to her, the Army captain murmured in her ear. "I guess you were right about my coming in here. Forward surveillance shows the Salik are pushing forward south of here, mainly along the C and D front lines. How much do you know about their movements?"

"They're just testing the waters," Ia murmured back, turning so she could speak into his ear. With the others listening to the lyrics and singing along with the chorus, the two of them had a fair amount of privacy. "They won't try a big push for three more days—they want the ground to be extra-muddy so that their mechsuits can handle the terrain troubles far better than our own. General Mattox should agree to my counterattack plans before then. They're tactically sound."

"You've only just arrived, and you've already worked up your big battle plans?" Roghetti asked her, skeptical.

"You have no idea just how much I can foresee, Captain, but you'll learn. I've been working on these and other plans for several years now, including a number of contingencies." She lifted her mug in salute. "All I need from you is to make sure you and your crew help out and don't commit any Fatalities along the way. I may have earned a little bit of trust from you and your people, but I'm staking a whole lot of trust *on* you, too. Just as I've staked it on my crew."

Her back itched, another memory dredged up in association with her words. The welts had long since healed scarlessly, but she still remembered the moment when everything had shattered. She wouldn't be punished with a caning if any of Roghetti's crew messed up, just for any big mistakes caused by her own, but there was something about the situation on Dabin that reminded her of that prickling sense of terror. Just a ghost of it, but that was enough to make her prod at the half-fogged waters of the near future.

Ia pushed it away, biting into her sandwich. Regrets were time-wasters. She was here to reassure her crew that their CO was safe and sound, fully in command of her faculties even if she'd deliberately destroyed their ship.

"You've been planning this day for a couple of years now?" he asked.

"Battle plans for Dabin for today and the next few weeks, battle plans for Zubeneschamali, battle plans for my capture by the Salik and my subsequent escape from Sallha . . . plans for this and plans for that. Plus contingencies upon contingencies, for those times when things go seriously wrong, and the free-willed actions of others toss my original plans out the nearest airlock," she added, answering his follow-up question before he could get to it. "I see percentages and probabilities, not absolute certainties . . . but I see *all* of them.

"I can also guide the dice quite a lot, but I can't always guarantee an exact outcome. Not without help from the people around me. Whatever rumor and my service record and even the Sh'nai faith might say about me, I'm still only one woman, Captain."

He shrugged, then changed the topic. Wrinkling his nose, Roghetti lifted his chin at Clairmont, and asked, "Why do your soldiers sing so much? Hell, some of 'em were singing even when they were doing KP, last night. The only thing they haven't done is sing while out on patrol or sentry duty, thank God."

Ia turned her attention back to Clairmont, bringing his song into its final verse. She was still enjoying it as background noise, despite the sometimes wildly inaccurate lyrics. The bit about her cutting her enemies into three wasn't always true, for instance . . . though in some fights, she had done just that. "It actually started as a cross-Branch rivalry."

"A rivalry? Over what?" Roghetti asked her.

"Soldiers in the Space Force Marine Corps sing," Ia told him. She touched her own chest. "I started out in the Corps, and their drill instructors use it as a method of building *esprit des corps* during Basic Training. But when I hand-picked my crew, I pulled in people from all four Branches.

"Their first chance to socialize in earnest off duty, some of the ex-Army members tried to mock the ex-Marines for it, and it got to the point that Private York—he's the one on comm duty right now," Ia reminded Roghetti, "he came and fetched me to handle it. I told the ex-Army members to either start singing themselves and outperform me and my fellow ex-Marines, or just shut up and put up with it. Since then . . . well, they've learned to integrate and work together. That includes singing."

He started to say something more, but Clairmont's performance came to an end. The private had a good voice, as good as the more professionally trained York, and that meant a fair amount of applause and a bit of cheering besides. Roghetti listened to the others calling for a new song, then turned back to Ia as soon as Clairmont settled them down and launched into his next *a capella* piece.

"Where do they all come from?" the Army captain asked Ia. Roghetti pointed at one of the gray-uniformed women listening raptly to the performance, Philadelphia Benjamin. "I thought I heard that meioa-e talking about her family back on Mars, yet they're walking around on Dabin like it's their native gravity. Mars is a major lightworld. They have gravity weaves underfoot almost everywhere you go, just so they don't grow up too weak to walk on another world, but it's set to Terran Standard. So she can't be from Mars."

"She *is* from Mars," Ia told him. "I spent the last two years slowly ramping up the gravity on our previous ship because I knew we'd have to come here to help the rest of you fight, and I wanted everyone acclimated enough that they *could* fight. Too many things can go wrong with a gravity weave if you wear one into combat, so I just made sure they could literally stand on their own two feet on this world." At his skeptical look, she shook her head. "Relax, Captain. You'll learn how accurate I am soon enough."

"If you say so," he murmured, sitting back against the edge of the table.

"You'd better go double-check on C and D Companies. They'll need supplies sent down the line in another forty-three minutes, after the shooting and screaming have stopped," she told him, leaning close enough to be heard without speaking over the new song. "Commander Harper was going to give your supply sergeants a list of what they'll need, but you'll still need to sign off on them as cross-Company requisitions.

"Use our budget authorizations, not your own. Master Sergeant Sadneczek should have included the codes for it in Harper's paperwork—oh, and don't forget the Salik will be shooting at us, too, shortly. You have about eight minutes, plenty of time to sign papers and redistribute the troops who haven't budged at Commander Harper's suggestion," she added. "Particularly Privates Ving and Hassan, and Lance Corporal von Mitt. The attack will be over after the seventh strike, then we can all clean up and get some rest."

Eyeing her one last time, Roghetti shook his head and rose without a word. Pulling up the hood on his poncho, he left the mess tent just as Clairmont reached the chorus of his next composition about his commanding officer.

Ia, Bloody Mary!
Place your body between your beloved home,
And the war's desolation . . .

The contents of her mug had finally lost heat. Ia sipped at the tepid caf' anyway. She had two more hours to stay awake before things would be calm enough for her to catch any sleep.

CHAPTER 2

Who? Oh God . . . Brigadier General José Mattox. Oh yes,
that name brings up some memories, doesn't it?

~Ia

"Captain—Ship's Captain Ia," Captain Roghetti corrected
himself. Lengthening his strides, the camouflage-clad man
caught up with her as she emerged from one of the spokes
of the tent-and-pod structures comprising his Company's
base camp. "Is there a particular reason why . . . Wait," he
muttered, frowning between her and the direction she was
headed. "So you *do* already know about the civilians insist-
ing on seeing you in person at the perimeter?"

"Of course. Before I hit the cot last night, I ducked back
into central command and asked my comm tech to make a
few calls," Ia explained. "Those civilians are bringing me

something I purchased and had stashed on this planet months ago."

She nodded at the gravel road that led away from the heart of the camp. In the light of local morning—though it was early evening Terran Standard time—it was easy to see that Roghetti had set up E Company's base camp in some farmer's unplowed fields. The local ground cover was a sort of reddish brown color and plush like moss. The mud was yellowish, and the gravel used to keep the landowner's tractor-bots from bogging down in that mud formed a ribbon of pinkish granite chips.

It snaked toward the brownish tree-equivalents bordering the camp, leaving Ia with the impression the landscape was the wrong color. She kept expecting the ground to have brown mud and bluish grass-stuff, not reddish brown and yellow. Even her own clothes looked a little weird since she kept expecting to see gray at the edge of her vision, not camouflaged yellow-brown-red, though she knew she'd be wearing them for the next sixty-three local days.

Chaplain Benjamin and Commander Harper had not only carried her belongings off the *Hellfire*, they had ensured the local Army equipment manufactories issued suitable camouflage clothing and equipment in her specific sizes. The only differences between her uniform and Roghetti's were the rocket-clutching brass eagles she wore on her shirt points and the fact that the outer edges of her sleeves and pant legs had a little streaking and sprinkling of neutral gray randomly seeded through the camouflage patterning, whereas his held hints of dull green.

Striding at her side, Roghetti followed her in silence, his gaze sweeping over the fields with their lumps of tents, container pods, hangars, and handful of vehicles in sight. The rain had quit at some point while she slept, and the ground was misting a little, the air cool but supersaturated with moisture. It wouldn't last long, she knew. Within the hour, water would be falling again. They were on the verge of full spring, locally, and that meant plenty of showers.

Roghetti finished his inspection and glanced at her again. "So, are you going to tell me what you're going to insist on letting in past my perimeter?"

"I'll not only tell you, I'll even let you use it," Ia promised. She tipped her head at the tunnel of the gravel road leading into the forest. "I directed the Afaso Order to purchase a portable hyperrelay unit and mount it in a hovervan for my use."

"You have a big enough budget to buy a portable hyperrelay?" he asked her, dark brows quirking under the bill of his cap. "Not to mention, last I checked, the Afaso were still nonmilitant, civilian-sector, monastic practical pacifists. Hardly the type to take orders from the Space Force."

"They're not. They're taking orders from the Prophet of a Thousand Years. And my operating budget was big enough to slag the single most sophisticated, expensive ship currently in the fleet after only two and a half years of operating it," Ia said.

The Army captain choked. Coughing, he cleared his throat. "You what?" he rasped. "What'd you do, blow up a capital ship? Is that what your ship was? But that can't be right. You said your entire crew is only 160 and you," Roghetti protested. "Capital ships require crews of several thousand."

"It was hardly a capital ship, Captain," Ia said. "The new Harasser Class is approximately the size of a frigate, with a normal crew complement of around five hundred. However, it hits with the firepower of somewhere between a battlecruiser and a battleship. The only problem was, I couldn't spare that many people to be on my crew. Too many were and are still needed elsewhere in this war. So I pared it down to the absolute minimum, with a pool of about twenty replacements available."

"Replacements?" he asked, confused.

She flicked her hand. "Nobodies. Talented, skillful, dedicated nobodies. People whose lives wouldn't make a single impact anywhere else, positive or negative, in the flow of time. At least, for the most part. They'd never make an impact anywhere else, but in *my* Company, Captain, they can, have, and will change the course of the future. For the better, if I have anything to say about it."

"You call them replacements, as if you *expect* your people to die," he observed dryly.

Ia stopped walking. Roghetti stopped a couple paces after her, turning to face her.

"We all die in the end, Luca," she said quietly, addressing him by his given name. "I am as mortal as you, or Private York, or your supply sergeants, or . . . or just about any Human out there. I can predict how to avoid death, and I can *tell* people how to avoid death . . . but that doesn't mean they'll follow through. And it definitely does not mean they'll succeed in avoiding it even if they do follow through. *Every* officer knows that the men and women under his or her command may die at some point.

"I've been lucky that, up until now, my crew has stayed mostly aboard our ship. I've been able to pilot it safely through every life-threatening engagement we've faced," she added, striding forward again. He turned to join her as she moved. "But now we're on the ground, we will have to scatter ourselves across a wide stretch of terrain, and we will face a very large number of the enemy. I can single-handedly control the flight of a starship less than a kilometer long. I cannot control a thousand kilometers of enemy-infested terrain."

They had reached the tree line. The perimeter checkpoint was another two hundred meters down the way. Such a large camp would have been difficult for her crew to have patrolled even with the use of surveillance equipment, but then Ia only had three Platoons, plus a small cadre. Roghetti commanded five Platoons of six Squads each and a full cadre, including Squad-level sergeants, supply officers, and so forth. The TUPSF Army could afford to be more support-heavy than the trimmed-down needs of the Marines, and when she had served in the Navy, Ia's support had been whatever Battle Platforms her small Delta-VX had touched.

Since neither she nor the captain strolling at her side were bothering to hide their approach, the sentries flanking the gate had plenty of time to identify them. One soldier, she could see openly; he gently cradled his stunner rifle as he stood by the fence gate, its bulbous black-and-white curves painted over in the local camouflage colors. She only knew the other soldier's location from the timestreams, for the woman had taken that much care to blend in with her surroundings.

Beyond the gate sat a beige hovervan. Next to it parked a hoverbike. Both sets of thrusters had been turned off, leaving them parked on their landing pods. Leaning against the front bumper of the van were a pair of batik-clad Human males.

One was dark-skinned, rather short, and boasted whipcord muscles, visible thanks to his sleeveless tunic. The other was about as tall as Ia, pale and freckled, but built like a brick door. Not quite as broad as Ia's brother Thorne, but meaty all the same. Both had their hair shorn close to their heads in buzz cuts that would have done any Space Force soldier proud, straight out of Basic.

The private at the gate nodded to them. "Captain, sir," he greeted Roghetti, then glanced at Ia. "Lieutenant Colonel."

"Ship's Captain," Roghetti corrected, lifting his chin at Ia. Or rather, at her collar points. "That eagle has a rocket. Navy insignia and rank, not Army."

"Sorry, sir. *Ship's* Captain, sir," the private corrected himself. The name patch above his shirt pocket read *Gulvigsson*. Like the two Afaso, he was stocky and muscular, bred for heavyworlder life, with pale skin and dark lashes.

"It's alright. Captain, would you like to inspect the van before permitting it into camp?" Ia offered politely.

Roghetti eyed it, her, the Afaso, then her again. "Will you vouch for it?"

Focusing her attention inward, down, and out in a peculiar mental flip, Ia checked the timestreams. Not to trace the future of the van—since she had plans for it—but to check its past. What took her a couple minutes within the expanse of her mind only took a second or two in reality. Nodding, she lifted her chin. "It's clean. Nothing's been tampered with."

"That's it?" Captain Roghetti asked her. "You just roll up your eyes for a moment, and that's it? You just know?"

"I've learned to be both very fast and very thorough at checking the past and future. That, and they are who they appear to be: vowed monks from the Eltegar City Dojo. Full Master Mark Saunders," Ia introduced. The shorter man gave them a short bow at her gesture, and the taller nodded. "And Senior Master Brian Apowain. Good morning, gentlemeioas. Thank you for bringing this out here."

The taller man bowed to her as his partner sagged back against the hovervan once more. Apowain fished a set of keys from the pocket of his wax-resist dyed trousers. The patterns on his clothes echoed the frilly leaves of the local Dabin-style trees, as was the usual custom for local monk batiks. "Good morning, Prophet. I believe these are now yours."

He tossed the starter keys, a pair of black plexi rods

connected by a ring, toward Ia. The high arc of it curved and fell faster than it would have back on Earth, thanks to Dabin's higher gravity, but it did clear the tall fence. Lifting her hand, Ia pulled the keys out of their arc telekinetically, slowing and wafting them into her grip. "Thank you. Return to the city and prepare to carry out the defense plans I sent to you. Remember to wait for the signal, and match it to the right plans before executing. Do not engage the enemy unless you absolutely have to."

Saunders smirked, pushing away from the van so he could saunter over to the hoverbike. "We're not that stupid. No offense to you Army types."

". . . None taken," Roghetti muttered, watching both monks mount the hoverbike. "Open the gate for the Ship's Captain."

Gulvigsson nodded and touched something on his arm unit. Static sparked not just across the gate but across the air for at least four meters above the gate, proving that the perimeter had been secured by more than just a mesh of cheap-looking, galvanized, chain-link steel. Saunders turned on the thrusters. With a quiet *thrum*, the hoverbike lifted up off the ground, then tipped sideways and took off. Ia stepped through the gate in their wake.

"I'll give you a ride back to camp if you want, Captain," she offered, unlocking the beige vehicle.

"I'll take that offer." Joining her, he climbed into the hovervan from the other side, then craned his neck to eye the machinery occupying most of the back. "You said I could use it?"

"My people will have priority, but yes. First thing's first. Get this back to camp and get my comm techs to start tuning its frequencies—buckle up," she ordered, strapping herself into the restraint harness. "It might be less than a klick back to the heart of camp, but this thing won't move until I hear that belt click."

"Sir, yes, sir," he quipped, pulling the straps into place for his own seat. "How long will it take to get the frequencies tuned? I have some reports I need to send to the DoI, and I'd prefer to send 'em by a more private means than lightwave."

"Probably about two, three hours. No more than three, most likely. Then I'll need half an hour to connect with Headquarters and give Mattox my battle plans." Starting the thrusters, Ia lifted the hovervan a meter off the ground and drifted it forward, navigating the gate gently to keep from knocking Gulvigsson's legs out from under him with the repulsor fields. She sped up a little once they were through. "We have twelve cable plugs for direct-line bandwidths available, with the capacity to project up to four pinholes at a time with this rig. But it has to be sitting still. The vacuum chamber is too small to compensate for anything more than the planet's own movement. You can have up to four of those twelve bandwidths if you know the exact connection frequencies."

"Not really, since we deal mostly in lightwave frequencies out here on the line . . . but I figure *you* might know. If your crew is right, and you really *are* that accurate," Roghetti added, glancing at her.

Ia shrugged. "I try to be. A lot more than I care to think about is riding every single day on my accuracy."

———

"Shakk," Captain Roghetti swore, staring at the screen on the back of the hyperrelay unit.

". . . Sir?" Private Mysuri asked, glancing between him and her CO. "Is something wrong?" It was her duty-shift hour to watch the van's contents, and her responsibility to make sure everything worked properly now that the hyper-relay had been programmed.

"It's alright, Private," Ia reassured her. "He's just realized he now has a direct connection to the Tower's hyperrelay hub on Earth."

"That explains why the machine is humming so loudly," Roghetti muttered, nodding at the thrumming bulk of white metal occupying the van's cargo space. He hesitated, datachip in hand, then shook his head. "I can't send this right now. I was thinking I'd get the DoI processing center on *Kelkirk* Station, which is where the Dabin relays connect."

Ia frowned in confusion. She trailed mental fingers through the timestreams, looking for what he wanted to send, and its potential repercussions. ". . . Ah. That report. Yeah, it'll get flagged for priority handling, coming in on this particular channel. You should probably speak with Colonel Matheson and Major Nikulu'a before you send it, double-confirm they'll be sending their own. Maybe even invite them out here to help file it in person."

"Yeah," he agreed quietly, staring at the chip. "It's easier to *v'shakk* away your career when you have at least two other officers willing to back you up. If it went to the *Kelkirk*, they'd also take a few days to process it since they have four or five battlefronts' worth of reports to wade through at any point, but this would happen a bit fast."

"As of tomorrow, six battlefronts," Ia quipped. "But three days after that, it drops to four. The volume from Dabin will pick up sharply, though."

"Are you pulling my leg?" the Army captain asked her. Ia smiled.

". . . Sirs?" Mysuri asked, flicking her brown gaze

between the two. Ia shook her head subtly, and she changed the subject. "If you don't need the DoI on Earth, Captain Roghetti, I'll set the ping to Admiral Genibes's office now."

He nodded, giving her permission. Stepping into place, Mysuri tapped in the address, then synched her arm unit. Text scrolled up the screen, response and counterresponse as she added more information. After a minute, she nodded. "Security protocols have been confirmed, Captain. We can use this. The distance involved limits us to three hours per liter, but we have a secured line to the chain of command now. The only thing you'll have to worry about, sirs, is parabolic audio surveillance. We don't have the vacuum of space and several cushioning layers between us and the enemy."

"Any messages for us?" Ia asked, curious.

"Just the one, sir, text from Admiral Genibes. 'Informed Mattox to expect your plans,'" she read, tapping open that file. "It looks like he's gone offline for sleep, sir. Did you want me to leave him a message?"

"Tell him 'I'm on it,' then switch relays to Dabin Army Headquarters," Ia instructed.

Movement caught her attention; it came from a figure ducking into the mouth of the tent sheltering the van. Like everyone else in camp, the tallish blonde woman had donned mottled camouflage clothes patterned and colored to look like the local terrain. Ia frowned, not expecting Jesselle Mishka's arrival right now. That was an off-the-wall percentile probability.

"Doctor?" Ia asked her.

The tall blonde woman waggled the datapad in her hand. "I finally got hold of the individual post-battle reports from Roghetti's Squad sergeants this morning, and do you know what I found, Captain? This Brigadier General Mattox's battle plans are a steaming pile of nonsense!"

Roghetti eyed Mishka, then glanced at Ia. "That's your Company physician. What is she doing discussing tactics?—Not that I disagree with your assessment, Lieutenant Commander," he added in a polite, apologetic aside to Jesselle, "but that's not normally a surgeon's area of expertise."

Ia held up her hand, warding off his doubt. "Dr. Mishka is a Triphid, not a mere surgeon, with a triple doctorate in comprehensive medicine from preventive care all the way through to post-op. As a result, she has a knack for putting disparate information together and coming up with an accurate summation of the underlying problem.

"*This* is why I insisted you study tactics for the last two and a half years, Doctor," she added, facing Jesselle. "I needed you to be familiar enough with tactics and battle reports to look at the fights here on Dabin and tell me what's wrong with my patient."

Jesselle waggled the datapad again, hints of a scowl pinching her otherwise-smooth brow. "What's *wrong* is that your patient is filled with self-inflicted wounds disguised to look like enemy-inflicted injuries. Somewhere along the way, someone started lying about it to the higher-ups. Look," the doctor added, tilting the pad so both fellow officers could see. "I cross-compared the official reports for the casualty ratings and the official tactical summaries pulled from the military Nets, versus the real reports from these soldiers.

"The types of casualty reports being passed up higher than the Legion level are being misrepresented for the types that *should* be felt in ground-based combat versus the Salik, given the officially reported battle plans," Mishka stated, thumbing the screen so that graphs overlaid each other. The tally counts and percentage bars did not match. "Almost every single one of these is like . . . is like *elective* surgery. Like ignoring a gut wound to augment the breasts. It looks pretty on the page, but it's all offensive pushes, trying to use overwhelming force to maneuver and destroy the enemy."

Ia blushed a little at her blunt analogy. She wasn't the only one. Roghetti coughed, and Mysuri bit her lip. The private cleared her throat. "We have a pingback from headquarters now, Captain Ia. Shall I put a call through?"

"Give me a moment, Doctor. Hopefully, my plans will fix the problem," Ia added. "Put it through, Private."

Mishka nodded. Turning back to the hyperrelay machine, Ia lifted her chin. Mysuri tapped in the commands to connect the link and shifted back so Ia could take her place. With this particular unit coded for direct contact with Earth, they didn't have the relay connected to any of Roghetti's communications net for security reasons. It could also be used to connect to a relatively close hyperrelay hub and bounce back directly to Army Headquarters here on Dabin, with the bare minimum in time lost and no risks of the enemy picking up the call via lightwave. However, using the machine meant using the one and only screen on the side facing the open back door of the van; that was the only way all the pieces could fit into a hovervan of this size.

Ia tucked her hands behind her back, echoing Roghetti's and Mysuri's waiting poses. Mishka folded her arms across her chest, datapad still in one hand. After a few seconds, someone answered the link. The woman on the other end was clad in Dress Greens, her formal jacket striped down the sleeves in Space Force Black; silver oak leaves decorated the collar points, marking her rank as a major. Behind her, Ia could see the bland beige walls of an office. The name pinned to her jacket said Perkins.

The major had started out with a smile, but switched it quickly to a puzzled frown as she studied Ia's face and local-colored clothes. ". . . Excuse me, meioa, but this channel and code are reserved for Command Staff–level communications. Who are you, and how did you get access?"

"I am Ship's Captain Ia, 9th Cordon Special Forces," Ia introduced herself. "Admiral Genibes of the Special Forces sent a message about eight hours ago on this same channel instructing Brigadier General Mattox to expect my call. I would like to speak with him, please."

A dog barked somewhere in the background. The pull of the planet's gravity was lighter than Ia's homeworld, but the sound wasn't much different from the yapping of a stubbie, the stout-legged heavyworlder dog breed found back on Sanctuary. For a moment, she thought it was a rather odd thing to have in a military headquarters, then had to remind herself she was on a planet, not a starship or a space station. Animals could roam a lot more freely here than they could on a ship, where they had to remain caged for their own safety in case of sudden maneuvers.

Major Leotta Perkins, checking something on a secondary screen, shook her head. She offered a polite smile. "I'm afraid he's not available at the moment, Ship's Captain. But we are expecting your battle plans. Please forward them to me now, and I'll make sure the General sees them as soon as he has a moment."

Ia didn't trust her smile. Not because it seemed insincere, which it didn't, but because of Mishka's sigh behind her. It was a *huff* of impatience mingled with disbelief. "I must insist on being put through for a face-to-face, Major. These plans have been approved by the Command Staff, and I have been instructed to deliver them to Brigadier General José Mattox himself. Since I am needed on the battlefront to help implement those orders as soon as they are approved and distributed, this puts me 643 kilometers from his location. If need be, I can hold this hyperrelay open . . ."

"Twelve hours, sir," Mysuri murmured from her position to one side. She pointed to the power display in the lower right corner of the oblong screen. "It's located right there on this model."

". . . For the next twelve hours," Ia confirmed, barely missing a beat. The configuration for the portable relay's screen wasn't the standard for military-issued ones, and she hadn't been the one to set it up. She had spent the last two and a half hours eating breakfast and conferring with the corporals and yeomen heading up each of her Company's Squads, going over what they had learned of the local terrain in order to match it up with her coming battle orders. "Considering he's just left the restroom, I think I can wait four more seconds for him to enter your office and become available."

The major's smile never slipped. "I don't know where you get your inf . . . oh." Major Perkins lost her smile at the corners of her mouth. She focused somewhere past her screen and spoke. "Brigadier General, there's a Ship's Captain Ia from the TUPSF Special Forces on the comm. She insists on speaking with you immediately, sir."

Her body turned, gaze lifting to follow the brigadier general's movement as he came around to her side of the desk. Bracing one green-sleeved arm on the desk and the other on the back of the major's chair, Mattox smiled into the pickups, deepening the creases on either side of his mouth. Aside from those lines, his round, tanned face was mostly wrinkle-free.

"Ah, the infamous Captain Ia. Bloody Mary herself, come to help out the Army. Pass on over those battle plans, will you?" he offered as the dog again barked in the background. "I've been looking forward to reading them."

Wary at his open friendliness, Ia took a moment to twist her mind onto the timestreams. Rippling waves of grass met her inner eye, crisscrossed by thousands of gleaming streams representing all the lives in her immediate reach. Mist scudded in tufts here and there, but Ia could see downstream into the future.

It looked like Mattox would indeed implement her plans. Satisfied, she pulled her awareness fully back into her body and fished for the datachip in her shirt pocket. "I have them right here, General. I'm looking forward to working with the Army on this."

Slotting the rectangle into the machine, she hit the download command. Major Perkins tapped a few controls, then nodded. "Download complete, sirs. Will that be all, Ship's Captain?"

"For now, yes. Make sure that gets distributed by the end of tomorrow," Ia added, removing the chip. "The timing is crucial."

"I'll look them over and deal with them right away. Welcome to Dabin, Captain," Mattox added politely. "I'm sure with you and your reputation on our side, the Salik won't be a problem for much longer. Headquarters out."

The connection ended with a tap of the major's hand. Ia blinked, then shrugged it off. She moved back to the other two officers, letting Private Mysuri shut the machine down. "Well, that went better than expected."

"That man is delusional." Mishka's flat statement made Roghetti blink and Ia frown. She lifted her chin at the now-blank screen on the other side of the black-haired private. "I've seen patients who refuse to acknowledge reality. He is far too agreeable in the face of the disparity found in these reports."

"I checked the timestreams, Doctor," Ia reassured her. "He will follow my plans."

Jesselle eyed her up and down, then shrugged. "Well,

you asked for my opinion, and that's my opinion. I'd almost judge him to be suffering from split-personality syndrome, but I'd need to examine him formally first . . . and *that* accusation goes no further than the four of us," she added, pinning Roghetti with a hard look. Ia and Mysuri, she apparently trusted. "I'm not inclined to piss away my career because of a bit of undocumented speculation."

Roghetti held up his hands, reassuring her. "I'm right there with you, sir. There's a handful of us who want to level charges of incompetence . . . but doing that even *with* solid proof guarantees our own conduct gets run through a Board of Inquiry."

Frowning at her crew member's words, Ia took a few seconds to slip back into the timestreams. Touching the waters of José Mattox's life, she checked it for signs of a dual personality, a happy Dr. Jekyll ignorant of a dangerous Mr. Hyde hidden inside. The fog was still there, but only in patches and mostly toward the edges of her immediate awareness.

She pulled back to herself with a shake of her head. "From what I can see in the timestreams, he's not suffering from any split-personality disorder."

"Well, *someone* is at Headquarters. If it's not a tumor in the brain of the snake, it's a cancerous growth down in the pancreas," Mishka muttered. "Presuming snakes have pancreases. I never studied herpetology."

"I'll keep my senses open," Ia promised her.

"You do that, sir. And do keep in mind he never *said* he would implement those orders," the blonde added tartly. "Just that he would look at them and handle them somehow."

Unsure if her Company physician was reading too much into Mattox's words, or lack thereof, Ia switched the subject. "I'll keep that in mind as well, Doctor. Captain Roghetti, if you don't need me, I'd like to walk the front perimeter with one of your sergeants, get a feel for the lay of the land. It's one thing to see it in my head but another to hear it, smell it, and feel it. Particularly before I have to go out and fight in it."

Roghetti checked the chrono built into his bracer-sized command arm unit. "There's a mixed patrol of yours and mine headed out in . . . sixteen minutes. We'll get you suited up to go out with them. If you'll excuse us, Lieutenant Commander?"

"Of course. Captain, I'll go review some more reports to see if I can diagnose exactly which element in the chain of command is causing the problems on this campaign if it isn't Mattox himself," Mishka promised. "That major might be one of your roadblocks. Try your best not to get hit, gentle-meioas. I'd far rather wade through piles of debriefings than have to perform surgery in a field hospital—no offense to your medical facilities. It's not a bad pod as far as portables go, but it's not a state-of-the-art infirmary."

"None taken," Roghetti replied. He held his tongue while he and Ia left the tent, aiming toward the section of camp where the patrol supplies were kept. When he was sure they were out of the other woman's hearing, he asked, ". . . Is she always like that? She doesn't seem to have the best of bedside manners."

"She does for the rest of my crew. She just has a problem with *me* throwing her into combat. She always has," Ia added candidly. "Jesselle came into my command thinking she needed to be safe and sound deep in the heart of some hospital in order to access her mental powers. Unfortunately, I need her out here on the front lines, able to think, act, and move."

"Huh. With a last name like Mishka, you'd think she was trying to act like a psychic, wanting to wrap herself in armored padding far behind our defensive lines," he joked.

"She *is* a psychic, a very strong biokinetic. That's why

she's not happy about being forced to use her abilities along the front lines. A good number of my crew are," Ia added when he glanced at her. "I disagree heartily with the PsiLeague's belief that psychics cannot learn to wield their abilities at the same time they're enduring the rigors of Basic Training, hostile-terrain scouting, and open combat.

"Twenty percent or so might honestly not be able to concentrate under such chaotic conditions, even with training, but that still leaves roughly eighty percent who could and should learn to do so . . . even if it means it takes them longer to master both mind and muscle. Mine have," Ia stated, following him into the first of the supply-and-armament tents. "Even if they didn't want to, they learned."

"Bit of a hard asteroid on 'em, are you?" Roghetti asked, smirking. "A real rough rider?"

Ia returned it wryly. "I'm harder on myself, but yeah. What good commander isn't?"

They walked in silence for a few more moments, then the captain looked at Ia. "So . . . precognitive. Precognition. Foretelling the future and all that."

Ia didn't have to be telepathic to know he had an oddball question on his mind. Not that she would read his thoughts without dire need; such things were not only rude, they bordered on outright illegal in the military. "Yes?"

"Something has always bothered me about that," Roghetti stated, clasping his hands behind his back. "You know, mucking around in time. I think ever since I first read *Oedipus Rex* back in high school."

She grasped what he meant right away. Nodding in understanding, Ia explained her own thoughts on the matter. "That story is responsible for some of the worst tropes in entertainment history—the idea that paradox will destroy the universe. Oedipus is born, his royal parents consult the

Oracle, who says he'll grow up to murder his father and marry his mother, so they cast the baby out with the bathwater, so to speak. He grows up *not* knowing who his father and mother are, slays some rude bastard in an oblivious roadside confrontation, and marries this sexy older woman who happens to be the dead guy's widow. He has kids with her, plays at being king for a while . . . and then finds out he's married his own mom and murdered his dad."

"Yeah, that's what I mean. You can't escape Fate. Paradox will bite you in the asteroid every single time," Captain Roghetti stated. She stopped and held out her arm, blocking him from progressing across a break between the tents. A hoverbike hummed past them, its rider swerving at the last second to avoid the pair. ". . . Thanks. So are your predictions really just probabilities, when they're going to come true anyway?"

Ia shook her head. "Like I said, that story ruined the tropes for everyone. It isn't inevitable. Fate is just what you're *handed*. What you *do* with it is your Destiny even if you choose to do nothing. If Oedipus's parents had chosen to do nothing about the Oracle's warning, kept him in the family and raised him, he probably wouldn't have slain his father because he would have grown up knowing and respecting the man. And even if he did, most Humans don't grow up developing sexual feelings for a mother they know and love as their mother. Even then, as an orphan not knowing anything, Oedipus could have not slain the man who turned out to be his father. He could have been careful not to slay *anyone* in case that person turned out to be his father in disguise."

"But doesn't that confirm the loop of inevitabilities?" Roghetti pressed. He gestured for them to continue moving toward the officers' barracks, where Ia's field gear had been stowed.

Rolling her eyes, Ia sought for a way to make him understand. "Okay . . . imagine you have a fortune cookie in your hands."

"A fortune cookie?" he asked, arching one dark brow.

"Yes, a fortune cookie," Ia repeated. "And you open it up to read the piece of paper inside. On that piece of paper you see the message, 'The fortune in this cookie is not true.' *Bang!* You have a paradox," she stated, snapping her fingers in accompaniment. "Because if the fortune is true, then the words state that it is *un*true, but if the fortune is a lie, then the words are wrong and fortune is *not* a lie. There's your paradox. *But.*"

". . . But?" Roghetti inquired when she paused for dramatic emphasis.

Ia shrugged and spread her hands. "But, the universe *isn't* destroyed by it. You are not caught up in a paradox. You aren't trapped in a causality loop or a bubble of illogic, because . . . you just aren't. It's just words on a page." Opening the door to the complex of crate-like tents, she gestured him inside. "The same thing goes for time travel. Yes, you *could* destroy your own grandfather, but then he wouldn't be your grandfather. Not because that would make you disappear, but because someone else would have stepped in to fill up that space, and your life would have rearranged itself to give you motivation to kill the guy who would have and should have been.

"Another way of looking at it is like this tangle of tents. You want to get to the command center, so you do have to open a door, but you don't *have* to always take the same door or path to get there. The job still gets done. You read the fortune in the fortune cookie, but you're not trapped in a logic loop of illogic." Ia opened another door in the series of container- and fabric-tents, gesturing for Roghetti to go first. She followed in his wake. "You can eat the cookie, toss the paper, and move on. Or you can eat the *paper*, toss the cookie, and move on. Eat both, toss both, find someone to hand them to . . . The cookie's job is done: it has delivered you a fortune.

"The key is to remember that what you do with the fortune you've been handed is *not* bound irrevocably to that fortune," Ia stated. "*My* abilities are simply a case of being able to see the shortest, easiest path to the heart of this complex for each person coming in from whatever angle of approach they might have. I can tell you how to get to the center in the most efficient manner possible from wherever you might be standing. I can also turn blue in the face telling you . . . but if you choose not to follow, there isn't a damned thing I can do about it without picking you up and dragging you there. Which I don't have time to do.

"All I can do is remind people that if they don't follow my instructions, a *lot* of people will be inconvenienced," she told him, stopping outside the door to her temporary quarters. "In fact, a lot of people will be literally inconvenienced to death. Which is why I want to go look at the perimeter, so I know exactly what our combined troops will *actually* be facing, rather than just taking a fortune-cookie-based guess. Information is the biggest source of power I have for making sense out of what I foresee, and in getting the fortune untangled, off the paper, and out into the real universe, where it can do a lot of good.

"Give me two minutes to grab my gear, Captain, and I'll be ready to hook up with that patrol," Ia promised.

Looking only halfway convinced, Roghetti gestured for her to proceed.

JUNE 6, 2498 T.S.

The tuft of vegetation was just a little too bushy to be Terran grass, but it served its purpose: camouflage and cover on the crawl toward enemy lines. Reaching it, Ia peered cautiously through the branching blades. Not more than forty meters away, a mechsuited figure with long servo-limbs coiled around a bulky, stunner-like weapon stood watch. Half lying over her legs, Private Ch'zun of Roghetti's Roughriders waited patiently for her to gauge the right moment to strike, as did his teammate, Private Pumipi.

That moment would come when Ia heard the telltale sounds of D Company bombing in the distance. Until then, their orders were to get within striking distance of the frogs and wait. Most of her crew picked for this assault had been broken up and paired with an Army team. Mattox's orders to this point had been for straightforward confrontations. She knew the TUPSF Army trained in maneuver-combat scenarios, but the Roughriders hadn't had a lot of practice lately, hence the partnering. Spyder practiced and led his people in nothing but small-force maneuvers versus larger forces; pairing the two would help refresh the old training memories for the Roughriders.

This approach was one such example. No matter how good modern surveillance gear was, it could always be fooled, particularly at a distance. By crawling in a slithering line three soldiers long and sticking to all the lowest points in the terrain, they could fool the Salik base sensors into thinking they were an allipede, a local, multilimbed cross between an Earth alligator and a very large insect in shape. Rather than using mechsuits, which bogged down in the muddy, soft soil, particularly near Salik encampments, Ia had ordered light armor to be worn under camouflage suits. The ceristeel plating would reflect infrared and sonar sweeps in ways similar to the thick-plated scales of the allipede, furthering the illusion.

They might be able to get closer in the increasingly dim light of the falling night, but Ia did not intend to risk a premature discovery. The clump of Dabin reddish beige bushgrass was a good one. When the missile strikes began somewhere off to her right, she would take the time to crawl her team forward another twenty, maybe even thirty meters to take out that sentry.

A well-thrown grenade would simulate a projectile strike in the confusion, adding further distraction. That would allow a second allipede-style team to crawl up to the base of the surveillance tower thirty meters beyond the sentry, where they would place a time-delayed bomb to take out the local node for lightwave communications. Other teams were scheduled to take out similar towers, plus listening posts, sentry stations, even projectile-gun bunkers.

All of it had to be done up close and personal, as quietly as possible. It was of greater individual risk to pit Humans in light armor against Salik in mechanized battlesuits, but not an impossible feat. It did, however, require timing and trust. While the flanking units distracted the Salik's main forces with a two-pronged, standard-seeming attack from B and D Companies, C Company and the Damned would run the greater risk of infiltration and sabotage. But she had the trust of Roghetti, and her Damned had the trust of the Roughriders. They would succeed.

As soon as D Company began their bombardment.

Any second now . . .

Ears straining, Ia waited for the telltale concussion shocks to boom in the distance. Nothing happened. She checked her chrono, subtly scraping away some of the mud smeared on her arm unit, and listened again. Nothing. Nothing but the itch of her instincts telling her *something* was wrong. It was faint, though, because there literally wasn't any threat for her to fight. Nothing for her battlecognition to target and analyze, even on a subconscious level.

Narrowing her eyes, she dipped her fingers into the waters of Time. If she hadn't had several years of practice under her belt, keeping her ears aware of her surroundings while checking the fog-dusted timeplains, she might have missed the boom. She could *feel* the projectiles being launched, both a few seconds into the past, and in the present, and into the future, could hear them reverberating through the waters of D Company's gunners as they loaded and launched payload after payload . . . but . . . heard nothing with her real ears.

Absolutely nothing out of the ordinary. A chirruping from bird-like creatures in the trees, the faint clicking of insects in the bushgrass, and the soft hiss and whine of the enemy's mechsuit servos as the Salik shifted his weight, independently pointing eyes surveying the horizon through his half-silvered suit dome.

"*. . . Sir?*" Ch'zun breathed as the seconds stretched into a full minute past the point where they should have been free to move forward.

She looked again in the timestreams, grateful their combined layers of armor and clothing were enough to shield Ch'zun from what she was doing. Pulling out again, she whispered back. "*Private . . . do you hear any bombardment, or have I gone deaf?*"

"*No bombs, sir,*" he confirmed.

Shakk. Something was seriously wrong. She could *see* the bombardment happening on schedule in *this* timestream. Her own timestream! But it wasn't happening. Dr. Mishka's diagnosis came back to her. *The patient is in denial . . .*

. . . Am I the patient? Have my abilities forsaken me?

Impossible. Not because she wanted to deny it but because her abilities had *never* worked like this. Under the cover of the bushgrass tuft, Ia opened her arm unit and sent a silent alert to the two Companies with a one-word message, along with her authorization code for the day.

Retreat.

Quietly closing the lid, she twitched her right leg four times, a pause, then four times again.

"Sir?" Ch'zun asked, a bare breath of sound. She repeated the pattern, and he passed it along to Pumipi. Without further protest, both he and the stocky man at the end of their fake allipede formation followed silently as she crawled in a careful, bush-hidden turn to make their way laboriously back over all the terrain they had just crossed. It would take a full hour or more to get far enough out of sensor range to be able to stand up and move, but that was the price of infiltration maneuvers.

———————

An hour of crawling, half an hour of jogging through night-darkened woods, and another half hour spent counting heads as each of the teams came back to the rendezvous point left Ia very frustrated. Another half hour of riding ground trucks did not improve her mood, though it did bring them safely back to base. Jumping off the back of the rearmost truck before it had even stopped, Ia strode straight for the shielded tent holding the beige van.

Once again, she reached Major Leotta Perkins. The brunette woman smiled politely. "Ship's Captain Ia. It's good to hear from you again. Is everything alright?"

"No, everything is not alright, Major," Ia stated without preamble. "I'd like to speak with the brigadier general right away."

"I'm afraid that's not possible," Perkins demurred, her

smile never slipping. "An emergency came up on one of the battlefronts. He won't be available for the next three days."

Dipping into the timestreams, Ia checked. According to what she saw, Mattox had indeed departed for an Army camp somewhere on the northern border of the war front . . . which . . . *wasn't* . . . what she had seen him doing while crawling for two-plus hours through the mud. But it was what he was doing right now. If the timestreams were to be believed.

". . . Are you alright, sir?" Major Perkins asked politely. "You look a little ill."

"I'm fine," Ia dismissed quickly. "Is this emergency the reason why Mattox did not deploy the troops according to the battle plans I gave him? Plans that were vetted by the Admiral-General herself?"

"I'm afraid I don't know the Brigadier General's reasons," the woman on the other end of the commscreen demurred, shrugging, "but any competent battle commander knows that whatever the Command Staff may decide for its troops to do does not always suit the ever-changing needs of the actual war front. No plan is ever perfectly tailored to actual circumstances."

"Mine are." Biting back a retort to say more—to snarl more—Ia confined herself to a deep breath and a calmer delivery. "I am a Command Staff–recognized precognitive, PsiLeague gauged in excess of Rank 84, Major. I have single-handedly wiped out three-quarters of a Choyan fleet traveling *in* faster-than-light. My accuracy is beyond a doubt."

Beyond a doubt . . . except reality and the timeplains no longer agree.

Shoving aside her doubts, Ia continued. "I will redraw the battle plans needed to win on this planet to account for this new delay. If need be, I will hand-deliver them to Mattox, and discuss their feasibility with him in person, so that he can have any questions answered. Tell him to be prepared for a visit from me in four days. Ship's Captain out."

A jab of her finger ended the transmission. Private Douglas, the current communications tech on duty in the tent, gave her a wary look. ". . . Sir?"

"Something's wrong. Something is *grievously* wrong," Ia muttered darkly, thoughts racing and probing, trying to find the source. Nothing but fog drifting slowly across the timestreams. She shook her head. "I don't know what, yet. Send a message to Admiral Genibes informing him that the first attempt at getting Mattox and the 1st Division to follow my battle plans has failed. Let him know I will be trying again."

"Aye, sir," Douglas agreed. She shifted to set up the connection all the way to Earth, then hesitated. The look she gave her CO wasn't quite anxious, but there was concern in her hazel eyes. "If the brigadier general won't be back for three more days, and you can't get the plans passed through him any sooner than four days from now, sir . . . won't that start to screw up the timelines too much?"

"We'll still have some leeway in the timing of things, Irene," Ia reassured her. "Don't worry too much about it. I'm going to go wash off this mud and get something to eat. Let me know if Admiral Genibes sends back a response."

"Aye, sir," Douglas said, resuming her task. With her back to her CO, she didn't see Ia's brief but confused, worried frown.

JUNE 8, 2498 T.S.

"And how does that make you feel?" Bennie asked her commanding officer. The quintessential psychology question was a valid one, given the circumstances.

"It's *frustrating*." Ia balled up another pair of socks, fresh from the sonic cleaner, and tossed them into her kitbag. "I keep going over it in my head. Over and over . . . I could *see* D Company loading their payloads into the mortars and firing them in every pertinent timestream connected to mine, but they weren't actually *doing* it when I watched with my eyes and listened with my ears.

"All I know is, my gifts *can't* have stopped working," she asserted, folding and rolling up a bra next. "I've never seen the timeplains so clear and bright before, except for those little scudding clouds of fog. They're like . . ."

". . . They're like?" her Company chaplain prodded. "What?"

"They're like little . . . Harper-clouds," Ia finally offered, finding the right words for it. "Little scudding knots of I-don't-know-whats. Or like those little optical illusions you get when you're staring at a grid of black squares on white paper, and you *see* the little fuzzy gray squares at the center of every intersecting set of white lines. But you only see them with your peripheral vision because when you stare straight at them, they vanish, and all you see is a clean white crossroads in the midst of all those black city blocks—does that make any sense?"

"It does," Bennie allowed. Leaning back against the head railing on her bunk-bed cot, she shook her head. "I'm afraid I cannot tell you if your gifts are working correctly or not. I'm not even a parapsychologist, let alone a parapsychiatrist. You'd be better off going to Jesselle for *that* kind of head-shrinking."

"Oh yes, *that'll* inspire confidence in my troops," Ia muttered, tossing in the last of her clean military-issue brassieres. "Tell the Company doctor I think I'm going nuts."

"Oh, piffle," the redhead dismissed, rolling her eyes. "I can tell you that you're not going nuts. You're relatively stress-free"—she paused while Ia snorted loudly—"*and* you're dealing with the source of your frustrations calmly and rationally."

"Except I'm *not* dealing with it because I have no idea what went wrong," Ia pointed out honestly. She realized she had mangled the folding of her camouflage trousers and sighed, shaking them out and starting over. Bunk beds on a heavy-gravitied world weren't usual, but Dabin's gravity was only 1.85Gs. The bottom bunks were also set lower to the ground, leaving the top ones lower as well. That meant she was free to use her bed as a sort of high, padded counter for folding things. "I'm just dealing with my frustration as best I can."

"So go see Jesselle," Bennie told her. "She's a paraphysician and a psychologist, as well as an outstanding medic. That's why you nabbed the best Triphid you could find, remember? Mental, physical, psychic, plus optical and dental health all in one . . ."

Ia wrinkled her nose. "God, don't remind me. I'm due for another checkup and tooth-cleaning. It'll have to wait until we're on the *Damnation*, though. I don't know if Roghetti's infirmary has the sonic picks, I *know* they don't have any supply of the right bacteriophagic cultures down here, and we're not taking the time to run her all the way out to a town with a dentist who does and has enough to spare us some."

"But you *will* take the time to talk with her about your inner-vision problem, right?" Bennie pressed. "She's also the ship's ophthamologist."

"*Inner* vision, Commander," Ia retorted. "Last I checked, she wasn't a paraophthamologist . . . if there even is such a thing." A moment of dipping into the timestreams out of pure curiosity ended in a sigh. ". . . Yes, there is. There's even one here on Dabin, but the nearest one is a good eight thousand kilometers away, give or take a few hundred. PsiLeague trained, of course. That is, if I'm not hallucinating his existence like I did Mattox's compliance."

"How cheerful. The most powerful psi on the planet is going for the broody, gothic-heroine theme." Pushing up onto one elbow, the middle-aged chaplain asked, "Should I try to wear a cowl, curl up my fingers, and command you to 'Give in to your uncertainties and fears! Let the power of the Doubt Side consume you!' . . . Hmm?"

Caught off guard, Ia laughed. Belly-clenching laughter. Gasping for air, she rested her face and arms on her bunk until she could breathe normally again, then stepped back. She tried glaring at her friend, but the sight of that gamine, freckled grin diffused her attempted scorn. "Okay, fine, I'll go talk to Jesselle. Just stop teasing me with ancient story tropes!"

"It's a quote, not a trope," Chaplain Benjamin asserted primly. Then relaxed, grinning again. "Okay, it's a *mis*-quote. Go on; go schedule yourself a paraphysician's visit."

"Only if you agree to fold and stow my clothes," Ia countered. She flicked a hand at the pile of laundry still waiting to be sorted on her bunk. "Any other officer of my rank would have a staff corporal to take care of stuff like this. Lucky me, I had to barter down my crew to the absolute bare necessity."

Uncurling herself from her bunk, Bennie stood up with a grunt. Unlike Ia, she hadn't been born a heavyworlder, though like all of Ia's crew, she had learned to adapt to the increasingly strong pull of their former ship's gravity plates. Patting Ia on the biceps, she nudged the slightly shorter woman aside. "Heave to, Cap'n," she ordered Ia. "You're lucky I'm already on your staff, and that my rank has a 'c' in it. Now *go*."

"Commander, yes, sir!" Ia quipped, smacking her fingers against her forehead in a fluttery mock-salute. Leaving her friend to fold her laundry, Ia left the barracks tent reserved for the top female officers and noncoms in the combined camp. *I'll owe Bennie a favor for that . . .*

The maze of tents, covered corridors, and expanded medical pods making up the infirmary complex wasn't far away, but it was damp outside. At the moment, the upper force fields were down. Her gifts *said* the weather would remain damp but not drenching, somewhere between a mist and a drizzle, but Ia wasn't sure anymore, so she grabbed a poncho from the stack hooked onto a tent post by the door and pulled it over her head and shoulders.

Are my gifts failing me? Am I going mad? Disconnected from reality and seeing things in my head that aren't really there? Seeing gray spots out of the corner of my eyes when there aren't any at the intersections of Time and probabilities?

Doubt wasn't a comfortable state of mind for her. It crawled up her spine like a trail of bugs from the Dabin mud, itching along her nerves. The feeling increased the closer she got to the infirmary tents, until Ia found herself spinning around, searching the camp and the tree-shrouded horizon for any sign of an incoming threat. It didn't help that she could see a cluster of technicians working on something at the base of the central projection tower for the shield generator. She did not like having that shield down, let alone down for repairs. Not with this itch of paranoia prickling her nerves.

Nothing happened, of course. Still, as much as she knew her chaplain, friend, and counselor was correct, she didn't take herself straight into the infirmary tents. Pushing the mottled hood of her poncho back from her face so she could use her peripheral vision without restriction, Ia studied the horizon. Ears and eyes strained, seeking anything that might be a telltale sign of an attack. She even sniffed the air, trying to figure out what was wrong.

Her battle instincts felt like something was plucking them, as they had *not* been plucked *en route* to that Salik sensor tower two days before. In the timestreams, she sensed nothing wrong . . . but she had sensed nothing wrong with her battle plans. *Circular thinking? Paranoia?*

At least paranoia saves lives. Raising her hands, she flipped open her arm unit, ready to contact the command center to see if anything had showed up on the scopes yet. Movement at the edge of her vision made her spin to the right.

A cluster of bird-things rose up into the sky, with long bodies and two sets of leathery, featherless wings evolved to handle the local heavy gravity. Their movement plucked sharply on her combat-trained nerves. Her fingers jabbed at the command unit's buttons, activating an open-channel broadcast. *"This is Ship's Captain Ia. Code India Alpha. Evacuate the camp. I repeat. India Alpha, evacuate the camp now. Fall back to Beta position. This is not a drill!"*

The camp roiled with movement. Bodies poured out of tent and pod openings, sprinting for the armory. Most of them had extra gray mottling their camouflage-hued sleeves, but enough of them were also green to satisfy her, reassuring Ia that Roghetti's side of things was willing to listen.

"Commander Harper, grab the special guns," she ordered, turning in a slow circle, searching for more spooked avians. *"Private C'ulosc, evacuate the van. Roughriders and Damned alike, fall back to Beta now. This is* not *a dr—"*

Bright orange light flashed out of the trees even as she spun on pure instinct. It slammed with searing heat into her left eye and scorched across her temple. Screaming as she dropped, Ia hit the ground in a squelch of wet moss-grass.

Instinct rolled her onto her side and stomach, pressing the wound into the damp plant life. Superheated flesh sizzled and steamed, adding a boiled aroma to the stench of scorched meat, as well as a fresh layer of blinding-hot agony.

"Captain!" she heard someone shout. "*Medic!* The captain's been shot!"

Teeth clenched against the pain, Ia grabbed the hand of one of the privates trying to turn her over. "*Run*, you slagging idiots!"

"*Shakk* that!" she heard one of her own soldiers swear; who, she couldn't see, and the pain was too much still to tell by voice alone. Hands snagged the belt strung through her pants, heaving her off the ground. "We're running *with* you!"

Somehow, she got her feet under her. It took her several meters of being dragged awkwardly, head throbbing with unholy agony and barely able to see out of her muddied, uninjured eye, but she got her feet under her. Shoving hard to the left, she pushed the three of them behind a tent, forcing the two men half carrying her into staggering and dropping in a bruising heap. A slap of her arm knocked the one on top of her back down just as he started to get up.

"Stay out of sight, you fools!" she hissed, vision streaked with coruscating bands of nerve-damaged pain. She couldn't see their faces as anything more than tear-blurred blobs. Behind her, she could hear the whining of servos, several startled shouts, and the tearing and tangling of fabric being moved. "I'm their primary target! Crawl *that* way!"

He rolled a bit more behind the shelter of the tent, then got up. Together, he and her crew member—Private Floathawg, she could see the burgundy blotches on his face—pulled her a couple meters past its edge. Sizzling sounds from laser rifles and the *tat-tat-tat* of projectile fire told her someone was counterattacking.

Blinking her right eye caused more pain in her left, but she saw a hand-shaped blur lift to a nonblotched face. Or rather, to his ear; the Army man still had on his headset. Hers was tucked in her shirt pocket. "Captain Ia, there are no other signs of an outright attack. It looks like it was just a lone sniper. Captain Roghetti wants to know if you want to cancel that evacuation order, sir."

Having her eye scorched out of her head hurt worse than being shot in the shoulder, but pain was nothing new. She pushed onto her knees, head swimming for a moment. A shaky check of the timestreams showed his report looked to be true . . . but her instincts were still demanding that they run. "No. The local bird-things flew up on the *northwest* side of camp, and that shot came from the east—evacuate the camp! That's an order!"

"With respect, Ship's Captain, you are *not* in our chain of command," the private retorted.

"With respect, Private, *shove it*!" she heard Floathawg snap. Wrapping his arm around her ribs, he hauled her to her feet with a grunt. "When my Captain says we all move, we *all* move!"

Forcing her legs to cooperate, Ia stumbled along at Harley's side as they left Roghetti's man behind. Her crewman kept the two of them to the edges of the tents. Getting used to the pain along the left side of her face, Ia moved as best she could with him. At least she could see more and more clearly with her right as the seconds stretched into a minute. She didn't need a mirror to know her left eye was gone; she had no depth perception, and her precognition wasn't working properly. But she did physically see members of her Company executing their retreat plan, grabbing packs of essential supplies, weapons, and whatever else they could lay their hands on that was of any use within a single minute.

An orange-speckled body moved up at her side, a field medic with the faint green stripe of the Army. "Sir, we need to get you to the infirmary. At least, the part not being *stolen* by that crazy chief medi—"

Something *boomed* in the distance. The sky crackled with momentary static. Orange light flashed, bright and strong.

Her instincts snapped again. Grabbing the woman, Ia flung both her and Harley to the ground with another shove. Something whistled in and *WHOMMED* bare meters away. Debris from the shelled tent showered down around them. The woman thrown prone next to Ia shrieked, peppered with shrapnel from the backsplash, but Ia's instincts said not badly, not lethally. Most of the impact had continued onward in the direction of the strike. Harley hadn't been touched, and she had only picked up a few stings, a cut on her cheek. She didn't know if anyone inside that tent had been injured or killed, though.

The blast left her ears ringing. Using her hands, Ia stroked the crying woman's face to refocus her attention, pressed two muddy fingers to her lips, then helped her onto hands and knees. Other concussions from exploding projectiles rumbled through the ground and the air, more felt than heard. Adrenaline made the pain in her head and body fade, allowing her to see and think more clearly, though she could still barely hear.

Pointing the way in pure instinct, she led three of them in a crawling shuffle through the smoke until they could gain their feet. Trucks were already on their way out of the field, swerving wildly to avoid the incoming rounds. Yanking the hood of her poncho up over her distinctive white hair, Ia tugged on the strings to bring it close to her face. That scraped the edge of the burn mark, blurring her vision from the pain. Teeth clenched, she ignored it, grabbing Harley and the Army medic by the shoulders.

"Run for it on three . . . *Three!*"

Shoving them forward, Ia tugged and pushed them right and left as her battle instincts demanded. Arms spread wide for balance when she wasn't grabbing one or the other either for avoidance or for support—her eyesight and her ears weren't doing too well, meddling with her sense of balance—she dodged as well. Laser fire scorched her poncho and bullets *paffed* through the soil at their feet, but they reached the bush-choked edge of the forest with no more real injuries. A handful of reddish-leaved branches scraped her face, searing pain across her nerves, but once past the sunlit, leaf-choked edge, most of the branches were high enough, she didn't feel like she was going to poke out her other eye just yet.

Movement caught her eye. Skimming through the shrubs at head height, someone pulled up a hoverbike next to them. It was Private Mara Sunrise, one of Sadneczek's full-time clerks and Floathawg's teammate. "Captain, are you alright?"

"*Yes*, some *real* transport! Permission to take that bike to cover our retreat, sir," Private Floathawg hissed, slowing down. He started to reach for the gun holstered at his hip and did a double take at his teammate. "Wait, how do *you* know how to ride a hawg? I thought you said they were too dangerous for your tastes."

"Stow it, Harley!" Ia snapped, pushing him forward. She squinted up at Sunrise and enunciated clearly through the agony in her head. "*Staff Sergeant*, our position is compromised. Grab whatever you need and ride ahead to secure the Beta site. If you cannot secure it, report to Lieutenant Commander Helstead on the situation why."

"*Staff* Sergeant?" Floathawg asked her, bewildered. His teammate, however, stiffened, blinked, and narrowed her eyes at their CO.

"Morning has broken, sir?" Sunrise asked Ia cryptically.

"Someone go fix it," Ia replied, sign and countersign. "Tag, you're it."

"Oh *rapture*. I finally get to violate my parole." Swaying the hoverbike closer to her teammate, the mousey-haired woman leaned down and snatched the projectile pistol from his hip. A second fast yank unsnapped the pouch of c-clips at his waist. Before he could do more than yelp in protest, she gunned the bike's thrusters and took off, *with* his weapon and ammunition.

"—The hell?" Floathawg protested, gaping as she left. "Captain? What the *hell* was that about? Why'd *she* take the hoverbike? And my gun!"

"Not *now*. Keep moving." Ia ordered. Her ears were now free enough from the ringing to hear the hissing of lasers striking into the trees, and the concussions of more missiles. Off to her right, thankfully within her functioning peripheral vision, she saw the nurse staggering, the torn fabric of her shirt and slacks showing patches of blood from her shrapnel wounds. Ia swayed that way to catch her. Harley followed her.

"Captain, you just sent a *clerk* to secure the Beta site," he hissed, moving to assist the Army woman. "No disrespect, sir, but did that laser penetrate your brain? Hell, *I'm* a better shot, and I'm a mechanic!"

"I just sent a *Knifeman* to secure that site, soldier," Ia countered grimly. "But you keep that part quiet; she's *not* supposed to violate her parole. And I'm not brain-damaged. The laser didn't strike that deep. Unfortunately, we have been compromised somehow, and right now, I don't know if the Beta site *is* secure or not."

The moment she said it, Ia realized she had used the wrong pronoun . . . *Not* we've *been compromised.* I've *been compromised. Little fuzzy patches . . . !*

She wanted to curse and scream, but didn't have the

energy or the time. Those scudding patches of fog that vanished whenever she looked directly, the gray patches of optical illusion on the grid, *they* were the reality, not the all-too-clear and clean crossroads she had focused upon. Her precognition had been compromised somehow, but *not* her battlecognition. One relied on direct examination of the timestreams, but the other relied on the paranormal equivalent of peripheral vision . . . where the scudding clouds of psychic obfuscation lay, and could not fully cover. Someone was messing with her ability to read the timestreams . . .

No. *Meddling* with her mind.

The underbrush thickened for a moment; the need to avoid impaling herself thwarted her rising anger. Emerging in the firebreak that contained the farmer's force-field-projected fence line, Ia nudged the two with her to the right. That fence was now down. About a hundred meters down the way, one of the escaping hovertrucks had stopped just on the other side of the inert pylons. Limping, the nurse stumbled that way. Ia and Harley helped her.

She spotted a member of the Damned and hustled them forward a little faster. "Private Jeeves! Front and center!"

The metrokinetic blinked, faced her, and started in shock. "Captain, your face—Medic!"

Two more soldiers swerved and came running at Jeeves's shout, one with a field kit in his hands. Ia pushed the Army woman at them. "Tend *her*, not me. My eye's cauterized, so it'll keep. Jeeves, get over here. KIman!"

Private Jeeves jogged over at her command. He was barely dressed in camouflage shirt and pants, his boots hastily knotted, and his long black hair unbound in a rain-dampened, tangled mess instead of pinned up in a neat bun at the back of his head as per regulations. He wasn't the only one who had been forced to make do with whatever they could grab to wear; others who had been on their sleeping shift wore haphazard gear, pieces of clothing, light armor, whatever they had grabbed without having the time to dig into their kitbags for full outfits just yet.

"Whatever you need, you got it, Captain," Private Jeeves offered. He extended his hand to offer her his personal energies.

"Not from you. *To* you. I need you to muck up the weather," she ordered, grabbing his hand. Or tried to; it took her two tries since she had no depth perception anymore. "Take my kinetic inergy, get on that truck, and wring the hardest rain you can out of those clouds. The Salik are hunters; they might like the humidity, but we need our ground tracks covered and their scanner range reduced, fast!"

He blinked, startled, but nodded grimly. Bracing himself with a deep breath, he said, "Ready, sir."

Closing her good eye—ignoring the pain caused by the reflex of trying to close the bad one—Ia spun kinetic inergy out of herself. It was something like the crackling sting of electrokinetic energy, and something like the cool wash of biokinetic, and carried the flavor of both, but much more personal. It was also a lot stronger than the weather-psi was expecting. His hair snapped and fluffed out despite the drizzling, misting rain trying to keep it flattened down.

She opened her eye just in time to see his brown ones rolling up and back in his head. Above them, the clouds boiled a little in the distance, darkening as he thickened their cover. Ia kept feeding him energy while more stragglers came out of the woods. She could still hear the Salik attacking the camp in the distance but didn't stop until she felt dizzy, until the timestreams fogged from depleted energy.

Releasing his hand, she clasped his shoulder, holding

him steady while he swayed, all of his attention still focused inward and upward. "KImen! I need two KImen!"

Two Army figures eyed each other, then jumped out of the truck, hurrying toward Ia. She felt a hand clasp her own shoulder. "We need to get *out* of here, Captain!"

"I know that, Floathawg—you and you!" she ordered the two approaching women, nodding at Private Jeeves. "Take this soldier up on that truck and you keep him psychically fed. Cycle in whoever you need to when you get dizzy. He'll be covering our tracks with a storm." Raising her voice as the two soldiers grabbed and guided him away, she shouted at the others. "This is a full-on retreat, soldiers! *Fall back!* I want an armed rearguard detail, but do *not* engage the enemy if you can avoid it.

"Everybody, move out!" Pulling Floathawg's hand off her shoulder, she tucked it behind her back, stuffing his fingers into her belt. "Get me to the nearest truck, Harley; I'm having trouble gauging distances at the moment."

"Sir, yes, sir," he agreed, picking up into a jog. The muscular ex-V'Dan didn't quite carry her, but he did guide her as they ran in tandem, keeping her on her feet as her boots stumbled over deceptive bits of terrain. "Heave up, sir!"

She pushed off the ground, yanked up indelicately by the belt as he boosted her into the back of the truck. Twisting around as she landed, she hauled him in as well, then awkwardly grabbed the hand of the man behind him, pulling that soldier in as well. A tree fell nearby, knocked down by an explosive blast. The truck started moving. Three more soldiers were still running their way, dodging bits of plant life turned into shrapnel.

With an Herculean effort, all three managed to grab the truck; Ia and the others pulled them inside. As soon as she could, she pushed them off her and tucked herself into the back corner of the truck, huddled up into as small a figure as she could manage. With her reserves either bled into Jeeves for manipulating the weather or tied into her wound to keep it biokinetically stable, she did not trust her ability to control the timeplains. She didn't trust *anything* about the timeplains beyond her deepest battle instincts anymore.

Somewhere out there, a Feyori had managed to sink him- or herself deeply enough into those same timeplains that they could occlude and rewrite temporal reality. It was the only answer to this mess that made sense. Not a direct touch because she *would* notice that. She'd touched more than enough Meddler minds to know exactly what their energies, their thoughts, felt like . . . but not on the timeplains before now.

As she had once told a certain lieutenant colonel of the Department of Innovations, back when putting her crew together, she was *not* the only person who could measure and manipulate the flow of Time. The worst of it, however, was the fact that she couldn't even run a headcount to see who had managed to escape the attack. Neither precognitively nor postcognitively; not and be sure she was seeing reality. If it didn't require instinctive, split-second battle timing, she was now effectively mind-blind.

The loss of her outer eye paled in comparison to the loss of the inner one, and her anger outburned the agony of her injury as the truck rolled and bounced in its rapid retreat.

CHAPTER 3

A tiny, petty part of myself still holds Brigadier General Mattox responsible for the combined Charlie Foxtrot which Roghetti's Roughriders and my Damned went through. But the lion's share, oh, that belonged to someone else entirely. Well, technically two someones. No commander likes a Charlie Foxtrot, and this one—what? Oh, that's archaic military-speak for when a situation goes seriously wrong. Charlie Foxtrot, the call signs for the letters C and F, is the polite shorthand for calling it a cluster f***—

. . . You'll actually have to bleep that one out? Sorry. I won't mention it again, then. Suffice to say, it's shorthand for things going very, very wrong, usually in combat. Regardless of how or when or why, we still have to deal with the resulting mess whenever we're handed one. My first concern was therefore the safety of the people under me, and by extension those under Captain Roghetti. My second was for the breach in the Army's line. It didn't help

that they kept pressing us back, and back, but at least they continued to pursue us rather than spread out and attack the locals.

I may have powers above and beyond most everyone out there, but I am first a soldier, and foremost an officer. Vengeance had to sit farther down the line and wait for its turn.

~Ia

JUNE 9, 2498 T.S.
KUN-BRELLER FOOTHILLS, DABIN

Ia listened to the hushed arguing of her officers and sergeants, though her gaze remained on the dark, wet forest beyond the knot of Dabin-style trees giving them temporary shelter. Jeeves's constant metrokinetic meddling had lowered the air pressure over the region long enough to bring in strong gusts of wind and soggy rainfalls up until now.

The resulting storms hid the two Companies' tracks alright, but the constant attacks by Salik, wind, and water left everyone wet and miserable. He also couldn't sustain it for more than half an hour at a time, with rest breaks for a handful of hours, and was now on the dregs of his mental reserves. Unable to do anything more, Jeeves now slept; this was the last of the ongoing storm he had summoned. The last chance for the weather to aid their situation by hindering their enemies.

". . . demanding that we return to the lowlands to protect the people of Eltegar City. I pointed out that while we're being hunted by the frogtopi, *they're* still more or less safe . . ."

At least her missing left eye didn't hurt anymore. They didn't have the facilities to regrow organs—those amenities were reserved for cities well beyond the current Salik invasion—but they did have emergency regeneration pads. With one of those strapped to her head over the wound, coupled with her modest biokinetic ability, the burns were healing. It wouldn't replace her eye, since that was too complex an organ for a mere pad, but it was working to turn the burned tissue into smooth, scarless flesh that would more readily accept a transplant once she did have time to get one regrown.

The loss of her eye wasn't the worst wound, however. Five members of the Damned hadn't made it out . . . and she didn't know if that was because they were lost in the wilderness somewhere, dead back at the abandoned camp, or because they'd been rendered CPE, Captured, Presumed Eaten, the military term for being chained up by the Salik so they could become a still-living lunch. Roghetti had lost even more than her, a good twenty-eight men and women out of his five Platoons.

Needlessly lost. She didn't know if they were alive or dead, either.

". . . don't 'ave th' forces, Doctor, an' you don' 'ave th' meds . . ."

Her precognition still wasn't working right. Her mind was thankfully unaffected; both Lieutenant Commander Mishka and one of the privates from the 3rd Platoon, Bibia Mk'nonn, had scanned her brain telepathically to look for Feyori fingerprints on her psyche. None had been found. She hadn't sensed an attempt to breach her mental walls at any point, but it was good to have it confirmed by two other psis.

Ia knew there were two Feyori playing their Games on this world, one for the Dabin colonists and one for the Salik invaders. If they had any influence on Ia, it was thankfully indirect at best, more a case of their obscuring the truth on the timeplains than of trying to Meddle directly with her thoughts. Unfortunately, that was more than enough to *shakk* all of her original and ongoing plans.

Ia would have taken some time to seek out and confront the Feyori in the timestreams, save for two things: her future self, who had warned her against contacting them directly on the timeplains; and the fact that the Salik had continued to chase them. There just hadn't been enough time to do so safely. As it was, they were all being forced to sleep in shifts with the most exhausted riding in the trucks while they continued to run, curving this way and that up into the nearby foothills.

At the moment, her instincts were telling her that they had two, maybe three hours to rest before the Salik struck again. She had forced herself to sleep for a little bit in the back of one of the trucks in the last six hours, but it wasn't the same as real sleep in a safe location. The others were even worse off; most didn't have alternate ways of resting and regaining energy.

Outlying scouts—mostly Private Sunrise, still somewhere out there on her hoverbike—reported that the Salik were ignoring the little burg of Eltegar City for now, a small but very important blessing. The fallback Beta site had been prepared with an ambush as Ia had feared, one a little too large for the former Knifeman to handle, but the ex-counterassassin had spotted it in time to alter their retreat to another location.

". . . going to need to resupply soon, or the grunts will start bitching about the food . . ."

That was Helstead's attempt at humor. One of the trucks that had escaped had been loaded with nearly haphazardly picked crates of weapons and ammunition, as well as Harper's special psi-guns; that alone, the ability to return fire, had kept the Salik from overrunning them. One had been loaded with boxes of rations, so at least they weren't fleeing on empty stomachs . . . but they *were* ration packs, as opposed to real food.

A third truck had already been loaded with light armor, which meant their rear guard and nearby scouts had a modicum of protection. Another had actually been the self-transporting surgery pod, retracted and evacuated by Dr. Mishka without a care for the tents connecting to it the moment Ia ordered everyone to move out. If it weren't for those latter two, their constant forced retreats would have suffered more fatal casualties . . . but that only covered so much. Their medical supplies, things like the gel-laden sponge strapped to her face, were now running low.

Morale was even lower. One eye was more than enough to see the dirty looks aimed her way by Roghetti's soldiers. The Roughriders' lack of faith, she could understand and forgive. They hadn't understood that when she gave an order like the one to evacuate, it wasn't on a whim. It was a real order, with a real need behind it. The stricken, puzzled, and angry looks from her *own* crew . . . she could understand those, too, given what had happened, but she couldn't forgive herself.

". . . heard some of Roghetti's talking the equivalent of *mutiny*, if we don't split up from them soon," she heard Rico rumble in that deep, quiet voice of his. The m-word pulled her attention back to the meeting behind her.

"Mutiny, hell," Sergeant Maxwell growled, "I've heard some of our *own* headed that way. I don't like that."

"Ia." That was the voice of her first officer. Harper's words cut her to the bone, striking into wounds already laid over the last few days. "You know I don't mean to doubt your decisions, but what *good* does this constant retreat do?"

Instinct said that if she didn't address the m-word problem *now*, they'd be in a world of hurt later. Despite how they'd done their best to elude pursuit time and again, the Salik had found them. In specific, whenever Ia started to *plan* some sort of counterattack, the Salik had still found them. When she *chose* to follow Roghetti's plans instead . . . the Salik had still found them.

She was getting tired of the Salik finding them. She was getting tired of the Feyori finding *her*. So she addressed his question obliquely.

"Commander Harper," Ia stated, turning to face the knot of her cadre. "Get me one of your guns."

He blinked, frowned at her, and asked, ". . . Just *one* of my guns, sir?"

"One gun. Now," she ordered, staring at her first officer.

". . . Sir, yes, sir." Shaking his head slightly, Harper moved out of the little dry patch formed by the closely spaced trunks, too closely spaced to allow any branches for the first five meters.

She didn't have to specify which gun, since there was only one type of gun which she would ask *him* to fetch. Any other kind, she would have asked one of the Platoon Sergeants to bring.

When he had moved away, Ia turned to her second officer. "Lieutenant Commander Helstead."

"Yes, sir." Helstead squared her shoulders, her gaze level and steady. Of all of them, she was actually the least restless right now. Then again, she looked like she'd had the least sleep of all of them, having volunteered for both coordinating the night watch and the sabotage efforts meant to slow, deter, or derail the enemy at their backs.

"There are twenty-five enlisted psis available in the Damned, not counting yourself and the doctor. Get them here," Ia ordered.

The petite redhead didn't even wait for a "now" from her

commanding officer. She just moved off, arms lifting to tap commands into her command unit, summoning the psis in question.

Spyder straightened his shoulders, coming to a modified Attention. He had forgone his favorite shades-of-green hair dye and had instead patterned his normally sandy brown hair in shades of brick, brown, and beige to match the local terrain. "Wha're your plans, Cap'n?"

"I don't have any." It was the honest truth, and it dropped Spyder's jaw. It also made Mishka's mouth sag.

Rico blinked, then narrowed his eyes. "There's something you're not telling us."

"There's a lot of things I'm not telling you," Ia admitted dryly. At least in tone; her clothes were damp despite the torn and scorched poncho she still wore to protect herself from the near-constant rain outside this little grove of trees. "But that doesn't matter."

"Then what *does*?" the large man pressed, shifting forward a step as if to loom over her. Lieutenant Rico didn't normally use his muscular height to intimidate; he was her Intelligence Officer, not her Combat Officer. He was, however, frustrated and angered by their situation.

She couldn't blame him for feeling that way. She felt the same. Unfortunately, getting angry would do absolutely nothing to fix the damned situation. Ia kept her tone calm, unruffled. Now more than ever, her troops needed to have faith in her. "You'll find out when the time is right."

"*Shakk* that," Sergeant Sadneczek muttered. He spat to the side, his grizzled jawline already growing a salt-and-pepper beard. Without the toiletry supplies found in a kitbag, several of the men in both Companies were starting to sprout stubble. His just grew faster. Her Company Sergeant eyed her, looking rough and ragged, and not ready for any *shova*-shoveling.

"Either you tell us now, or you're gonna start losin' our faith, Captain."

"*After* the psis have come," she countered, keeping her thoughts calm. A plan was starting to form. She squelched it firmly and just breathed while they waited for the others to return.

Filling her senses with the sounds and the sensations and the smells evoked by each breath, she focused on just breathing, until Harper returned with a bulky case containing one of the brass and faintly glowing crystalline guns he had created. Until twenty-five curious, limping, exhausted, angry, patient, sullen soldiers crowded in as best they could under the patch of dryness their officers and noncoms had appropriated. When instinct said the moment was right, Ia stopped focusing on her breathing and spoke, without a single thought in mind for what lay ahead.

"Right. My ability to predict things has been compromised. I cannot tell you how, nor what I'm going to do about it, as that would tip off the enemy to the one card still in my hand," she clarified, as her opening statement caused startled looks and uneasy shifting among the men and women around her, enlisted or otherwise. "Until I can do something about it, you psychics are hereby ordered to implement Company Directive 'Mary Had a Little Lamb' until further notice. Try to include Roghetti's Roughriders if you can, but only while they're in range.

"Otherwise, I want every last one of our fifteen Squads covered, and two of you shielding your commanding officer at all times, starting as soon as this meeting is over." Ia paused, then smiled wryly. "Whoever thinks of the worst, most annoyingly catchy earworm of a jingle to project and protect with will earn a full-pay-grade raise as a bonus when this is all over and done. Take a moment now to start thinking of which ones you'll use."

While they looked at each other, from Private Jeeves in the 1st Platoon all the way through to Private Mittletech in the 3rd, Crow and his teammate Teevie already started humming a faint duet that sounded suspiciously like the theme song for a certain popular, long-running Gatsugi comedy show, *Red Is Green*. Ia turned to Harper. Lifting her chin, she looked at the case. He set it on the ground, used his thumbprint on the scanner locks, and opened the latches.

Helstead moved up next to him. "Do you want someone to fire it, sir?"

"Nope. I want you to organize a party," Ia countered. That earned her more than a few odd looks. Crow and Teevie stopped humming, blinking in astonishment. Ia shifted her gaze to include them, before moving on to the others. They quickly started humming again. "You *all* heard me right. This Company is dangerously low on morale. You desperately need a day of rest. As your Commanding Officer, it is my prerogative as whether or not to give you one . . . and I am going to give you one. Inform Roghetti's Roughriders that I will be giving them a day of rest as well."

"And how, exactly, are you going to do that?" Commander Benjamin questioned her. The taller of the two redheads in Ia's cadre, the chaplain adopted a pose near identical to Helstead's: hands on hips, head cocked, and brow furrowed in confusion. "There's a whole bunch of frogtopi after us, in case you've forgotten the last few days. We shook them off for an hour or two, but they *will* catch up and find us again, and they'll do it soon."

"You have your orders, people," Ia stated, ignoring the question. She stooped to pluck the odd, oversized, *pi*-shaped gun-thing from the padding lining the case. Hefting it onto her shoulder, she balanced it muzzle up with one hand. "You will all take a day off, save for rotating out the perimeter sentries. You will enjoy whatever sort of party you can scrape together. And you will *rest*.

"One more thing. I am dividing the Damned into two Companies. Until further orders, Commander Meyun Harper is now officially in charge of A Company, 1st Legion, 1st Battalion, 1st Brigade, 1st Division, 9th Cordon Special Forces, as of this date and time . . ." Lifting her left arm, the one not balancing the heavy gun, she checked her chronometer, "19:13 Terran Standard, being 6:23 Local Dabin Standard. I'm still in overall charge, but B Company will be under my direct command, and A under Harper's."

"B Company?" Harper asked her, frowning and rising from his crouch. "Who's going to be in B Company, besides you?"

She gave him a blithe shrug. "Commander, I have no clue. I have not a single damned thought in my head on what I'm going to do . . . because I cannot even *touch* the timestreams without betraying our position to the enemy—and don't say the 'F' word. *That's* why they've kept chasing us all this time. So I am going to go for a little walk in an attempt to clear my head and shake them off my trail." Ia didn't clarify whether she meant the Feyori or the Salik. Either way, it didn't matter. "*You* will have a little party while I'm gone. Your priority is now Company morale."

They gaped at her. The Salik were mind-blind as a race, not as mere individuals. That the strongest psi among them was admitting the Salik could trace her precognitive efforts was an impossibility, but only because she didn't dare mention the F-word to them. Feyori. She faced her first officer.

"Harper, you are the *only* person whose moves I cannot predict," Ia told him, taking advantage of their stunned silence. "I need you to take over and lead A Company for me because they're trying to predict *us* based on *me*. But the Damned also need a day of rest . . . so my one order for the lot of you is to take that day of rest. After that, *you* get to decide what the larger share of our two Companies will do. In the meantime, B Company is going for a walk. I'll be rejoining you shortly," she promised, thinking firmly about doing so within half an hour. Believing she would do so. "I just need to go for a little walk first and clear my head. I won't go far, but I do need to get away."

Turning, she started picking her way through the trees, bizarre gun on her shoulder. Behind her, Helstead filled in for the still-stunned first officer. "You heard the Captain! Teevie, Crow, shadow Captain Ia. Mankiller, MacInnes, you're with Commander Harper. The rest of you, we have no one covering 1st E Squad, and no one covering 2nd D Squad, until those four are relieved of their duty."

"I'll take 2nd D Squad, Commander," Mishka volunteered. "We've caught up on all the current injuries, so I have the inergy to spare."

"Alright, then I'll take 1st E," Helstead stated. "Thank you, Doc."

Ia heard footsteps crunching over the dried leaves on the ground. It wasn't just Crow and Teevie, who had shifted up to flank her on either side, humming the theme of their favorite show, but Harper as well. She didn't face him, though. "You have your orders, Commander. Take over A Company, give them a day of rest, then do as you see fit."

"And if I see fit to order the Company to follow you anyway?" he asked.

She swung around to face him and tangled the oversized, lumpy muzzle of her gun in the branches of a waist-high bush. Dislodging it impatiently, still lacking depth perception, she lowered it far enough to look at him. "They are using *my own abilities* against me, Meyun. You are therefore the only person with any hope of slipping past them unseen. However, everyone in this Company is exhausted. You *need* a day of rest. We all do. Go organize a Wake or something, and use the intervening time to figure out what you're going to do. Just make sure it's nowhere near me."

"And what about the enemy, while we're sitting still?" Harper asked her, one hand catching and holding back a branch as a gust of wind threatened to sway it into his face.

"If you try to rely on my precognition, you will die. Which means I am left with *no* plans for doing anything but to go stretch my legs by taking a walk. Teevie, Crow, keep humming psychically," she directed her male-and-female shadows. "I'll see you later, Commander."

"Be sure that you *do* see me later," he ordered, pointing at her. Flicking his hand at the two female psis shadowing him, he headed back to the others.

Ia meandered her way toward the perimeter of their make-shift resting spot. Teevie took a brief break from her humming as they drew near the sentry line. "You really have no clue what to do next, sir?"

"Not a damned thing. My mind is as blank and direction-less as an autumn leaf . . . and it is a very uncomfortable place for me to be." She fell silent as they passed the resting figures of a clutch of Roughriders.

Thankfully, Teevie didn't ask anything more. She did clear her throat as Ia almost walked into a branch—stereoscopic vision was beyond her capabilities—but her danger sense allowed Ia to sidestep it at the last moment. Another two minutes of walking brought them to a spot between the light-armored soldiers straining to see any enemy movements through the rainy gray twilight of dawn. They were counting bushes and trees manually, checking the few portable scanners they had managed to snatch up during the evacuation, and were keeping themselves as discreetly hidden as their skills could allow, but she knew they were there.

"Right," Ia murmured. "This is where you two and I part company. Report back to your Squad, and follow Commander Harper's orders."

"Sir?" Corporal Crow asked, still following her. "You're not seriously going to walk out of here alone, are you?"

"I'm merely going to go for a little walk," Ia promised. "One just far enough to clear my head."

They exchanged a look. No doubt they were also exchanging telepathic words because both firmed their jaws at the same moment.

"We're not leaving you, sir," Crow stated, flanking Ia's other side. "Lieutenant Commander Helstead ordered us to shadow you, and she's in charge of all psychic operations."

"And I say you're staying here—I am *still* in your chain of command, meioas," Ia growled when they didn't peel off. "Return to camp, soldiers, or I will break off the nearest branch and cane you myself for Fatality Five."

Again, an exchange of looks. Crow cleared his throat. ". . . You won't be gone long, will you, sir?"

"I'm *just* going for a little walk," she repeated, and started forward. "You have your orders. Do not disobey them."

She kept moving. After a few seconds, she heard her two shadows turn and start back. Walking steadily, if obliquely forward through the forest-cloaked valley, Ia waited until her instincts said she was out of sight of the sentries. As soon as she was, she sunk her electrokinetic senses into the crystals and the e-clips of the gun-thing, and pulled energy out of all of them.

Electricity crackled into her blood, stinging her nerves with a hint of seared eggplant, but it also softened the tough mineral. She pulled the thick, crystalline goo out of the weapon telekinetically, pooling it in her left hand. Bits of brass and other metals dropped off the gun as she did so. Ia left them in a scattered trail, crushing the more delicate components underfoot so that even if they were found, no one would know what their purpose had been.

When only the housing was left, she tossed that into a thicket of Dabin-style brambles and focused her kinetics on the biomineral. At one point, the crysium in her hands had been a fine, matter-based dust cast off by the Feyori back on her homeworld of Sanctuary. Energy-based beings, they had mastered the trick of accelerating themselves to the squared speed of light and back, transforming into matter and back . . . but there was always a little bit of one or the other left over.

Excess energy and the ability to manipulate it usually got bred into whatever matter-based species they chose for a brief mating. That was why Ia and the other psis had psychic abilities, which by definition were the direct manipulation of energies by a sentient mind. The Salik and the Choya had no such abilities, and Ia had never bothered to find out why, but the other races had them.

For the Feyori, excess matter got dumped out whenever a Meddler skimmed a world heavy enough to pull the bits of leftover mass from their silvery soap-bubble bodies. Dabin's gravity wasn't quite high enough to pull out all of it, though some of it would fall. Parker's World might have been, being 2.98Gs, but Sanctuary, her home, came with an excess of electrical energy in the air as well as a decently high gravitational pull. Restaurant and restroom all in one place.

No one but Ia knew how to manipulate crysium, the incredibly tough crystals that grew from that discarded matter-dust. She guided it under her clothes by withdrawing enough innate energy within the mineral to make it pliable under a touch of telekinesis, then restored that energy, forming plates of armor. Like its creators, crysium ate energy, including laser fire. It was more impact-resistant than ceristeel. And it was definitely lighter than her old exercise weight suit, though not nearly as light as a matching suit of plexi would have been.

She didn't know exactly what she was going to do, that was the truth, but that was just fine. Picking up into a steady, ground-eating lope, Ia ran as quietly as she could through the forest. Somewhere up ahead, a Company of fully armed and armored Salik soldiers were taking a brief break from pursuing the two undergeared, highly demoralized Human Companies in desperate need of rest behind her.

Her plan—her only plan—was to tap so far into the future that no Feyori could possibly follow her to spy on her choices. Not to find the right path in the nearest timestreams to get through the trap of misinformation they had laid for her but to find the right person with the right instincts to get herself alive through the next several hours. She wasn't a one-person army, capable of taking on whole Companies, even Legions on her own . . . but she did know of someone who *was*. Or rather, someone who one day would be. A life located so far into the future, no Feyori alive could even hope to reach even a quarter as far . . . which meant it was a life they could not hide precognitively.

All she was going to do—which she kept firmly in her mind as she moved rapidly through the woods—was plug herself into the life-stream of that ultimate one-person warrior and go for a walk on Dabin. She would just do so by walking in a way that would ensure her and Roghetti's Companies would be able to have that promised day of rest.

JUNE 10, 2498 T.S.
SALIK 1117TH INFANTRY BASE CAMP SH-SHWUUN-GWA-GISH
DABIN

A line of flexible, translucent peach-gold dangled from her right wrist in an elongated, lethal parody of a Salik's tentacle-limb. Other bits of transparent gold gleamed in the thin sunlight where it struck the holes torn and scorched in her muddied, bloodied uniform. Dragging the makeshift whip slowly along the ground, flicking it occasionally forward in a sinuous line, Ia stalked through the smoldering, bloodied rubble. Stalking her prey.

Her mind had split itself into three layers. One layer focused purely on her senses, from sight and sound all the way through to the instant *knowing* of battlecognition. The second layer stayed tapped into a life-stream nearly three hundred years down the way, connecting her thoughts, her instincts with a mind far more attuned to the Now than Ia's own ever could be. A life-stream no Feyori could reach or predict, it lay that far ahead. Time, after all, was *her* best battle arena . . . even if her greatest enemies here on Dabin had blasted huge, invisible craters into her path, hoping to make her stumble, fall, and break her metaphorical neck.

The third corner of her mind reserved itself for pure tactical analysis. She honestly didn't know what she was going to do until the upper two layers absorbed her surroundings and processed them down to that bottommost level. It made her highly unpredictable, almost mindlessly so, but still kept her actions on a three-phase track.

Step one, hunt down the nearest cluster of Salik. Step two, discern their strengths and weaknesses. Step three, distract them during her approach, divert their attention from the Damned, and destroy everything she could, all as swiftly and as simultaneously as possible to narrow down whatever reactions the two Feyori counterfactioning her might use. Preferably by using sapper and other infiltration techniques, followed by outright attacks. Once the current knot was handled, she started the process all over again, but not on a predictable pattern or discernible path.

She had distracted and diverted the forces closing in on the Damned and the Roughriders, destroyed more than enough of their vehicles, munitions, and equipment to piss them off, stolen a Salik-style hoversled, and led them in a chase all the way back through the demolished remnants of Roghetti's camp to their own base in the last nine hours. She was tired, hungry, and tingled all over from sucking on stolen e-clips and power cables for sustenance, but it didn't matter.

Her current prey was a crawling, whistle-burbling Salik officer trying to push himself away from the ferally grinning Human. He wasn't getting very far; she had already sliced off one of his flipper-feet to the backwards-facing knee, cauterizing each slice with the Salik-style laser pistol gripped in her left hand. Her mind sliced into his, digging via xeno-telepathy for anything that might give her a location for her true quarry.

It was doubtful any of these Salik knew where to find a Feyori, but that was alright. He was dead anyway. She didn't mind taking her time getting him there—or rather, *Ia* minded, but she was channeling someone else's attitudes right now.

Instincts twinged; her left hand snapped up and fired off a shot. Someone screeched in the distance, paying the price yet again for trying to sniper her. A tiny corner of her mind wondered why they were still trying after seventeen fai— *eighteen* failures. Her right hand lashed up, swinging the crysium whip. Not to destroy the inbound projectile, since she knocked that off course telekinetically while it was still several meters away, but to strike through the crawling alien's thigh, severing part of it. Her left hand came back down and seared across his flesh in an orange line of hot alien laser fire, keeping him from bleeding to death.

It pushed the alien too far. His mind shattered from too much pain and too much fear. Rather than images of commanders and orders and authorities that might have come from or been influenced by one of the Feyori she was hunting, she got an image of his huntress-mother, of hunkering in an underwater cave for protection . . . and of a longing for his old youthful classmates to be the ones to tear out his guts. It would be, she read in the cold, jumbled thoughts of her prey, a far less shameful death than being sliced apart but *not* eaten by an all-too-worthy foe.

Disgusted, she pushed a wave of Salik-style pity—a wave of you-were-not-worth-my-time—into his brain with her modest xenopathy. He keened and curled up protectively, shamed by the truth. Her ears pricked at the approaching hum of a hovercraft before she could raise her right arm to deliver the death lash he had earned. Her left hand, however, did *not* twitch up in the instinct to counterattack the driver of the incoming vehicle. Turning slightly, she looked with her one good eye for the source of the sound.

The hoverbike drifted into view among the smoldering remnants of Salik-style pods and tents. The one she had stolen several hours back in a previous fight had died in a fiery collision, crashing into the camp shield generator, but this one was intact. Its brown-haired rider ducked under a sagging pole formerly supporting an artificial tree's worth of sensor arrays. Hazel eyes fixed on Ia's upright stance, switched to the now-curled-up ball of frogtopodic misery at her feet, and blinked. One brow quirked upward. Mara Sunrise brought the bike to a stop a short distance away, letting its thruster field relax enough to rest the bike on its landing struts.

A *boom* in the distance was followed by a chain of louder explosions. Several clouds of smoke and flame billowed up from somewhere beyond the edge of the camp. The Salik hadn't moved their projectile munitions fast enough to avoid the returning missile Ia had mentally smacked back their way.

"You did all of this by yourself, sir?" the ex-Knifeman murmured.

The question was a distraction. Ia brushed it off with a shrug. Not to deny, but to dismiss. The attempt at conversation, however little there was, made it difficult for her to continue to channel that future life. Finally, she sighed and shook her head to clear it of its connections. Now that she wasn't concentrating, she could feel every ache, every bruise, every cut and burn that had gotten through her defenses. Everything hurt. "Yes. Most of it."

Private Sunrise nodded to herself, listening to the faint whistling screams of the aliens wounded by the counter-attack. "I'm impressed."

Lifting her arm, Ia slashed down. The thin whip cut straight through the alien's limbs and gut. It embedded itself half a meter in the muddy earth. A tug pulled it free of both. A second, more gentle flick slashed it through the not-grass, cleaning the reddish stain from the faintly glowing flail.

"Orders, Captain?" Private Sunrise asked her. A former Staff Sergeant from the Knifeman Corps, the Space Force's assassination/counterassassination bureau, she didn't flinch at the blood pouring from the alien's body. Her gaze did flick away more than once from Ia's face, but only to survey their surroundings with an eye for potential danger, not to glance at the dying Salik.

Ia didn't give any orders. She didn't dare give any. Turning away from the bleeding body, she started spinning. Right arm slashing up and down, she carved letters into the trampled path that had served the Salik as a makeshift road between their camp structures. The pain wasn't important, only the message, and the outlet of her anger in each hard-slashed blow against the unflinching ground. It wasn't meant for the Salik to read, though the survivors would eventually regroup and see it before fleeing. It was meant for the Feyori who were tracking her through the timeplains, trying to keep up with her wherever-the-wind-blows, nearly mindless movements.

SAVAA'NN SUD-DHA.

As the *Savior* wills it. Not the usual, commonly found *Ia'nn sud-dha*, As the Prophet wills it.

. . . Let them try to track that *in the timestreams.*

Pulling the whip from the last line of that block-printed A, she moved toward Sunrise's bike. A sweep of her gifts sucked the crystalline cord back up under her right sleeve, restoring it as a bracer. Her command arm unit had been scorched into uselessness on her left limb at some point during her stolen sled ride to this camp, and half-healed wounds caused her to limp her way over to the hovering bike, but she was alive and able to move. She also smacked into the side of the machine, thrown off by her lack of perspective.

". . . Orders?" Sunrise repeated, carefully not saying a word about her CO's clumsiness, or her strange weaponry.

Grabbing the back of the bike, Ia hauled herself onto the padded seat. "None whatsoever, Sergeant. The Feyori do not have any hooks into my brain, but they are watching the timestreams for *anything* I choose to do. You can give me a lift out of here, but after that, you're on your own."

Revving the thrusters, she lifted them off and swerved between the sabotaged tents. "And then what'll you do?"

"Whatever my instincts tell me to do. They're the only advantage I have left at the moment." It felt good to sit down. "I hope the others enjoyed their day of rest."

"They did, sir. They were rather surprised that they *were* allowed to rest without pursuit, but then were deeply grateful for it." Sunrise fell quiet for a few minutes as she navigated toward the edge of camp. The officer wasn't the only Salik Ia had cut down in her rampage through the enemy, and the bike rose and fell a little, its thruster field bumping over the carnage and debris strewn across the ground.

Ia wasn't quite in her mindless, future-tapping fugue anymore, but neither was she trying to actively think. Not that she could concentrate much since there were several spots where her makeshift crysium armor hadn't completely covered under her uniform, narrow strips of skin at various joints that had been scorched, scraped, bloodied, and burned. Her biokinesis was working hard to seal and repair what her body naturally could, but it was taking a toll on her.

At least she wasn't forcing herself to ignore the pain in order to fight, anymore. Like her Company, she, too, needed a day of rest. Until then, a few minutes' ride on the hoverbike would have to do.

Finally, Sunrise spoke again. "You know, that sounds rather pleasant, sir."

"What does?" Ia asked.

"Following one's instincts," Sunrise clarified. "Mind if I do that, too?"

"I don't mind, Sergeant," Ia allowed. "Unless and until Helstead revokes your current operating parameters and yanks you back home, which means back under Commander Harper's purview in A Company . . . you're free to do whatever you want. Just try not to violate your parole too much."

Gunning the thrusters, she skidded them up into the sky,

reversing course toward the north. Ia clutched at her, then dug her hands down beneath Mara's belt, anchoring herself in place. One of the wounds was on her inner thigh, making it painful to clutch at the body of the bike that way.

The parabolic arc Sunrise used sailed them over the latest column of smoke but didn't land them in the woods. She brought the bike down among the tufted and spiked tops of the local trees but didn't go any lower than that.

"Go to sleep, sir," Sunrise directed her, speaking over her shoulder so Ia could hear her. "Or at least get some rest. I promise I won't crash us into any trees."

"I know you won't. Just don't *think* about where you're going while you're busy not-crashing," Ia instructed the other woman. She had voluntarily blinded herself to the sights of the timeplains since they were no longer reliable, but her instincts were still there. The Feyori could play tricks on her eyes but not on her innermost instincts.

"I've run more than a few missions against enemy psis, sir. I know how to keep my mind free," Mara stated. She had to raise her voice since between the hum of the bike and the whistling of the wind, it was getting hard to hear anything, but she spoke lightly all the same. "Mostly, I think about crackers. There are thousands of varieties of crackers out there, you know, both plain and tasty."

"You do that, soldier. I think I'll join you, too," Ia stated. On impulse, she added, "Welcome to B Company, Sergeant. You'll eventually have to return to being a Private in A Company, though."

"I know, sir. I also don't envy you explaining to the Command Staff why you activated me, when the terms of my release were that I remain hidden in your Company," Sunrise stated. "Particularly if a certain Provincial Governor ever hears about it."

"That's because he's a *skutting shakk-torr,*" Ia snorted. "If he tries to get you locked up a second time for being 'politically inconvenient,' I'll either blackmail the *shova v'shakk* out of him, or I *might* let you take him down for being detrimental to the welfare of the Terran Empire."

"Ooh, sir," Sunrise mock-purred. "You make it sound like Christmas just might come early!"

She'd forgotten what Sunrise's true personality would be like, without her mousey, quiet clerk of a cover story. "Hush, or I'll convert you to Taoism. I only said *might.*"

"Technically, if you want me to think of nothing, then shouldn't you be converting me to Zen Buddhism?" Sunrise quipped.

"Just drive, soldier," Ia ordered. "And think about crackers."

Tucking her cheek against the other woman's back, she turned her own attention inward, focusing on her biokinetic self-awareness. Ia didn't care that the move smeared blood, both her own and alien, against Sunrise's shirt. Not caring was part and parcel with not thinking.

Except she couldn't help but glance into the immediate, immutable past. The Salik's thrust through the Army's line had been broken. The Damned and the Roughriders hadn't been pursued or pestered in any way about two hours after she had left the others behind. She very carefully did not look to see *what* either Company had done in the last nine hours. But she did peek enough to know the Salik weren't able to continue their Feyori-backed persecution. For now, at least.

Tugging her fingers firmly out of the timestreams, she forced herself to think about crackers as well. Just in case the Feyori Meddling with her timestreams was still waiting to thwart and follow her. *Big ones, little ones, square ones, oblong ones, flavored with vegetables, flavored with sweet-*

eners, thick fluffy airy ones and thin hard brittle ones . . .
nothing but crackers as far as the mind can see.

A moment later, a soft chuckle escaped her, the sound of it almost lost to the wind. *I'm definitely going crackers.*

JUNE 11, 2498 T.S.
LANDING CITY

"Wakey, wakey, breakfast shake-y . . ."

Ia hadn't exactly been asleep, but neither had she been fully awake. Unnervingly enough—and perhaps proof the Feyori were still trying to suppress her gifts—not once had she triggered a dip onto the timestreams, postcognitively or precognitively, despite being snugged up against Sunrise's cloth-covered back for hundreds of kilometers. Drawing in a deep breath, she uncurled herself slowly from Sunrise's back, stiff from her half-healed wounds. "Hmm?"

Mara eased back on the bike's thrusters, bringing it down to rest its support pods on the plexcrete surface of a parking lot. She nodded to her left. "Restaurant, Captain. Where we can find breakfast. You know, real food? Or at least a reasonable facsimile?"

They hadn't needed to stop for anything other than three brief breaks, once to eat a couple of ration packs which the officially-still-a-private had liberated at some point during her long-range scouting forays, and twice more to use the bushes. Like all modern transports, the hoverbike itself ran on a compact hydrogenerator; a liter's worth of water was enough to keep it running for two or more years. Only its riders needed frequent refueling.

Skimming the treetops in nearly random directions for hours, the pair hadn't otherwise touched down or even selected a conscious heading, as far as Ia had been able to tell. With her precognition locked firmly away, and her others gifts worn down from constant use during those nine hours, Ia had taken the time to reinforce her mental shields while her companion thought most firmly about a thousand different varieties of crackers, and all the things one could do with them: eat them, destroy them, bake them, top them with objects both edible and indigestible, even use them as building materials in various different ways both decorative and practical.

But at some point in their meanderings, Mara Sunrise had pointed the hoverbike toward the colonyworld's capital, or rather, to the section of the hundred-year-old town where the Terran Space Force, Branch Army, had appropriated a stout, four-story office building for its Division Headquarters. Specifically, to the parking lot shared by the restaurant and the grocery store across the street from that building.

To Mara's surprise, as soon as her CO dismounted, Ia didn't head for the smaller, green-painted building. Instead, she headed for the intersection.

"Sir? Restaurant? . . . Food?" Reversing course as soon as she noticed, Sunrise followed her toward the crosswalk zone. Shrugging, she gave up on the subject of food. "Sir . . . before we get into trouble—not that I'm going to start any, but I'm always prepared for it—I just wanted to say thank you. For pulling me out of that holding brig on the Moon. What I did to wind up in there wasn't *wrong*, so much as . . . as . . ."

"Politically inconvenient?" Ia offered. Both women shared a brief, wry smile. The light changed, permitting them to cross the street. "I don't believe in letting anyone with good, useful talents go to waste."

"What, everyone? Even serial killers?" Sunrise asked, glancing her way. Across the street, a four-winged bird-thing tried to fly close to the building. It smacked into the unseen force field covering the upper floors of the structure with a shower of sparks and an indignant squawk. Undulating rapidly, it flapped off to find a safer perch.

Ia, watching the Dabin-style bird flee, nodded. Her brother was doing exactly that, back home. Under her orders. "If they're particularly good at it, yes. Provided they're willing to cooperate and toe the line. There does come a point where they could stop being useful and start being harmful . . . and at that point, I'd take 'em out and find someone else to carry on with their job."

"I guess I can't complain, then. And I know I've been useful, even as a mere 'mousey, boring clerk.' Of course, rumor has it the first batch of Knifemen *were* alleged serial killers," Sunrise added. She offered her arm unit to be scanned by the sergeant guarding the nearest door into the office building. "My history teachers told us that they and the people who became the first Troubleshooters were recruited to fill the gaps in the various old Earth intelligence and counterintelligence bureaus that got broken up and amalgamated into the TUP's one-world government. There's a couple divisions similar to the Troubleshooters in the Peacekeepers' organizations from what I hear, but nothing quite like the Corpse."

Knowing she meant the Knifeman Corps, Ia nodded and turned her attention to the building. Instinct had brought her here—Sunrise's instincts—but now that she was here, she might as well go in. However, there was one slight problem. "You'll have to use a palm scanner instead of my ident," Ia told the sergeant waiting at the door they had approached. She lifted her left arm, showing the blackened case of her arm unit. "Mine got slagged in combat."

"I'm surprised your whole arm didn't get slagged, sir. Those units are tough, but they aren't meant to be armor," he stated. Poking through a couple of the pockets scattered over his fatigues, he found and extracted his portable palm scanner. His brows rose after the beam swept over her upturned hand. "—Ship's Captain Ia? Sir! Brigadier General Mattox has standing orders regarding *your* visit, sir."

Ia had no clue what those orders were. There were too many possibilities, all of them ruined by certain meddling forces. Clamping down on the reflexive need to check the timestreams, she shook her head. "Oh, we're not here to see the brigadier general. That's a visit for another day."

"Sir, the Brigadier General left strict orders for you to be escorted upstairs right away," he stated. Touching his arm unit, he spoke into the pickup wire on his headset. *"Sergeant Kukley to Major Tonkswell . . . Yes, sir, it's important. I have Ship's Captain Ia at the southwest entrance . . . Yes, sir, right away, sir."*

Opening the door, he leaned inside the foyer and called out a name. "Corporal, front and center!"

A clean-cut man in crisp fatigues and lance-corporal stripes jogged out to join them. Saluting the sergeant, he held himself At Attention. "You needed me, Sergeant?"

"Lance Corporal Aston, escort these two meioas to the Brigadier General's office," Sergeant Kukley instructed, saluting back. He then saluted Ia with one hand and opened the door with the other. "Ship's Captain Ia, welcome to the 1st Division 6th Cordon Army Headquarters. I hope you have a nice day, sir—you, too, Private."

Ia saluted him in return, then followed Sunrise and the lance corporal into the building. They were halfway to the bank of lifts when Mara murmured in V'Dan, *"Ma'a ni-uol s'tiettra a'amul'o, neh-yah-veh?"*

"Neh-yah-veh," Ia agreed. She, too, thought this warm welcome was rather odd coming from a man and his staff

who had deliberately lied to them about their willingness to follow Ia's battle plans. It was definitely going too smoothly.

Mara gestured at a door recessed a couple meters from the lifts. Ia nodded; it was an instinctively better choice. They swerved to the side. It wasn't until the heavy door clicked open that their escort realized they were no longer following him to the elevators.

". . . Sir? Sir! The lifts are over here, sir," he called out. Hurrying to catch up with them, he pushed the closing door back open in their wake. "Captain, why are you taking the stairs to go *up* on a heavyworld? You'd be pushing almost 4Gs with each step!"

"Lance Corporal, I used to take the stairs on *my* homeworld," Ia stated briskly, mounting the stairs at a steady pace. "That's over 6.4Gs of pure upward force, every single step."

"But it's four full floors up, and the lift is faster," he protested.

"My Captain is being kind by accompanying me," Sunrise interjected. "She knows I dislike small, enclosed spaces. Don't worry; we'll meet you on the fourth floor."

He hesitated so much, they got a full floor ahead of him before the two women heard his exasperated sigh. Footsteps echoed up the stairwell in their wake. Glancing back at Ia, Mara rolled her eyes, but she didn't stop climbing the stairs. They both knew the reason why Sunrise had picked a different way to get to the top floor. Laborious as it was, no one could cut power to a stairwell and trap the people trying to use it, like they could to an elevator car.

Ia very carefully thought about the rubbery, cushiony nature of the plain gray plexcrete under her feet, instead of whatever she might do when they reached the top floor. Aside from resting long enough to catch her breath, of course. Sunrise rested with her in the alcove. There was a drinking fountain in the same alcove as the stairwell door, though neither touched it. There was also a power outlet. Standing with her arms behind her back and her back to the wall, Ia extruded a bit of crysium down to the holes and plugged herself into the circuit. Electrical energy pulsed up the hidden line, as refreshing and filling as a long drink of cool water.

Politely waiting for the lance corporal to regain his breath once he emerged from the stairway, Ia discreetly extracted the line when he straightened and nodded. She could just start to see the edges of energy fields around her but would need more for true Feyori-style vision. She didn't ask for more time, though.

Politely, the two fatigues-clad women followed the Dress-uniformed man away from the banks of lifts and the fire-door alcove. There hadn't been many signs of the Army's presence down in the foyer, but up here, everyone was dressed either in the local reddish camouflage hues with the extra speckles of Army green down each pant leg and sleeve, or in formal Dress Greens with black stripes down the outer seams—mostly in Dress uniforms, suggesting the brigadier general was a stickler for formality. By comparison, Ia and Mara were muddy, even bloody; Ia in particular not only had rents and burn holes in her garments, she still smelled of munitions powder as she walked blithely along with a dingy regen pack strapped to her head. No one they crossed paths with commented, though a few did double takes, sniffed, and stared.

One of the rooms they passed thrummed audibly from the force of the hydrogenerators working inside. The sign posted on the door read *Shield Generator Room 2*. Another was filled with rows of workstations filled with transparent screens displaying tactical information ranging from the colorful hues of real-time radar maps to tiny, crowded rows of words and numbers too small to be easily read at that distance. Ia wanted to see what those screens said, to try to match it up to the timeplains, but carefully refrained.

"Hey, Ginger!" Stooping, the lance corporal held out his fingers to the short-legged, slightly pudgy canine that came trotting out of the open door at the end of the hall.

It was a stubbie, the breed of well-adapted heavyworlder dog descended from a mix between a beagle, a boxer, and a Labrador. With stout, strong legs covered in short, reddish beige fur and cinnamon brown eyes, she looked very much like her namesake, only sweeter.

"Heya, girl, how are you? This is Ginger," he stated, looking back at the two women. "She's sorta our mascot here at HQ. Someone found her rooting around in the garbage bins out back, took pity on her, and brought her inside. General Mattox has a soft spot for dogs, so he let 'er stay. She's really sweet, too. She's also getting a bit fat, but then we spoil 'er. Aren't you, girl? Who's a sweet lil' fatty?"

He patted her flanks, and the dog just lapped it up, wagging her sleek little tail. The dog moved closer to the newcomers, nostrils flexing in the effort to sniff them. Sunrise didn't stoop to pet her. That surprised Ia. She hadn't thought the woman a dog-hater.

"Aren't you gonna say hello, meioas?" their escort asked, giving them the civilian honorific, since Ia's and Mara's ranks were too different to lump together.

Sunrise folded her arms across her chest, doing her best to ignore the canine sniffing around her knees. She didn't even look at the stubbie, staring instead at the end of the hall. "I'm a cat person."

Without warning, the dog yapped happily and scampered down the hall, dashing past Ia without so much as a hello sniff. A glance back showed the canine rushing up to a pair of men with enthusiastic displays of body-wiggling and tail-wagging.

Both soldiers stooped to pet the stubbie, giving her the same enthusiastic greetings that Lance Corporal Aston had.

Once upon a time, Ia had longed to have a stubbie for a pet. But pets and restaurants did not mix well when it came time for health inspections, so both of her mothers had forbidden it. Living as she did now in the military, with most of her time spent on a spaceship, Ia still didn't have one. The only animals allowed on board were all in life support, usually a mix of fish and fowl, and were meant strictly for food, not for companionship. It was against the rules and regs to turn any of them into a pet.

Shaking it off, she moved toward the open door at the end of the hall. Inside was a modest front office with a man seated behind the front desk. The name tag pinned to his Dress Greens said Major Tonkswell and his gray-streaked hair formed a wiry halo around his dark head. Behind and to the right stood a pair of fine wooden doors, suggesting this office had originally been meant for some sort of business executive. One of the doors stood slightly open but not enough to see into the next chamber.

Ia recognized the wall behind the major's chair and felt a brief wash of relief that it wasn't Major Perkins who was currently on duty. If she'd had to face that woman's artificially constant smiles, she might have done something a little *too* instinctive. Maybe even downright impulsive. As it was, she had no idea what she was going to say to the head of the Army's 1st Division, 6th Cordon.

"Major Tonkswell, this is Ship's Captain Ia, and . . . Private Second Class Sunrise," the lance corporal introduced them, taking a quick moment to peer at the name patch stuck to the front of Mara's mottled shirt and the single stripe on her sleeve for her rank.

"You're both Branch Special Forces, yes?" Major Tonkswell

asked, eyeing the two women. Ia and her companion nodded. He gave them a brief smile. "Welcome to the Dabin Army HQ. The Brigadier General will be free in just a few minutes. Can I have the lance corporal get you anything?"

"Some water, please?" Sunrise asked, giving the lance corporal a shy, mousey-clerk sort of smile. "I should've drunk from the fountain."

"I'll take an electrical outlet," Ia quipped.

She'd half meant it as a joke, but with only a brief, bemused look at her odd request, the major pointed at the wall to her left. Glancing that way, she spotted the socket holes. Since it wasn't a bad idea, Ia shifted that way, crouched, and pressed her hand over the opening. Leaving just enough room under her palm, she shifted the now faintly peach-hued, transparent gold bracer tucked beneath her right sleeve, extruding a set of prongs on a self-flexing cable.

Plugging it into the wall, she drew firmly from the outlet, rather than gently as she had earlier; having permission meant not having to hide any energy-drain spikes on the maintenance-system monitors. The overhead lights dimmed a little, though the effect wasn't overly blatant in the daylight glowing through the windows over the outlet. Stuffing herself with energy, Ia didn't stop until their escort had come back with a clutch of bottles. By that point, everything was glowing firmly.

Restoring her bracer, Ia straightened and accepted one of the bottles the lance corporal offered to her. His short hair fluffed up a little with static energy as their hands briefly touched. It amused her. It also drained a tiny bit of the glow. Stepping back with the bottle in hand, Ia cast her gaze around the room.

She could now see the power conduits in the walls, the convection currents caused by a mix of warm sunlight streaming in through the windows and the cooling effect of the building's ventilation currents, the glow of all four bodies in the room, and a blob-shaped hint of a glow from the next room to her left, which looked like it could have been the brigadier general seated at his desk. More glows radiated through the thermal patches of the walls in the other direction. One of them trotted their way, low to the ground, very bright and pug-shaped, replete with a happily wagging tail and panting jaws.

Ia watched the stubbie approach, mind carefully blank. Or as blank as a mental dissertation on the ratio of flaky crackery crunch to savory thickness could get. Her precognitive sense was still locked down, wrapped up in a tight ball so that she didn't try to touch the timeplains. It made her head feel oddly lightweight, and not in the least bit clearheaded.

It felt a bit like mentally holding one's breath in hope that the monsters under-the-bed/in-the-closet wouldn't hear.

As the bright-hued dog came through the front office door, she found herself asking lightly, "Private Sunrise, do you suppose Melba toast counts as a cracker? Or is it too bready? What do you think?"

Turning to face her CO, Sunrise opened her mouth to reply. That brought her right hip into Ia's reach. Without a thought in her head, Ia plucked the gun from the other woman's holster, flicked off the safety, and fired, all in a swift, smooth motion. The *bang* of the gun echoed loudly in the small room, accompanied by a puff of acrid smoke and a sharp *yipe* of pain from the stubbie as it was flung back across the floor by the force of her shot.

CHAPTER 4

I'm quite sure I was equally memorable, and I know I am equally to blame for some of the actions on Dabin—it was not so much a matter of breaking any rules or regs as it was a matter of shocking and appalling the meioas around me.

In hindsight, it's easy to claim I had a purpose for what I did, but at the time, it was nothing more than the sheerest instinct to deliver an horrendous, overwhelming shock. A slap to the face to wake everybody up. And . . . maybe a touch of revenge. I am mostly Human, after all.

~Ia

"The *hell*?" Major Tonkswell bolted up from his seat, only to grab for his gun and crouch behind the bulk of the drawers holding up one side of his desk. Out in the hall, voices shouted and footsteps thundered, some fleeing, others drawing near. "Put down the gun!"

Lance Corporal Aston also gaped and blinked, then grabbed for his own pistol. Both men aimed their weapons at Ia's head. She didn't move, just stood there with an unopened bottle of water in her left hand and a smoking projectile weapon in the other, still aimed at the dog. Silently, she studied the last gasping breaths from the dying animal. A third gun poked through the opening of the brigadier general's office, this time the muzzle of an HK-74 laser rifle, replete with the faint whine that said it was charging. Only a narrow strip of its wielder could be seen, however.

Blinking a couple times from shock herself, Private Sunrise finally shrugged and answered her commanding officer's question. "I'm . . . not really sure, sir. It's usually about the size of a large cracker, it *is* crisp, and you can certainly spread things on Melba toast like a cracker . . . but it technically does start out as bread, first. Yeast-risen, not sodium or some other means."

"What the mossy red *hell* is *wrong* with you two?" Aston demanded, hands no longer shaking, though sweat now beaded visibly on his brow. "You *shot* the General's dog, and you're talking about *toast*?"

"Put *down* the gun, sir!" Tonkswell asserted loudly, his own hands quite steady.

Ia didn't take her eyes or her aim off the still-glowing, dying canine. She could see the potential chemical energy in the explosive powders of the projectile cartridges loaded into Aston's, Tonkswell's, and her borrowed handguns. The glow from the power conduits in the walls lit up the nearby walls in angular bars, and the glow from the brigadier general's now fully charged laser rifle was even stronger as it poked past the edge of the inner-office door . . . but none of those were as bright as the dog's glow. Paradoxically, that glow kept getting brighter, not dimmer as the creature twitched and bled.

Still, Corporal Aston's question deserved an answer. As did the major's demand. She answered in a tone as dry as the toast in question, though her gaze never left the dog. The little hitches of Ginger's bloodied rib cage were slowing down.

"I apologize, gentlemeioas. It *would* have been an instant kill, but I am missing an eye, and the bitch moved at the last second. And technically, the subject is *crackers*, not bread. As for the gun . . . Private Sunrise?"

Reversing the gun, she held it grip-first to her companion, gaze never wavering from the dying dog. In Ia's mind, "Ginger" was a modern-day leprechaun; she didn't even allow herself a moment to blink. She couldn't get close enough to touch the dog, not with so many weapons aimed at her head, but Ia didn't blink and didn't look away.

She did, however, address the ex-Knifeman. "I am surprised this wasn't still loaded with splatters, Private. That would've made this a lot faster."

"Sorry, sir. I swapped 'em out at our last rest stop when it occurred to me we were deep in civilian territory," Sunrise admitted, taking the pistol back. "Controlled expansion bullets are frowned upon by most Peacekeeper forces, sir. But . . . now I'm wishing I'd kept them in there. I brought us here because a part of me realized someone in Mattox's immediate environment had to be controlling him."

"*Controlling* me?" Mattox demanded from behind the shelter of his office door. "Nobody's controlling me."

Sunrise ignored him. "For the record, Captain, I had picked the dog, too . . . but mine was just a paranoid guess. Ah . . . not that I doubt you, but I *do* hope your choice is the right one, sir. I'd really rather not be incarcerated for this."

The stubbie finally stopped breathing. Her awareness of the other energy sources in the room was starting to fade, but the dog's glow only increased. Eye itching from the need to blink away the mounting dryness, Ia counted down inside her head from ten. "Oh, I *know* I'm right."

"Right about what?" Aston demanded. "About hating a poor, sweet dog so much you . . . you . . ." A flash of light made him whip his head to the side. *"What the* shakking . . . *?"*

The stubbie's corpse had vanished in that flash. Even the blood spatters were gone. Had anyone looked closely at the faux-granite pattern of the plexcrete flooring, they might have noticed a thin dusting of tiny golden specks, which hadn't been there before. No one bothered, though; everyone but Ia gaped at the oversized, mirror-smooth, dark soap bubble that now hung in the air in the absent dog's place. She knew the dust had been left behind, but only because she knew Dabin's gravity was just barely high enough to pull some of that residual matter out of the alien hovering in midair.

"I will give you one warning, Meddler," Ia stated calmly, eyeing the dark gray sphere. "Drop your faction with Miklinn, swear a new faction to *me*, and I will arrange things so that you *gain* position in the Game. Run from me, or continue to counterfaction me, and I will—"

The Feyori turned and bolted out through the window. Ia spun and dashed after it to the window, hand slapping against the broad pane just centimeters short of touching that sphere. It slowed a few meters away at the shield boundary, causing a cascade of sparks to arrow down into the slowly brightening alien as it fed briefly, then zipped off into the sky.

"Slag!" Ia growled, watching the bubble shrink into the distance. She thumped the transparent plexi pane again, this time with a curled-up fist. *"Shakking v'shova v'carra v'slag!"*

The cursing didn't alleviate her frustration. Nor did it

add anything to it. Unfortunately, her anger wasn't nearly enough to tip her over the energy/matter border. Part of what held her back was how a little too much of the excess energy had bled away. Part was from the realization that she would be leaving Private Sunrise in a very indelicate position if she did leave to go bubble-chasing across the planet.

The rest came from acknowledging to herself that she now had the mess of the 1st Division's blatant contamination by Meddling to clean up. The Admiral-General would expect nothing less of her. So would her parents, in a lesson Ia had learned long ago. *If you are the one who saw the mess, that means you are the one expected to clean it up, and you're not allowed to just walk by and leave it to rot . . .*

I love you, Mom and Ma, but sometimes I wish you hadn't dented such a strong sense of responsibility into my head!

Her hand slapped one last time into the plexi surface. Drawing in a deep breath, she let it out again slowly. Stepping away from the window, Ia turned to face the others . . . and found a host of weapons still pointed at her. Tonkswell had tilted his gun up, pointing it ceilingward as the only safe direction, but Aston, Mattox, and the cluster of soldiers filling the front doorway continued to aim at her. Rolling her eyes, Ia shifted her hands to her hips.

"As you just saw for yourselves, I did *not* shoot anybody's dog. I shot *an enemy spy.* You have all been contaminated by Feyori Meddling, thanks to 'Ginger' disguising herself as a friendly canine. *Think*, meioas, about what you have all just seen." She waited for them to lower their weapons. When they didn't, she firmed her expression. "I have been authorized by Admiral-General Christine Myang to deal with the Feyori, including the right to intercede in covert Human-Feyori interactions. My actions are completely within the realm of my orders."

They didn't move. Excepting Sunrise, the men and women around her looked dazed, as if not quite registering her words. It was possible "Ginger" had implanted a last-minute telepathic suggestion. Ia could only guess, though; telepathy was not one of her strengths by any means. Still, every word she said was true, under her terms of *carte blanche* and the Admiral-General's awareness of her dealings with the Feyori.

This would be so much easier with Helstead on hand. I am not *a psychodominant . . .*

"You will put. Your weapons. *Away*," she ordered, her tone edged with the authority Myang had entrusted to her. (*Now!*)

That single thought pulse, hard and forceful, jolted through them. It also drained the last of the glow, leaving Ia with nothing more than normal senses and a faint, burgeoning headache. Like a slap to the face, they shook their heads and drew in sharp breaths. Blinking, the men and women slowly lowered their weapons, looking as if they had just woken up from a weird dream. Ia wasn't completely fooled; the subtle depths of Feyori mind games would take more than a single mental demand from her to wipe them away. But they did activate the safeties on the projectile guns and shut off the e-clips for the energy ones.

Most pointed the muzzles up, the one safe direction on the top floor of a building. With her peripheral vision, she could see Mara narrowing her own eyes at the few who pointed their weapons down. Ia let her handle that violation. She kept her gaze on the brigadier general while Mara spoke, her tone cold with highly displeased authority.

"I see a few of you have forgotten the Rules of the Range, meioas." The ex–staff sergeant hardened her tone when they didn't move. "Stunners don't go through floors and walls, but *those* are Hecks and Jellies. Muzzles *up*, soldiers!"

They snapped their guns up. Ia turned slightly, addressing the man still lurking mostly behind the inner door. "Brigadier General Mattox. In light of the revelation of the Meddler's presence in your Headquarters, I strongly suggest you and your entire staff submit immediately to psychic examinations and treatments. Failure to comply carries with it automatic accusations of Fatalities Nineteen, Collusion; Six, Subversion; Three, Espionage; Thirty-five, Sabotage; and possibly Fatality Two, Treason . . . and I'll remind you that Fatality Two is automatically an accusation of Grand Treason, given that we're currently at war. Possibly Grand High Treason, depending on how much damage you have done to the war efforts while under Ginger's influence."

Major Tonkswell spoke up. "We're the Army, Ship's Captain. We have zero psychic attachés on our staff. The Brigadier General . . . ah . . . *shova*."

"Brigadier General Mattox had asserted that they would not be necessary, yes, I figured as much the moment you said there weren't any," Ia finished for him. "Whether or not this was before or after 'Ginger' officially arriving on the scene is immaterial. The Feyori could have hidden in that restaurant across the street and still been able to influence his mind. *All* of your minds. They do have a limit to that range, but that's more than close enough."

Aston frowned at that. "Then why did she bother to disguise herself as a *dog*?"

"Conservation of energy," Sunrise told the corporal. "It's a lot easier to spy on your game pieces and keep them playing in all the right ways when you're right there at the gaming board."

"Exactly," Ia agreed. "Nobody would suspect a dog of being a spy, she wouldn't need to have her identity checked and confirmed, and those extra-sensitive canine ears would give her an increased chance to eavesdrop on anything important—Brigadier General, would you please put down the gun now?"

Mattox wasn't aiming it at her, and in fact was now cradling it against his chest, but it was still fully charged. Despite the naturally tanned hue of his skin, he looked pale, shaken by what had just happened. "I . . . I just want to be ready. To shoot her. If she comes back . . ."

Ia wasn't the only one to roll her eyes at that. Private Sunrise did, too. "That was a *Feyori*, sir," the ex-Knifeman scorned. "You're wielding a *Heck*. That'd be like smacking a starving, feral dog with a *sausage*."

He flushed under the sting of her derision, the color rushing back into his sallow cheeks in splotches. "Your insolence, soldier, is—"

"—Is exactly what you need to wake up to the fact that you have been *controlled*, sir," Ia interjected, defending her crew member. She softened her tone a little. "Now, I believe this situation can be salvaged. It does require everyone in this building undergoing psychic scans, behavioral evaluations, and a review of every decision you have made for as long as Ginger was here, plus an extra month or so before that point so we can pinpoint when your actions began to change under her influence."

"And where are we going to get the psychics necessary for such evaluations, Ship's Captain?" Major Tonkswell asked dryly. A flick from his hand dismissed the crowd at the door, Aston included. "If you haven't noticed, we've been blockaded by the Salik fleet. We can't exactly call them in from another system."

"This is a well-established colonyworld with plenty of resources," Ia reminded him. "Until we can get formal evaluators out here from the 6th Cordon Psi Division, we'll use a mixture of civilian contractors and certain members of my crew. I brought plenty of psis with me, knowing I'd have to deal with the two Feyori on this world. Some of them are qualified to do formal mind scans, and I'm willing to attach some of them to Headquarters until we're all reasonably assured that the impact of the Feyori's Meddling has passed."

Brigadier General Mattox frowned. "You aren't in the Space Force Army, let alone in our chain of command."

"That will not be a problem, General. All it will take is a few moments of chatting with a member of the Command Staff to authorize my assistance. My immediate superior, Admiral John Genibes, would certainly qualify," Ia replied. "He knows the various capabilities of my Company and can craft the necessary orders."

Letting his rifle drop so that it dangled from just one hand, Mattox stared at her. "Captain, we don't *need* your help."

Ia raised one brow. "Did you hear yourself, just now? You have been *compromised*, Mattox. Yes, you have just had a terrible shock, when I shot your so-called dog—and I apologize for the shock of it—but you have been in close proximity to a Feyori for months, and most likely have been brainwashed by that Feyori. Follow *procedure*, Brigadier General."

He looked away. She didn't have to be a precognitive to know what would happen if he didn't follow through. Ia deliberately reminded him of it when he continued to hesitate.

"That procedure means being examined as soon as possible by a qualified telepath of Rank 9 or higher, or two of Rank 6 or higher, to determine the extent of influence the Feyori known as 'Ginger' had on your brain. Now, I can pull in Private Mk'nonn, who is a Rank 11 Telepath, and *maybe* pull in Commander Mishka, who is a Rank 9 Triphid, but that depends on whether or not my Company needs her more as our chief medic. The next best I can offer you are pairs of my soldiers who are Ranks 8 to 6 in Telepathy.

"Beyond that, you'll have to go into the civilian sector. Psis who are vetted by the PsiLeague and the Witan Order *may* be trustworthy, sir," Ia said, pointing at the floor under their feet, "but every brain in this building has been working in the heart of the Army's efforts, and those brains have been in close proximity with a Feyori for *months*. By offering my soldiers first and foremost, I can guarantee that whatever secrets the Army has left on this planet will remain within the Space Force. You have no such guarantees in the civilian sector, but the sheer number of people who will need to be scanned means we'll still have to call in outsiders to scan the lower ranks, particularly the enlisted."

"What's the difference between a civilian psi and a *mere private* scanning the mind of a Division leader?" Mattox asked sarcastically. He flipped his hand at Sunrise. "Your people might be in the Special Forces, but *you* don't have the kind of clearance it takes to read the secrets in *my* mind."

Private Sunrise braced her palms on her hips, her look sardonic. "Begging pardon, General, but *I* have a higher clearance rating than you. We *all* do in the 9th Cordon Special Forces."

José Mattox snorted. "Now that, I highly doubt."

"Every single crew member in my Company is rated at High Class 9A at the very least," Ia stated bluntly. "The only clearance higher is Ultra, and there are five . . . sorry, seven . . . who are rated for Ultra Clearance. Three of them are Ultra Class C, two are Ultra Class B, and two of us are Class A, including myself."

She didn't have to add that only a handful of generals and admirals at the top of the Command Staff had Ultra Class A clearance . . . and that Mattox only had a High Class

9B clearance. The widening of his eyes let her know he knew that much. The narrowing that followed it warned her there were grooves of stubborn resistance worn into his brain by the paws of his so-called pet dog.

"*Follow procedure*, Brigadier General," Ia repeated firmly. "Whatever you may be thinking or feeling right now, you have an obligation to follow the orders and procedures of the Terran Space Force. As a high-ranking officer, your resistance only proves you have been contaminated. Follow procedure, while you still have a choice in the matter."

He looked her over and gestured with the hand holding his rifle. It was still powered down, and the muzzle pointed at the floor, thankfully. "You're not here to make friends, are you, Ship's Captain?"

Lightly folding her arms across her chest, Ia turned to her companion. "You know, everybody keeps asking me that question. Do you know what I always tell them, Private?"

"Sir, yes, sir. I do know what you always tell them, sir. I've heard you say it several times when chatting on the comms with any number of stubborn idiots." Sunrise looked at Mattox and answered his question for her. "Ship's Captain Ia is here to save lives. Why are *you* here?"

"Insolent little—!" he growled.

"More like extremely accurate," Ia stated blandly, "considering I've already asked the Admiral-General that very same question twice to her face."

"And you still have your rank?" Major Tonkswell asked her, one of his brows rising in a skeptical frown.

"The first time I asked it, she bumped me from Lieutenant First Class to Ship's Captain," Ia admitted, glancing his way. *The more this drags on, the more I wonder at just how much the Feyori have Meddled, and what they have blocked me from seeing in the timestreams . . . which means fixing this mess may be beyond* my *capabilities, given the constraints of time . . . which means I'm going to have to bind the Feyori to do it for me. Somehow . . . and I have no idea how, right now.*

Slag.

"But not the second time?" Mattox asked shrewdly when she said nothing more, deep in thought.

"I didn't need to go any higher," Ia dismissed, "and I obviously didn't go any lower."

"I still wanna know why *he's* here, in the Army, on Dabin," Sunrise muttered, lifting her chin at the brigadier general. "Are you here to serve the selfish interests of a Meddler? Or what?"

Mattox frowned at her. "I am here, soldier, to *win* this war. Why are *you* here?"

The question didn't phase Mara. "I'm here to help Captain Ia save lives while you do just that, sir."

"General, not to rush your decision, but we are running out of time," Ia pointed out, rubbing at her temple. "Let me have access to the comms here at Headquarters, and I'll get you the cross-Branch authorizations you need. That way we can pull in a few psis from my Company, a few from the PsiLeague, and get your headquarters cleared to proceed.

"If you do not follow procedure, I will be forced to contact the Admiral-General herself to have you removed, and I *really* don't want to have to do that," Ia insisted. "You are not a psi, you were not trained to shield your mind, and you have had *zero* chance of guarding your thoughts from being scrambled by a Meddler because you had no clue Ginger was anything other than what she seemed and thus no reason to guard your brain. *Follow procedure*, sir. Your removal from command is the only other option here."

Mattox grimaced, clearly not liking the choice ahead of

him, but nodded. "You can use the comm out here. And get my . . . the damned not-a-dog's blood off of you."

"Oh, this isn't canine blood," Ia dismissed, flicking a hand at her brown-stained uniform. "Ginger took every scrap and droplet of herself with her across the mass-energy barrier when she shifted back into a bubble. This is Salik blood."

"Salik blood?" Mattox asked her. "When did you pick that up?"

"When I went out for a walk a couple days ago. Specifically, when I went on a walk through the Salik 1117th. They took out one of my eyes, so I took out a few hundred of theirs. Let me get those orders processed first, sir, then I'll go looking for a clean uniform." Moving around to join Tonkswell on his side of the reception desk, Ia lifted her arm unit to transfer the contact codes . . . and wrinkled her nose at the scorched lid. "Slag . . . I forgot I still need to get this thing replaced. I'll have to do this electrokinetically. Private Sunrise, don't let me leave Headquarters without a new arm unit."

"Sir, yes, sir," Sunrise promised, reverting to her efficient-clerk persona. "I'll get one requisitioned for you right away, sir, along with a fresh uniform."

Getting hold of Admiral Genibes was relatively easy even if it took an extra hyperrelay hub in rerouting and a couple minutes' delay for him to respond. Getting hold of her Company was another matter. Her instincts didn't twinge when she thought about them, but it took Ia half an hour of trying to contact them via the comm relays in a conference room to give up waiting for any sort of swift response. The only other recourse was to check what her crew were doing via their timestreams.

Wary of what she might find, she flipped herself into the timeplains . . . and found not a single scrap of fog. Standing on the right-hand bank of her own stream, she didn't move immediately to search for the rest of her crew. Instead, she treated the view she had of the rolling, river-streaked prairie and its golden sunlight as warily as she would have an expanse of enemy territory.

Is everything too clear and fog-free? Are those double shadows cast by the grass? Are things moving at the right pace, or just a little too slow because they're trying to feed me false information at my normal accelerated speed?

It was difficult to tell.

Wary of the too-tranquil scene, Ia pulled back into herself. Silently, she surveyed the conference room she and Private Sunrise had been given. Mara sat off to one side with a portable comm similar to the one in front of Ia. From the sound of things, the other woman was finalizing the hiring of a quintet of high-ranked PsiLeague telepaths to come by Headquarters for mind scans. Dressed in clean clothes after a quick, sketchy wash in one of the building's restrooms, Ia should have been happy to finally have Mattox's cooperation. She wasn't because she still could not trust anything she could foresee.

Mara ended her call. Glancing up from the portable screen, she lifted one brow. "Something wrong, sir?"

"I'm not sure. I can't see any fog patches in the time-streams. I don't know if it's because the Feyori aren't trying to cloud my vision anymore or if it's because both of them have joined forces to further enforce a false reality on my view of the fourth dimension. If that makes any sense," Ia added, catching the wrinkle in the private's brow. "They're not in *my* mind, so much as they're attempting to alter my view of reality on a higher plane of consciousness. Like they're pasting layers of illusion over the buildings I'm trying to look at in the distance."

"It makes sense," Sunrise demurred, though she didn't lose the frown. "Sir . . . I don't really know how your, ah, time sense works. Does it take a lot of energy out of you to access the timestreams?"

"Me? No," Ia said. At Mara's skeptical look, she considered the question more carefully. "Well, not really. Not anymore. I've been doing it since I was an infant. Of course, that was more involuntary than anything until I was fifteen and had a sort of . . . breakthrough. But I had three years of solid practice before I hit the Marines," she continued, shrugging off the unpleasant memory, "and even then, it was more a matter of learning how to concentrate and focus my thoughts. I'll admit it's easier to limit my scope to a matter of minutes and hours when in the midst of battle, but ten minutes or ten thousand years, it's all one and the same to me now, and no more or less exhausting than concentrating on any other task. Paperwork, calisthenics, breathing . . ."

"Well, what about the Feyori? If they can access Time itself, how exhausting is it for them?" Sunrise asked next. "How far into the future can they push themselves, and how deeply? Do you even know?"

"Based on what I'd investigated prior to coming to Dabin . . . it's relatively exhausting for them. As exhausting as juggling large objects telekinetically. Particularly if they try to push into the future," Ia told her. "The farther ahead a Feyori tries to push, the heavier the metaphorical objects become in their juggling act. It's much easier for them to peek backwards into the past because the past is more or less complete, and thus lacking in as much psychokinetic resistance, trying to push their way through alternate possibilities. They can access it a lot better than the future . . . but still only by so much."

"Oh? How so?" Mara asked, bracing her elbows on the edge of the table. "And what about their supposed ability to time-travel?"

She gave it a few moments of thought, trying to find the right analogy to help the other woman understand. "Think of viewing or even touching the past like it's a river winding through a valley edged by mountains. You can shift the course of the river along the valley floor by digging a new channel or two on either side," Ia explained, using her hands to shape the images in her words; she had zero holokinetic abilities, so it was the only way to show Sunrise her meaning. "But there comes a point where you just cannot fight the pull of gravity.

"The farther up the valley—into the past—the closer the mountainsides are to the river, and the harder it is to reach that point and change the river's course. So they *can* send someone back in time to the past, but that person can only change the course of that river by so much. It takes a handful of Meddlers to send just one of them back . . . and it almost always costs the life-force energies of at least one Feyori, if not more. Fifteen thousand years cost twenty Feyori lives out of over five thousand cooperating."

Mara thought about it for a few moments, then nodded slowly. "So the future is more like a river that's free of the foothills and is now trying to cross a wide, flat plain. There aren't any mountains holding it to a single valley, and you can dig as many experimental canals as you want, exploring said future. But because there are so many possible places you can put the water, you—or rather, they—cannot afford the energy expended in trying to explore them all. Right?"

"More or less," Ia agreed. "The analogy breaks down a little at that point, but it's close enough."

"So . . . to overlay an illusion of normalcy on this broad, flat plain," Mara murmured, working it through, "a Feyori would have to expend a lot of effort. Particularly one detailed enough to fool *you*. Right, sir?"

"Right. Most Feyori can only see a few weeks ahead, maybe a few months at most," she confirmed. "And from what I have seen, the fog patches currently clouding my view only extended a couple weeks outward because the concentration required to paint realistic falsehoods no doubt takes even more effort and energy—although they're damned good even when blanking out just a few weeks," Ia admitted wryly. "They weren't quite touching my mind, but they did cloak whatever I looked at. 'Ginger' was too busy interacting with the real world, so whoever the other Feyori is, *that's* the one I have to watch out for."

"Can this 'Ginger' assist the other one?" Mara asked next.

"Quite possibly," Ia allowed, rubbing at the frown creasing her forehead. She sighed and shrugged. "The Feyori can do a close-faction gestalt not too dissimilar from our psychic gestalts, boosting and augmenting their abilities beyond what either one could add together . . . but while the whole ends up greater than the sum of its parts, it's not by *that* much. Scrying and overwriting the future is an uphill struggle."

"I'm amazed you even try, sir," Mara said dryly.

"*I'm* trying to work *with* the flow of Time," Ia said, flicking her hands emphatically. "I'm not trying to make any rivers climb any mountains. I'm just building canals and levees to guide the course of events down a valley-sized swath of those vast plains." She paused to think for a moment, then quickly lifted a hand to smother a yawn. "'Scuse me . . . been up for too many days straight."

"Ahh, 'To sleep, perchance to dream,'" the private quoted. "Although if I'm tired enough, I just snap the sheets up over my head to block out the light, and I drop like a stone."

The imagery conjured by Mara's words made Ia pause and frown. Sunrise gave her a bemused, inquiring look. Ia started to shake it off, then stilled her head. "*That* just might . . ."

"That just . . . what, sir?" Mara asked.

Without waiting to think about it, Ia closed her eyes, flipped her mind onto the timeplains, grabbed hold of temporality, and heaved with a fierce mental shout.

(*TIME!*)

Everything rocked. Dust snapped up from the too-clear fields and streams around her—no, not mere dust, *fog*. She snapped again, harder, shoving everything into a massive tapestry sheet instead of a vast prairie. Yanking up a strip of her own life-thread, Ia spun and cracked it like a whip for her third attack, visualizing hard the task of removing anyone else from actively scrying the future. The sine wave of her efforts smacked into one, two silvery soap bubbles, flinging the aliens off that sheet with outraged telepathic screeches. A fourth, hard lash of the timestreams . . . met no resistance.

Dropping back into her body, Ia landed with a nauseating *bump*, like the way she sometimes woke with a jolt from a dream about falling. From the stunned, pale look on her face and the hard way Mara swallowed, Ia's little trick had resulted in a mind-quake. Taking advantage of the cleared timeplains, Ia quickly dipped her hands back into the waters, checking to see just how far out her efforts had rippled.

. . . *God! A three-block radius. Only three blocks . . . and brief enough, no one was injured,* she realized. Relief washed through her. The move had been rather foolish without checking for that sort of thing first, but she hadn't dared *think* about it first. Thinking about it beforehand meant carving a possibility canal in the timeplains, one which the Feyori could have checked in advance and maybe compensated for.

But given how easily I snapped them loose, how hard and far they were flung off . . . I don't think they can cling to the timeplains in the face of another, similar attack even if they know it's coming, Ia thought. *Not that I'm going to let myself get cocky and assume I can fling them off at will. Not when it churns my stomach and disrupts everyone around me. And next time . . . I think I'll confine it very much to just the timeplains, now that I know I can shake them loose.*

I guess Time really is just one more form of energy . . . and as a half-breed Feyori, it's an energy I can manipulate as well as touch.

As for why it had only covered three mere blocks instead of many kilometers, she could only guess. For one, the mindquake had been under her firm control, not triggered involuntarily. For another, she had kept it short. And for a third reason . . . she realized there was no crysium on this world other than what she herself wore under her clothes. Nothing was there to be absorbed into the local diet, and nothing radiating excess, psychically sensitive KI into the aether to amplify and piggyback her efforts.

Sucking in a shuddering breath, Mara Sunrise blinked and shook off the aftereffects. *"Shakk,"* she cursed under her breath. "I just . . . I *think* I just saw the future. I don't . . . I've never . . . Sir, did you *do* something, just now?"

It wouldn't do her any good to deny it. "I think I've figured out how to get the Feyori off my back. At least temporarily. And it took actual effort from me," she admitted. Touching her stomach—or rather, touching the cloth covering the crystalline plates covering her stomach—Ia muttered, "I'm feeling nauseated like a trip through OTL, so I know I spent at least some kinetic inergy."

"How long will it last? Getting them off your back, I mean?" Sunrise clarified.

"I'm not sure. I'll need to check the timestreams while they're still clear." Closing her eyes, Ia focused her thoughts inward once more. She had almost forgotten *why* she needed to check the timestreams: to find out what had actually happened to her Company. But the first thing she needed to do was search for the life-paths of the two Feyori.

Spotting the waters of their lives, she stayed firmly on the bank. Without touching the rippling surface, Ia watched the images flickering inside each alien's life. She had an impression of some sort of facility with huge, blocky, metal objects, maybe an industrial manufactory. They seemed to be reeling, and didn't seem inclined to reach for the timestreams again for at least an hour, maybe longer.

Satisfied they would stay put for the moment, she turned her attention to A Company. Ia couldn't see much of Meyun Harper's life, just snatches here and there, but she could see the others. What she saw raised her brows. Her former Academy roommate, a man renowned for his brilliance when it came to mechanical problems . . . had taken the men and women under his command into combat?

He's actually carrying out combat maneuvers right now? Well, that would *explain why I couldn't reach them. Infiltration, sapper activities, and covert skirmishing do require long-range comm silence . . . Oh-ho! That's the excuse he used?* She double-checked the recent past, admiring the argument Commander Harper gave to Captain Roghetti. *"If Captain Ia can 'take a walk' and stomp all over the Salik forces pursuing us all by herself, why can't we do the same as a whole Company in her wake?"*

Except Roghetti's crew stopped to reclaim their camp, and split off a couple Platoons to mop up the stragglers among the 1117th. So at least the perimeter's secure once again. My crew overran the area far enough to give Roghetti's Company a good buffer, came back just long enough to pick up fresh supplies, get a good night's rest, and are now "taking a walk" themselves. She grinned for a few moments, watching them fight from a dozen riverbank viewpoints consolidated into a single, water-rippled image for convenience . . . then lost the urge to smile.

The recent past. My five missing crew members. Right . . .

Bracing herself, she headed upstream, traveling across streams shrunk down to rivulets for easy crossing. She moved back just a few days, to the moment when everything went to hell.

The first one she encountered ended in a dried-up streambed. She knew the woman. *Helenne Franke . . . Private First Grade, 3rd Platoon C Alpha, served in the Navy five years, and very good at managing life support. Saved our lives at least twice in the last two years by keeping the fish alive in the fore-sector tanks. Liked playing Mozart when she was on duty, swore the plants grew better by it. Death by . . . oh God . . .*

She forced herself to look at the last few minutes and hours of Private Franke's life. *Eaten by the Salik, post-battle. Caught off guard in her sleep, she didn't make it out of the tents before one of them collapsed, trapping her just long enough for the Salik to catch up to her.* Grim, Ia forced herself to move on, to look for the other four.

Two died at roughly the same time. *Private Second Class Cald Feldman, C Gamma of the 2nd Platoon . . . dammit, a fantastic cross-discipline engineer even if he had that horrible temper problem.* Like Sunrise, he had once been a sergeant. A Buck Sergeant. In his case, he had been reprimanded and demoted for nearly killing the drunken murderer of his fiancée, even though the man had sobered up enough to surrender himself to the Space Force's military peacekeepers afterward. *At least he died fighting, right alongside . . . oh,* shakk.

Private First Class Philadelphia Benjamin. A Epsilon, 2nd. Dammit! I liked her. She . . . dammit! Dammit dammit dammit . . .

Closing her eyes, Ia didn't quite block out the timestreams, but she did give herself a moment to grieve. *Her family has already gone through too much . . .* Ia counted the stout, wrong-limbed bodies falling around the pair in the waters of the past, holed up at the camp armory. *She and Feldman died back-to-back, taking out a good . . . wow, a good twenty-five mechsuited Salik, that's impressive for having no armor other than a couple of ceristeel breastplates.*

She checked the other streams nearby, then the alternate version, if things had worked out differently. What she found gave her a grim, unhappy satisfaction. *It took the Salik a fair bit to bring 'em down. Not in vain, either; it looks like they focused enough of the enemy's attentions to delay the main pursuit after us. If they hadn't holed up and held off, it looks like the rearward three trucks would've been attacked, possibly even destroyed by incoming projectiles. I was on one of those trucks. I owe them my life . . .*

Shakking *slag. Rearguard Stars are not a good thing when you have to hand 'em out to their family members along with the Black Heart. Two more deaths to lay at the metaphorical feet of those damned Feyori and their stupid Meddler politics! Why can't they just believe that I want to* help *their damned Game continue? Yes, I don't like it how they think of matter-based beings as nothing more than bugs to be toyed with or squished, but even* they *have a right to still exist five hundred years from now!*

She couldn't do anything about any of that right now, though. Her ears were picking up a conversation, slow and distorted thanks to the racing of her mind. Pulling back from the timeplains just enough to grasp what was being said, she found a woman in Army Greens asking her and Sunrise if any "weird visions" had happened to the two of them as well. Giving her a curt nod, Ia flipped her mind back into the sun-drenched grass and went looking for the last two missing soldiers.

Private Second Class Cynthia Gadalah, D Beta, 1st Platoon, and Private First Class Juan del Salvo, E Alpha 1st Platoon . . . and . . . oh thank God; they're both still alive, she discovered, seeing both streams still flowing strong, side by side, well into the future. Entwined, even. Frowning, she moved closer, peering down into their life-waters.

Oh. Oh my . . . Startled and amused, Ia politely left them to their activities in the farmhouse's shower, and backtracked their history from the homestead where the pair had taken refuge. She didn't blame them for taking advantage of their current moment of peace and rest. In fact, she found it amusing. Gadalah and del Salvo had been showering—separately—when the evacuation call came. Hearing it a bit late, they snatched up a few bits of clothing and ran, both dripping wet and naked, for the tree line.

Ia watched as, in the past, the pair joined up with Private Pumipi of the Army: he remembered the trick they'd tried to play on that first, aborted sabotage mission, back when Mattox had been handed his first set of Ia's battle plans. All three quickly coated themselves in mud, festooned their bodies with bits of flora, and crept their way in a tight line through the woods while the Salik searched for survivors.

Shaped more or less like yet another allipede, the trio had evaded discovery and pursuit by moving slowly but steadily along every bit of cover they could find until they were well beyond detection range. Right now, in the present, Pumipi was downstairs in the same home, in the laundry room of their colonist-host, sorting through old clothes for the other two to wear when they finally got done showering. He was the only one with an arm unit, and had checked in with Roghetti not an hour or so before. Roghetti hadn't been able to pass along the news of the other two surviving for the same reason Ia hadn't been able to reach her Company: covert combat operations in enemy territory required comm silence for the duration of the mission.

So the question about those two is . . . do I have to swap team pairings between those two, in case they've decided to bond romantically? . . . No, I don't have the time to decide right now. That was a question for another time. Specifically, for when she had the freedom and luxury of picking new crew members to replace the three she had lost. There was another task awaiting her, first. The unpleasant one of tracking down the missing members of Roghetti's Company. He would want to know what happened to the rest of them, too.

Before she began, Ia pulled back enough to check on her surroundings. Private Sunrise was now sitting quietly across from her. Utterly unlike Helstead, who would have been wiggling or tapping or fiddling with her little hairpin knives, Mara Sunrise just sat there patiently, watching her CO, her borrowed workpad set aside for the moment.

". . . Back in your own head, sir?" she asked, noting it the moment Ia focused her gaze on the other woman.

"For a few moments. Privates del Salvo and Gadalah are

alive. Privates Benjamin, Feldman, and Franke . . . are not. I
don't know when the Feyori are coming back to muck up the
timeplains again, so I'm going to take a few more moments
to find out what happened to Roghetti's missing crew," Ia
added.

Sunrise shook her head slightly. "I don't envy you that
task, Captain. I have, however, been thinking about Feyori
energy requirements. If they want to be able to blanket the
timestreams so much that *you* cannot see reality . . . then
they'll need to be parked in or next to a large pool of energy.
Probably more than one type since they surely need different
types like we need different types of food."

Ia nodded. "That's more or less correct. And I see where
you're going with that. Cross-reference all major sources of
energy: hydrogenerator plants, smelting foundries, maglev
trains, chemical plants, wind farms, solar farms . . . Coordinate with civilian resources to find any anomalous dips
in power outputs, thermal measurements—even ask around
to see if a bunch of hydrogenerators have been purchased
recently, or gone missing. Keep up Protocol Mary Had a
Little Lamb while you're doing it."

"Of course, sir. I'm still thinking about crackers in my
uppermost thoughts," Mara agreed, pulling the portable
workstation back into position in front of her. She flashed a
quick smile. "Though I may have to move on to contemplat-
ing various cheeses if this takes much longer."

Ia returned the smile ruefully. The quip was funny, but
Sunrise was also right about the task on her own plate. No
one would ever envy a Commanding Officer who had to
compile a dead-or-missing report. The only good thing in
this whole situation was how clear her head now felt, her
thoughts free to trail mental fingers and toes in the waters
of past and future for the first time since the rout at Roghetti's

camp. And to snap the sheet-like surface of Time every now and again, to keep it influence-free.

————————

The "bursts of strange visions" were the talk of the restaurant, when Private Sunrise finally insisted—politely but very firmly—that her CO go across the street and get some real food. The waiters and waitresses were greeting their customers with the typical aplomb of career servers, but they spent a few extra minutes chatting at each table about who had seen what and where they had been.

Ia merely shrugged and ordered a pot of caf' and two of the largest brunch specials on the menu for her caloric needs. After a quick glance at her commanding officer, Mara carried most of that conversation with the waiter serving their table, mentioning she'd seen herself crossing the street outside, going somewhere, but didn't know where. Both women got an earful of local gossip about business calls preseen, conversations preremembered, and at least one averted traffic accident since the person had chosen to stop by for a slice of pie and a change of travel plans.

All in all, Ia thought, barely listening to their waiter chatting about the mind-quake, *at least it's a much more pleasant experience for these people than the Fire Girl Prophecies everyone back home got. But I suppose that's because the crysium in everyone's diet is augmenting the visions back home.*

Her arm unit beeped, using the two-tone signal that said it was audio only. Fishing in her pocket, Ia pulled out her headset, hooking it over her ear. The waiter noticed her taking the call and smiled and excused himself, giving the two women a bit of privacy.

"Ship's Captain Ia, go," she murmured.

"Oh Captain, my Captain," a very welcome, male voice murmured in her ear. Commander Harper sounded like he could have used a good ten hours of sleep from the roughness in his tone, but it couldn't disguise the satisfaction coloring his mood. *"I understand you tried to get ahold of me a little while ago?"*

"Yeah. I gave up when I figured out how to clear the timeplains. Unfortunately, it's only a temporary solution. You're still in charge of A Company, with all my trust and confidence. Privates Benjamin, Franke, and Feldman are dead. Privates del Salvo and Gadalah are still alive. They had one of Roghetti's with them, Private Pumipi."

"Yeah, I just heard about del Salvo's group. Dunno if you know, but on my end of things . . . Doersch is touch-and-go right now. Mishka's holding him together," Harper promised, *"but he got crushed by a tree knocked over by enemy fire."*

"Then keep Mishka, by all means. I do, however, need Privates Mk'nonn, Jjones, Yarrin, Theam, and Rayne sent to Army Headquarters," she told him.

Harper's tone sharpened a little. *"Ia . . . those are some of the strongest telepaths we have."*

"Yes, and I need them stationed at HQ for the next two weeks to mind-scan everyone here, to certify them as Feyori-free." Opening the lid on her newly issued arm unit, she tapped in a couple commands. *"I'm sending you a copy of Admiral Genibes's orders for cross-Branch cooperation on a subchannel."*

The waiter came back, a pair of bowls in his hands. He delivered the fruit salads with a smile, then took himself off to greet the next set of arrivals.

". . . Received," Harper murmured. *"I'll see what I can do. We don't exactly have reliable transport out here."*

"Make it a priority," Ia ordered. *"Beyond that, keep doing whatever you think best—I'd take Crow and Teevie, but they're a gestalt-pair. You might need all their extra nontelepathic strengths. Plan carefully, Harper, whatever you plan to do. Until I can get the Meddlers to stop being my enemy, you're still safer on your own, but that isn't the same as safe. Watch your back."*

"Helstead filled me in a little on 'Private' Sunrise's background," Harper told her. *"Your messages said you'd transferred her to B Company. Good choice . . . but remember your own words. Safer isn't the same as safe. Watch your own back."*

"Aye, aye, Commander," she quipped. *"Anything else?"*

"Figure out a way to extract a good old-fashioned pound of flesh from the Feyori for each of the meioas we lost. And come back safe and sound. Beyond that . . . I can't think of anything. Good luck, Captain. Harper out."

Ia closed her arm unit and unhooked the headset. The style used by the Army wiggled weirdly against the side of her head whenever she chewed, so she tucked it back into her shirt pocket.

"Any good news?" Sunrise asked her.

"Everyone we know who made it out is still alive," Ia relayed. "Private Doersch, 2nd D Alpha, took a bad hit, but the Doc's holding him together."

"Heh. Probably complaining about the 'primitive working conditions,' too," Mara joked. She caught the wrinkling of Ia's nose. "Something wrong, sir?"

Ia tapped the table between them. "I dislike being here. I need to be out *there*, and soon, before everything starts unraveling too much for me to stitch back together."

"Well, I'm still working on Operation Think About Cheese, sir," Mara quipped. She sort of shrunk into herself, shoulders slumping slightly, her competent air evaporating into a look of boredom. Within the span of three breaths, she was no longer an ex-Knifeman but was once again nothing but a mousey military clerk, better suited for a desk job than anything rife with danger or intrigue. "I can't make up my mind. Should I count the processed cheese-flavored spreads, or not?"

Amused despite the seriousness of their situation, Ia let herself smile for a moment. "Don't take forever making up your mind. I *think* I can bludgeon Mattox into letting me revise all his battle plans now, but there isn't a lot of leeway in Genibes's orders since even a Command Staff rank has to be careful about directing a brigadier general to take orders from a mere Ship's Captain."

"He has a bit of an ego," Mara agreed. A shrug of her shoulders and a quirk of one brow resettled her confident persona back in place. "You'll have to be careful. Point out that the Meddler clearly influenced him to ignore your perfectly sound battle plans but don't make him lose any more face than he already has."

Ia wrinkled her nose again. "I *hate* politics. I'd much rather deal with people who can see reason on the first try— I'll point out that Harper's using similar tactics to chew a successful little hole in the Salik perimeter, so clearly the Feyori didn't want him doing anything of the kind to the Salik since they know he'd see how effective it would be if they hadn't clouded his thinking . . . gah!" She grimaced and reached for the ice water in front of her. "Pandering to the general's ego—I'm getting a nasty taste in my mouth just thinking about it."

Mara tried but failed to keep her expression straight and somber. A smirk curled up the corner of her mouth. "We all have to make sacrifices, sir."

That put things back into perspective. Sighing, Ia picked up her fork and poked at the locally grown slices of fruit in her bowl. "Compared to what the Benjamins—Philly's family back on Mars—have gone through, I have no right to complain." At the loss of the other woman's half smile, Ia moved the subject back to business. "Sorry, didn't mean to be depressing. You said the first of the League psis will be arriving tomorrow?"

Nodding, Mara filled in Ia on what she had arranged.

CHAPTER 5

No, I told you, Ginger wasn't a dog. I did not shoot a real dog. I like dogs, particularly stubbies, and I certainly wouldn't harm one without a very serious cause. What I shot was a Feyori Meddler, who did not die, so therefore there is and was no possible way that I could have killed a real dog that day. And I didn't kill the damned Feyori that day, either.

. . . What? Don't be ridiculous. Of course you can kill a Feyori, and I do mean for-real kill it. Dead-dead kill it. It's just . . . really difficult, and comes with a high price attached. Particularly since a Meddler's death upsets the balance of their precious Game. And no, I'm not going to tell you how to do it. They have just as much right to live as you or I . . . and yes, I know the irony of that statement, coming from me of all people.

~Ia

JUNE 14, 2498 T.S.

"Daytime maneuvers?" Ia asked the battle techs around her. "*Seriously?* Where did you get your tactical playbooks, from Westerners back at the turn of the twenty-first century?"

"These tactics work brilliantly when we have the home-field advantage," Lieutenant Colonel Kiang-Smith countered. "Which, being native to Dabin, we do."

"These tactics *only* work when you have a vast number of bodies you are willing to *throw away* in the face of enemy fire—do none of you remember your history lessons? The Battle for Iwo Jima, Old Earth World War II? There is a *reason* why the current flagship of the Navy's 1st Cordon is named the TUPSF *Kuribayashi*, after the military leader who planned the defenses for that bloodied hellhole.

"*Yes*, your tactics would work, if you threw two-thirds of the 1st Division at *this* point," Ia allowed. Jabbing at the screen, she slashed her finger over the battle lines, electrokinetically streaking it with different colors than the ones already proposed. "But you'd be leaving every other flank, and all the citizens beyond them, vulnerable to one-quarter of the Salik ground forces pushing at any point they wanted along several hundred kilometers of undermanned perimeter!"

"The perimeter will remain secure," one of the lieutenants argued back. "The Salik will be busy containing our attack."

"Not once they see how lightly it'll be defended. Unless you plan to conjure up extra troops from your magician's hat? Where did you think you'd get the extra bodies needed to man the rest of the battle lines?" she asked tartly. "From farmhands? They're having enough problems with the not-cats and the regular wildlife, and the enemy patrols that *do* slip past our people, and that's with a full-on containment perimeter. We're lucky we even have that much.

"The Salik want to keep as many people alive, and as much of our infrastructure intact as possible, so they'll have an easier time setting up their own colonists on this world. *I* want to keep as many people alive as possible because to do it any other way is not only a criminal waste of resources, it is *immoral*." Bracing her hands on the edge of the display table, Ia glared at the others through the transparent screens projecting the holographic image of the chunk of continent occupied by the Salik. "Frankly, the thought that you *are* willing to throw so many bodies at this problem without a thought or a care for finding a better way *sickens* me."

"You're not here to make friends, are you?" Kiang-Smith asked, folding his arms across his chest.

"Get in line," she muttered. Straightening, she raked a hand through her locks. Once again, the bangs were getting long enough to fall across her eyes. Shoving the white strands out of her way, she flexed her shoulders. "Okay. From the top. Throw out *every* plan you have made since Ginger-the-not-a-damned-dog showed up in this building. Every single time you *start* to return to those plans, remind yourselves, 'These plans are what the *enemy* wants me to do.'"

"How do *we* know that's what the enemy actually wants us to do?" one of the junior lieutenants asked, her tone suspicious. "We just have *your* word for it. Sir."

"Can you not *see* the—? *Gah! Eyah, ginsa screama!*" It took her a moment to realize she was so frustrated, she was starting to channel her distant descendant again. Covering her right eye with her hand—the left had a fresh regen pack on it—Ia forced herself to breathe deeply, slowly. Recentering her mind, she strengthened her mental shields. *I am* not *from the Barros of Gyp City. I am* not *a massive self-made sociopath. I am* not *in combat and do not* need *to be a massive self-made sociopath . . .*

The Feyori weren't touching the timeplains. Not with Ia snapping the fourth dimension at random intervals to give herself room to work. But this mental stubbornness on the part of the Human men and women around her was undoubtedly a sign that their telepathic influence was still at work.

It was the only reason she could think of for her fellow officers being so *stupid* about their strategic and tactical analyses. She did have the requested psis from her Company to help scan minds for Meddler fingerprints, plus a quartet from the PsiLeague, who were mostly focusing on trying to blanket the building in the mental equivalent of counter-surveillance jamming, but it clearly wasn't enough.

"Okay. Please remember that everyone in this building has been influenced by a Feyori. That you are *still* being influenced by a Feyori digging its silvery-soap-bubble fingerprints into your brains. With that said, your strategic analyses *are* accurate. We *do* need to disrupt all attempts by the Salik to further entrench themselves on this world, and you have identified the key targets," Ia praised them. "You have done very good work with that.

"Now . . . step *back* from the battlefield and hand off the *tactical* implementations of those strategic targets to the Companies who *actually have to pull it all off*. Decentralize all tactical command decisions, so that you can *guarantee* the Feyori cannot influence everyone here on Dabin. They *do* have a limit on how large an area they can blanket with their mind tricks, and a limit on how many people they can manipulate with their mind games," Ia told the dozen or so men and women around her. "Whether or not they *are* still Meddling with Headquarters is not as important as whether or not they *can* still Meddle with Headquarters."

"You're asking us to put our trust into people who are

not trained in tactical analysis," Lieutenant Colonel Kiang-Smith stated.

Ia shifted her hands to her hips. ". . . Excuse me? Are you telling me that the *Army* has failed to train each and every soldier in the basic Space Force requirements of Squad-, Platoon-, and Company-level tactical comprehension and implementation? When I know for a fact that the Army devotes half of Basic Training to it, the exact same as the Marine Corps?"

"According to your Service file, you've *never* served in the Army," one of the male majors scorned. "What does an ex-Marine know about the Army?"

"I know that the Army *specializes* in ground-based combat, unlike the Marines, who specialize in ship- and station-boarding maneuvers. Those soldiers out there may be *rusty* at making their own tactical decisions," she added, pointing off to one side, "because you've robbed them of their right to make on-the-scene, real-time changes and corrections for who knows how long. But I also know they still have the skills to get the job done. They wouldn't have graduated from Basic if they didn't! Tell them what the endgame goal is, then *let* them accomplish it as they were *trained* to do."

A new voice joined the argument. Brigadier General Mattox stepped into the room. "Your orders are to advise us on the *Feyori* problem, Ship's Captain."

Ia turned to face him. He had taken the time to decorate his Dress Greens with half glittery, one of each medal as well as his Service zone pins. Compared to her camouflage clothes, he looked like he *should* be in charge. Ia was starting to doubt that, though. If he wasn't thinking clearly, if he wasn't willing to cooperate and return to his non-Meddled brilliance, then far too many of her plans would have to change on this world. Too many were being forced to change on the fly as it was. Still, his statement had to be answered.

"Brigadier General, yes, sir; I know very well what my orders are, sir. I am *telling* you that this centralization of command decision and power, of concentrating it into a single building here at Headquarters *is* a Feyori problem, General," she stated. "If *I* can blanket three whole blocks with a mind-quake, then covering and influencing a single building's worth of mind in ways too subtle for a nonpsi to detect is child's play to a Meddler."

"Your Service file also states that *you* are half-Feyori," he argued back.

Some of his attachés gave her uneasy looks at that. Ia didn't let it faze her. She was long past the point where she had to hide her birthright.

"That just proves my point on how much more a full Feyori can interfere," she stated, spreading her arms. "I am here to advise you how to avoid further Feyori contamination. There is a limit to how much territory and how many minds a Feyori can cover. If you want to be *sure* the 1st Division's battle plans are not being influenced by the enemy, then you *decentralize*. Your strategies are perfectly fine, but maintaining this top-down level of micromanaging for your tactics is not.

"In order to thwart further Feyori influences, I am advising you, flat out, to pass the tactical planning on how to carry out those goals into the hands of the people in the field, who know best how to adapt their maneuvers to the immediate needs of the terrain, their personal resources, and the enemy forces they face. A method which we already know works well, and which we have known for centuries works very well." Dropping her hands to her sides, she waited for him to make up his mind. A dozen people under Feyori influence might be hard for her to sway with just words, but this was the man in charge.

"Ship's Captain Ia," Mattox finally said. "Please leave the tactical room."

They *were* still under Feyori influence. The handful of psis struggling to shield the building weren't enough.

"Now, Captain," Mattox ordered.

"Then I'm sorry, but you leave me no choice," she started to say. A thought interrupted her. One which was not, and yet was, her own.

(*Don't even think about it. Not while the Feyori are still here.*)

Blinking, Ia revised what she was going to say, uttering a non sequitur instead. ". . . I think I'll go take up cheese-making. I'm sure it'll be more productive than this."

Not bothering to give him a polite nod, Ia stepped around Mattox and left the room, as requested. Taking the stairs, she flipped open her arm unit, typing in a command. She was all the way down to the parking garage, within sight of the hoverbike, before Sunrise caught up with her.

"You called, sir?" the ex-sergeant asked, not quite running but not dawdling either as she strode up to the bike.

"Get on, drive, and think about cheese," Ia directed her. "I want us well out of Meddler mind-control range before I start ranting so hard, I'm foaming at the mouth."

"Aye, sir." Mounting the bike, she waited for Ia to swing into place behind her, then started it up. "Any particular type of cheese? Gruyère? Swiss? Dabinian purple cheddar?"

"Dabinian purple cheddar. With jalapeños," Ia added, gripping the bike seat with her hands as well as her thighs. "At least thirty kilometers' worth."

"Hang on to your curds and whey, sir." Guiding the bike up out of the underground garage, she hit the thrusters and pointed the bike toward the nearest road out of town. Both women winced at the wind kicked up by their passage until the shields activated, warping some of the airflow around the front of the bike.

TRONDHIN LAKE MUNICIPAL RECREATIONAL PARK

"Nice place you found," Ia observed, coming to a stop near the edge of the modest lake.

It was indeed nice; someone had coaxed Terran-style grass and bushes to grow, making a splash of soothing green against the beiges, purples, and reds prevalent locally. The color even spilled down into the lake, if only by reflection. They formed a stain of green that didn't go too badly with the blue of the sky and the russet of the local foliage.

Seated beside her on the ground, Mara shrugged. "It's on the local tourism map. Just used my arm unit to find one. It didn't say why no one would be here, though. It's a good time of day for parents with young children, or people taking an early lunch break." She looked around at the peaceful, empty park, then shrugged. ". . . At least it's quiet. Private enough to vent, too, if you need it."

Ia nodded curtly but didn't start. Too many years of keeping temporal secrets to herself had left her with few moments where she felt comfortable venting herself verbally. Instead, she surveyed the cattails, water flowers, and bushy trees in the distance. Aside from the wind-swayed foliage, the only other movement came from the occasional trundling of a little gardening robot, the kind that was just smart enough to find and remove anything resembling a grass seed from the lawn, so that the foreign plants couldn't spread beyond the garden's boundaries.

She tried not to let her impatience get the best of her. Until she could figure out what to do about the Feyori—until she could *find* and thus deal with them—she was stuck in an uncomfortable sort of limbo. She didn't like this inactivity. She did not like the mess back at Army HQ, either. Unable to change things, Ia settled onto the ground, frustration escaping her in a heavy sigh.

"You sound like I feel, sir," Mara observed quietly. She pulled loose the end of her braid, unbinding it and finger-combing it out. Even with a partial shield on the bike, the wind stirred by their flight had rumpled her neat hairdo. She didn't use stiletto pins like Commander Helstead did, but she did have to remove several ordinary bobby pins as she worked.

Ia looked at her. "You're frustrated as hell, too?"

"Every time I think I'm closing in on a possible Feyori location, the energy imbalances drop back to normal, and I'm left without a location for you," Sunrise confessed. She patted down her pockets and finally pulled out a small travel comb. "If Helstead were here, and if she knew the locations in question, she might be able to teleport you there in time to catch them, but . . . Well, at this rate, I'd be more useful back in the field, running scouting forays for Commander Harper. Maybe not as a mousey, ordinary clerk, but as a scout, yes."

"I'd be a lot more useful in the field, too, but not while I'm blocked by all the damn Meddling they're still free to do." Bracing her elbows on her knees, Ia dragged her fingers through her hair. She no longer needed a regen pack on her left eye socket but had been given a patch to cover the tender pink skin, shielding it from accidental bumps and scrapes. At some point, she would need to schedule an appointment with a biotank company to grow a new eye, but right now, getting Mattox and his meioas to stop being idiots was her top priority . . . yet she couldn't even manage that much. "I block them from interfering on the timeplains, and they interfere with the minds of those around me. I move to block them from the minds around me, and they go back to Meddling with the timeplains. I'm a Dutch boy with a mere mortal arm span not even two meters long and a pair of dike leaks at least fifty meters apart. I can only plug the one leak for short periods of time before I have to run off to the other side of the levee."

"Well, I'd *think* the Prophet of a Thousand Years could at least lock them out of Time itself," Mara pointed out, pausing briefly between strokes to gesture at Ia with her comb. "Can't you layer an illusion over the fourth dimension? Or shield it somehow? You've all but said you're a far stronger precognitive than any Feyori out there."

"It's not something I'm practiced at. I'd be spending all my time watching and shielding the timestreams so they couldn't notice my next few steps," Ia pointed out. "But that means I wouldn't be able to *deal* with them. I'd need a steady source of energy to feed me, too, and that means staying put somewhere."

"What about the other psis?" Sunrise offered, setting her comb aside in favor of replaiting her hair. "What if they banded together? There are plenty of stories of psis kicking Feyori off-world, out there."

"Even if the others *could* access the timestreams, that's only a temporary solution," Ia dismissed. "They'd just come back and do it all over again the moment the psis relaxed. It'd work the other way around a lot better since I know I can take on a Feyori, but I can't teach the rest of the psis how to shelter the timestreams, so they don't know what's coming to hit them. Even the best precog in the League cannot access Time the way that I do."

"Hm. A pity you can't duplicate yourself. If there were two of you, one could shield the timestreams while the other hunted," the ex-sergeant muttered.

A pity . . . if there were two of you . . . Ia slapped her forehead on the undamaged side. Mara gave her an odd look, but Ia didn't explain. She just twisted and flipped her mind into the timestreams, diving in deep. Grabbing the local tapestry, she gave it a hard snap—and felt at least one Feyori dislodge. As soon as it was clear, she let her mind and body race over the threads, plucking at various possibilities. *When when when*

when when . . . *aha! October 21st, 2498 Terran Standard,* sic transit *to the Dlmvla homeworld . . . yes, and there I am. I can do this.*

Rising out of her own future life-stream, clad in a simple gray T-shirt, and exercise pants, the older Ia smiled wryly at her younger self. A glimpse at the waters showed the older, future version of herself lying on a bed in their next ship's infirmary, being monitored physically while she guarded everything mentally. (*Got it in one go, and an excellent moment in time for it. You figured out which one to confront yet?*)

(*Miklinn,*) the younger Ia confirmed. She hadn't given it any thought until that moment, but could already see the effects such a choice would have on the webwork of lives and actions around her. (*These two are lackeys. Loyal, but stupid. I need to catch and control the fanged head of this serpent, not waste my time wrestling with its coils. And it'll be either a case of conversion to my cause, or . . . yeah.*)

(*Yeah,*) older Ia agreed. (*Either path will end up with you here, being me. But be careful all the same. Remember, to see the true path ahead of you, you'll have to come to* this *point in time, and work your way back upstream. Not just for this case, but for all other instances, too.*)

(*Understood. Ready?*) she asked her older self.

(*I am.*) The October Ia lifted her hands, shifting the shape of the Plains into a copy of Trondhin Lake. From there, Time expanded outward, forward and back, up and down, left and right. Her elder self settled on the grass in a position not too dissimilar from the younger one's stance in the real world, and began to meditate. A last whisper of thought reached her. (*Go get 'em, meioa-e . . .*)

The visualization of the lake faded, reducing itself down to a small eddy in her future self's life-waters. Marking it in her mind, Ia shifted the stream into a thread, grasped it, and peered up the weave, looking for her quarry. Two Feyori on Dabin, one watching over the Salik, one the colonists, and neither giving a damn for the fact that their pawns were people, not cheap, replaceable game pieces.

When she had all the information she needed, Ia swung herself back up into her body. At her side, Mara Sunrise was still slotting a couple pins into place, securing the coil of her braid to the back of her head. Male or female, any Human could grow long hair in the Space Force once they were out of Basic Training. They just had to keep it up off the collar to ensure it would stay out of the way of a pressure-suit's O-ring.

"Done thinking about cheese and crackers, sir?" Mara asked.

"Not only done, but ready to eat it, too. I figured out a way to cover up everything we do in the timestreams over the next few hours. I had to borrow a couple days to do it," she added, not bothering to explain, "but that's alright. Do you know how to get to the Petran Company Alloy Manufactory Center?"

The ex-sergeant blinked. "That's one of the companies on my target list . . . so yeah, I have the address in my arm unit."

Pushing to her feet, Ia offered her hand. "Then let's go."

Mara accepted it. "I'm glad you had us adapt over the last few years to the local gravity. Just standing up would've been a chore, otherwise." She grinned and slapped her abdomen through her camouflage shirt. "Not to mention I wouldn't have these fantastic abs."

Shaking her head in amusement, Ia started up the hill, Mara at her side. Halfway up the landscaped slope, Ia slowed. The hairs on the back of her neck were rising. She looked to either side, but the flower-strewn bushes were growing too thickly together to see anything concrete. It didn't help that the worst of the danger sense came from her left, her blinded side.

Instinct flexed her gifts through the crystalline bands beneath her clothes—and a heavy weight slammed into her side and back, claws grooving and teeth denting the half-pliable biomineral even as it formed a collar to protect her shoulders and neck. If she hadn't been so strong, the blow would have knocked her to the ground and possibly broken a few bones from the weight of the beast and the local gravity. As it was, she staggered, grunting under the impact.

"Shakk!" Whipping around, Sunrise pulled out her gun, only to hesitate, since Ia's head was in the way.

Ia didn't have time to reply; pain scored her chest as the not-cat got enough of its claws dug under the shifting plates to spin her around. That finished her half-thwarted fall. Thumping into the ground in a controlled slump, she managed to solidify the plates enough to protect herself while the alien beast shredded her shirt.

Three loud *bangs* slammed into the predator. The first thumped into its hip, making it flinch and roar at Sunrise. The second ripped off its stinger-loaded tail half a meter from striking the other woman in vengeance. The third caught it in the left eye-stalk socket, and the size of the exit wound spraying across the lawn proved the ex-sergeant had swapped the contents of her cartridge clip from standards back to splatters.

Shoving hard, Ia pushed the slumping beast aside before it could finish collapsing on top of her. Mara was strong for her modest frame, but she would've needed help to get the not-cat off her commanding officer if it pinned Ia in place as a literal dead weight. Lying there, panting for breath, Ia rested. After a few moments, Mara finally shifted from pointing her gun at the not-cat to pointing it at the ground off to the side, away from anything other than Terran-transplanted grass.

"Well." Mara sighed. "Now we know why people weren't using this park. How badly are you injured, sir?"

Ia managed a wry smile. "I think I'm going to have to decree that the mousey clerk be put away. I much prefer your normal self even if we'll have to keep calling you Mara for discretion's sake."

"I'd appreciate that, sir. That, and I like my new name . . . but you haven't answered my question," Mara repeated doggedly, staring down at her supine CO. "How badly are you injured, sir?"

Grunting, she managed to heave herself into a sitting position and winced as the move stung the scrapes on her chest. Given the wounds she had received in the past and the fact she no longer had to hide her biokinetic powers, she gauged the severity of her wounds as modest at best. They would just hurt for the next hour while the scratches healed. *Not like a laser to the shoulder, or the loss of an eye, thank God.*

"The beast got to me in a few small spots, but I'll heal up within the hour," she promised her crewwoman. She looked over at the not-cat, studying this one in the light of day, as she had not been able to view the first one on that rainy night. The hide was a ruddy shade of mottled brick and dull gunmetal, well suited to blending into the shadows of Dabin's reddish version of greenery, and heavily scaled, the muscles underneath still evident despite the limpness of death.

Mara frowned at her, then knelt and brushed at the shredded bits of Ia's camouflage shirt, baring bits of translucent golden peach. "You know, I've been meaning to ask, what are you wearing underneath your clothing, sir?"

"None of your business and well beyond your pay grade, *Private.*" Gathering her strength, she pushed to her feet. The shirt would need to be replaced, but it still covered enough for modesty's sake once she was upright. "Not-cats are usually solitary hunters once scattered into the wild, so all we have to do is report this one to the Peacekeepers. They can come do a tracking sweep to be doubly sure and dispose of the body while they're here. Good shot, by the way."

Sunrise grimaced, holstering her weapon. "Not really; the first shot was meant for the abdomen. I think the equivalent of a pelvis stopped the bullet before it could finish expanding."

"I won't tell Helstead your first shot was off if you won't tell her it got the drop on me anyway," Ia promised. "You might want to do some quick-draw shooting drills on the targeting range next time you get the chance."

"That's already on my To Do list, Captain, don't worry," Mara said. After a few paces, a thought made her frown. "Question, sir—that is, getting back to the original topic—but, wouldn't my coming along with you tip off our arrival to the Feyori? I can think about cheese and crackers and fruit all day long, but won't they notice me thinking it as soon as I come into range? Your cloaking trick is only good on the timeplains, right?"

"I'm going up against them as a fellow Feyori," Ia told her. "Which means we'll have to stop somewhere with enough of a power supply that I can get ready to manifest on cue. All you have to do is think of me *as* a Feyori, coming to challenge them face-to . . . erm, bubble-to-bubble, so to speak . . . and they'll have to leave you alone. Meddling with someone else's pawns during a direct challenge is a serious *faux pas*. It would mean they're too weak to face *me*, and no Feyori would admit to that when facing a half-breed. Of course, if they do try, I should be strong enough to free you."

"I'll try to keep in mind the whole direct-challenge thing, sir, so we don't have to risk that option. Can we pick up lunch along the way?" she asked, unfazed by the gore they were leaving on the grassy slope behind them.

"Sure. I could use a little something to help these cuts and bruises heal. Sandwiches okay?" Ia asked.

That earned her a rolling of Mara's eyes. She continued trudging up the slope toward the parking area. "Sandwiches? *Ugh*. According to your bridge crew, that's all you ever fix!"

"Hey, they're lucky I *can* fix sandwiches," Ia argued back, following her. "And sandwiches are portable, which is why I suggested them. Besides, not everyone is born with cordon bleu cheese running through their veins."

"Ugh," Mara scoffed. "That's not even a decent pun."

"I'm just trying to drive you crackers," Ia quipped. That earned her another snort of disgust and a half-stifled chuckle. She couldn't help her quirky moment of good humor, spurred to the surface by the jolt of adrenaline from the not-cat's attack. She was alive, and she had a plan to put an end to her current biggest problem.

With her future self's help, Ia finally had a way to deal with her Meddler-based problems, *without* their realizing it in advance. For that matter, the weeks she had spent as a teenager, combing through alternate realities, poring over past activities, and puzzling through the more obscure of Feyori customs would finally come in handy. Her Right of Simmerings was about to come to a full-on boil.

PETRAN COMPANY CAMPUS

"Gotta love M-class colonyworlds," Sunrise murmured, letting the hoverbike drift to a stop a hundred meters from the force-field fence separating the Petran Company from the rest of the planet. "Fresh air to breathe, livable gravity, and all the space you could want for sprawling out. One hundred square kilometers of homesteading territory picked from land and sea for each registered firstworlder, to be divided and inherited tax-free . . . or not divided, in the case of this company, as owned by the Petran family."

"Yes, and all you have to do to get it is put up with the native wildlife, survive untested pathogens, endure a dearth of modern amenities for the first couple of decades, and on heavyworlds, tread carefully around the fact that tripping and falling can literally break bones and crack open skulls," Ia agreed. "The Quentin side of the family initially snagged a big patch of coastline, before they discovered just how dangerous sea-based life is on Sanctuary. They successfully refiled their claims for the eastern side of the mountains, as did everyone else who thought to claim a chunk of the seaboard. The Jones side grabbed a solid chunk of the midplains south of the capital. But that's on Sanctuary, this is Dabin, and we're nowhere near any large bodies of water."

"So how do we get in, Captain?" Mara asked, lifting her chin at the fence. "If we try to fly over that, those stunner towers will smack us silly. Or rather, they'll smack *me* silly since I'm the one flying this thing and you're the one with the antistunner whatsit ability."

"And how do you know about that?" Ia asked, amused.

"*Captain* Helstead showed me your full personnel file. At least, the amount she has clearance for . . . which does beg the question of who has the other Ultra Class A clearance," the ex-Knifeman mused out loud. "Or the Class Cs, for that matter."

"The Class C clearances are for our trio of shiptechs who worked on the original Harasser-Class project," Ia explained. "Their clearance is limited to ship functions only; the rest is the same as most of the crew. The two Class Bs are Harper and Helstead, and the other Class A is Lieutenant Rico."

"Why Rico? I'd understand if it was Helstead, given what she used to do in the Corpse. Even I as a former Staff Sergeant had a higher clearance than anyone else in the Company, back when I was still a Knifeman," Mara said, confusion lacing her tone. She even craned her neck, frowning back at Ia. "But Lieutenant First Class Oslo Rico? Why is his clearance higher than your first officer's?"

"Rico's the chief spy for the Admiral-General in the Company," Ia reminded her.

"*Oh*, right," Mara murmured. "I'd forgotten that. Sorry, sir, it won't happen again."

"Don't worry about it. He has that clearance simply because if you're going to spy on a woman with Ultra Class A clearance, you need someone who *also* has that level of trust, in case he overhears anything that would otherwise be above his pay grade. This way, he can investigate anything I get into and gauge whether or not it's a threat to the security of the Space Force."

"So I guess he's sort of an honorary Troubleshooter in that sense—the man's way too nice to be a Knifeman. Okay, so how do *we* get in there?" Mara repeated, returning her attention to the fence. They hadn't followed a road, though there was one off to the right that led up to the gatehouse. "If they're smart little soap bubbles, the Feyori will be keeping a mental finger on the thoughts of the security teams. We try the front door, and they'll probably know we're here within moments. Presuming they don't already."

"The thing about front doors, Private, is that the polite thing to do is to find and ring the doorbell. Which I will do telepathically, not physically."

Sitting back from the other woman, Ia centered her mind. It had taken them barely an hour to get here, even with a quick stop for lunch. With the boost in energy from her meal, she had enough strength to divide her mind.

One part dipped into the timestreams and split in half. One of those halves looked at the current overlay, while the other darted ahead to a specific, park-like moment a handful of months ahead, before burrowing back upstream. That gave her a view of both the real universe in all its four-dimensional glory, and the false one overlaid by her future

•

self. The other part reached outward, seeking the minds of the two Feyori a kilometer or so away.

It wasn't easy, even with her temporal sense guiding her. In fact, it wasn't possible. There were too many minds, and a kilometer was over her limit for telepathy. If she could use the timeplains, she could do it easily, but she couldn't. Shaking her head, Ia pulled back into herself. "We need a power line. I can't reach that far on my own."

"Why power lines?" Mara asked, consulting her arm unit briefly before moving the hoverbike off to the left. Ia drew in a breath to answer, and the private shook her head. "I'm not talking about your needing to siphon energy; *that* part I get, sir. I meant, why do they have overhead lines at all? Most worlds I know of have their power lines buried for safety reasons."

"Dabin's still a bit young in some ways, or rather, cash-poor, to be able to afford such luxuries. The local ground is too wet three seasons of the year to bury the cables in reasonably cheap pipelines, and it's easier for large holdings like this company to sell excess energy to the nearest neighborhoods than it is for each and every family to have its own hydrogenerator," Ia explained. Her half brother Thorne knew more about things like this, but she knew enough to answer the other woman's question. "In cities, it's cheaper for the government to supply the power through a public utility that they can afford to bury in properly sealed and maintained pipelines. Most colonists go that route unless it's a business or building that depends heavily on a steady supply of energy, such as a hospital.

"But when you get farther out, it's cheaper to run lines. Plus, the local businesses can take the place of a public utility, if they have the funds for a large hydrogenerator plant, or the right sort of terrain for an old-fashioned wind farm or hydro-electric dam," she added. "The Petran family runs power out to its neighbors for a reasonable fee . . . and there they are, the lines I need. Get close to the struts, will you?"

"The lines on those struts are forty meters off the ground, sir," Mara pointed out, though she did maneuver the bike as requested. "If you fall, I'm not catching you—and need I remind you that you only have *one* good eye at the moment, sir?"

"I still have two, if you count my inner eye," Ia quipped. As they came into range, the humming from the lines could be heard. They could also be felt, at least by Ia. Easing off the bike and onto the tower scaffolding, she balanced herself carefully and contemplated the wires. "Actually . . . I think there's enough power in two of these, and they're just enough within reach, I can fully manifest. You'd better back off and get grounded, just to be safe—and don't try this at home, soldier. You are *not* a high-ranked electrokinetic."

"I don't *want* to be," Mara snorted, before dipping the bike toward the ground off to the side.

Ia smiled, not at all surprised the other woman didn't want to be a psi. Mara Sunrise was more the type to want to rely on her own skills rather than "cheating" through Meddler-bred advantages. Balancing carefully, mindful of the modest breeze, Ia reached up, first with her left hand, grabbing the high-tension cable bending its way around the insulated tower anchors. The shock of energy was indeed high, crackling over her skin with a stinging heat not unlike miniaturized versions of the pain from her most recent lasering.

She was a much better electrokinetic than she was a pyrokinetic, however. Forcing herself to breathe steadily despite the power crackling through the line, stinging her nerves, she stretched herself out, then hopped a little, snagging the other line. Energy snapped through her as she bridged the two lines with a bright, writhing flash. Fingers clenched tight, feet dangling, she let the power turn everything a glowing shade—and snapped into Meddler-form.

The first coherent thought to cross her altered state of mind was that the dual electrical current tasted vaguely like a piping-hot cheese pizza, the kind Philadelphia had sometimes baked for the crew for Wake parties. The second was that the drain on the power loop was about to be noticed by the two Feyori in the distance. Her third thought was a pulsed one, pure Feyori and very much the equivalent of a doorbell being rung . . . or rather, more like the hand of a government official knocking sternly on a private home.

(*What? Who's there?*)

(*Who—? Oh, it's* you.)

The two voices weren't overly gender-oriented, but the latter one had a flavor of disgust and irritation that said it had to belong to the ex-stubbie, Ginger.

(*Yes, it's me,*) Ia stated crisply, now that she had both of their attention. She tensed herself, prepared to lunge. (*Pass the word along to your little master. I call the Right of Leadership Challenge on Miklinn, faction head to faction head . . . and be grateful I choose to bypass the two of you.*)

(*I don't have to—*)

The Feyori broke off with a yelp as Ia dove her mind across the distance between them, striking just hard and fast enough to grab and pluck on Ginger's faction-tethers. A twist plucked at the other Feyori's strings, and a third, longer one pulled on her own as she retreated the bulk of her thoughts back into her body.

(*I don't give a plasma fart what* you *think,*) Ia retorted. (*I call the Right of Leadership Challenge on Miklinn. He has two local days to respond. You, being in faction to him, will cease all movements against me and those in faction to me, until this Challenge is settled.*)

(*You don't have the rank to pull a Leadership Challenge, half-breed,*) the other Feyori stated.

He hadn't given her his name—and a Feyori often used several over its life span, rarely just one—but Ia could sense it. Teshwun was what he called himself among the Salik. She could also sense something of the timeplains about him. He was a strong precognitive for the Feyori . . . but a lousy postcognitive, she realized. Not everyone who could read the future could read the past, and vice versa. There were plenty who could, but not this one. He was ignorant of what had happened just a short time ago.

(*Actually, Teshwun, I have over twelve hundred Feyori sworn in faction to me,*) she stated matter-of-factly. (*To me, not to any cosponsor or any other Meddler. It is Miklinn who is too lowly ranked to directly challenge me. But since he insists upon disrupting my Right of Simmerings, I have the right to confront him directly. Now, if the two of you are not so important in his factioning that you cannot contact him directly, I'll just keep pulling strings, and strings-of-strings, until I find someone with enough rank who* can.)

Withdrawing abruptly, she returned her mental presence to the scaffolding. Down on the ground—off to the left of her sense of self, though she could see all around her, as well as up and down—Mara had lowered the bike to its parking struts and had pulled out a small datapad. Sharpening her attention, Ia probed the small, electrical glow, curious as to its contents.

It tasted like braised salmon in some sort of tangy sauce, electrically. Materially, it was something entirely different.

. . . *A romance novel?* It reminded Ia of a time several years ago when she had discovered that her first official partner in the military had to smear goop on her face to cut down on breakouts of acne. Not something she'd expected to learn. *Huh. I never really thought of Sunrise as being that type. Her teammate, Floathawg, yes; that man has a romantic streak a full klick wide . . .*

A dark gray bubble popped into existence at her side. It—he—dipped down between all five lines, soaking up energy until his surface brightened to a silvery mirror shine. (*Your timing is inconvenient for Belini right this minute,*) Kierfando stated. (*But she'll be along eventually. You're lucky that I'm free . . . and does this stuff taste like cheese to you? I swear, this power current tastes like cheese.*)

(*Cheese pizza, to me,*) Ia agreed, looking up at the power lines. (*I think it's some subresonance in the amplitude.*)

(*In concept, the very idea of cheese is revolting, the curdled, moldering lactations of bovines and other mammalian ungulates. In practice, it is disturbingly tasty to a Human-shaped palate,*) Kier muttered, before getting to the point. (*So what, exactly, caused you to pluck our cosmic strings, little one?*)

(*Right of Leadership Challenge. I'm tired of Miklinn getting in everyone's way—tired, and angry,*) she explained. She swirled her surface, the equivalent of lifting a chin at the buildings in the distance. (*I figure where "Ginger" and Teshwun are currently camped would be a good spot for the confrontation. There's plenty of electrical, thermal, and kinetic energy for everyone to draw upon before, during, and after.*)

(*That's a dangerous battleground. You're only a half-breed,*) the Feyori reminded Ia. (*He has far more practice at drawing on energy sources than you do.*)

(*He's becoming far too dangerous to every faction, Kierfando,*) Ia stated quietly. (*He has only two choices at this point. I don't like limiting his choices to just those two, but he's driving everything to the precipice, and that was his choice. All the energy on Dabin won't be enough to help him if he refuses to give up this counterproductive grudge.*)

Kierfando swirled, a surface-style chuckle. (*You do have sparks as big as a star system, half child. Have you ever been wrong?*)

(*Multiple times. But not in this.*) Pulling out of the wires, she drifted down to Sunrise. Her previous telepathic sendings had been focused specifically for Feyori minds. She now gentled her "volume" so that it wouldn't hurt the other woman's head. (*Sunrise, I'm about to go inside. I might be there for half an hour, or I might be there for up to two days.*)

She sighed, touched the screen to mark her spot, and looked up at the silvery sphere of Ia's altered body. "You need me for backup?"

Thinking about it, Ia dipped into the timestreams. There wasn't much the woman could do physically to a Feyori, but perhaps she could interrupt the power sources . . .

On the false timeplain, she saw a confrontation that split into a trio of possibilities; one path had Ia as the winner, the other had Miklinn winning—a possibility she could not and would not allow, ever—and the third had Miklinn releasing his grudge. That was the smallest of the three streams. On the true timeplains, however . . . there was a very odd streak. A static image of herself, and . . .

Fascinating. I hadn't realized I could do that now . . . but it does make sense. It's also far easier and faster than what I had planned, with far less risk to me . . . and all because he insisted I manifest. How ironically apropos. Pulling back to herself, Ia found Mara squinting up at her with a distinctly dubious, uncertain look. (. . . *What? What's wrong?*)

"You just went all . . . all golden, sir. Instead of silver, like you are now," Sunrise pointed out, still eyeing her sphere warily. The sonic energies of her voice tasted like a savory puff pastry with some sort of mushroom filling. "I've never once heard of a Feyori turning gold. Begging pardon, Captain, but you are actually starting to unnerve me a little."

(*You know I wouldn't harm you unless you did something that would harm the future. And yes, I already know you're not that suicidal, so that won't be a problem*,) she added at Mara's derisive snort.

(*They're arriving*,) Kierfando warned her, still floating up at the top of the nearby tower. (*And she's right, that was a little unnerving to watch*.)

(*I'm going inside now*,) Ia told Sunrise, sending a pulse of acknowledgment to Kierfando.

Mara frowned a moment, then asked, "Sir . . . does your arm unit continue to record while you're shaped like that? Because you were missing a good six hours on the old one, and it just occurred to me that the Admiral-General might want to examine anything you do when your unit's not recording."

(*Ah, slag . . . no, it doesn't, and even if it did, it'd run the risk of me misremembering events electrokinetically. I could bring you along, but you'd still miss out on most of the conversations, since the things don't pick up telepathic conversations . . . I'll cross that bridge when I come to it*,) she thought, sighing. (*Get yourself comfortable somewhere, Sunrise, and keep your comm ready. I'll call you when I'm through*.)

"Aye, aye, Captain." She tucked away the datapad, then reached for the hoverbike controls. "I am in the military, so I do know the drill. 'Hurry up and wait, hurry up and wait' . . ."

(*As Roghetti's Roughriders like to say, "Infantry gets out of the way when the Artillery comes out to play."*) She added a mental image of an old-fashioned, sailing-ship-style cannon clad in Dress Grays and a white wig, and heard Sunrise's laugh. Humor was the best way either of them had to keep their morale up in the midst of this Meddler-based mess.

The thruster field from the hoverbike as the private revved its generator tasted like herb-baked peas. Hungry, Ia made a mental note to sup on some thermal energy during the coming wait.

————————

It took seven hours, fifteen additional Feyori bubbles string-tugged into range, and a good twoscore dazed Petran Company technicians before Miklinn deigned to show up. The Humans and Solaricans manning the power plant and the smelting factory placed next to it watched the silvery soap bubbles swirling around their equipment with gaping confusion. One or two could successfully hide themselves—and the pair had—by nudging all those minds into "not looking" their way, but more than two dozen Feyori was a little too much to ignore.

Kierfando, acting as Ia's highest-ranked supporter of the ones to show up, manifested as his graying-haired, dark-skinned version of a Human. He patiently explained to the two plant supervisors, security personnel, and even the planetary Peacekeepers who showed up that this was, ". . . Just us Meddlers having a little party. We deeply appreciate your tasty thermoelectrical snacks here, but there's nothing to worry about, folks. We'll be gone soon enough, don't you worry."

Undoubtedly, he used a bit of telepathic Meddling to get them to calm down since after an hour of nervous surveillance, the Peacekeepers finally left. He couldn't keep the technicians from gawking at the mirror-bubbles floating overhead, though. Nor from flinching whenever a soap bubble swooped through the generators, dimming the lights a little, or through the melting vats, cooling the molten alloys a tiny bit. But when Miklinn did finally arrive, the swirling and swooping stopped.

Ia wondered if the sudden stillness of the Feyori as they

spread themselves out and hovered in two broken, concentric arcs unnerved the technicians all over again. She couldn't, daren't take her eyes . . . well, her attention . . . off the newcomer, though she did peek out of the sides of her more or less 360-degree, highly alien view. Several tails among the Solarican employees twitched, and a few sets of ears pulled down and back. More than one Human brow was furrowed in worry, though they all kept monitoring their stations between furtive looks.

It was an impressive sight, too; more than three Meddlers in any one spot was a very rare sight, on the few occasions they allowed themselves to be seen. As it was, twenty Meddlers showed up. Ia wound up placed at the center-point of one arc, the smaller one, with Kierfando and the belatedly arrived Belini anchoring either end.

Miklinn took his place at the center point of the other, with Ginger and Teshwun forming the endpoints as the two local hosts. Both sides waited for the confrontation, hovering in pewter gray bubbles a meter or so off the plexcrete floor. Miklinn surveyed Ia, swirled his soap-bubble surface in contempt, and did not speak. Since he would not, it was up to her, the one who had called the Leadership Challenge, to speak.

(*Miklinn, you and I are in deep counterfaction to each other. This counterfaction has grown strong enough that our contentions threaten the very nature of the entire Game,*) she stated in preamble, carefully pitching her telepathic sending to each Feyori in the room, though the bulk of her attention remained on her enemy. (*There is a point at the start of the Right of Leadership Challenge where one of us may offer apologies and attempt amends.*)

He pulsed a thought at her, a mental scoff of derision that denied the thought that *he* could possibly owe *her* an apology.

(*No, Miklinn. I owe* you *that apology.*) This wasn't the
larger of the two main probabilities ahead of her, but in order
to stick to her principles, Ia had to try. (*I wronged you when
I exposed you. It was selfish of me to use you as a distraction to protect my own faction-standing among my pawns,
and it was wrong. I ask you to end our counterfaction by
allowing me to help strengthen your standing above what
you lost, and above what you now hold, in exchange for you
leaving my own efforts alone, without further interference
from yourself or your cofactions.*)

(*Will you forgive my mistakes, Miklinn, put an end to
this contention between us, and permit me to help you?*) she
asked formally.

Another contemptuous swirl.

(*Will you forgive my mistakes, Miklinn, and join me in
a factioning that will restore any lost ground and even add
to your plays in the Game?*) she repeated.

Contempt; his surface focus was no longer fixed upon
her. Silence stretched between them. She did not dare make
her request a third time since her faction numbers were too
great to stoop to such weak pleading. Twice was enough, so
Ia waited in silence, trying not to let her own contempt, her
rising anger, get the better of her.

(*You must answer the Challenge question, leader to
leader,*) Kierfando finally reminded the younger Meddler.
(*Or lose in rank.*)

His surface brightened, blocking out extra energy. (*I do
not faction with* half-breeds.)

Ia checked the timestreams. That percentage was now
lost. There was now only his winning the duel, or her winning, and the future could not afford to allow him the win.
More than that, his contempt was going to make it hard for

her own cofactions to hold her in high esteem, because she *was* a half-breed. Unless she defeated him *as* a half-breed.

(*So be it.*)

Energy arced inward from the cables and the machines spaced around the room. Bright lines crackled into her darkening sphere a second time as the dynamos recharged. Three siphonings were enough to allow her to pop back into matterform. She dropped the half meter or so to the floor, knees bending to cushion and steady her landing.

"You're right. I *am* a half-breed," Ia stated openly in Terranglo as she straightened, making the technicians lurking at the edges of the humming machinery blink and stare. "As you insist on viewing my birthright as a weakness, I will destroy you *as* a half-breed, to prove to all of you that you are wrong. *As* a half-Human, I am stronger than *all* of you."

Lifting her hand palm up, as if inviting him to step down and join her, Ia pulsed the wordless challenge in the Feyori way, the version with the ultimate price for the loser: to the death, either hers, his, or even both of theirs if they both spent too much in the contest.

(*Fool!*) Belini hissed in her mind on a tight telepathic pulse. (*You're risking everything with that!*)

(*He can suck your biokinetic energy right out of you in that form,*) Kierfando added. (*He'll do it as fast as you can blink.*)

"You shouldn't have forced the issue to make me manifest to prove myself in the first place, Miklinn," Ia told the sphere floating just a few meters from her, ignoring her cofaction leaders' warnings. "I have tried to apologize and sought to make amends. You have been rude and uncooperative. All that is left now is for the two of us to fight. Get down here and fight me, or lose all status."

He swirled his surface in her direction, then swirl-snorted

and "looked" away. (*Your tele-*pathetic *powers are weak, and your words meaningless. Even if you were strong, I don't deal with pawns who cover themselves in* shit.)

She'd forgotten she was still picturing herself covered in crysium plates under the loose fit of her now unshredded, whole camouflage clothes. Crysium dust was discarded matter from Feyori who made the transition to solid form and back. That meant she was literally armored in Meddler-made waste, so his words, while arrogant, were undeniably true.

Blinking, Ia belatedly realized she also now had two whole, sound, and perfectly functional eyes, left as well as right. As much as she wanted to touch the left side of her face in absent wonder, she refrained, keeping her right hand lifted toward her counterfaction foe, the other resting at her side. In the seven hours she had spent as an energy bubble, plucking at cosmic strings to get this one silvery-sphered idiot to show up . . . she had apparently forgotten her own injuries. Returning to matter-form had restored her to the way she normally thought of herself, as whole, sound, and strong. Human.

A pity I can't use that trick on anyone else, she thought privately. *I don't have the time to learn how.* Marshalling her telepathy, she projected once more to all the Feyori gathered around her, though her words were aimed at only one. She let her irritation and disdain stain her mental tone as she did so. (*I have challenged you to the death, Miklinn. Are you afraid to die?*)

He ignored her. Ia felt her jaw tighten, hard enough to grind her teeth. Seven hours of waiting, days' worth of plans disrupted, untold life-streams altered, and the *galaxy* at stake . . . and he was ignoring her?

(*If you don't face her, I'll spread the news far and wide that you're afraid of a mere* pawn,) Belini taunted, speaking for her. The pixie-like overtones in the alien's mental voice

took on a dark tone, the kind found among the cruel, dark
Sidhe of the Unseelie Court, not the Seelie.

One of the Human languages had a word for it: *Schaden-
freude*. The enjoyment of someone else's suffering. Of
course, Belini could afford to enjoy the moment; she was
merely a peripheral, a spectator. Ia, on the other hand, felt
different emotions: irritation, resentment, even a face-heating
level of anger rising within her, but she could not afford to
give in to rage.

(. . . *Hell, even* after *you lose, I'll spread it. You're no
leader, and she* knows *it. That's why this is a Leadership
Challenge, not a mere personal Challenge*,) the bubble-
shaped sprite added when Miklinn made no move.

(*A half-breed has more ability to lead in our Games than
you do, child*,) Kierfando added, his mental tone soured
with disgust. He pulsed an additional thought that was a
mental *tsk*.

(. . . *I am distressed to agree*.)

The sending came from one of the Feyori on Miklinn's
side of the broken ring. He—or she, the gender was
ambiguous—swirled into one of the humming hydrogenerator machines, sucking up enough energy, clearly preparing
to depart. He wasn't the only one. A second one moved.

(*Faction yourselves to me*,) Ia broadcast to the two of
them, (*and you will have my assistance as the Prophet of a
Thousand Years*.)

Her offer finally got Miklinn's attention. (*That will be
difficult to do, little molecule*,) he growled telepathically,
descending in a slow glide toward her still-upturned hand.
(*As* you *will be dead*.)

"I truly am sorry, Miklinn," Ia murmured before he
reached her. "I *did* want you to live."

Massless metallic silver brushed golden tan skin. The

moment his sphere intersected her fingers, his outer surface darkened in preparation to suck her bioenergies out of her flesh. At the same instant, Ia yanked both of them onto the timeplains. This time, however, she did *not* cushion his presence, nor did she shelter his mind as she always did with a guest.

(*You made your own mistake, Miklinn, when you forced me to fully manifest,*) she whispered in that precious pause between life-beats, hers the pulse of a heart, his the pulse of a spark. She could feel him still straining to gather his energies to drain her, but she wasn't helping to accelerate his thoughts and reactions here on the unshielded prairie accessed only by her mind. Ia merely sheltered her own, as she always had. (*You gave me unprecedented power when you made me unlock my full grasp of* Time.)

The timeplains heaved beneath them, bucking them forward even as she snapped the temporal fabric to make sure Teshwun wasn't trying to interfere. Using the upheaval, she dragged the unsheltered Miklinn into the future, barreling through his own waters, splashing life-energy up and over the banks of his stream.

Sparks flew, burnished off the surface of the darkened sphere touching her fingertips, spewing in a bright shower in every direction. Ruthlessly, she skidded him through the future, ripping him past the streams of everyone he would have touched. Carried him all the way into the barren wasteland that was the destruction of their galaxy, past the slender, green garden that was its salvation. Past a hundred years, past three hundred . . . past a thousand, and three thousand more. As she had told Sunrise, all she needed to do was concentrate, and she had gotten very good at that over the years.

Unshielded, the scrape of Time itself against his senses

abraded his energies, wearing them down through sheer frictional entropy. Four thousand three hundred eighty-seven years into the future, into the one future where he would have survived the coming invasion had he cooperated with her, Ia took him *past* the point of his otherwise-natural death. Forced him to live—or rather, *not* live—through the last possible point where he would have ever been alive.

Miklinn turned a sickly amber gold in her grip, then to a dark umber. In the span of just a second or so, his sphere shrunk down, darkened—and popped. A fine, faintly glittering mist dropped to the ground, lingering remnants of whatever matter Miklinn hadn't managed to convert back into energy during his last transformation.

Flicking her fingers to rid them of that dust, Ia checked the timestreams, grimaced, and opened her eyes to the real world. Both eyes, including the left one restored whole after its loss, the least of her recent hardships. There were many shattered lives and vastly altered streams to be paid for, after all . . . and not just by Miklinn.

Her attention had fixed on the two Feyori who had been stationed here. Not just here in reality, but on the timeplains as well. She stared at a smug sonova Meddler, who was boasting that he had *bested* the Prophet on the timestreams. At the one who *gloated* over the deaths of her "pawns" . . . her soldiers. Her friends.

Now that she was in their actual presences, she knew exactly which one of the two had the power to disrupt Time itself. The power to undo everything she had fought for since turning fifteen. It wasn't a guess anymore.

However, she did not act completely precipitously. Acting without any forethought, without checking the timestreams first, was what had *gotten* her in this Miklinn-Meddle mess. So Ia paused, took a full heartbeat in real time to examine the eons that lay ahead, carefully considered her options and their possible outcomes versus her desires, and only *then* acted.

Never again, Meddler. Never again.

(*I claim the Right of Personal Challenge against Teshwun,*) she asserted, letting her anger rise high enough to flavor her projection.

(*You might want to quit while you're ahead, girl,*) Kier cautioned her privately.

Ia ignored the advice. If the two percent failure rate she could foresee actually happened, she could regain it later. Right now, she was too angry to play cautious. Not when this *would* drive home the point to everyone here, and everyone these Meddlers spoke with in the next few years.

It was worth the risk, and then some.

"Teshwun interfered not only with my Game plays," Ia stated out loud, lifting her hand toward the leftmost Feyori still arrayed on Miklinn's side of the broken ring. She pointed at the silvered sphere. "But *this* Salik-factioned Meddler is directly responsible for the death of hundreds of thousands of *my* pawns in the five-hundred-year Right of Simmerings I bartered for, a promise garnered from roughly twelve hundred of your kind. In addition, Teshwun is responsible for the deaths of a handful of my crew, my direct underlings . . . and the deaths of hundreds of good soldiers of the Terran Army who should *not* have had to die."

(*With the death of the faction leader who ordered those moves, I can claim the Right of Absolution,*) Teshwun stated flatly. (*And I do.*)

Smug, silver . . . !

"I *deny* you that absolution," Ia retorted just as implacably, switching back to telepathy to keep the details of the Game from the other matter-based beings straining to listen at what they hoped was a safe distance. (*Each Feyori has a*

*territory which she or he holds. Kierfando holds the public
interstellar commerce of the V'Dan. Belini holds the Terran
entertainment industry. Even "Ginger" over there has had
the right to influence the inhabitants of Dabin . . . which
currently includes the 1st Division 6th Cordon Army stationed here.* My *rights cover the monitoring* and *manipulation of Time itself . . . and you will* never *Meddle in my*
territory *again!*)

Her hand twisted in a snatching motion. Despite the six or
so meters of open air between them, Ia snagged him psychically and dragged him onto the timeplains. Dragged him
unbuffered through the entropy of Time, far, far into the Future,
until he, too, darkened and shrunk in a desperate attempt to
suck in enough energy to survive . . . and popped into a fine
mist that scattered over the floor. That took over two seconds,
not one, since she wasn't touching him directly . . . but she did
kill him in a spark-skittered pair of heartbeats.

The other Feyori swirled and bobbled in shock, eyeing
the empty air where their companion had been, and—meters
away—the Human-shaped body that had killed him. Without
any direct contact.

It felt good to kill him. Disturbingly good, for it satisfied
most of the anger that had simmered deep down inside from
the first moment she realized Brigadier General José Mattox
had not followed her battle plans for this world.

(*You didn't give him a chance to apologize and offer
faction-amends,*) Belini chided her, the first to recover from
the shock of it. (*That was not fair of you.*)

Most of her anger, but not all of it. Ia unleashed the rest
of it on the Feyori around her.

"You're right. This *isn't* fair. This is me being a vindictive
bitch. I am *done* with being fair!" she snapped, staring at
the other members of Miklinn's former faction. This part,

she spoke out loud so that the technicians at the station would spread rumors of what happened here, furthering the legend she had to become. "This is me warning *you* that I can kill *any* of you, any*where*, any*when*.

"I have *tried* to be nice. I have tried to be *helpful*." She jabbed her finger at the second faint smear of golden dust on the polished beige plexcrete floor. "This is to remind you that *I* am the Meddler of Time, faction to *all* of you. You will tell the others that there is *no* neutral anymore, and that I will *not* tolerate a second counterfaction!

"Obey me, faction yourselves unto me, and I will be benevolent, both generous and merciful. Counterfaction me again, and I will be merciless in removing *all* obstacles from my path. You have been warned, Meddlers," she added softly, so softly some of the Feyori farthest from her swirled and darkened their surfaces a little, just enough to pick up the energy-impacts of the noise she did make. "I will let you know when I need you, and what you will need to do. Until then, you will return to your plays in the Game."

(*You will not dictate the rules of the Game to us, half-breed,*) one of the orbs on the other side of the room stated. Named Chule'eth, his mindvoice was masculine, deep with disdain. (*One on one against us, you may be strong—*)

(*I dragged over two thousand of your kind onto the time-plains to show them why you all need to heed me or lose your entire game when the Zida"ya come,*) Ia warned him, cutting him off. (That *was me being kind. I can just as easily drag two thousand more onto the timeplains to* die, *just like Teshwun and Miklinn. But do get it through your stubborn, slow matrices: I am trying to* help *you.*)

(*We don't take orders from a—*) Chule'eth started to repeat.

Grabbing him with part of her mind, Ia dragged the

male-voiced Feyori unshielded through the waters of his own timestream. He screamed telepathically. The other Humans and Solaricans in range clapped their hands over their ears, though it didn't help. Ia, braced by her anger, ignored it. Ruthlessly, she dragged him up to the desert-dead span where the Zida"ya came and destroyed everything. Only then did she shield him, and forced him to See what his choice of refusing to obey would cost.

She had to hold him there in the desert for a few actual seconds because dragging him unshielded through Time was the equivalent of having three hundred years of his life force abraded off, and had to wait for the shock of it to wear off. She wasn't fully immersed in the streams this time, either. With her physical eyes, Ia watched the silvery orb vibrate and turn a dark gold, casting off strange dark amber sparks like a manufactory saw cutting through gilded metal. Until they reached that point three hundred or so years ahead, where she held him still, cushioning him just long enough for him to be able to comprehend, before pulling him forward another two hundred years, to when the destruction of the galaxy would be complete if she failed in her task to save everyone. She cushioned him so that he could *see* what those two hundred years held, but she dragged him forward ruthlessly to the end.

She listened with her mind as he cried out again from what he saw of that ugly, barren, energyless future. Watched with her eyes as his sphere wobbled like a slow-struck bell. Pulling Chule'eth out, she let his sphere return to its normal, if now slightly smaller, silvery state. As she did so, his fear and agony faded, leaving the Meddler a pulsing, dark pewter orb, shaken by the visions and by her power over him. Her words echoed slightly when she addressed him, spoken loudly enough to be heard over the humming of the generators.

"I have just removed three hundred years of your life, Chule'eth. I would *prefer* to keep you alive and incorporate you into the new Game . . . but I *will not* tolerate any more insubordination. You are dehydrated horses, not stubborn jackasses. *Drink* when I lead you to water!" she said, looking at the others.

Some of their surfaces swirled with chastisement, others with indignation. The movements were subdued, however. Ia softened her tone.

"I am honestly, sincerely, truly trying to help all of you so that there will still *be* a Game to play, and pawns to play with, in your future. Interfere with that again, and I will have no choice but to destroy you, so that I can save all the rest of the lives in this galaxy. For now . . . For *now*, what you were doing before you thought up the idiocy of opposing me is acceptable," she said, looking at the beings floating around her. "I have calculated it into the plays awaiting us, so go back to what you were doing before deciding so short-sightedly to oppose me.

"Go back to being *smart* Meddlers. Your race lives for thousands of years. If you oppose me again, none of you will live past the next five hundred . . . and all *I* will have to do is step aside and let you die. On that, you have my Pro-phetic Stamp," she told them, her tone somewhere between gentle and implacable. "Cooperate, and you will live for thousands of years more, as you rightfully should. If things change, I will let you know what you must do to preserve the Game, and your roles within it. For now, I just want to help you with what you were originally planning to do, until it is time for you to assist me in saving your damned Game.

"Now, get off the damned planet and get back to work," she ordered, letting her irritation show through once more. "We *all* have more important things to do—not *you*, Ginger," she added as one of the Feyori off to her right started to move toward the generators along with the others. "*You* will stay and receive your new position in the Game from me. The rest of you, take whatever energy you need, and go."

(*You have deeply frightened them today, child. I'll admit even I am a little nervous in your presence now,*) Kierfando observed quietly, privately to Ia. Around them, the spheres moved toward unoccupied generators, and the overhead lights dimmed, shadowing the room deeply, making it clear that the sun had set outside at some point. (*But . . . you have subdued them as well. This group, at least. There is no guarantee for those not yet in open faction to you.*)

(*I know. But I have truly lost all patience with your kind, and you all need to know it. I am* not *kidding, Kierfando. You know what's at stake. The rest* must *comply.* There is no neutral faction with me anymore,) she stressed, projecting that part of her thoughts to the other silvery spheres as well. (*Anyone who tries to counterfaction, I will know it, and they will die. And as you just saw, I don't even have to be on the same planet, anymore.* That *is the price Miklinn made* all *of you pay when he forced me to manifest as one of you.*

(*Do* not *be stupid enough to make me collect on those dues.*)

He had nothing to say to that. Nothing he could say, and nothing the others could say. Speaking out loud, Ia gave the Meddlers around her one last warning.

"Spread the word to all the rest. The entire Feyori race has just been drafted into the war to save our mutual home galaxy, and *I* am your Commander in Chief. I will *not* tolerate any more insubordination in the ranks. Thanks to Chule'eth, you have all just *shakked* away your second chance," she reminded them harshly as the lights flickered and dimmed, flickered and dimmed. "The punishment for further treason is temporal abrasion, and death. I will not stay my hand again with you. There is no place, and no time, that puts you beyond my reach within this galaxy, present, future, *or* past. *That* is your final warning. *Dismissed.*"

The lights stuttered, dimmed, and blacked out completely, generators whining with the strain of being drained. When the power came back, lightstrips winking back on in twos and threes, most of the silvery spheres were gone, and the remainder were moving away. All but one, the one who had lived for a while as a dog named Ginger.

Ginger did not speak, though Ia could tell from the swirling patterns on the alien's silvery skin that she—for lack of a better, more accurate gender—was watching her. Ia knew the threat of death kept the Meddler in place. Ia had not been gentle with either Miklinn or Teshwun. Worse, killing the latter at a distance rather than at a touch had indeed frightened the others. If Ia didn't have to physically touch a Feyori's energy-sphere to use Time itself as a method of execution, then she *could* reach out and grab *any* of them, anywhere, anywhen.

Part of her felt sick from having to kill two Meddlers. She needed their help; she wanted to spare their lives. But she could not afford any more interference. *Morals versus expediency . . . ethics versus efficacy. Damned personally if I do, but damned far worse for everyone else if I do not.*

Closing her eyes, she centered her mind, and flipped downward, inward, and out onto the timeplains. Heading downstream, she found her future self sitting on the bank of her own life-waters, meditating next to the channel that was the most deeply etched in Time. Ia ducked into the point where her future self had started laying the false visions over everything, and emerged in the true timeplains. She dropped onto the green and yellow grass with a sigh.

"I have a lot to do now. I'm hoping Ginger can fix what-ever's wrong with Mattox, though if we go that route, that

*does run up against the Space Force's need to keep him
from being Meddled with any farther."*

"You know I'm not able to give you many hints without
muddying my own streams," her older self stated, opening
her amber brown eyes. "I can only say that there is a difference between altering what is not there to begin with and
augmenting what already is."

Younger Ia winced as the timeplains dimmed, threatening
exactly that. The elder one smiled ruefully. Or maybe sardonically. Pushing to her feet, the version from October
flexed her wrists and hands. Her false overlay pulled off the
true timeplains like a transparent sheet being pulled into a
wadded bundle between her palms.

"Go on. Start figuring out how to fix all the rends and
tears in the system," her older self directed. "I have the Dlmvla to finish courting."

"Good luck," her younger self said. She turned to head
back upstream. "See you when I am you, if not at some point
again on the timeplains."

The older one chuckled and vanished into the water. Free
to alter Time, Ia shifted everything into a giant graph chart.
Her older self was right about one thing; there were a lot of
proper streams that were now off course. Most of them were
here on Dabin. Many more stretched into the future, onto
other worlds. People who should have given little points of
influence were either now dead and gone, or their life-paths
altered so much that it would be a blatant artifice to send
them where they originally needed to go, which in turn
would cause more problems. Unless, that was, she spent a
lifetime making subtle corrections.

If she'd had the time and the life to spare, Ia would have
made all those necessary corrections herself. As it was, she
didn't have even the resources needed to direct her normal

agents, the Afaso, to make all the changes. But she *did* have
someone who could stand in for her and them, someone who
could *subtly* nudge minds and alter the courses of all those
misplaced lives. Resolving Time back into a stream-scattered
plain, she explored all the near-future conversations and
efforts she could, should, would, might, and will have had
with the Feyori named Ginger.

The most damning thing she found clarified the reason
behind the dull, dusky golden hue of the timeplains. Ginger
hadn't forced Brigadier General Mattox into a completely
different set of tactical strategies. As her future self had
obliquely warned, the Feyori had merely *emphasized* what
was already there. Mattox wanted to be a modern-day General George Patton.

The problem was, the war on Dabin just wasn't going to
work that way. Ia needed the 1st Division Army to disrupt
the Salik entrenchment efforts, force them into the open by
damaging and destroying their bunkers and shielded facilities, and maneuver them into a position where they had no
choice but to be driven off-world. Straightforward, daylight-
based, full-on confrontational warfare was *not* going to get
the job done. In fact, it would only drive the Salik into en-
trenching and fortifying their positions.

*I cannot fix all the damage that Ginger and Teshwun did
to the timestreams. Not personally. I have only enough time
to fix the damage Mattox has been doing to the Army and pry
him out of power.* She searched side-streams, and sighed in
disgust. *Slag. It's now to the point where I'll* have *to do things
by the book to salvage my standing in the military . . . which
means leaving everything else in Ginger's soap-bubble hands.*

Standing there on the grassy bank of Mattox's life, Ia
folded her arms over her chest for a moment, then rubbed
at the ache forming in the middle of her furrowed brow. The

crease felt like it was trying to iron itself into her flesh. Only twenty-six years old, and she was already on the verge of feeling forty-six going on sixty-six. Drawing in a deep breath, she ordered her mind, centered and grounded herself, then pulled up every single nexus point relevant to Dabin that *had* to be achieved in the next three hundred years, despite the loss of all those lives and all their influences.

Once she had them in her grip, she shifted them into a tapestry of brocaded threads, then flipped most of her awareness back into her body. A minute or so had passed in reality. Ginger was still floating a few meters from her. The lights were fully back on, and the technicians lurking in the background looked far less nervous than before and far more curious now that there was only one Meddler left in the generator room.

(*Come here,*) Ia ordered. Cautiously, the Feyori floated closer. When the silvery soap bubble was in range, Ia reached up and hooked the alien into the timeplains with just two fingers, flipping them both into the sepia-toned prairie. (*Your position in the Game has now changed. You will still influence the people of Dabin, but only as directed, and far less along the original lines than you believed. Instead, you will spend the next three hundred years managing every single crisis point your stupidity-induced interference has created, both here and off-world.*)

Wrapping the threads through the alien's energy matrices, Ia bound Ginger to the purposes she had isolated. It was a variation on the death-by-temporal-entropy drag; a true geas in that if Ginger resisted, the alien's very life force would be abraded away for as long as she tried to resist. Belatedly, the Feyori realized what was happening and tried to extract herself. Ia seized her firmly and wove the temporal directives deeper into her energies.

(*Stop resisting this, Ginger,*) she ordered. (*You will either comply, or you will die.* These *are your assigned duties for the next three hundred years. The harder you try to resist, the more years you will scrape away from your life with each tug of your struggle. The more you cooperate, the longer you will survive past the point where the last of your tasks are done.*)

Snapping the last thread into place, she surveyed the timestreams, then added a few contingency lines. Like archaic bungee cords, there was some give and flexibility in what she had done. If the Feyori hadn't been a being of energy, Ia wouldn't have been able to do it. But she could, and did. Ginger *could* free herself . . . at the cost of cutting off about a thousand years' worth of her life. Considering she had only two thousand or so more years to live, that kind of freedom wasn't much of a bargain, a thousand for a mere three hundred.

To be sure the Meddler understood what Ia had done, Ia teased up a thread of mortal awareness and tied that in as well. It would not tell Ginger how or where she would die, or at what exact point in time. Rather, it would feel like an hourglass. The more Ginger resisted, the more the alien would realize how much more sand was being shoved down through the waistline by her own actions, and how little sand remained in the reservoir.

Any sufficiently advanced science, psychic science though it may be, can feel just like magic . . . and here I am binding a former enemy in an old-fashioned, Celtic-style geas. Marshalling her thoughts, she pinned the Feyori with a hard stare. (*You* can *break free of these bonds, but they will shred and slice away half your remaining life span if you try. This is your choice: spend three centuries making up for the* shova v'shakk *you've caused, or lose a thousand years or more of*

*rank and strength in the Game. Assuming you don't piss me
off to the point I hunt you down and kill you outright, of course.*

*(And don't count on waiting a hundred years, long after
I'll be dead and gone, before trying to undo everything I want
done. I am the Master of Time, and I can kill you at any point
in Time now that I have manifested in full. It is your choice,
of course . . . but if you want my advice, I'd say you've been
acting like a mindless idiot for long enough. Try being smart
enough to know you've just been given a last chance.)* She
lifted her chin at the generators. *(Take what energy you need,
and go. If you are uncertain, call me, but you should know
through these bindings what you're supposed to do next.)*

The surface of the silvery sphere shifted only slightly, a
subtle drift of reflective energies along its curves. Some of
those energies gave off golden glints. Ginger didn't say anything, but after a few moments, she did swirl and glide
toward the hydrogenerators. Ia followed the alien's movements with both her eyes and her mental hands trailing in
the waters of the timestreams, holding her breath a little.

It escaped with a faint sigh of relief. Ginger would do as
she demanded. Not entirely happily, and she would resist a
few times, testing the bonds laced throughout her energy
matrix, but she would obey. *One more success salvaged
from this disaster. Yet more* trompe l'oeil *painted over the
cracks on the walls of reality, if not in as painstakingly exact
a match as Hollick's sacrifice . . .*

Perhaps she could bind a fellow precognitive, as well as
a Feyori? Ia made a mental note to investigate that possibility
soon. There certainly would be plenty of precognitives in
the future on Sanctuary, ones who could help carry forward
Ia's work on that world. None with her sheer strength and
ability, but if Ia could tie their awareness into her workings,
that would help solidify things. Precognitives elsewhere as

well, ones living among the PsiLeague and the Witan Order, the Seers of Solarica and the crested priest caste of the Tlassians, to name but a few.

Any magic is but an insufficiently understood science. If I had another lifetime to spare—and there probably is an alternate-me life-stream out there with this knowledge—then I could work out the how of what I can do right now by instinct. But that would require more Time than I can spare in this life, save for whatever I can scrape out of my Company's travels sic transit *between our many destinations.*

. . . Tele-pathetic powers . . . heh. That was *funny . . .* Miklinn's crack at her relatively weak telepathic powers amused her for a brief moment. It was the truth; Ia wasn't much of a 'path, xeno- or otherwise. Her smile faded as she watched the movements of the last Feyori in view.

The alien's surface slowly shifted from polished gunmetal to gleaming platinum. Finally, Ginger lifted up out of the generator she had picked. Swirling once in a not-quite-rude farewell, the energy-based being darted up through the ceiling at an angle. The moment she was gone . . . Ia's legs trembled. Sinking to the floor with a knee-bruising thump, she slumped in place, palms braced on her thighs. She had been strong while the enemy had stood . . . floated before her, but now her adrenaline spike was a crash.

I have not done a good thing, today. I was cruel. I was brutal. I was spiteful and vindictive. But I have done a necessary *thing,* she acknowledged silently, waiting for her nerves and her reserves to recover. *They'll hate me for it, and fear me for it, and I really did* not *want to have to . . . to murder . . .*

There was no denying that murder was what she had done, particularly to Teshwun. She had challenged Miklinn and killed him more or less fairly according to the Feyori rules for such things. She had done so only after giving him a chance to repent, which he had refused of his own free will to do. But the timestream-meddling Feyori? That *was* her being a vindictive bitch, exactly as she had said. Lifting her fingers to her face, to her whole, healed, two-eyed, scarless face, Ia buried her awareness of the world in the heels of her hands.

Ah, God . . . Yet another stain on my soul . . . and all I can give in payment for all of this is what I've already pledged to give. I could've spent an hour convincing Tesh-wun to work with me, and I probably had the hour to spare, but . . . It was a shortcut to her goals, expediently executing the second Feyori in front of his peers. However, it was not nearly so noble as, say, hunting down a fellow recruit. Returning her hands to her lap, she focused on her breathing, ordering her thoughts. *I shouldn't waste the hour I've stolen with the loss of his life, then. Even with Ginger handling most of the damage for me, there are still days' worth of damages to control . . . and a certain brigadier general to deal with. Somehow.*

"Ah . . . parrrdonn me? Meioa Feyorrri?"

Opening her eyes, Ia looked over her shoulder. One of the felinoid technicians had approached tentatively, coming within three or so meters of her. His dark brown ears were down and back a little in uncertainty, but his whiskers were forward and his tail tip twitched, visible bravery in the face of a potential adversary.

Ia climbed to her feet, shifting to face him. "I'm only a half-breed, meioa-o. The rest of me is fully Human and quite happy to remain so. You have a question?"

"Ah, yes. Will there be anny morrre of, ah . . . your kinnd drrropping by? Using our gennneratorrs?" he asked, one ear flicking.

"Not really, no. Maybe a single one in the future, but he,

she, or it will be more discreet in what they take. For now . . . consider it a wartime appropriation of civilian resources. If your company wishes monetary reimbursement, I can arrange for it," Ia told him. "I have the authority to reimburse you for your production losses. But you'll have to let my Company clerk onto the property so she can give you the necessary paperwork. If that's alright?"

The Solarican studied her a moment, then nodded curtly. "Fairrr enough—annnd we *will* give you a bill for all the powerrr you took."

Ia nodded her acceptance. At the moment, all she wanted was to have Mara come pick her up, maybe wait long enough for the paperwork to be filled out and filed, then head somewhere for a rest and a bit of solid, matter-based food. Tomorrow, she would have to find a formal uniform to don so that she could face off against Mattox. It was possible she could try to shift herself a set of Dress Grays or even Dress Blacks by turning from matter to energy and back, but now that the crisis was over, she was too tired to want to bother.

She also didn't want to be a Feyori for any longer than she absolutely had to be. The longer she stayed in that form, the more she *thought* like a Meddler. Her Human nature, her humanity, was too precious to be set aside so quickly or easily.

CHAPTER 6

I did not go into the military because I liked the politics.

~Ia

JUNE 16, 2498 T.S.
ARMY HEADQUARTERS
LANDING CITY, DABIN

It took two days for her polite, formal, repeated requests to see Brigadier General José Mattox to actually get her a moment of his time. Enough time for Private Sunrise to leave Headquarters, track down the rest of the Company, and bring back the hovervan with the hyperrelay packed inside. By the time he let her into his office, clad in formal Dress Grays with her half glittery of one medal type apiece—fetched from the recovered remains of their camp by Mara—Ia was more than ready for the confrontation.

It went about as she expected, too.

Mattox listened politely as she outlined her latest set of battle plans, carefully pointing out all the advantages and rare few disadvantages of each. He listened—frowning, but he listened—while she explained the far fewer advantages and far greater disadvantages of his own most recent series of battle plans. All of which she carefully recorded on her arm unit, along with his response. It came after a deep breath and a wry smile from the brigadier general.

"Well. I certainly appreciate how much thought and effort you have put into your arguments," Mattox stated politely, tipping his head ever so slightly. "However, your job was to handle the Feyori threat. Since you seem to have chased them off, and ensured ways for us to avoid being taken over by their meddlings in the future . . . your services and attempts at advising a ground-based war are no longer necessary, *Ship's* Captain."

"I have *also* been directed by the Admiral-General to assist you in removing the *Salik* presence from Dabin within the next month," Ia reminded him, keeping her tone as polite as she could, in the face of what she knew was coming. "I have offered you several battle plans to achieve this goal over the last few weeks, plans which have been low on risks and casualty rates and high in probabilities of success. Each one has been adapted to the needs of that moment, the terrain involved, the personnel and equipment available, and tailored to reduce the risks to life and limb for soldiers and civilians alike, sir, as the Admiral-General requested of me."

"*I* have been placed in charge of all military matters on Dabin, Ship's Captain Ia," Brigadier General Mattox stated crisply, coldly. "Your services are no longer required. Withdraw yourself from my Headquarters . . . and withdraw your Company from my battle zone."

Ia drew in a breath to remind him of one salient point. He cut her off before she could.

"That is an *order*, Ship's Captain. *Dismissed*."

And that is your fatal mistake, General. Sealing her lips on any possible reply—on any possible *acknowledgment* of his order, for that matter—Ia rose from the chair across from his and left his office. The obnoxious woman was on duty in the outer office. From the smirk on her face, Major Perkins had heard her CO's words, or at least had been forewarned of his plans in advance. Ia ignored the other woman aside from that one quick, assessing look.

Once she was out in the hall, she tucked her headset in place and activated her arm unit. *"Captain Ia to all Damned personnel at Army Headquarters. Report to the parking garage immediately. I repeat, report to the parking garage immediately."* She kept her voice low, barely above a subvocal murmur. *"Ia out."*

She took the stairs down out of homeworld habit. Not the same stairs she and Private Sunrise had used on their first visit, but instead a different set, one that went all the way down into the underground garage located beneath the appropriated office building. Two levels down was where Sunrise had brought the hovervan with the hyperrelay unit tucked inside, picked up in exchange for her hoverbike when she had gone back for Ia's uniform and half glittery.

Private Floathawg had taken over the bike with some glee, according to Mara. The part-time clerk wasn't overly attached to the machine, though it had been useful at the time; her teammate, on the other hand, loved the things. Ia didn't mind giving it up; she had two solid reasons for appropriating the van and its cargo. Not to transport herself and the handful of psis who had come to help with the Feyori problem, not to take them away from Headquarters as *ordered* by the Army Division's head, but for something more important.

Something much more awkward. Sighing roughly, she lifted her chin at Mara, who was lounging by the back doors. The private opened the panels, revealing the relay occupying most of the cargo area. Ia took her place in front of the control panel, and warmed up the machine. By the time the device was ready, the others had gathered behind their silent, grim commanding officer, dropping into modified versions of At Ease and Parade Rest. Pressing the last key, Ia listened to the hydrogenerator whining faintly as the relay strove its best to project a tiny pinpoint hyperrift all the way to Earth from deep inside the vacuum-sealed depths of the machine.

Admiral John Genibes was not particularly happy to see her when his face finally flashed onto the hyperrelay screen, but he didn't do more than sigh. "Ship's Captain, Ia. Which is it this time, fire, famine, or flood?"

Ia didn't respond to his weak attempt at a joke. Lifting her arm unit into view, she flipped open the lid and touched the buttons inside. "Admiral Genibes. I am synching my arm unit's latest recordings to you on subchannel beta, along with several pertinent files. They contain the results of my last meeting with Brigadier General José Mattox, commanding officer of the Army's 1st Division, 6th Cordon here on Dabin."

She had to pause to ensure the entire meeting had fully uploaded, but she also used the seconds to take a discreet, bracing breath. Finally, Genibes nodded. ". . . Yes, I've got it. I take it there's a specific reason why you've sent me this recording while I'm in a meeting with several generals of the Army, all of whom are listening in as we speak?"

Squaring her shoulders, Ia nodded and clasped her hands behind her back. Truthfully, she hadn't considered those reasons; she had merely checked the timestreams to make sure she wasn't presenting this report at an utterly inappropriate moment. If those generals had not been with Genibes, then they would have found out about it in swift order anyway, as this report had to be made, regardless.

"Admiral, Generals, yes, sirs," she stated crisply. It wasn't entirely a lie even if it wasn't entirely a truth. "I have uploaded both the results of my latest meeting with the brigadier general in question for your immediate perusal, as well as all available records of my activities from the point of landing on Dabin up to this meeting to your data files regarding my and my Company's activities.

"With this unaltered, unexpurgated, unedited information placed in your hands, it is my regret-filled duty to inform the Command Staff, in my very carefully considered estimation as an officer and a duly acknowledged precognitive . . . that Brigadier General José Mattox is no longer fit for command of the 1st Division, 6th Cordon Army," she finished after taking a steadying breath.

She had more to say, but waited the full five seconds of lag time. As the highest probabilities had predicted, the other men and women meeting with Genibes began exclaiming and arguing off-screen. Behind her, she could hear Privates Mk'nonn, Jjones, Yarrin, Theam, and Rayne shifting restlessly, though none of them said a word. Private Sunrise neither spoke nor moved. Then again, she'd been privy to more of the problems behind the scenes than the psis had and was smart enough that this moment probably didn't come as a surprise.

The babble on the other side of the comm link, that was Ia's main concern. Not her troops' reactions. Genibes allowed it to continue for several long seconds, then cut through the heated arguments of the others with a few choice words of his own, mostly a demand for silence while he interrogated *his* subordinate. When the unseen generals were quiet again, he faced Ia's image on his own viewscreen, scowling at her.

"Ship's Captain Ia, this is a *very* serious accusation for anyone to make. It is all the more serious for someone not placed within the brigadier general's chain of command. Are you *sure* that you wish to make this accusation, with all the attendant investigations that will be required for it?"

"Admiral Genibes, I have no choice left but to make it," Ia said grimly. She could feel the anger starting to boil again within her over this whole mess but shoved it back down, leaning on her sense of duty to keep her outward self reasonably calm. "Brigadier General Mattox has consistently and repeatedly shown not just an inability to grasp superior tactics as best adapted to the 1st Division's actual circumstances, but an outright *refusal* to consider any tactics or strategies other than his own. He has done so in the face of tactical analyses that have shown his plans will decimate the 1st Division's ranks by a casualty rate of one-half to two-thirds," Ia stated, listing all her reasons. "He has done so repeatedly in the face of several offered plans which would each reduce the 1st Division's casualty lists to less than one-tenth its current attrition rate.

"He has refused to accept advice tendered to him by a Space Force–acknowledged precognitive and battlecognitive of the highest rank. He has refused to acknowledge that this advice was tendered because this precognitive was *ordered* to give it by a member of the Command Staff, being yourself, *and* ordered by the Admiral-General herself to provide said advice, being her command to help remove the Salik presence from Dabin in a timely and lifesaving manner."

She paused, squared her shoulders, and gave the last damning bit, the straw that would break Mattox's back.

"And he had the temerity to not only dismiss said pre-

cognitive advisor, being myself, but to *order* my Company
and I, being the A and B Companies, 1st Legion, 1st Battalion, 1st Brigade, 1st Division, 9th Cordon *Special Forces*,
to remove ourselves from *Army* Headquarters and quit the
battlefields of Dabin immediately. Brigadier General Mattox's order qualifies as a direct nonchain countermand to
my and my Company's standing orders from our superiors
in *our* chain of command.

"He has done so to my face while I wore *this* uniform,
my Dress Grays, without consulting with any member of
the Command Staff, let alone my immediate superiors in the
proper chain of command. Brigadier General Mattox of
the Space Force Army has taken upon himself to exercise
a level of authority over the Branch Special Forces which
he does not possess, sirs, in addition to demonstrating a
palpable inability to grasp the shifting needs and carefully
husbanded resources of a battlefield command. He *is* unfit
for his duties, sirs. If he is not removed from his position
and replaced immediately—and I say this *as* a Space Force–
acknowledged precognitive of documented accuracy—he
will be responsible for losing the entire planet of Dabin,
civilians and soldiers alike, to enemy hands and enemy
appetites.

"I repeat, this is no joke, sirs. This is a very serious
charge." She kept her chin square, her gaze level, as Genibes
and the officers unseen on the other end of the comm link
considered her statements.

The Admiral shook his head after eight or so seconds.
"Are *you* prepared, Captain Ia, to undergo the same level of
scrutiny that your accusation of fitness for command will
engender? *Any* accusation that a commander is unfit for his
post requires the accuser's own career and choices to also
be heavily examined."

"I am prepared, sir. While I am not the only Space Force officer on Dabin who feels that Brigadier General Mattox is unfit for command, sir," Ia stated, "I am the one officer best placed to make these accusations. I have spoken with more than one Army officer who has expressed similar sentiments since arriving on Dabin and assessing the Army's position as a combat-trained and tactically experienced officer. Most understandably, they have hesitated to speak up against their Division commander. They have the loyalties of their troops and the concerns of their duties weighing on their minds and staying their hands.

"Being outside their immediate chain of command, I have been free to assess the situation without concern for my own rank and standing . . . and because I am outside the Army Division in question, any repercussions that may fall upon myself, and my Company as a consequence, will not harm the Army's efforts any further than the brigadier general's own failures already have. However, the brigadier general's choices have already had grave impacts on the lives and strategies of the soldiers sent to defend Dabin from the Salik invasion. In good conscience, I *must* stand by my accusation, sirs, whatever the consequences to myself and my career.

"I state once more for the record as an officer and a precognitive, sirs, that Brigadier General Mattox of the 1st Division, 6th Cordon TUPSF Army is unfit for command, and must be removed immediately for the good of the Army's war efforts here on Dabin," she finished.

Admiral Genibes sat back in his seat with a rough sigh. "Lovely," he muttered. "Over half the stuff *you* have done is Ultra Classified, Captain . . . Generals," he addressed the men and women off-screen, "would it be acceptable to you, as members of the Army, if we limited investigating Ship's

Captain Ia's own activities strictly to her time on Dabin? She has an Ultra Class A clearance level for a reason, most of which has taken place off-world, and most of which will have no bearing whatsoever upon the situation on Dabin concerning her accusations."

The assent came in a ragged set of murmurs. Ia spoke up before Genibes could turn back to her.

"I have also uploaded all pertinent personal recordings to your data files for virtually my entire time here, Admiral," she reminded him. "But I must state at this time that I am missing two periods of recorded time. One period was due to the disabling of my arm unit in combat on a solo mission. I was able to augment some of the recordings from enemy surveillance footage and the arm unit of one of my privates, who joined me at the end of my mission, but during those four-plus hours I could not, I have no immediately accessible means of independently confirming my activities.

"The other period . . . I was negotiating with the Feyori to mitigate their interference on Dabin, part of which includes the direct mental Meddling with Brigadier General José Mattox's mind, a fact of which he has been apprised and which he has chosen to dismiss as not an ongoing concern. As a consequence, my arm unit was unable to record anything for approximately seven hours of the earlier stages of those negotiations. It also could not record some of the telepathically conducted conversations that took place.

"I was able to transcribe most of the missing information, and have sent that on to your data caches as well, but there is no other record than my own written report, sir," Ia confessed. "I mention it not only for the Meddling with Mattox's mind, but because the involvement of the Feyori on Dabin contains Ultra Classified material of a potentially disruptive nature for those who do not know the particulars of *why* that meeting had to take place. I therefore respectfully suggest that the inquest into my actions be a closed investigation made by those members of the Command Staff with a Class A rating."

"We will take that under advisement, Ship's Captain," the Admiral replied neutrally. "Anything else?"

"Sir, yes, sir. My Company and I cannot be dismissed from our assigned duties by Brigadier General Mattox, nor can any of my orders from you or your superior be counter-manded by a non–Command Staff officer from another Branch," Ia reminded him, speaking quickly to cover the two and a half seconds of lag from her to him. From the way he opened his mouth to say more, then subsided, she had spoken in time. "Under the discretionary powers I was given by the Admiral-General herself, the majority of A Company, 9th Cordon has been placed under the command of Com-mander Meyun Harper, which is why I specifically men-tioned my command having been split into A and B Companies.

"They are currently undertaking the task of breaking up the Salik invasion forces in preparation for pushing them off this planet, which is the task we were ordered to under-take by yourself and the Admiral-General. As a result, I have less than a Squadron of soldiers under my direct com-mand in B Company here at Army Headquarters. What are your orders for my full Company, now that I have made these accusations, sir?"

He frowned, thinking about it. "You said everyone but you and a handful are in the field under Commander Harper?"

"Yes, sir. They are currently undertaking covert opera-tions deep within enemy territory, Admiral. I have no means of contacting them for the next two days without a high probability of alerting the enemy to their presence. I would rather not lose them to an unexpected and utterly unnecessary lunch date, sir," she stated flatly. "But I will attempt to pull them out of combat if you request it. That is what the brigadier general tried to order me to do . . . but I obviously cannot follow *his* orders, sir."

John Genibes twisted his mouth, as if tasting something sour. He tapped his screen for several seconds, reading something, then addressed her question.

". . . Pull them out *after* they have completed their current mission, Captain, when it is appropriately safe to do so. Take up residence in the capital near Army Headquarters. Your Company will be placed on Modified Leave under your command once they have been extracted as per Section 119, paragraphs b and c, and you yourself shall be placed on Restricted Leave, Section 119, paragraphs f, g, and j, from this moment until further notice," he instructed her. "Continue to record everything you do, and expect to hear from me at approximately this time tomorrow, Terran Standard . . . whatever that translates as in Dabin time."

"Sir, yes, sir. For the record, I am sorry I had to do this," she offered, softening her tone for a moment. "I would far rather have had Mattox's cooperation in salvaging this whole mess. One last thing, Admiral. As a duly registered and acknowledged precognitive, I warn you that this matter *must* be resolved by the start of this July, Terran Standard. If it is not, this planet will fall, and we will *all* bear the burden of all the lives that will be lost. Furthermore, my Company and I must be on board our next ship by the end of July, or many more worlds will be lost. You are of course free to accept my warnings or not, as is your prerogative. All I can do is give them to you, with the same accuracy with which I have always given them."

"Again, we will take all of that under advisement, Ship's Captain. You have your new orders. Genibes out," he instructed her. Leaning forward, he tapped the link off.

Mindful of the eyes watching her, Ia sighed slowly, quietly. She tried to release the tension in her back muscles subtly; this was not the moment to show weakness in front of her own troops even if there were only a handful of them. Predictably, it was Private Sunrise who broke the silence.

"Well, as far as *shova*-storms go, sir, that wasn't too bad," Mara offered mildly. "And Modified Leave *is* still Leave. I'm sorry yours is Restricted, but that's still better than what that one certain sergeant we both know of went through."

Sighing more deeply, Ia shrugged, loosening up her back. "True. And it's not like I got stuck with paragraphs h or i," she agreed, turning to face the others. "But I am still under surveillance from here on out, with *everything* I do destined to be poked, prodded, and questioned.

"Private Sunrise, start looking for a suitably large hotel or university dormitory which we can rent, and drum up the paperwork to do it. Mk'nonn, start looking up restaurants and cafeterias. Cross-reference to each other; I'd prefer something conjoined in some manner even if we have to rent a convention-center kitchen and staff it ourselves. Jjones . . . contact vehicle-rental companies, and try to find something with enough seats for everyone in this little group, minus one driver and one guard for the van. Since it'll be kept to the city, you can go ahead and pick a ground car to keep it cheap, but keep in mind that we might need to rent larger vehicles.

"Private Theam, contact Roghetti's crew to see if they can spare transport for the Company in two days' time, or if we'll need to go pick up everything ourselves. Yarrin, Rayne, hit the restrooms; when you get back, you'll be on first watch over this van, and yes, you have permission to draw your guns. Sunrise, issue them that pair of trank clips I know you've got hidden on you."

"Guns, sir?" Theam asked, wrinkling her nose.

"Tranks, sir?" Sunrise asked, lifting one brow warily. She fished the requested cartridge clips out of her uniform, double-checking for the blue feathers stamped into the sides of the factory-loaded cases, but she did give Ia a questioning look.

"The last thing we need is Mattox trying to commandeer my privately purchased hyperrelay, especially once he gets official word back from Earth on what I've just done," Ia told her crew. "If he's truly gone over the deep end to the point where he's acting deliberately in ways that will sabotage the Space Force's best interests in favor of his own agenda, whatever that may be, then he may want to silence me. Or at least breach the relays and falsify my reports.

"I don't want to have to fight the Army, but the codes being used in this hyperrelay are beyond Mattox's clearance level. You are therefore instructed to keep it out of all hands but this Company's," she told Yarrin and Rayne. "Given our limited supplies at the moment, tranquilizer cartridges are the best option we have since none of us have any stunners on hand."

Rayne wrinkled her nose. "You don't *really* think he'd sabotage a claim like this, do you, sir? That'd only get him into even worse trouble."

"It's just under a two percent probability, Private," Ia told her. "I don't think it'll happen . . . but I didn't think I'd get shot in the shoulder on a mere three percent. He doesn't *know* that I've already sent on a record of everything that has happened up to this point, and he doesn't know that we have this hyperrelay on hand to send even more incriminating files on a near-direct link to the Tower back on Earth. But I'm taking no more chances. Neither should you." She gave them a sober, unhappy look. "We've lost far too many people and far too much of the timestreams as it is."

JUNE 19, 2498 T.S.
LOXANA HOTEL AND CONVENTION CENTER
LANDING CITY, DABIN

The transport trucks looked like they shouldn't fit under the modest hotel portico. They did, of course; each private manning the controls brought their ground truck to a halt with deft accuracy, neither brushing the columns nor the bushes. Single file, they disgorged soldiers and gear, all of which were off-loaded with swift efficiency while the men and women employed by the hotel's valet corps watched in bemusement. No doubt they wondered if *they* would have to be responsible for parking the vehicles.

Ia didn't give them the time to worry. She emerged from the lobby with Yarrin, Theam, Jjones, and Sunrise in tow the moment the first vehicle in the convoy appeared. The hotel staff watched with some apprehension as a motley collection of men and women emerged from the backs of the trucks. Some were soldiers clad in the local camouflage colors, many of them covered in dried streaks of reddish beige Dabin mud and a few in brownish dried blood. Some sported bandages holding regen gel packs in place. Others were clad in dark silver mechsuits, donned solely to be used as stevedore suits.

Activating her arm unit, Ia linked to the Company as a whole.

"This is Captain Ia to all members of the Damned.

Welcome to the Loxana Hotel and Convention Center," she announced over her headset. *"At least one member of each team will report to Private Sunrise at the main entrance before 1500 for housing assignments and room codes. All personnel in charge of mechsuits, report to Private Yarrin for mechsuit-storage arrangements in conference halls Whiteflower and Greenwater.* Walk lightly. *Only the ground floor of this facility is solid plexcrete; no mechsuits will be allowed on any other floors, and do not go into close-quarters situations. Stick strictly to the broadest paths. Private Yarrin will direct you along the sidewalks to the proper exterior entrances.*

"All personnel in charge of all other nonpersonal or nonmechsuit supplies, report to Private Theam; storage facilities will be in Redleaf Halls 1–4. Coordinate with the mechsuit teams and Private Yarrin for carrying heavy cargo around the exterior perimeter," she continued briskly. *"All wounded and infirmary personnel, report to Private Jjones. An infirmary station has been set up in the west wing conference halls Waterfall, Fountain, and Lakeshore. Company Command and the Company boardroom will be located in the Olympic Ballroom.*

"All personnel will remain on the premises until further notice . . . and do remember that you will be moving among civilians. Be on your best behavior at all times; that includes this afternoon when some of you are in the pool, and this evening when some of you are in the hotel bar. All meals have been prepaid through the Crystal Gardens restaurant; if you want something different, you'll have to pay at one of the other restaurants, and that includes the bar.

"The Company has bartered for the use of one *laundry facility, located on the eighth floor, to be used by Company personnel. Otherwise, all extraneous room services will*

come out of your own *pocket,"* she warned dryly. *"Your hotel rooms will still be subject to Inspection by Squad leaders and Platoon Sergeants every morning at 0700 Dabinian Standard local. There will be a cadre meeting in the ballroom at 1500 hours; otherwise, your orders are to settle in and enjoy your Modified Leave. Captain Ia out."*

The first pair of trucks, now emptied, rolled out; most were being driven by Roghetti's soldiers and had to be returned to the front. Barely missing a beat, the third one—which was still being unloaded—pulled forward after a warning shout from the driver to the men and women unloading the back; the next two pulled in behind it. Commander Harper jumped out of the cab of the fifth ground truck as soon as that one stopped.

Striding up to Ia, he saluted, his tanned face pale and grim, scratches on the left side of his forehead and cheek, his uniform as muddied as the rest. "Commander Harper, reporting in with . . . with most of the Company, sir."

"I know," Ia murmured, then repeated herself out loud, knowing the others were covertly watching their two seniormost officers. "I know. At least the Feyori are no longer a problem. The timestreams are finally free and clear to me. If our battle plans for the Army as well as ourselves had been implemented, then there would have been only a third of the casualties we've suffered, and none of the lost lives. But we weren't given that option, and I *know* you did your best with what we were given, Commander."

He shook his head, eyes gleaming with tears he would not shed. "I tried. I planned for everything, tried to think of every . . . I'm sorry, Ia."

There were many things she could have said to him. That no plan ever survives intact after actually engaging the enemy. That she could *see* in the streams that he had done far better than could be expected, with roughly half the losses and injuries most other plans would have sustained. That it wasn't his fault that the Feyori had robbed them of her precognitive advantages. That he had truly done the best he could.

But that would not bring back Corporal Svarson, who had died while acting as a paramedic, pulling out wounded comrades from crossfire before being shot himself. It would not bring back Yeoman Nabouleh, third-watch pilot and another favorite crew member of Ia's. Nabouleh had been smashed under a toppled enemy tower when the munitions depot ignited and exploded, thanks to a poorly aimed shot from a Salik weapon.

Ia could see each of their deaths, knew each one as an unforeseen, unavoidable tragedy, but words would not change any of that.

Stepping forward, she wrapped her arms around her second-in-command, hugging him. It was public, it was not part of protocol, everyone was watching their two seniormost officers . . . but he needed it. Wrapping his own around her waist, he dropped his head to her shoulder and shook silently with the grief and pain bottled up inside, corked beneath the ever-present duty of an officer and pressurized by the knowledge he had failed in that duty.

"I know," she murmured, thinking of her own failures in the wake of all that Feyori meddling. He had lost two soldiers under his command. She had lost three, plus all the lives in Roghetti's Roughriders who hadn't made it out, either. "I *hate* that we've been so helpless in the hands of Fate."

He clung harder, reacting to the intensity in her murmured words. This was his first solo command, the first time Meyun Harper had been completely in charge of any of his missions. From the gathering of intelligence to the forming of battle plans, from their initial execution through to the retreat and cleanup stages, it had been all his, and only his.

Prior to this, he had been a lead mechanic, a logistics officer, a chief engineer, a junior officer, a third-in-command, her second-in-command and first officer . . . but not *in* command. Not the one ultimately responsible for every drop of blood shed by those under him. Ia knew she had placed a huge burden on his shoulders when she had handed over the majority of the Company to him, a burden she hadn't been able to lighten with any precognitive advice.

As she stood there, embracing and supporting him, one of the bodies crowding around Private Sunrise eyed the two of them, then moved closer. Private Nesbit, a regen patch strapped to his cheek, clasped Harper on the shoulder. Ia eased back from her first officer. Meyun straightened a little but kept his head down, not yet ready to look at the other man.

"It's okay, sir," Nesbit murmured, his tone gentle. He couldn't speak with great animation thanks to the regen goop doing its best to heal the scorched line marring his face, but his tone conveyed what his expression could not. "We all knew the odds of a bad die roll were high. Hell, most of us are surprised we didn't lose a lot more. But you planned your best, and we gave you our best. Sometimes, the dice just roll like *shakk-tor*, s'all."

He started to say more, then just squeezed Harper's shoulder and moved back over to await his room assignment. He wasn't the only one to speak up. So did one of the noncoms, stepping over to join them.

"Captain Ia. The Commander did his best to give the enemy hell while getting most of us in and out alive, sir," Sergeant Santori stated, moving up from the other side. The woman had her left arm in a sling with the telltale lump of a regen pack tucked inside. She looked at Ia as she spoke, but her words were as much for Harper's ears as the Captain's. "I'm giving him highest marks in my post-battle reports, sir."

Ia dipped her head in acknowledgment, her gaze still mostly on Meyun. He drew in a deep breath, squared his shoulders, and lifted his chin. One tear had escaped while he had rested in her arms, but only one. Hardening his expression, he didn't bother to wipe it away. He just looked at her.

That moment of grief was walled off again. *Now* he was ready to be an officer once more. Her second-in-command. She could see it in the way he looked at her, competent but ready to be relieved of command. "When do you want to debrief me, sir?"

She nodded but otherwise didn't acknowledge his brief lapse in discipline. Harper had to deal with his grief in his own way, much as she had learned to deal with her own. "Fifteen hundred, so all the officers and noncoms can hear all the news, all at once. In the meantime, coordinate with Private Sunrise on overseeing the settling of the troops in our temporary quarters. If you need me, I'll be in conference hall Waterfall. Dr. Mishka still has a lot of patients to tend. At this point, she can do a lot more with me as a KIman, boosting her biokinetics, than she could if we tried to commandeer a hospital. The civilians will have their hands full soon enough."

He nodded, then touched her arm as she started to move away. "When do you want to take back full command of the Company?"

She shook her head. "I can't. I contacted the Command Staff three days ago to file a formal charge of incompetency against Brigadier General Mattox. The rest of you are on Modified Leave, but I'm on Restricted. I cannot lead this Company effectively under those conditions. Not until they're lifted. The Damned are safer under your control for the time being, so you get the others back under A Company, too."

She meant safer out of the line of political fire, not enemy fire. Meyun frowned a little, then nodded in understanding. ". . . Right, then. Thank you for finding us accommodations, sir. You said Private Sunrise is the one to coordinate with?"

"I put her in charge of hotel-Company liaisons, since she's so good at doing the clerk thing," Ia stated dryly. Harper's mouth twitched. As her first officer, he knew Mara's true background and knew how much her other talents were being wasted. Ia's quip did have the right effect, though; the touch of humor lifted him out of his grief enough that he could get his work done without feeling like an instrument string tuned too tight—still tense, but not ready to snap.

The line of trucks pulled forward, bringing the vehicle with the patients too wounded to be ambulatory under the cover of the portico. Just in time, too; the gray clouds looming over the capital of the colonyworld started dropping a light drizzle again. Ia paused long enough to catch Harper's elbow, though.

"One more thing. I've taken the liberty of arranging for your family to come in for dinner tomorrow night," she told him.

His brown eyes widened in surprise and pleasure. A smile ghosted across his face. "Ah, thank you, Captain."

"I know you've been keeping in touch with them via the comms, but since you're on Leave, and they're less than a hundred kilometers from here, I saw no reason why the Harpers shouldn't come into town for dinner. My treat," she added. "You've earned a night off, and a bit of Leave. Loxana's Loft, the rooftop restaurant, 1830 hours sharp. Your family will arrive by 1810, tomorrow. I've made all the arrangements, and I'll be picking up the tab."

"You'll be there, then?" he asked her.

"Only if you're prepared to have everything recorded and dissected by the Command Staff," Ia reminded him, tapping her arm unit. He wrinkled his nose, thinking about it.

Restricted Leave meant she could do some civilian things, but *everything* she did had to be copied from her arm unit's black-box memory files and passed along for analysis. Previous accusations by some officers against other officers had proved quite telling when the accuser's private moments had been analyzed; some of those officers had apparently instigated their accusations for reasons of personal dislike, ambition, and even sabotage . . . and had forgotten their every move had been placed under watch.

Ia *was* willing to be recorded and analyzed. This was the one time in her career, post–Godstrike cannon, that she would be free to have everything analyzed by others. She wasn't on an Ultra Classified ship doing Ultra Classified work. Of course, she wasn't going to stop being who and what she was; she wasn't going to change her actions. The admirals and generals assigned to investigate her half of the case would interrogate her soldiers as well as herself via the hyperrelay now tucked into a large storage closet attached to the ballroom. They would do so to look for any discrepancies between her current behavior and her prior actions in years past, but that was fine with her.

They would find none, save only the hardship that Mattox had caused her.

Harper finally shook his head. ". . . I'd rather not risk it. The moment my parents realize you're trying to get Mattox out of command, they'll unleash their opinions. Father's retired Army. He does *not* like how Mattox has been running things, and I don't want his rantings coloring your situation. Perhaps another time, Captain?"

"Perhaps," she agreed, giving him a polite nod. Unspoken between them was the chance that his mother, perceptive as parents tended to be, might notice the chemistry between her son and his immediate superior. Even if she kept silent verbally on her suspicions, Ia didn't need the woman's facial expressions analyzed, and she was fairly sure Meyun realized it, too. *A pity; I would have liked meeting the rest of his kin, not just Sergeant Tae . . .*

With the gurneys now off-loaded into waiting hands, the paramedics and nurses attending the seven patients unable to walk were being organized by Private Jjones and Dr. Mishka. Ia joined them. Mishka gave her a relieved look; Ia nodded in return, answering her unspoken question. Without a word, Mishka directed the soldiers carrying the gurneys toward the makeshift infirmary.

The other woman looked exhausted, shadows under her blue eyes, her blonde locks falling haphazardly out of the knot that normally skewered them to the back of her head. Her personal energies had gone toward ensuring that only two members of Ia's Damned had died and that the rest were stable enough for transport. None of the seven would be *well* until they could get missing limbs and nonvital organs regenerated, but they would survive.

They should have been shipped to a hospital. Ia knew that as well as Mishka, and Mishka knew that Ia knew it. But the doctor had finally come to trust Ia's judgment. Ia hadn't commandeered a civilian hospital for her troops for a reason. Not a good one, but a reason. Without the Damned playing sabotage-style distractionary tactics in the field, the Salik would be free to resume attacks on both the Army and the civilians around the edges of the battle zone hundreds of kilometers away. All the hospitals between there and here would soon be full of patients needing far more care than her crew required, injured though many were.

That knowledge would go into the information discussed at the cadre meeting in a little while, and thus into the recordings for the investigation. Ia would have to be careful to speak calmly about those losses even though each wound, each lost limb, and each lost life, seared her nerves with such senseless, brutal, arrogance-inflicted waste. She couldn't do anything about preventing the attacks and the injuries without violating her orders, and had to show to the Command Staff that she was still rational, still capable of being a competent leader, unswayed by anger or thoughts of vengeance.

Part of her did want to pound the brigadier general into a paste . . . but just like the luxury of going insane, it was only a feeling. An indulgence which she did not have the time for. It had to be set aside and ignored.

JUNE 24, 2498 T.S.

"No, sirs," Ia stated, shaking her head. She flexed her knees subtly as she did so. This was her fourth hour-long interrogation session today, and her knees were not enjoying the strain. At this rate, the hyperrelay's tank would have to be refilled soon. "Until post-battle forensics uncovers more enemy surveillance footage, I cannot corroborate anything I wrote in my mission transcripts during the hours I lacked a functioning arm unit on the tenth of June. The additional enemy footage will not be available until the Salik are kicked off Dabin, and this situation needs to be resolved long before then."

General Amalyn Gadalah, chief justice of the Special Forces' Judge Advocate General division—and no relation to Private Gadalah—frowned at Ia. "You claim that you 'tapped into' someone else's life in order to combat the Salik. I don't understand how that works. If you tapped into someone else's mind, did they not tap into yours, compromising your security clearance?"

Ia shook her head. "No, sir. It is not a form of telepathy, which you may be thinking it is. Instead, it is a form of immersive postcognition, and is a passive, one-way reception only, not an active two-way—it's the equivalent of borrowing lecture notes for a class you yourself were unable to attend. There is no way via mere notes to interact with the professor giving the lecture."

"Lecture notes?" Lieutenant General Chun Hestin of the Psi Division asked, skeptical. There were four high-ranked officers interviewing her, not the usual three, but then the person Ia had accused was a high-ranked officer himself. Hestin sat to the left of Gadalah on Ia's screen, Sranna to Gadalah's immediate right, and T'Tkul perched to the far right.

"That is the simplest and shortest explanation I can give, sir," Ia told the Psi Division officer. "Trying to explain what I do is the equivalent of attempting to describe an entire three-dimensional, three-hour-long entertainment program in a simple, single, two-dimensional line drawing. I can only say that I have always used similar versions of temporally advanced postcognitive alternate life-stream analysis to determine probability rates during the last eleven years." Her knees hurt, and the soles of her feet hurt. "Adding in superior battlecognitive sensitivities plus combat skills and reflexes borrowed from the best Human warrior in existence is merely an extension of those same skills."

"I thought *you* were supposed to be the best soldier the Space Force will ever have," General Sranna stated. "Or were my earliest impressions of you all the way back when you were a mere sergeant in the Corps wrong, Ship's Captain?"

Sranna was there to represent the Army's interests in the investigation. From the start, the white-haired general had taken a belligerent stance during the proceedings, despite the way he had been friendlier when working with Ia in the past. She suspected he had been asked to be hostile but didn't know for sure. As it was, she had to deal with how he acted right now, not with how he was supposed to act.

"With respect, General, over half the soldiers on the Command Staff have been, are, and will continue to be better soldiers than I will ever be. If you refer to the unnamed individual whose skills I borrowed . . . she, too, will not have been the best soldier in the Space Force's history," Ia stated, twisting her grammar awkwardly around the future-perspective tenses. "She will, however, have been the best *warrior.*

"With my precognitive abilities blanketed by the Feyori sabotage efforts, there was no way I could rely upon my own battlecognition, which is based upon my ability to read the Future," she said. "So I borrowed the battlecognition of someone whose skills will be based on her ability to read the Now, and whose reflexes will be so tied into that awareness that, despite being a Sanctuarian heavyworlder with all the attendant reflexes, I myself could not achieve that level of instantaneous awareness-response without her . . . ah, without her 'lecture notes,' as it were. Disrupting the Salik forces so that my Company could have a badly needed day of rest in the face .of their unchecked aggressions required more than my skills alone could achieve."

"'Unchecked aggressions.' Again, we come back to your accusations against the brigadier general," General Gadalah stated, turning over a printout on the desk in front of her. "Are you sure you wish to describe the Salik pursuit of your forces in such a manner, Captain?"

"Sir, yes, sir," Ia confirmed bluntly. "We received zero support action from any of the Companies flanking Roghetti's command when the camp was overrun, General. I know postcognitively that you have already received and analyzed the communications from Dabin Army HQ to those Companies in question, and have noted the orders given to maintain their position. Had the lieutenant and captain to either side been allowed the leeway to react with tactics appropriate to the moment, they could have pincered the Salik 1117th and crushed them within a matter of hours. As already noted, we were instead forced to flee for two days straight before I handed over command of my Company to my first officer and went back to personally disrupt the enemy's advance and turn it back on itself."

"You said you did so to pull the temporal attentions of the Feyori . . . Teshwun," General T'Tkul stated, consulting a datapad.

While the majority of the Terran military was filled with Humans, there were sections in which the alien races could and did serve as Terran citizens-turned-soldiers—an entire Division set aside for each of the non-Human species in the 2nd Cordons of each of the Army, Navy, and Marine Corps, in fact. The sandy-furred, spider-like general lifted the pad with a forelimb, indicating the material on it, and chittered, letting the small translator unit attached to the blue-striped black vest wrapped around her thorax project her words in Terranglo.

While the K'Katta could not physically pronounce the Alliance trade tongue, they could become quite fluent-sounding in it with the aid of translation programs, and a K'Katta's mind wasn't too terribly different from a Human's.

T'Tkul had therefore been included as the most neutral observer possible. Her questions so far had been to the point, and her next one was no different. "You stated you wanted to turn the enemy's attentions away from the battle plans of your Company. Yet you claim you could not foresee the future at the same time . . . so you were, what, guessing?"

"General, yes, sir." Ia didn't know how many times she would have to answer the same or similar questions over and over again. Mustering her patience, she refrained from rolling her eyes, though she did flex her knees again.

On the screen in front of her, General Sranna narrowed his eyes as the five-second delay transmitted the slight shift in her posture to him and his reaction back to her. ". . . Are you bored with these proceedings, Captain?"

"No, sir."

"Do you need to visit the nearest head, Captain?" Lieutenant General Hestin asked her.

"No, sir. I'm just flexing my legs to assist my circulation. The gravity may not be as high as my homeworld, but it does still wear on the knees a bit, sirs," Ia added. "You were saying?"

Gadalah looked up at Ia, her dark eyes narrowed in a piercing stare. Wherever the trio were seated back on Earth, the room was dark enough that it shadowed their expressions half the time. Ia suspected the effect was deliberate. The only one whose expression was not affected either way was General T'Tkul, but then it normally took a fellow K'Katta to read their physical nuances, and Ia hadn't bothered to learn anything but the basics everyone learned in school.

Don't show your teeth when you smile; the Solaricans, Tlassians, and Gatsugi will all think you're being aggressive when you're not. Don't hold both your hands high over your head for any length of time, the Chinsoiy will think you're

*mocking them. Don't lie on your back with your legs and
arms folded in like a dead Terran bug, the K'Katta will* not
be amused . . .

"Are you *sure* the Feyori will not interfere from this point
onward?" General Gadalah asked her. Ia pulled her attention
fully back to the proceedings.

"I am very sure, sirs. They know I can kill them at a
distance, now. When they are needed, I will call upon them,
and they will obey. Until that time, they best serve the needs
of the future by continuing with what they were doing before
some of them tried to counterfaction me and interfere," Ia
explained patiently, yet again.

"You seem very confident they will obey," T'Tkul stated,
shifting a little on her abdomen-seat so she could curl one
of her forelimbs in an almost Human, circular gesture. "Why
aren't you using the Feyori to remove the Salik from Dabin?
You *say* you can call upon them and that they will obey,"
the alien pointed out logically. "So why not use them?"

Ia breathed deep and let it go, trying not to look or sound
too impatient with the question. At the edges of her awareness, she could sense the pitfalls of assumptions behind the
general's query. "That would be like using a Starstrike-class
laser cannon to light all the votives in a cathedral sanctuary,
sir. At the end of the battle, you'd have scorched the altar
boys, melted half the wrought-iron railings, most of the
votives would have been vaporized, and the pews and
the choir loft would be on fire.

"I have always been interested in the most *efficient* use
of the resources at hand. The most frugal use in the sense
that I will use to their fullest extent whoever and whatever
is available, yes, but also the most frugal in the sense that I
will use only what I *must* to get a job done. Anything else
is a waste of resources that others will need," she told them,

keeping her demeanor calm and rational. Logic and meta-
phor had to sway her superiors. "I may have to borrow a box
of matches from a civilian and a taper candle from the priest
to get the job done, but it is far safer to take the time to light
those votives by hand, rather than haul in a starship-class
cannon, sir."

"Regardless of whether or not *you* care to use them, if
they are now under your command, then the Feyori are under
our command," General Sranna stated.

Ia spoke on top of him, mindful of the two and a half
seconds of delay in the current relay system. Her timing was
intended to cut off the orders he was about to give . . . which,
as a member of the Command Staff and thus in command
of all four Branches, she and her troops would have been
required to obey. "I'm sorry, General, but I cannot do what
you were about to say. The Feyori will obey *my* orders
because they have been forced to recognize me as a fellow
Player in their infernal, alien Game, but I have in turn been
forced by the same rules of their own Game to limit the
moves *I* can make strictly to my own area of influence.

"*You* are a bug," she stated flatly as he fell silent, frowning
at her image on his screen. "No offense to our K'Katta allies,
General T'Tkul . . . but you are all nothing more than an
ant to them. An insignificant centipede, something either
to be stepped around or stepped upon. As you yourself would
not take orders from a tiny bug, they will not take orders
from *you*. Nor could I successfully pretend that your orders
for them are my idea because those orders are not the task
for which we will need them.

"I am obligated, by my vows as a soldier and an officer,
to inform my superiors when their battle plans will cause
far more harm than good. I am further obligated as a precognitive to refuse to carry out any orders that I can foresee

will do far more harm than good. The JAG rulings of the military case for Sergeant Casey MacOwens versus the Terran Army during the AI War permit the use of Johns and Mishka versus the United Nations to be applied in such cases.

"I would rather not have to use that ruling, sirs," Ia stated levelly. "So I am telling you, as a duly registered and Space Force–acknowledged precognitive, that trying to get the Feyori to fight our wars for us above and beyond the limited role which I already have planned for them is a *bad* idea. They might get the idea they can swoop in and take over, sirs. That, and it will cause too much harm. As I said, it's like taking a Starstrike cannon to an entire cathedral when all you need is a handful of candles lit."

Sranna sat back in the shadows, folding his arms across his chest. "So what, exactly, are we to do with the situation on Dabin, Ship's Captain Ia?" he asked her. "You want us to remove Mattox and his top brass for incompetency and conspiracy to support incompetency. But whom do we put into their place? *You?*"

"I can only stay on Dabin until my new ship is ready to be crewed, sir," Ia reminded him. "My job here has always been to provide the best possible battle plans, not to lead. If the troops are given the leeway to resume the tactical flexibility they should have been employing from the start, with my precognitively enhanced plans assisting them with advice on how to regain all the territory lost, then my part of the job will be done. *They* will get the job done. Any competent strategist and leader from the 1st Division 6th Cordon can take over at that point."

"Yes, but *which* competent soul should be picked to take Mattox's place, in your opinion?" Gadalah asked. Unlike Sranna, who remained leaning back in the shadows, she leaned forward, fingers interlaced as her forearms rested on the table.

Grateful for the opening, Ia fished a datachip out of her pocket and slotted it into the relay's workstation, transferring its information to the tribunal officers. "I have prepared a list of candidates to fill in the gaps in the 1st Division's echelons, in different arrangements for the Department of Innovations to look over for their analysis and approval. They're being transmitted on subchannel alpha . . . now. Most of the suggested officers will require promotion, and several of them by more than one grade. Of the twenty-seven possibilities, I have earmarked three top contenders here on Dabin, particularly if they follow my battle plans for clearing up the mess Mattox made of everything. After that, they should be competent enough to handle the rest of the war on Dabin on their own without any further guidance, which is my ultimate goal.

"I have also included two higher-ranked alternates in the top five, ones who could be brought in from outside when the planetary blockade has been broken if none of these three are deemed acceptable by the Command Staff as replacements in the long term. However, by immediately assigning strategic goals, then decentralizing the command structure on how to apply the tactics needed to achieve them, the various Companies of the 1st Division 6th Cordon Army will be able to handle each portion of each task under their own purview," Ia stated. "They won't need a Division commander right away."

"Decentralize?" General T'Tkul asked, her translator box adding a slight lilt, no doubt translating literally the K'Kattan equivalent of skepticism.

"For at least a month Terran Standard, sir," Ia told her. "The apparent chaos of so many disparate Companies acting on their own will be mitigated by inter-Company cooperation in tactical planning at the local level. That is, *if* they are given leave to organize things as they themselves best see fit, being the ones actually familiar with the local problems they face.

"Such methods haven't been used on Dabin under Mattox's command, but every single soldier in the Space Force Army has been trained since Basic for the flexibility of maneuver warfare, which is what this is," Ia said, her gaze more on the shadowy form of Sranna than on the well-lit ones of Gadalah and T'Tkul, or the half-lit figure of Hestin. "The enemy is like a hive of wasps that is busy trying to build a nest. We need to shake them up and smash their hive, destroying their budding infrastructure so that when the blockade is finally broken, they will be unable to dig in and resist when it is time for them to be driven from this planet. That strategy calls for individual sorties, sapper attacks, and sabotage efforts, maximizing the Army's efforts while minimizing wasted resources and reducing unnecessary casualty lists."

"And again we come back to your claims of efficiency and frugality," General Gadalah said, her tone dry. To the left of her, Hestin looked like he was reviewing the lists Ia had transmitted, using a workstation embedded into the tabletop. Gadalah seemed to prefer paper. "Tell me, Captain. Which was it that prompted your actions when you *hugged* Commander Meyun Harper, according to not only your own arm unit, but the units of several others in your Company a few days ago? Efficiency, or frugality?"

"Neither," Ia admitted calmly. "It was my humanity."

"Please," Lieutenant General Hestin snorted, lifting his gaze from his screen to the pickups for their communications link. "You claim to be the commander in chief of the Feyori nation, you freely admit that you are half-alien and that they acknowledge you as a fellow Meddler, yet you claim your *humanity* caused you to embrace your second-in-command? I'd say it was your past relationship with him."

"I have never allowed any relationship, past, present, or future, to interfere with my sense of duty, General," Ia said, flexing her knees slightly. "Until coming to Dabin, Commander Harper had never served as a Commanding Officer. As an officer, yes, but never the one in command. He lost two of our soldiers in the most recent engagement, under *his* command, using *his* plans. It may have been a very long time since you yourselves, sirs, lost that first soldier under a solo combat command directed under your own plans, but I am quite sure that if you cast your minds back to that day, you will remember the anguish, guilt, and grief over the fact that you could not change their deaths.

"In the light of my own memories of those days, how could I not give my first officer a moment of comfort?" Ia asked the quartet of officers on the other side of the relay. "He came to me to report their deaths. To report his *failure* as an officer. If I, who can foresee nearly everything, can still be blindsided and fail from time to time, how can I *not* be sympathetic to someone who cannot foresee yet still tries to do his best for his soldiers with the information and orders given to him? I may have convinced the Feyori to heed my commands as a half-breed, but I am *still* very much a Human being. It was as one Human to another that I gave him a moment of understanding and sympathy when he needed it most.

"I don't know what military you may want to run, or what kind of a war you think this is," she stated, allowing some of her anger to show through in the way she narrowed her eyes in a frown and by the slight edge she gave her words. "Maybe you think of this colonyworld, which is just one among scores of worlds being attacked, as a list of the numbers that come in every time someone relays you a report on supplies used, objectives lost, or casualties taken. But from where I stand, I am in the trenches on my first officer's homeworld, where the next set of casualties—the next day's *lunch*—could be his own family. I am in the middle of a very tangible war, with all the psychological and emotional and physical impacts that you are not feeling. This is a very Human war.

"Forgive me, sirs, for taking a moment to support my first officer in his hour of need." Ia paused briefly, checked the timestreams, then added, "And I wouldn't call a thirty-second comfort-hug in full sight of soldiers and civilians alike a moment of *fraternization*. Unless you want to call the one he received from Private Sunrise, who was Corporal Svarson's Platoonmate, a breach of Fatality Forty-Nine for wanting to show she understood he had done his best as well, or the way Private Nesbit put a hand on Harper's shoulder in sympathy, or a dozen other, similar, *Human* displays of sympathy, comfort, and understanding that have been expressed toward him."

"I would think such displays would be better suited if they came from your Company chaplain," the lieutenant general stated blandly.

"Our Company chaplain was gut-shot helping to extract Svarson's body under enemy fire," Ia returned dryly, though not blandly. "For the record, I went to her and gave her a hug, too, returning some of the same comfort and support she has given me over the years. We are Human beings, sirs, not machines. Morale is the single most important tool we have, Generals. Or at least, that's what I learned in Marines Basic. I learned it at the Naval Academy, too. Does the Army operate with a different toolkit?" she asked, lifting one brow. "From what I and my crew observed, Captain Roghetti's soldiers could certainly use a good dose of positive morale right about now . . . and they're not the only ones on this world."

General Gadalah lifted her hands and clapped slowly three times. Leaving them clasped, leaning on her elbows, she drawled, "How neatly turned, Ship's Captain Ia. So *very* neatly turned back to the problem at hand."

"Life is a cycle, General," Ia said, again shifting her knees. The closet, roughly as large as her quarters had been back on the *Hellfire*, was fairly well lit, but the floor was a thin carpet over some type of plexcrete a little stiffer than the kind used on Sanctuary. "It is a series of circles and spirals, like the turbulence found in a stream. Some religions say the reason that we come around again and again to face certain problems is because we simply haven't learned how to surmount and move past them yet. We don't know how to get out of the eddy."

"Are you getting restless, soldier?" General Sranna asked.

Ia debated how to answer that question. She could go with the one that her knees and legs could use the break but decided to admit a more serious concern. "I understand that at the end of the day, each of you goes home to your family, or out to dinner with your friends. That at the end of the day, each of you gets to lie down on a comfortable bed and that you have seated yourselves on padded chairs while you conduct these interrogations.

"Unfortunately, while you take your ease, sirs—which your years and rank have rightfully granted unto you—a *lot* of the 1st Division's soldiers are facing the dangers of being blown apart by projectiles, seared by laser fire, and the very real possibility that they will be eaten alive, one bloody bite at a time, tonight. Every day, every hour, and every minute this investigation goes on, with no change in tactics or orders, is a day those men and women out there run the very real and immediate risk of dying.

"My *duty* is to stand here and submit to these inquests," Ia added firmly as the leader of the four officers drew in a breath to protest. "And I will do my duty, sirs. But as much as standing here for long spans of time wears on my knees, the knowledge of just how many members of the Army are losing their lives and their limbs wears on my conscience. I wish I could be like you, far removed from the consequences, the sights, smells, and sounds of the front lines. But I am only a couple hundred kilometers from it, not a couple hundred light-years. My *conscience* is not comfortable with how long this is taking."

"Tough it out, soldier," Gadalah ordered her, her jaw set, her brows lowered in a grim line. "We're not done with you yet, and Mattox is still in charge. Those lives or deaths are on his conscience, not yours."

There was nothing Ia could say to that. She knew General Gadalah wouldn't understand that they *were* on Ia's conscience. That because she could see ways around such unnecessary things, it was *her* responsibility to help those men and women avoid such fates . . . and that Fate demanded she ignore far too many that she *could* have helped, for simple lack of time. *Those who see a problem have the responsibility to help correct it. Preferably in a way that benefits the greatest number of people.*

Thank you, Mom and Ma, for instilling in me such a solid sense of conscience and humanity, she sighed mentally, part complaint, part truth. *I'd go insane from this if I had the time to waste.*

Consulting her pieces of paper, the JAG officer began the next set of questions. "On the afternoon of the fourteenth of June, you encountered a 'not-cat,' one of the genetically modified creatures recently introduced to Dabin by the Salik.

When you killed it, were you in any way envisioning José Mattox as the target of your aggressions?"

Ia rolled her eyes. "*No*, sirs. All I had on my mind at the time was the desperate need to survive, since at that point in time, the Feyori named Teshwun was still manipulating the timestreams, concealing my precognitive awareness of all immediate dangers in my vicinity. Contrary to what you may expect me to feel in my situation, I do *not* hate, loathe, despise, or otherwise wish to harm the brigadier general."

"But you claim you are Human, and that you are suffering emotionally because of the war on this colonyworld," Lieutenant General Hestin stated, pouncing on that. "So how *do* you feel about Mattox? For the record, Ship's Captain. Be completely honest."

"To be completely honest? He is an *annoyance*," Ia stated bluntly, letting her tone convey how candid she was being. "He is wasting lives, he is wasting time, and he is wasting my energies, trying to improvise time after time to perform some kind of . . . of *damage* control for all the harm he's been so willfully doing to the war effort on this world. Get him out of command, and I will gladly wish him a long and happy life—*Hellfire*, I will give him all the information he needs to live a long and happy life! Just get him *out* of command before he causes the death of every single person left on this planet."

"Well. Isn't that a nice piece of hyperbole?" General Sranna quipped, leaning back into the light, his mouth twisted in a sardonic hint of a smile. "Do you honestly expect us to believe he'll cause the death of everyone on Dabin?"

"*Vladistad*, General," Ia stated flatly, giving him a hard look. "That bomb killed and harmed millions of innocent civilians . . . and I can see far, *far* more than Giorgi Mishka ever dreamed of in his wildest nightmares. I wish to God it *was* hyperbole. The Salik *cannot* be allowed to entrench on Dabin. Ask whatever you will of me, but the clock *is* ticking on that particular bomb."

"We will," Gadalah replied dryly. "Let us discuss your so-called offer to ensure Brigadier General Mattox lives a long and happy life. Are you talking prophetically guided advice on what to do with him?"

"General, yes I am, sir," Ia said. She paused, then added, "Of course, if you want me to actually do that right now, you'll have to give me a minute to search the timestreams and program it into a data file."

"What, you don't have it prepared already?" Sranna asked her, lifting his brows.

"No, sir. I would rather give the brigadier general free rein to choose whatever path he wishes to take," Ia stated. "I could pick out *your* life in clear detail, but that would be interfering with your right to live it your way. You have the right to rise or fall by your own actions," she admitted. "I cannot, however, stand by in good conscience when a person's poorest choices destroy so many *other* lives. I will not stay silent while Mattox *v'shakks* away the lives under his command and the civilians under his protection by using outmoded twentieth-century tactics coupled with such a rigid, inflexible command structure as he has imposed upon the local branch of the Army."

And again we come back full circle, Ia thought, struggling to hide the urge to roll her eyes. She could do so where it was absolutely appropriate, such as that absurd question about her feelings during the not-cat's attack, but not when it would be deemed an act of insolence toward her superiors.

Flexing her knees once more, she reached for the bottle of water someone had left for her on the table to one side. They wouldn't be done with her for another half hour at least for this session, if not longer. And when this set was done, the quartet currently interrogating Mattox would switch to interrogating her in a few more hours, just as they had done before and would do again. All eight would eventually compare notes and observations, and like a jury, come to a decision on what to do with both the accuser and the accused.

It wasn't at all physically exhausting like Marines Hell Week had been, and it wasn't nearly as mentally taxing as Navy Hell Week, but it did wear on her conscience and her heart in its own way. At least in the hours when she wasn't being interrogated, she had plenty of time to refine her eventual tactics for this world. There was enough time to write extra prophecies, contingencies to cover everything being messed up on this one world by Mattox. Unfortunately.

JUNE 29, 2498 T.S.

Ia waited in front of the hyperrelay station, as tense as a wall-harp string tuned far too high. All but holding her breath for the Admiral-General's verdict. There were several possibilities clouding the moment. Most led forward in the direction the future needed to go. She had contingency plans for a good eight or so of them already plotted out; all she needed to know was which one Christine Myang intended to choose.

The older woman's stare gave nothing away. She sat at the center of the screen, hands clasped lightly in front of her, with the shadowy presences of the other eight officers of the dual tribunals seated around her. General Sranna once again sat to the right, General Gadalah to the left, and the remaining six at a higher table in the back.

"Well," Admiral-General Myang finally stated, "you've certainly managed to waste our battle-planning time with this matter."

Ia didn't know whether Myang was addressing her or Brigadier General Mattox, who was sharing the same relay channel so that both of them could hear the verdict simultaneously. On her side of things, Ia had moved the hyperrelay into the main part of the ballroom so that her entire Company could witness the verdict. Supposedly, Mattox was broadcasting the results of the hearing to everyone in Army Headquarters as well, though Ia knew it was actually only being broadcast to a few high-ranked officers.

Off-screen, she heard Mattox speak. *"I apologize, sir, but I really have had no control over the insanities of this loose cannon from the Special Forces save to get her out of my Headquarters. I would not have wasted your time otherwise."*

Myang lifted one gray-salted brow. "Brigadier General Mattox. After having reviewed the evidence collected from Ship's Captain Ia, her Special Forces Company, and several of the Army officers in the 1st Division 6th Cordon who have stepped forward with brave honesty about your actions over the last year, it is the joint decision of the Space Force Command Staff that you be relieved of your command immediately, under the charge of incompetency."

She paused a long moment, giving Mattox the seconds needed to reply. It came as a very subdued, *"Admiral-General, yes, sir . . ."*

"When the blockade is broken," Myang continued, "you will be extracted from Dabin to face psychological evaluation to determine whether your actions were undertaken by deliberate arrogance or by sheer stupidity, in addition to being swayed by Feyori Meddling. This charge is sustained by the Command Staff of the Terran United Planets Space Force, and sealed by my hand." Shifting one hand to the sensor pad to her right, Myang affixed a scan of her thumbprint to the order. With that done, the Admiral-General clasped her hands in front of her. "Ship's Captain Ia."

"Sir, yes, sir," Ia stated, shifting from At Ease to Attention in front of the relay's screen, with the bulk of the hyper-relay machine placed in one corner of the ballroom. A second, much larger screen had been unfurled next to it, giving the men and women seated in the chairs lining half the chamber a clear view of the proceedings. Boots together, hands at her sides, she waited to hear which of the possible choices—almost all now in her favor—would be selected by the head of the military.

"Captain, you have said all along that the Salik must be pushed off Dabin by a specific date in order to preserve the lives of everyone on that planet," Myang stated.

"That is correct, sir," Ia said, shoulders square and chin level.

"What would you do to prevent it?" Myang asked her. As Ia blinked and absorbed the off-the-wall question, the older woman asked again, "What would you do to prevent this great tragedy you foresee?"

That was not a question she had anticipated. It was not only an extremely small probability, less than a hundredth of one percent, it was the exact same question Ia had been asking herself since that horrible morning back when she was fifteen. A question that came with the one answer she had decided upon long ago, the only answer she could live with for the rest of her life.

"Anything," Ia said, mind caught up in the memories of that fateful decision. "Anything within the constraints of Time itself, mindful of the demands of my duty, and bearing up under the weight of my conscience. Within those boundaries, sir . . . anything at all. Ask it, and I will give you every single bit I can."

Myang waited two and a half seconds as Ia's reply was forwarded to her through the tiny pinhole of hyperspace connecting their two disparate worlds . . . and nodded to herself, as if expecting Ia's answer. Ia had a strange feeling of suspension as she watched the older woman; the timestreams had turned mist-gray, though every path out of the knot led fully, firmly forward. As she watched, Myang removed her elbows from the desk and tugged on her jacket hem, straightening her all-black uniform. Inhaling slowly, she let it out and nodded a second time, just once but firmly, as if making up her mind.

". . . Very well. Ship's Captain Ia, you are hereby promoted to the rank of four-star General, and placed in direct command over the Army's 1st Division 6th Cordon immedi—"

"—WHAT?"

Caught in the act of gaping, Ia winced away from the speakers built into the struts supporting the membrane of the larger viewing screen. It didn't help; Mattox continued to protest at full volume.

"You're making that white-haired freak *a* full-blown general *in charge of* MY Army?!"

The one good thing about his vehemence was that it cleared the shock from her mind. It also cleared the fog from the timestreams. They stretched now before her as bright and clear as the middle of a summer's day on Earth. Stepping forward, Ia touched the workstation controls. Sinking her electrokinesis into the command pathways, she leapfrogged it to Army Headquarters via the infrared carrier wave, and from there, sparked screen after active screen into switching channels.

"Admiral-General," she stated over Mattox's continued protests, "would you please repeat *both* verdicts? I think everyone at Army HQ needs to hear this from you directly."

"*—And if you think I'm going to let you get* away *with this* madness—"

"Our techs are no doubt trying, but can you reduce the brigadier general's audio feed from your end of things?" Myang asked dryly over the two and a half seconds of lag, speaking as best she could through his ranting. It cut off while she was still speaking, thanks to that lag. "I presume it's within your abilities, and that you'll be faster at it?"

Ia nodded. "Already done, sir. I've shifted it to subchannel alpha; I'm sure you'll want a recording of whatever he's saying. Now, if you could repeat everything, starting with your verdict regarding the brigadier general, sir? I have ensured that *all* of the workstations at Army Headquarters here on Dabin are receiving your transmission."

". . . Of course. It is the verdict of the Command Staff that Brigadier General José Mattox, commanding officer of the 1st Division 6th Cordon Army, is to be immediately stripped of his command on grounds of incompetency . . . and possible mental instability," Myang added dryly. "He will be remanded into Space Force custody to await full psychological evaluation as soon as the blockade on Dabin has been broken. This verdict has been sustained and sealed as of two minutes ago, Terran Standard.

"Ship's Captain Ia of the 9th Cordon Special Forces is hereby promoted to the rank of four-starred General and placed in direct command of the 1st Division 6th Cordon Army forces which are stationed on Dabin, in addition to her command of the 9th Cordon Special Forces—your black uniform, General Ia, will have both a gray and a green stripe, in addition to those four stars. You are hereby ordered by your peers of the Command Staff to take charge of the situation on Dabin, and do anything necessary . . . within the boundaries of your conscience, your duty, and your grasp of Time itself, as you have said," Myang stated dryly, ". . . to amend the damages wrought by Brigadier General Mattox, and to correct the situation to save the maximum number of lives in the most efficient manner possible."

As much as this highly unexpected promotion vastly— *vastly*—simplified things for her, and opened up a whole host of possibilities under the purview of her new rank, Ia's conscience burned. It prodded her like a white-hot poker into speaking. "Sir, with a promotion to the rank of four-star General, and with leave given to do anything and everything that I must . . . I *will* take the bit in my teeth and run with it, sir. You *do* know that, right?"

"I know that I am placing a great deal of faith in you and your abilities, meioa-e," Myang told Ia, holding the younger woman's gaze over the lag-seconds and light-years between them. "Do not make me regret this decision. But do show me what you can do with no more constraints holding you back, save for your conscience, your duty, and that unholy-strong psi of yours, *General*."

"Sir, yes, sir!" Hand snapping to her brow, she saluted the Admiral-General. Myang saluted her back. The moment she was free to drop her hand, Ia snapped in a crisp left face and addressed her Company, mind racing—leapfrogging— after every possibility now opened up before her. "Attention, Damned; you heard the Admiral-General! You have exactly one hour to pack up your combat kitbags and be prepared to depart. Report back to the ballroom in whatever light armor you can scrounge, ready to travel. I will have individualized orders ready for each of you by then."

"Capta—er, General, sir?" Commander Helstead corrected, raising her hand in inquiry as the others rose to obey. "What *will* we be doing?"

"I'm sending each one of you across the Army as tactical consultants. We are finally going to get this war done, and we are going to get it done *right*. The seven still on the seriously wounded list will be remaining behind, along with Private Jjones and myself—yes, Dr. Mishka, I expect *you* to go into combat as a consultant as well. Ramasa is still missing his left foot and is therefore unfit for combat, but you are uninjured. Everyone who can go *must* go, and you are going in his place. I will remain here to coordinate everything above and beyond the orders I will give you, and I will oversee the reorganization of the Army from this end.

"Xhuge, Douglas, and Togama, get on the comms immediately and contact every rental-hovercar agency in town. I want each and every pairing heading into the field to have their own vehicle—Private Floathawg, contact the hovercycle companies to see about leasing bikes to those personnel you know are licensed to ride. We're going to wipe out half the rental agencies in the city, but it must be done. Clerks, file all payment vouchers on my *carte blanche* ticket with Sergeant Sadneczek.

"You have your orders, meioas. Dismissed!" Turning back to the hyperrelay as the others scrambled out of their seats, Ia nodded at the screen. "If you'll forgive my eagerness and please excuse me, Admiral-General, you have just changed the *entire* list of game plays I had drawn up. I wasn't expecting to be given such a free rein. If I'm to uphold your faith in me, I and my people need to get to work immediately, and I have a *lot* of plans to rewrite in the next ten hours."

Myang was already nodding, listening impatiently to Ia's

relay-lagged words. "General Ia, you are dismissed to your new duties."

"Thank you, sir. Thank you, Generals, Admirals. I'll try to keep your faith in me. Ia out." Ia touched the controls again as the Admiral-General and the generals flanking her vanished from the screen. The blue-and-gold logo of the Space Force took their place, though the link was still active, if rerouted. "To the men and women at Army Headquarters, these are my first set of orders: Colonel Zirenja of the Military Peacekeepers, you will place Brigadier General José Mattox under house arrest, escort him to his quarters, and keep him there under armed guard. He will be allowed no visitors and no unrecorded communications. He may call or contact whoever he likes, but all communiqués are to be recorded or copied and shipped to the Command Staff on Earth unaltered.

"To Major Xiayan, the officer in charge of HQ Supply. Please issue me a set of Dress Blacks with the requisite green-and-gray stripes, and a set of four-star pips. Your department already has a current set of my measurements, so that shouldn't take you long. Colonel Satsuke, have the communications department relay to all Companies of the 1st Division copies of the orders containing the change-of-command. I want them to know that *I* am in charge within the next ninety minutes Terran Standard.

"Colonel Zirenja, please also place the general's chief assistant, Major Leotta Perkins, under house arrest as well as the brigadier general, under the exact same conditions. There's a sixty-seven percent probability she'll try to sabotage my orders and efforts at Headquarters. I will allow nothing and no one to interfere with the salvation of this colonyworld," Ia stated bluntly. "Please do remember, I have just been given the authority and the freedom to do whatever

I must by command of the Admiral-General herself. Make no mistake, I am in full charge now—and gentlemeioas? I will *know* if any of you fail to comply. If you do, you will also be placed under house arrest.

"Follow my orders to the spirit and the letter, and I will make you the heroes of Dabin," she promised, staring into the camera pickups, though there was only the TUPSF logo for her to look at. "Get in my way, interfere with my calculations, and I will take you out of the equation. This is *not* the time to get petulant and commit a whole string of Fatalities, gentlebeings. Expect me at Headquarters in one hour twenty-eight minutes local. You have your orders. General Ia out."

Shutting off the relay, Ia turned to find Meyun waiting patiently at her elbow. There was still a trace of shock and wonder in his brown eyes, but he didn't let her abrupt promotion faze him. *This* was why he was far more suitable as a first officer than any other choice the DoI would have made. Too many off-the-wall things happened around Ia, and she knew it. So did Harper, and he of all choices had the flexibility for it, even if she still couldn't predict most of his life.

"So what exactly *is* the new plan, sir?" Harper asked under his breath.

"Each and every single one of you will have to contact and deliver very specific orders to twenty-three Companies within the next three days. That's per person, not just per team, which means that working in pairs around the clock, you'll have to deliver orders to and brief forty-six Companies within sixty-eight hours," Ia explained to her second-in-command, fingers and toes trailing mentally through the timestreams.

"That is a lot of Companies to reach," he admitted.

"There are almost thirty-five hundred Companies here

on Dabin, and they *all* need to know what each and every one of them and their neighbors can do about removing the Salik presence on Dabin—and it's thanks to something *you* told me about that'll make it that much easier to remove them. You handed me a brilliant idea for a shortcut to this planet's part in the war, which will make up for all the time Mattox lost for us. Unfortunately, it will only work if they're not entrenched."

"Something *I* told you?" Meyun asked her, puzzled.

Ia flashed him one of her rare full grins. "Don't worry about it right now, Harper," she said, clapping him briefly on the shoulder. "I've had the civilian sector working on it for months, just like I had this hyperrelay bought and stashed for months. So long as we can disrupt the Salik efforts to entrench by breaking up their wasp nests—and we *can*; we have just enough time left for that, if we all work hard—then we can kick them off your homeworld for good."

"I'll trust you, Cap . . . *shakk*," Harper muttered, shaking his head ruefully. "*General.* That is going to take a *lot* of adjustment. You have got to be the single youngest four-star General in Terran history—how the hell did you pull that off?"

She spread her hands, letting him see her sincerity, and a touch of her giddiness. "I honestly haven't a clue! I was fully expecting to remain a Ship's Captain, or maybe get a promotion to Vice Commodore, *maybe* even promoted to be a Commodore here on Dabin after Mattox kept screwing everything up. And I was only supposed to be a Commodore at most until at least the last few months of the Salik War, when I was supposed to be promoted to a Rear Admiral at that point. But here I am, *General* Ia . . . and I *am* going to run this war how I see fit.

"Go get packed," she ordered, pointing at him. "Change

your clothes for combat zones, grab a quick bite from the buffet, and do whatever you need to do. I'll have your team-mate assignment by the time you get back."

Nodding, he headed for the door. That left just Private Jjones still in the Olympic Ballroom with Ia. She cleared her throat, standing in a very proper, soldierly version of Parade Rest, though she had started her military career predominantly as a surgical nurse. "Sir. What do you want me to do? You said I was to remain behind with you. Do I accompany you to Army HQ?"

Ia shook her head. "No, you'll be in charge of our make-shift infirmary, which means you'll stay and anchor our base as the one fully mobile member left here. I'll be busy splitting my time between here and Army HQ. Commander Benjamin is almost ready for desk duty; when she is, she'll take over monitoring everything from this room with Ramasa's assis-tance. I couldn't predict these injuries because of Meddler interference, but I knew I *could* plan for plenty of flexibility across the crew."

Jjones lifted her brows briefly and shrugged her broad shoulders. "You put in some commands in my version of the Company bible way back when we first boarded the *Hellfire*, things that convinced me you really could see the future. It wasn't pleasant to find out even you could be blinded—metaphysically, not just physically—but even so, I'll still follow your orders, sir. You're a good officer even without the psi stuff."

Ia swallowed. She was touched by the transgendered wom-an's faith but couldn't dwell on it more than briefly. Too many plans had just changed. "I'll try to be worthy, Private."

Moving away from the hyperrelay, Ia headed for the office supplies stacked in the other corner at the back of the room. Fetching out an empty container and a box of datachips from under one of the tables, she pulled out the first dozen of the thin little rectangles with a touch of telekinesis. Light as a feather, they floated up and out, forming a halo around her hand.

"In the meantime, stand guard and make sure no one interrupts me. I have over three thousand sets of orders to revise and make perfect, and just over an hour to get it done."

"I'll have the hotel staff bring in a lunch sack for you at that end of the hour, something you can eat on the way to Army HQ, and I'll fetch a couple energy drinks for starters, sir," Jjones stated, her paramedical training coming to the fore. She moved out of her Parade Rest stance and headed for the door. "You'll be burning through a lot of kinetic inergy to do that, so you'll need food to replace whatever you use."

"Thank you, Private," Ia told Jjones, in between flipping her mind back and forth between reality and the timestreams, altering the orders inscribed on each of the many, many chips. This would indeed exhaust her if she didn't replace all the energy spent. "I'll have to commend you to the DoI for your thoughtfulness and good planning . . . along with everyone else who survives this debacle."

CHAPTER 7

To this day, I still do not know what prompted the Admiral-General to pick such a long-shot option. I know I have been a pain in her plans, the ache in her head, the wrench in her neatly ordered works. I have been belligerent, uncooperative, devious, obstructive, and blunt. I have withheld vital information repeatedly, snuck around behind her back, and bent the rules on multiple occasions, and she knew all of this . . . yet the woman still elevated me to a higher rank than even I had foreseen as probable. She gave me virtual free rein to do whatever I wanted, beyond all hopes and expectations for it . . . and a good thing, too, because I needed it, on Dabin.

So yeah, you bet your sweet asteroid I ran with it. Like a horse given its head and a long flat stretch to gallop in, with nothing to hold it back but the wind and the weight of its burdens, I ran. Clenched the bit in my teeth and ran as fast and hard as I could, because while I still don't wish

Mattox any harm, I do wish to heaven and back that he hadn't done nearly so much damage on Dabin. I've piled as much of the repair work on Ginger as I can, but a fair share of the meddling—that's with a lowercase "M"—that fair share of meddling also belongs on his shoulders.

Still, the Admiral-General took him out of the equation, for which many on Dabin thanked God, and gave me my shot at running the war on that world in the best ways that I saw fit. And maybe that's my answer, right there. What would you do to set everything right again, or as right as the vagaries of Fate would allow? . . . Or rather, what would you let someone else do if you thought there was a chance they could do it?

                                                                    ~Ia

JULY 2, 2498 T.S.

"You're on, sir, in five, four . . ." The technician held out his hand as he looked up, counting down silently with his fingers. This was a broadcast to the entire Division, something that would be picked up and eventually decoded by the Salik forces on Dabin in spite of the heavy encryptions used by the military, but it was something she couldn't avoid.

Waiting a beat after he silently reached *one,* Ia addressed the dozen hovercameras floating in front of her. There was no corresponding viewscreen because this was a broadcast, not a workstation-to-workstation comm link. "Greetings. I am General Ia of the Space Force Command Staff. As you were informed by dispatch within the last few days, Brigadier General Mattox has been retired from combat command, and I have been appointed by Admiral-General Myang in his place."

Retired was a euphemism that would hopefully smooth things over between those troops who were still loyal to

Mattox and those who wanted him gone. The messages delivered by her own soldiers had contained official news of the change in command and a set of preliminary orders that would get every group currently being engaged by the enemy out of immediate danger in time for this broadcast, as well as certain specific orders and general directives for the coming weeks.

This broadcast would cover the new command structure and the types of orders that they would now have to follow. First, though, she had to get the unseen ranks of men and women in almost thirty-five hundred individual Companies to trust her.

"As sometimes may happen with a major change in combat command," Ia stated calmly, "there comes a change in command structure, strategies, and tactics . . . and yes, I do know the Salik are decoding this broadcast even as I send it. I do wish them good luck in figuring out what I am going to have you do, for they will need it."

Mattox had approached his organization top-down, from the Division level to the Brigade, to the Battalion, the Legion, and finally down to the Company level. Below that were Platoons and Squads and teammate pairings. A good fifth of what Ia had sent out were Squad-level orders, but only when they absolutely had to have direction. What she needed now was to remind every single soldier listening to this broadcast, either right now or on a replay later, of what they had been taught to do back in Basic.

Not the hand-to-hand combat or the target practice, and not the monkey-gym antics of the confidence courses, but the group practices. Things that *weren't* openly discussed in the civilian sectors because they were the *real* weapons in the hands of the Terran military. Battle tactics, the kind that depended on the on-the-spot information only a Squad,

Platoon, or Company would know in time to make decisions that would do any actual good.

Her plans hinged on each person being able to act independently because she literally did not have the time to direct each and every piece of combat personally, second by second. It would be polar opposite to what Mattox had done to them and expected of them. Ia needed to remind the men and women watching this broadcast that they did have the training for this task.

"I realize many of you have little reason to trust a complete stranger. But while I have never served in the Army before now, I began my career as a Marines grunt, enlisted, ordered about, and expected to shoulder my share of the combat burden just like you. The Marines aren't that much different than the Army, save that they're mostly stuck in space, while you have the advantage in knowledge and skills when it comes to planet-side fighting, and a far better support system at your backs."

A lie, but a face-saving one. The Marines and the Army were different in many ways, some blatantly so, others subtly. But morale, as she had reminded her interrogators, was the single most important tool in their hands. These were soldiers who had suffered heavy losses, restrictive orders, and a planet-side top brass who hadn't given a damn for their suffering or their ideas on how to alleviate it, save where it would enhance Mattox's own biased ideas of glory and strategy.

"If you are unsure of my reputation in small-unit tactics as General Ia . . . well, I know that many of you have at least heard of my reputation as Bloody Mary," she said, smiling slightly, wryly, for the cameras. "Rest assured, I have kept that reputation fresh and dripping from my first week in Marines to my field promotion as an officer in the Navy, all the way to my years in the Special Forces. My service in the Army here on Dabin will be no different. I promise you this: follow my orders, and the enemy *will* bleed before we are through."

Her nose itched. She couldn't take a moment to rub at it, as that would spoil the tough, confident image she was trying to project in her newly issued Dress Blacks, with her half glittery gleaming down her chest on both sides of a medal apiece for each type, and a veritable rainbow of service-zone pins. She and her previous ship, the *Hellfire*, had pretty much covered all the Terran and jointly Terran-V'Dan star systems, along with many of the systems among their alien allies, in the first few years of the war before winding up on this world. She wanted the soldiers watching her to see that glittery and believe she had more than enough experience to back up her commands.

"For those of you doubting my claims, particularly when my predecessor made similar ones which did not come true, I would like to speak of some of the tactical plans I have enacted. Plans which *you* will now use. Listen *carefully*:

"Water Buffalo. Pitchfork. Cone. Cloud . . ." She enunciated each one calmly and levelly.

The important points of her speech were buried in plain, open Terranglo. The genius of her orders lay in the fact the Salik wouldn't understand the images she was evoking, because they didn't use any of these images in their battle-training simulations. Cryptography was easy enough to crack if one had time and a powerful enough computer, but a stenographic message always depended on knowing what each word secretly stood for.

She continued calmly, reciting words with images and associated meanings that each soldier, male and female, would remember very clearly from their months of training.

"Clapboard. Triple-C. Chevron. Chevronelle. Drawbridge. Racetrack. And finally . . . Guerilla, Mobile, Positional."

Save for those last three terms, the definitions for which the Salik *would* understand, each of the previous words in her list was a mnemonic: simple words defining the images of complex sets of instructions every recruit and cadet learned in Basic, regardless of Branch, all of which she wanted to evoke in each soldier's mind.

The Water Buffalo was a slowly building central front of attack, the bulge in the middle distracting the enemy from the two "horns" which would attempt to encircle and flank their foe for a three-pronged pincer. The Pitchfork was for parallel thrusts through cluttered terrain, such as a heavy forest or an urban jungle, necessary since there was more than one town that had been captured and occupied by the enemy. The Triple-C was a series of nested firesacks, layered regions where the enemy would be forced to go through heavy defensive crossfire when attacking.

The others were similar memes, each one an image etched on a display screen during the many tactical lectures of Basic Training, each a combat maneuver that had been practiced and practiced and practiced back in their earliest days. Such things were learned purely by rote, doing them over and over and over until it was as much a soldier's reflex to think along those lines as it was to block and throw a punch. More than that, throughout a combat soldier's entire career, every single post-action report had to include a tactical analysis of what happened, what went right, what went wrong, and what could have been done to improve upon that action. It was a highly flexible, incredibly skilled method of continually training the soldiers of the Space Force across its four Branches, a training method very few militaries could match.

Her last three words were stated plainly to place these mnemonics in their context as small-unit tactical maneuvers . . . and as a reminder of the Space Force's normal, bottom-up way of organizing any fighting force.

"Cast your minds back to when you first learned these things, and all the times in which you analyzed and improved them," Ia urged in a calm, confident tone. "These are the parts of your training that required you to exercise and utilize all six of your senses *and* your minds, not just your muscles or your machines. I know that these things are the exact same as what I myself learned in the Marines as a recruit, and learned again as a cadet in the Navy. I know you will remember them, and execute them as well as any soldier I have been privileged to fight alongside."

Again, a small lie; Marines training was far more intense, more focused on ship-to-ship or ship-to-station battles. It was very much more focused on small-unit tactics than the far larger movements and maneuvers of an army the size of this one. But she knew that in the Navy and the Special Forces, where such things weren't strictly necessary to learn for certain jobs, the crewmen and service personnel all had to train in the same set of tactical understanding before anyone was allowed to leave either enlisted Basic or an officer's Academy. In a pinch, even the Chaplain Corps would know what to do, provided they could remember it under pressure.

But aside from some of the focus and the intensity level, the Army was no different than the Marines, and far better trained than the auxiliary forces. The trick was to remind the unseen men and women watching her of these things. Ia nodded slowly as she stared into the hovering cameras, confirming the understanding dawning in most of the men and women listening to her words.

"That's right," she urged, knowing via the timestreams

that they were indeed beginning to understand. "You know exactly what sort of commands I am giving you. Commands *very* different from the brigadier general's. With that said, here are your *strategic* objectives:

"The Salik are building wasp nests in the ground and in the trees. Break them up and drive their occupants into the open. Work in coordination with your nearest brothers and sisters so that you do not step on each other's toes or attempt to throw a rock at a nest in the wrong direction at the wrong moment of time . . . but break those nests wide open.

"Go for a *walk*, meioas," she urged the unseen men and women watching her broadcast. "Take a stroll through these Dabinian woods and smack down every hive you meet. I took a similar walk past an enemy nest a few days ago, and did just that. Now it is your turn. Focus on my words and understand their meaning. Those are your *strategic* objectives," she repeated, wanting them to understand that *her* command structure was very much not going to be top-down. She was not going to dictate anything tactical, save for those hand-delivered, temporally vital messages that had already gone out. "For the rest of it . . . you already know what you need to do. I am ordering you to go do it.

"One more thing. Do not feel anger for the enemy, though as you fight deeper and deeper into their territories, you will see the atrocities which they will use against you, too, if they catch you," she stated, meeting each camera pickup in turn to give the impression she was meeting everyone's gaze. "Do not waste your energies on hatred. Anger clouds the mind, wrecks the judgment, and pulls all your plans out of alignment. Instead, if you must feel anything toward them, then just pity them. Because of their arrogance and their species-centric blindness, they are a dying race. Their time is drawing to an end. Crack open their nests, shake them loose from the soil of Dabin, and brush them away. That is all you can do, and all you need to do.

"I am the Prophet of a Thousand Years, and your duly appointed Commanding Officer for this fight . . . but while I can see what needs to be done for us to succeed, I am just one person. I can only tell you what needs to be done; the rest is up to you to carry through." Squaring her shoulders, she gave the center camera a level look. "You have your orders, soldiers. You also have my trust. Get to it, and get it done as soon as you can. General Ia out."

The technician touched a control on his portable workpad. Tiny red lights on the cameras blinked off. He nodded, confirming the transmission was done.

". . . We're off-line now, sir. Begging pardon, General, but . . . that's a very strange set of orders. In fact, it didn't even sound like a set of orders. Not like . . . ah . . ." He trailed off, blushing a little.

"Not like what the brigadier general loved to give, no," Ia agreed. She removed her cap and unbuttoned her jacket, relaxing from her formal stance. "I have a degree in military history, Sergeant. Mattox's strategies were used by Western commanders in the twentieth and early twenty-first century. Very heavy on the top-down command structure, with the generals making all the decisions from hundreds and thousands of kilometers away and not allowing for a lot of the flexibility needed to adapt to the actual situations found on the smaller scales, at the Company, Platoon, Squad, and individual team units.

"You can look at a bunch of trees, and say, 'Hey, that's a forest; have everyone in the Legion climb the nearest trees right now,' but without knowing exactly which tree each Squad will face in that forest, some of your soldiers will end up facing a stingersap tree," she told him, setting cap and jacket on the end of the table. Lifting her chin at the freckled man, who was catching and shutting down the hovercams to conserve power, Ia asked, "You're a native of Dabin. Would *you* climb a stingersap?"

"Hell *no*, sir," the sergeant agreed, catching another machine and stacking it with the rest on the table at the back of the small broadcast room. "Not without full protection. Not unless I wanted my hands to swell up and split open. Not even the *jungen* virus can stop that kind of an anaphylactic reaction."

"That's why the Space Force chose to emphasize more of the Eastern tactics of that same era, planning for flexibility at the local level. In a military two billion strong spread out across countless light-years and covering dozens of different colony-worlds, you cannot hope to give an order at the Command Staff level and expect the Squadron level to know exactly what to do to carry it out under the conditions at hand *unless* they are trained to understand *and* given leave to implement a broad range of independent, easily tailored maneuvers," Ia said.

She stepped forward and caught one of the higher machines, finding and pressing its off button to help him shut everything down. He gave her a surprised look, but Ia didn't stop speaking. This conversation would be repeated among the lower ranks here at Headquarters and would eventually spread outward. She wanted everyone here in the Army on Dabin to understand *why* she was so completely changing the way Mattox had run things.

"Mattox had an ego problem he was desperate to feed, and the Army here on Dabin suffered from it. I have a desperate need to get the job done, period, by the most legal and expedient means available. My ego is *not* allowed to stand in the way, not when others have the time to spare and the brains to do all the planning they need." Catching the third hovercam, she shut it off, set it on the table, and nodded to him as she spoke. "The next broadcast will be in two days, forty-one minutes local. I can foresee you'll do an equally good job at that time, but until then, you're dismissed to return to your normal duties, soldier."

"Sir, yes, sir," he said, his expression thoughtful.

Hundreds of thousands of soldiers all at once . . . and one soldier at a time, she thought, sighing. *Eventually, I'll get the full job done.*

JULY 8, 2498 T.S.
. . . AND MARCH 19, 2497, AMONG OTHER DATES

(*Don't exhaust yourself,*) October Ia admonished one of the other versions. Once again, she sat on the embankment of the future stream, projecting an air of normalcy over everything seen from any other point in time. (*Pace it out over several of us.*)

(*You're not the one trying to sneak in an extra ten minutes' help between enemy engagements,*) Mid August Ia stated. (*And this* is *me pacing it out over several of us.*)

The one from early July stooped and trailed her fingers through the stream of a lieutenant colonel, altering the words on his workstation so that he received a direct communication from General Ia, replete with security codes. There were far too many battles for just one Ia—the youngest Ia—to keep track of at the moment, not on her own. The battle with the Feyori had taught her something about herself, that she *could* use Time itself to alter time. She was therefore going to use it. To run with the bit firmly caught in her teeth, as she had told the Admiral-General.

Hopping over a cluster of thread-like rivulets, she enlarged another and touched it. This time, the headset of a private caught behind enemy lines snapped to life. Ia projected her voice—gently, ever so gently—into his life. *"Sandusky, there will be a ten-second window thirty-six seconds from the end of this transmission. You will have just enough time to grab Dostoyer and bolt for the tree line while the enemy reloads, but you both have to be ready. Thirty-six seconds from mark."*

The image in the stream showed the wide-eyed private babbling something to his teammate. If they didn't move, they'd both be stunned and eaten, and several minor but still-influential sets of descendants would have their lives altered in the wrong ways. The little stream shifted as soon as she withdrew her fingers, realigning itself to correct the damages wrought to its original channel from Mattox's efforts. She didn't stay to see if Sandusky would move; the shifted streambed told her he would, and had.

(*Could be worse,*) December Ia offered. Like August and October, she was on a ship *sic transit*, headed from one engagement to the next. (*We could be wasting our youngest self's breath trying to convince these people well in advance of what to do, instead.*)

(*This is only working because I used up all the time I would've spent fighting, verbally and physically, on writing prophecies while waiting for that verdict,*) Late July Ia stated, moving to yet another stream, this time a yeoman pressed into corpsman service, driving the wounded back from the front lines in a civilian flatbed hovertruck for lack of anything better.

(*You're all welcome,*) Early July quipped. December, the most relaxed of the lot, stuck out her tongue. October Ia *tsked.*

Physically, their youngest self sat in a recliner chair hauled into the Olympic Ballroom by the hotel staff, wearing plain camouflage Grays, no sign of her new rank on her person. Her physical ears could hear Bennie and Ramasa coordinating things with Army Headquarters, and faintly in the distance, very faintly, they all heard the *cha-whomp* of the city's defensive cannons firing, plus the hissing *tzzzzng* of building shields repelling projectiles that exploded like the crack-and-rumble of thunder.

The Salik were trying to press all the way to Army HQ to take out the new commander, convinced that if they cut off the head of this Human serpent, the waters of their tactical plans would be safer to swim in once again, as they had been under Mattox. The Loxana was halfway across the city from the office building occupied by the Army, on the far side of town from the enemy engagements, but she could still hear the sounds of all that battle. Thankfully, most of the citizens were safe in bunkers and cellars underground.

Army Headquarters itself had been evacuated by two-thirds, with the various departments and their equipment broken down into subunits and spread out among several other hotels. Her preferred choice was not only to decentralize the tactical command structure, but the entire chain of command. Certain towns and homesteads had been alerted in advance and evacuated, most of them along a path that was designed to *let* the Salik advance toward Landing City. Many buildings in the capital itself lay empty for the day, including the restaurant and grocery store across from Army HQ.

It had not been easy to get people to shut down businesses and hide elsewhere while their homes and shops were bombarded and besieged. But for those who would not go, Ia's orders had been straightforward. *Stun them all, drag them off to the shelters, and let them sort through the wreckage when it's all over and done. Homes can be rebuilt, and in worst-case scenarios, food can usually be foraged for on an M-class world, but their irreplaceable* lives *must be saved.*

She had ordered, the Army had obeyed, and the civilians were safe in those shelters which she knew precognitively would not be hit. In the physical world, she was supposed to be lining up supply manifests, anticipating needs based upon the fallout from the combat taking place right at that moment in time. In the realm of the timeplains, she was doing so much more.

(*Hey, Early July,*) Mid October called out. (*It's about time for you to go meet your March mad self.*)

(*I'm aware.*) One last trail of her fingers through a stream, and she straightened.

She staggered a little, too. Touching so many lives, altering so many streams and strands in high speed, had a mental as well as a physical cost. Righting herself, the youngest Ia headed downstream to October and twisted across the curtain just in time to feel a rippling snap from her younger self. Dipping down into her own life, she inhaled deeply to center herself briefly in her physical body, sipped from the energy drink Jjones had left for her, listened to her chaplain explaining something to one of the tactical officers visiting from the Army, and flipped back onto the timeplains when nothing needed her attention in the real world.

She could sense her younger self—March from the year before—about to dip into her own point in time, and spoke. Or rather, projected into her other mind. (*About time you showed up.*)

For a moment, she saw her younger self, still on board the *Hellfire* and startled beyond words. Waiting patiently for the younger version to return, Ia addressed herself again.

(*Don't freak again. You really* are *hearing me,*) she added dryly. (*Your future me, talking to you.*)

Feeling the press of her own curiosity, Ia—the July Ia—pushed up out of the water and onto the grassy bank of their own stream. Seeing her own jaw drop, those amber eyes opening so wide that the whites could be seen all the way around . . . well, it was funny. She grinned at her younger self and remembered what she had said.

(*Don't you look shocked . . . wait until you can see your expression from* this *side of things*,) she added. Part of the elder Ia was amused by her own earlier amazement, reliving things from the other side. It really was funny, seeing her more innocent self being flabbergasted by this new trick. But they didn't have a lot of time. They never did. So she held out her hand. (*Come on. Sit up. I'm going to share with you the list of things you'll need them to buy and stash, and a couple extra places to stash them.*)

There was so much she wanted to say to her younger self, and so much she couldn't. Even the Feyori knew better than to meddle casually with the Past. There was *always* a price to pay for such things. It was the price of entropy itself, that a balance would eventually, inevitably be achieved, pleasantly or unpleasantly—a grandparent *could* be killed before even the parent was born, since a new one would simply slip into alignment, along with a new reason to go back and slay that former relative . . . but it always came at a cost as one's past consequentially changed. So she spoke of the few things she could address, things from her past and March Ia's future that were the same in many, many versions of reality, plus things for the future of both of them, and more.

When the meeting between her and her first temporally awakened self finally ended, July Ia sunk back into her stream, headed downstream, and submerged in mid October. More than just the Feyori influence had to be concealed. More than just the battle to free Dabin from unwanted Meddling had to be fought. (. . . *Right, that step is done. How's the fight going, August?*)

(*Just a few more touches from all of us should see it done,*) December answered, since August Ia had her fingers in the waters of four resized streams simultaneously. (*I haven't noticed any serious or sudden deviations outside our plans, so we must be doing it right.*)

August Ia let out a raspberry-snort as she straightened. (*Just because you do not see an enemy disguised as a bush doesn't mean the enemy isn't sitting there, clothed in branches and leaves. I'll feel better when Early July has become Late July, and Mid August, and Mid October, and all the way to you, Eldest.*)

December Ia flipped a rude gesture at the implication that all the responsibility rested on *her* shoulders but otherwise didn't respond.

Late July Ia finished touching a few vital life-streams, then straightened with a sigh. (*Right. That's my part done. The V'Dan Fleet has been alerted to the exact placements of the Salik blockade within the Dabinae System. They'll emerge from faster-than-light with guns blazing. Try not to screw things up, my other selves. The farther away we try to reach from our exact physical body and personal point in time, the more exhausting this is . . . and trying to contact the right people on a ship moving faster-than-light from several light-years out is not easy, even if I—if we—can access all of eternity in this galaxy.*)

(*Understood,*) the youngest of them, the one from the start of July, promised. The others nodded. Turning her attention back to the tangle of streams on Dabin, Ia felt for more knots in need of untangling in the tapestry they were trying to weave.

She emerged ten physical minutes later, not having moved save to drink sips of the vitamin-and-caffeine-laced water at her side but as exhausted as if she had been working for two hours straight in a full-battle simulation. Which in a way, she had. Stifling a groan, Ia levered herself up out of the chair, rested a moment with knees locked, then downed the last of the fruit-flavored liquid Jjones had found. Only then did she amble toward the tactical screens set up around Private Ramasa, slowly stretching limbs that felt as if they had been stuck sitting still for hours instead of minutes.

Ramasa normally sat at the gunnery post on the bridge of her ship for first watch, rotating along with three others so that each man or woman could stare at the boards and screens with fresh eyes. For the moment, though, they didn't have a ship. He also didn't have his left foot, and was making his way around from screen to screen by scooting his chair on its rollers with little pushes from the intact right one. It was certainly faster than using the cumbersome, time-consuming crutches Jjones had scrounged up for him, but he did have to keep moving to keep track of it all.

She gave him an approving nod as he pushed with his good foot from station to station, consulting the list of timings and target coordinates she had given him earlier. His job was to coordinate with the city defenses, manned in part by the Peacekeepers and in part by the Army. He was doing it rather well, too. Ia wasn't going to interfere.

Modern medicine ensured the wound wasn't a painful one, and it would eventually ensure it wasn't a permanent one. Once they were on board the *Damnation*, Jesselle Mishka would work herself and her infirmary crew long and hard to replace every organ and limb lost via the new ship's regeneration vats. Ia's eye would have still been on that list of replacement parts needing to be vat-cloned, but she had taken care of that herself.

If she'd had any confidence in her ability to replace Yung Ramasa's foot the same way, by Meddling deliberately, she would have. The problem was, it hadn't been deliberate. Ia hadn't realized she was restoring her eye and repairing her shredded clothes when it had happened, nor did she have a truly detailed grasp of biology, never mind Human male biology. She was not about to experiment upon her own crew through the awkwardness and potential horrors of trial and error, when they could simply wait a few more weeks and undergo the normal reconstructive sort of surgery, augmented by bio-kinetics.

"Yes!"

The shout startled all of them, though Private Ramasa only looked up briefly from his work, his eyes bulging like the Frog Prince he was nicknamed to be. Christine Benjamin, Chaplain Bennie, waved her hands in the air, dancing as she sat in her own wheel-footed chair. Ia strolled that way, smiling back at her friend's open grin.

"We got 'em, sir! The 6th Legion, 2nd Battalion, 5th Brigade just imploded the whole complex at the Sur Chelle Vineyards, General," she reported, while the major at her side frowned at the information scrolling across her broad bank of screens. Her task, not too dissimilar from Ramasa's, was to monitor communications on a list of channels which Ia had given her. She touched her headset and nodded. "Scan sweeps are reporting complete collapse of all openings, and a prolapse of the hill over most of the complex. If the surviving enemy's not buried alive, the 6th says they'll be highly surprised."

"Tell them they have two hours to salvage and pull out," Ia told her. "Remind the 6th of the fighting they'll still have to do to get the prisoners out of the feeding pens, and that there'll be White Hearts to earn, as well as White Crosses, if they're not careful about keeping themselves out of the enemy's traps. Then start passing along the word to the distractionary teams to shift into rearguard action so they can pull out."

The major, a stout, dark-skinned fellow with a receding hairline as the only sign of his advanced age, shook his head. "This is so very different from what we were doing before . . . Massive chaos over the first four days. I honestly thought the Salik were going to break through the original containment line and through the sides of that corridor you then set up for them to get all the way here," Major Tumseh confessed. "I'm sorry to say I did not have as much faith in my own troops as you, sir."

Ia ran a hand through her hair, wincing as another bomb exploded somewhere in the skies nearby, making the hotel windows and doors rattle a little. Her fingers trembled, and her head ached inside her skull, feeling stretched and bruised. She needed a meal and a rest soon, but wouldn't get any food other than snack bags for another three hours. That was when the kitchens finally opened in the morning, and the nap wouldn't happen for another five hours. Bracing herself subtly against the edge of one of Bennie's tables, she shook her head, then reached for one of the energy drinks in the case Jjones had directed the hotel staff to leave out for the crew members on duty in the ballroom.

"It's a failing of genius, and of supposed genius," she murmured. "If you start believing in your own successes too much, you start believing in the hype and forget the hard work and careful thought that went into building that kind of reputation. Mattox was good at tactics and strategy, but he was also too proud of it. The Feyori played up that flaw, widening the gap between his belief in his own abilities and the realities of the situation he was in." Giving the major a pointed look, she opened the bottle. "Unfortunately for my sense of ego, I cannot avoid seeing the results of any mistakes I make. In fact, I am forced to foresee them, as probabilities and possibilities. I am not insulated from my own failures at any step along the way, with rare exception.

"But I can and will use the reputation I have built. The moment the Salik here on Dabin realized that General Ia was the same Lieutenant Ia who destroyed their uppermost echelons back on Sallha a few years ago, I knew they'd be eager to wipe me out. Any Salik who could claim to have captured or slain *the* Bloody Mary would be given the highest honors, and the right to eat my liver one screaming slice at a time if they could catch me alive." Saluting him with the drink, she swallowed some of it down. The flavor was chocolate, but not as dark as she normally liked. That meant it was a little too sweet for her tastes. She drank anyway.

"Yes, with a dish of beans and a glass of wine on the side," Major Tumseh muttered, grimacing. Not getting the significance, Ia gave him a questioning look as she drank, but he shrugged it off. ". . . Classic literature reference."

"Ah." It was all she could say. There were many things in the universe which she just didn't have the time to understand. That wasn't her task this time around. Beyond the ballroom, beyond the windows visible in the corridor just outside, the first of a solid week of heavy rains was beginning. Finishing her glass, she said, "As for trusting them, isn't that why we train our soldiers so hard and so well? *Any* man or woman can rise up from the bottommost ranks to become the next Admiral-General. *All* of them need to know how to fight, and why, and when and where and how."

"And we as officers just need to step back and *let* them fight, once we assign them their objectives," Tumseh agreed, sighing roughly. "A flaw in our own thinking, swept up in Mattox's self-importance. Surfing the tide of his enthusiasm, and blind to the fact the breakers were dashing our own soldiers upon the rocks."

Ia nodded. "That's why you're here with me." Tumseh shot her a questioning look. She smiled briefly. "You'll be replacing me when I leave with my Company. You're the best man for the job because *you* see the flaw, and will remember the flaw, and do your best to keep it from clouding your own thinking."

Tumseh shook his head, hands tucked behind his back. "Oh, I hardly think I'm the right man for the job. I'm an analyst, not a strategist. I'll tell you what needs to be knocked down, but . . ." He stopped, thought about his own words, eyed the markers on the central screen showing the general placements of various Army groupings, and realized what he had just said. ". . . *Ah.* I see your point."

"Precisely. They're doing a fine job, now that they're *allowed* to do their job as they see fit," Ia allowed, watching the tiny little shifts of color that indicated enemies engaged and objectives nearing completion. "As I told one of your sergeants a few days ago, a general leading from the rear can order his subordinates to climb the nearest local trees all he or she wants, but if he expects the soldiers out on the line to climb a stingersap tree simply because it's closer than a beech-bark, then he is leading far too much from the rear. *I* lead from the front . . . even if I'm stuck in here for the moment, coordinating the few far-flung bits that still need it."

"You do realize that, once you've had a year's full worth of service in the Army, they'll expect you to spend a year teaching at a Camp or a Fort or an Academy?" Major Tumseh asked her.

Ia knew what he meant by that. He thought she was being groomed for the Admiral-General's post. Christine Myang herself thought she was grooming Ia for her own post. It was a very flattering idea, she had to admit.

"Yes, I do realize that, and all that it implies." Ia changed the subject. "Right now, however, my intent is to drive the Salik fully into the open. They will be permitted no permanent structures, no long-lasting shelters, and no self-contained atmospheres that can last longer than two days. So. As my top and most sensible analyst . . . what pockets of resistance do you think should be tackled next?"

"The Sharriah Valley," Major Tumseh stated after only a few moments of thought. Extending an arm, he traced a route along the map on the largest screen. "Now that you've driven them out of the caves in the hills, that's their fallback position. It's deep within their territory, though. Not an easy location to reach."

"You have a plan?" Ia asked.

"Bomb random spots to distract them sonically, form up at least three push spots along the perimeter to look like real attacks, and use sandhogs to tunnel all the way to the base under the noise and confusion."

"Get on it," Ia ordered. "Wait—I almost forgot." Opening her command bracer, she programmed it for a formal recording. "As a member of the Command Staff, I hereby authorize the immediate field promotion of Major Michel Tumseh to the rank of Brigadier General, 1st Division 6th Cordon Terran United Planets Space Force Army." Logging it with a touch of a button to include the needed timestamp, and a touch of another to issue it to the local Army database, she snapped the lid shut again. "You'll still report directly to me and follow my orders until I and my Special Forces troops leave, but this will get people used to looking to you for leadership. Particularly with this valley plan of yours. Once I'm gone, you will report to Major General Louise Xenadra of the 6th Cordon, and be fully responsible for the conduct and effectiveness of the 1st Division."

"Sir, yes, sir!" he acknowledged, snapping into a salute. "Thank you, sir. I'll do my best."

She saluted him back. "You're welcome, and congratulations on your promotion, Brigadier General. Be mindful of both your first and last duties as an officer, with equal weight and care: to get the necessary objectives done, *and* get your soldiers back home again, as alive and well as possible. But do understand I wouldn't have selected you if I foresaw any problems. Providing you put your mind to the tasks and responsibilities ahead, and *remember* that your own strength lies in analyzing what strategies must be sought, not in what tactics must be used."

"Yes, sir, I will remember that, sir," Tumseh agreed briskly. "With your permission, I'll go issue the orders about the valley."

Ia nodded, relieved to see him go willingly to his work. He was a good soldier, and would be a better officer with those warnings in his head. He would do well here. God knew she couldn't stay beyond the appointed hour on this world, whatever happened between now and then. Too many other worlds hung in the balance, not just Dabin. The fiasco triggered by Private Sung back in the Helix Nebula had proved that all too well.

JULY 10, 2498 T.S.

"Beware the Ides of March," Ia murmured. She had replaced Bennie at the tactical station, which had been rigged with eight more screens forming a faceted half dome over the station. Each of the six large secondary screens flanking the main screen showed a scene being covertly scanned by a tiny surveillance drone. The images were all dull in colors, Salik campsites barely lit by the twilight of burgeoning dawn.

"The Ides of March?" Brigadier General Tumseh asked her. He sipped at the cup of caf' in his hand, standing next to her chair, shadowing her faithfully as she continued to teach him a different command style than the previous brigadier's. "Pardon me, sir, but isn't today the tenth of July, Terran Standard?"

"On Earth right now, it's either summer or winter. But right here, right now . . . we're about to experience the full glory of a Dabinian spring." She lifted her chin at the image on the largest screen, the primary one. It showed a close-up reddish-hued plant with tiny leaves and fuzzy stems, and tiny, bulging yellow buds, many ready to burst. "For the last four days, it has been both dry and hot, locally. You've been on Dabin for, what, three tours now?"

"Three and a quarter," Tumseh admitted. "I could've been switched out at the end of my third tour, but the blockade hemmed us in, so Mattox kept me on. General, *why* are we staring at an enlarged close-up of passion moss?"

"Yansuun di'esh Shio-ma A'tun, na'ala bura g'jong jungen g'vesh; atta tu-shia oua V'Sh'nai melunn li-a'ethnakh soth-ve druzh ka'a'oua t'tournei g'attesh." At his puzzled look, Ia explained what she had learned in her cross-cultural classes as a child. "It's archaic High V'Dan, one of the praise-prayers from the Sh'nai faith of V'Dan. Basically, it means, 'Praise be unto the High One, for the miracle of *jungen*; we the Faithful shall live happily and well for the rest of our days with each lungful drawn in and each mouthful consumed.' It's a very appropriate saying for this moment, on a world that was jointly founded."

Sunlight struck the edge of the moss, creeping over the blossoms. As they watched, two of the blossoms quivered, then snapped open, releasing puffs of orange-yellow mist. Three more followed, and a cluster of five.

With each pop-and-puff, Ia's subtle smile grew in its satisfaction. Movement in the skies on the secondary screens drew her attention. Great spheres of vat-grown leather had just been launched into these enemy camps from special cannons hauled as close as certain Companies and Legions had dared to get them.

The actual weapons were contained within leathery spheres because the presence of metal objects inbound from beyond the enemy's perimeters would have triggered their antiprojectile defenses. As it was, most of the bird-sized spheres fell short of camp. But that was alright; when they hit, they exploded much like the blossoms had, puffing huge clouds of yellowish orange dust into the air. The mist dispersed fairly quickly in the morning breeze, turning the view slightly hazy. It didn't vanish completely, but it did spread and thin out.

Most of the Salik in view reached for their weapons, bulging eyes pointing this way and that on their heads, trying to ascertain where the next attack would come from. When nothing else happened, they eyed the mist warily. Most stayed back from it. A few moved forward with breather masks firmly settled on their alien heads and scanner tech extended in their tentacled grips, trying to analyze the mist for danger.

That was when the real missiles came arrowing in from outside, along with laser fire scorching through the trees, scoring through force-field projection poles and toppling support towers. None of these attacks would actually decimate the Salik forces. None of the others would, either. Ia's loyal crew members had hand-delivered strict orders to sow only confusion and distraction today rather than death among the enemy.

Those missiles and their accompanying streaks of light

did, however, tear into the tents and container structures, puncturing holes and venting the air each contained. She hadn't given orders preventing the Army from taking out whatever they could of the frogtopusses in their way. Mostly, some of the metal-wrapped missiles made it through only to explode in golden puffs rather than in dark smoke and bright fire. The rest destroyed random targets as real missiles would.

"You're bombing the enemy with . . . with passion-moss spores?" Tumseh asked her, one brow quirked in confusion. "They're not Dabinian animals, General. They won't go into a mating frenzy. Frankly, given the viciousness I've heard about Salik females compared to the relatively calm temperaments of their males, I would *not* be inclined to make them sex-change in the middle of a war."

"Have you ever fed onions to a dog or a cat?" Ia asked him, ignoring his quip about the quirks in Salik biology.

"What? No!" the brigadier general denied harshly. "That'd kill the poor animal—not even Ginger would've deserved that. Shooting her was a bit extreme, but at least it was a *quick* death. So to speak, since you can't actually kill the silvery bastards," he added under his breath. "Onions would be a slow and painful death in even modest amounts, and no animal, no sentient deserves that."

"Precisely. Onions contain a compound called . . . thio-sulfate, if I remember right," Ia said, eyes still on the screens. One of them jolted and fuzzed with static, going dark as the hidden drone became a casualty of random battle shrapnel. The scanner techs sending them this feed switched to a different camera's view. "It causes the blood cells to burst. Symptoms include lethargy, breathlessness, diarrhea, vomiting, even paralysis of the extremities, particularly the legs . . . It can go away given enough care and time, but it can also build up in the system in small doses spaced out over a matter of days. Humans aren't affected; we can eat all the onions we want. But not cats and dogs.

"The Salik possess hemoglobin-based blood, the same as we do, but in some ways they are more like cats and dogs. Their cell structures are a bit different, and the compounds in passion-moss spores are not exactly like thiosulfate . . . but they will have a similar effect after roughly two weeks of exposure. All we have to do is keep harassing them so they cannot maintain any airproof shelters. It won't work on the Choya, who have hemocyanin-based blood," she admitted lightly, "but then they aren't here, and they won't fight as tenaciously as the Salik. Thankfully, they will be slightly easier to drive off the other colonyworlds, once the frogtopi are forced to flee."

"The Choya, yes, but not the . . ." Tumseh broke off, frowning at her. "Wait, are you planning on releasing Dabinian passion-moss spores on *other* worlds?"

Ia nodded slowly, still watching the combat chaos on the remaining screens. A second went abruptly dark. It, too, was replaced by a new surveillance angle. "They are indeed being released on other words as well, with passion moss grown and transported on a wide variety of ships and scheduled for release today. And yes, I *do* know I'll have the various colonial environmental agencies screaming at me for it," she murmured, flicking him a brief, wry look. "I accepted that stain on my soul years ago. But clearing passion moss out of an alien planet's ecology will be a *lot* easier to deal with than what will happen if the Salik are allowed to remain on any of our worlds.

"We—and by we, I mean the Dabinians I contracted with to grow the stuff in sufficient quantities over the last few years—already know how to kill the moss quickly and cleanly—if tediously—with targeted counter-rhiozomes.

Thankfully, the war will be over before the Salik can develop an effective counteragent of their own in any quantity large enough to do them any good. In the meantime . . . every breathable world they touch down on that isn't theirs must be rendered *un*breathable for them."

"So you say," Tumseh muttered, his tone disapproving and skeptical.

Swiveling her seat, Ia met his gaze evenly. "So I *know*, as an extremely high-ranked precognitive." Returning her attention to the screens, Ia nodded at the chaos. "But that is a job for another day. The release of all these spores today, here and on other worlds, is only the start of the end, not the actual end. Today, you and I must focus on Dabin. Now that we have the Salik pushed back into eight main lobes, which bottlenecks would you recommend cutting through, to further disorient and isolate them, Tumseh?"

"It'll depend on the Sharriah Valley sappers. Lieutenant Colonel Xenaria said she was going to try to tunnel through the east side of the camp as well as the west, but that depended on whether or not her engineers could get the two broken machines running again. *I'm* not a massive precog and cannot get instantaneous, reliable information on her movements," he added dryly.

Ia twisted her mouth in a half smile. "Okay, I deserved that one. They'll have made it halfway to the east by the time you can get some troops into position, and nine-tenths to the west. The northern tunnels are doing fine."

Tapping a few controls, she switched the central image from passion moss in bloom to an overlay map of the broad valley in question. Green Army icons and red Salik markers indicated the current known placements for both forces. Programming the map to display an approximation of the sapper forces' works far below the main Salik encampment, she zoomed out the view to show the approximate battle lines for that moment.

"Presuming they can step up the pace and get into range . . . these two lobes, this one, and the north ones. That'll leave Sharriah with three main battlefronts still attached to the south and east. I'd want to cut off this one in the middle as well," Tumseh stated, eyeing it in regret, "but there's no way to do it without compromising the retreat zone for the sappers."

"Just as well; the enemy will need an approach vector from orbit for the evacuation of their surviving forces," Ia stated. "Since my crew destroyed a number of their hidden crèche stations, plus the big push to destroy their main base in the Helix Nebula last year, the Salik are slowly being forced to consider every adult warrior still alive as an asset to be preserved. It'll only get worse by the end of the year."

"Care to share with the rest of the class what you know, General?" Tumseh asked, giving her a sardonic look.

Ia shook her head. "Wish I could, but once I'm gone, you won't be able to rely upon me anyway. You'll have pockets of lingering Salik resistance to stamp out, and all those not-cats to hunt down. They won't be as badly affected by the spores as their creators, but they're still dangerous. Don't leave them for the civilians to handle. You have far more resources and enough firepower for it than they ever will. And Brigadier General . . . your orders are to ship any prisoners off-world by the end of this year . . . and by the start of the new year, your orders are to *kill* all Salik found on this planet, whether or not they surrender. *Kill*, not capture."

"Begging pardon, sir, but that isn't exactly in concordance with Alliance sentientarian regulations. Mind you, I don't think a second Interdicted Zone will work again. I'll put *some* trust in you," he murmured, studying her warily. "I'd do the same anyway about the Salik, kill them if we can't kick them off-world, but . . . kill them even if they surrender?"

She held his gaze levelly. "You do not want to see what will happen if a second landing attempt succeeds on this world. You will not survive it . . . and you have my Prophetic Stamp on that, General. Consider it a strong incentive to round them all up and ship them off-world before New Year's Terran Standard . . . and a standing order, Brigadier."

Unsettled, he looked back at the images she was still monitoring. "I'd think making a big show about killing off the not-cats might help more toward repairing the Army's reputation . . . but I will comply. Thank you, by the way," he added dryly. "I can now see the day when we *will* kick the Salik off Dabin—preferably by New Year's—and that means I can start planning to put my troops to work in rebuilding the war-damaged buildings and infrastructures out there. I'm good at long-range strategic and logistics planning . . . but I suspect you already knew that, didn't you?"

Ia nodded, pleased that he was able to see beyond the immediate applications of her suggestion and the distasteful horror of her order. *He'll do. I cannot be everywhere or do everything, but he'll do in my stead.*

JULY 24, 2498 T.S.

No one but Ia saw the V'Dan ships slipping into insystem space. Certainly not the Salik, not until it was too late. Plenty of people saw the explosions in the local predawn sky, however. Many of them were civilians, not just soldiers. Once again, Ramasa found himself busy at the comm station in the Olympic Ballroom, coordinating a stream of civilian inquiries with V'Dan battle reports being beamed their way

as their interstellar allies smashed through the orbital
blockade.

By Ia's command, the Salik ground troops were permitted
to board their drop ships in an attempt to leave. Any ship that
fired at forces on the ground was ruthlessly shot down, of
course, but the evacuation transports that didn't attack were
permitted to flee. Thankfully by this point, the men and
women of the 1st Division 6th Cordon were willing to follow
her commands even if they didn't understand the point.

The point, cruel in the end as it is, she thought, face tilted
up to the late-afternoon sky, *is to give the Salik hope that
they can regroup elsewhere long enough to recover and
come back. That puts them in clumps that our various allies
will more readily be able to destroy . . . once I convince
them to do it.*

Now, at the end of the long day that saw the Salik being
forced firmly off-world, at a point in time just a few hours
after the last alien transport had hastily departed the system,
Ia lifted a hand to hold her cap in place as the winds stirred
by the thrusters of the descending ships kicked up dust and
stray blades of reddish local grass. The local college, Landing
City University, had given them the use of their athletics fields
for landing sites since the city's spaceport had long since been
abandoned, destroyed in various enemy attacks during the
lengthy blockade. The local ground cover smelled somewhat
like soap when cut, and vaguely like chlorophyll, but it was
the sweet, burned-plexi smell of passion-moss spores that
saturated the artificial wind whipping through the campus.

The LCU marching band had also been brought out for
this moment, and civilians thronged the stands along one
side of the fields, staying at a distance respectful of the huge
orbital shuttles with their silvery ceristeel hulls and red
Imperial logos. Ia and her crew, arrayed in their cleanest,

neatest post-battle uniforms—some in Dress Grays, some in camouflage, whatever was available—stood on the edge of the football field. Behind them, forming a second, double wall of soldierly protection, stood troops from the Army. Over half of them were from Roghetti's Company, who had more than earned this break from ground-based combat.

Between the civilians and the soldiers stood a knot of waiting government officials and a clutch of local reporters, hovercameras busy swooping over the crowds and the heads of the Army and Special Forces arrayed between them and the incoming ships. They did not fly any closer, though. As it was, Ia had placed her soldiers in the front with the order to keep everyone back from the V'Dan vessels. Thruster fields weren't too dangerous at a distance of more than fifteen or so meters, but the orbital shuttles were large and heavy, with a slight chance that one or two might wobble out of formation. Thankfully, they didn't, but it didn't hurt to be prepared.

The moment the great whining rumble of the thrusters shut off, and the wind died down, the bandmaster raised his baton, beginning some triumphant-sounding piece with plenty of brass, wind instruments, and thumping drums. It was a short piece, just long enough to welcome the V'Dan as the ramps descended from the ships. The melody switched to the Imperial Anthem the moment a double line of V'Dan soldiers marched down each ramp, the officers clad in their formal red-and-gold uniforms, and the enlisted soldiers in reddish gold camouflage meant to blend in with the local foliage.

There weren't many of them compared to the Terran presence, just a hundred or so, but it was enough to cause the crowd in the background to erupt into a great cheer. At their head, in a crisply cut coat decorated with extra thread-of-gold, strode the admiral of the large Fleet that had just cracked apart the blockade keeping Dabin from receiving any off-world support. He searched along the line of soldiers, checked the approaching knot of planetary officials, and headed for the same spot as the governor and his aides: the black-clad, medal-draped figure of Ia in her full Dress Blacks, centered in front of her carefully spaced troops.

Ia didn't begrudge them those cheers for their V'Dan saviors. Morale was important for civilians, too. Being *able* to regain interstellar commerce and travel was vitally important to these people. They could use their own weapons against the Salik on the ground as civilian defenders—and many had—but could not attack anything above their skies. Even the men and women in the Army were cheering the arrival of the V'Dan since it was something they, too, hadn't been able to change while stuck on the ground without insystem support.

Stopping a meter from Ia, Admiral Donsuu V'Chech lifted his hand to his brow in a very good approximation of the Terran salute. As the visiting officer of roughly equal rank, it was up to him to salute Ia, the incumbent officer, first. Since she was a Terran, it had been decided long ago by the protocol officers that the Terran salute should be used in such cases. Ia saluted him back while the band brought the V'Dan anthem to an end, then shifted her flattened hand into a fist, thumping it onto her chest in the V'Dan version. He returned her second salute with a smile for the courtesy.

"General Ia. His Eternal Majesty speaks highly of you, and the help you have already given the Empire," the golden-skinned Human stated, his accent faint, but his vocabulary well educated in the trade tongue of the Alliance. He ignored the trio of cameras swirling around them, recording every-thing in three dimensions for broadcast. "I am deeply pleased to see you have helped our shared world with equal diligence during your time here. As sorry as they will be to see you go, it will be our pleasure to host you. I trust you will give the

Imperial Fleet more of the same superlative aid as we transport your soldiers to their next destination?"

Clasping the hand he offered, Ia nodded. "You may assure His Eternal Majesty that I will continue to do my best for the V'Dan people, for they are as dear to me as the people of Dabin, my fellow Terrans, and all Alliance members. Please, let me make you known to the Governor of Dabin, Meioa Cole von Straschen," she introduced, stepping sideways with a slight pivot to begin the local introductions. "Governor, this is Admiral Donsuu V'Chech of the V'Dan Imperial Fleet, head of the forces which have just driven off every Salik starship they can from your skies. Admiral, Governor Cole von Straschen of Joint Colonyworld Dabin."

Letting the governor wring the admiral's hand in enthusiasm as he began a speech for the hovercams, Ia stepped back two paces and gestured for Tumseh to join her. Unsnapping her jacket sleeve, she opened her arm unit and tapped in a few commands. Under the cover of the more formal greetings going on, she addressed the green-clad man at her side, keeping her voice low.

"Brigadier General Michel Tumseh, at this moment in time, I am formally handing over the full command of the 1st Division 6th Cordon Army and all its subordinate and ancillary ranks into your command, and I am attaching your chain of command to Major General Louise Xenadra. She may reassess and reassign you, but it will be at her discretion from this point forward."

"General, yes, sir," he agreed, saluting her. "I accept full command of the Terran Army's 1st Division 6th Cordon, and will report to Major General Xenadra."

She saluted him back, allowed him a chance to log the changeover on his own arm unit, then extracted a datachip from her unit to hand to him as a more tangible record of the matter.

"Remember to heed the precognitive recommendations I have handed into your care, but take care to craft and carry out such plans as you believe will best serve the remaining war effort here on Dabin. Particularly be mindful of the safety and prosperity of the civilians of Dabin, whom you and your soldiers pledged to guard the moment you put on those uniforms."

"Sir, yes, sir," he confirmed briskly. "The Army will not fail you in our duty, sir."

"Good." Leaning in close, Ia added in a murmur, "You also owe every last Company in the 2nd Battalion, 2nd Brigade *big* for being willing to keep the fight going tonight on the remaining Salik forces stuck planet-side, so that the rest of us could enjoy this party tonight."

Tumseh nodded firmly, grinning. "Sir, yes, sir. I've already started the paperwork for a Battalion-sized barbecue two days from now, when the rest go back to work."

"Good. Speaking of which . . ." Turning back to the admiral and the governor, whose praise was finally winding down to an end, Ia gestured at the college gymnasium in the distance. "Gentlemeioas, I do believe the kindhearted staff and students of the LCU have arranged for a little victory celebration. We still have a lot of fighting left to do in the morning, and for several mornings to come . . . but for tonight, we celebrate the liberation of Joint Colonyworld Dabin."

"Ia'nn sud-dha," Admiral V'Chech agreed in his native tongue . . . and then paused, smiling ruefully at Ia. "As *you* will it, Prophet."

Knowing she had more of that to put up with on the ride out of Dabin, Ia let it pass. She needed people to believe in her only as much as they needed to in order to heed her prophetic directives. The importance lay in the messages she could read in the shifting waters of Time. Turning crisply on her heel, she addressed the assembled troops. "Soldiers! Dismissed!"

A second, broader gesture from her toward the gymnasium broke the rigid At Attention postures of both her crew and the troops of the Army. With a second cheer, the civilians took that as the signal to surge forward and greet all three sets of soldiers with an enthusiasm stirred up by renewed hope. Among them were her first officer's parents, who were already hugging their son, looking strong and handsome in his Dress Grays.

She just had to keep up a polite, friendly, but otherwise neutral personality in front of the Harper clan. They, in turn, simply had to keep their mouths shut on any of their suspicions. Thankfully, the vast majority of probabilities were on her side. They *would* be circumspect . . . at a 98 percent chance.

Then again, this time if the instincts of his parents picked up on any hints of a relationship between the two of them, Ia wouldn't have to worry about anyone analyzing to death any recordings of this night's meeting. This time, chatting with them would be as private as a public celebration could make it, contradictory though that was.

"Ah! Meioa General, sir!"

. . . *Unfortunately, I now have to deal with the Press.* Managing a polite smile, Ia turned to acknowledge the local reporter catching up with her. Denora de Marco and her hovercamera operator hurried up, her own smile broad, polite, and polished, known locally for her occasional piecework for Interstellar News Network and her brave reports from the battle lines, though she wasn't yet a big name off-world. What she wanted to do would *make* de Marco famous, however.

Famous enough, it'll come back around to try to bite me in the asteroid . . . but like so many other things in life, I'll just have to turn it into a useful tool, in the end.

"General Ia, since you now have a few moments, I was wondering if we could get an interview with you?" the brown-haired de Marco asked. "I'd love to do an even longer one, but I was given to understand you'll be departing soon."

"For a longer interview, I'm afraid you'll have to wait a while, but for a brief one right now . . . You will have eleven minutes and thirteen seconds, then I will be needed inside," Ia stated, checking the timestreams and nodding at the reporter's companion. "I'm ready when you and your cameras are, meioas."

The other woman fiddled with her controls, and nodded, flicking her fingers in a brief countdown at de Marco, who smiled brightly and began. "This is Denora de Marco for Interstellar News Network. I'm here on Dabin, the formerly besieged but now liberated Joint Colonyworld, thanks to the combined efforts of the V'Dan Imperial Fleet, which has finally broken the Salik blockade, and the efforts of the Terran Space Force Army here on the ground. With me is the recently promoted four-star General Ia, formerly an officer of the Special Forces, and now attached to the Army. General, it is an honor to have a chance to speak with you."

Ia dipped her head briefly in the direction of the cameras floating over the operator's brown curls. "Meioa de Marco, the honor is mine. I admired your work on the Chansonné scandal last year."

The reporter gave Ia a genuine, warm smile before launching into her first question. "Thank you. General Ia, you've been acknowledged by the government and major figures of the Sh'nai faith as the Prophet of a Thousand Years, one of their most iconic and ancient figureheads," de Marco pointed out. "How do you reconcile your place as a religious figurehead to the V'Dan people with your duties and responsibilities as a major Terran military figure?"

Joy. Well, with the V'Dan here, I should've figured she'd

want to explore that *twenty-eight percent angle first* . . .
"They go hand in hand, meioa. My duty as an officer compels
me to carry out my orders with the least loss of life possible.
I do so by using my precognitive abilities to assess the possible outcomes and their potential risks. The biggest difference between myself and the other generals and analysts in
the Terran military is that I simply see more . . . but they do
generally see quite a lot even without any added abilities."

"A thousand years' worth, or so you say," the reporter
clarified, making her statement a partial question.

"Yes, though technically I see a lot more than just a thousand years. In this case, I foresaw the need to kick the Salik
off Dabin. The Army still has a ways to go before the last of
the enemy has been driven from Dabinian soil," Ia
warned lightly, "but with careful planning and hard work,
we, both the Terrans and the V'Dan, have finally removed
the bulk of the enemy. The majority of the Salik have fled
both the planet and the system, and only a fraction remain.
It's a modest respite since the Salik will still continue to wreak
damage and endanger lives until the last ones are caught or
killed. But the meioas here have earned the right to at least a
little bit of celebrating before they get back to work."

"You say 'they' get back to work. Will you not be staying?" de Marco asked. She likely knew the answer since it
wasn't exactly a secret at Army Headquarters; instead, her
question was for her viewers' benefit. One which Ia patiently
answered, mindful of the press of time and the obligation
all officers were under to make the military look good in
civilian eyes.

"No, meioa, I will not be able to stay. Now that the one
particular spot of difficulty we came here to deal with has
been handled, my crew and I are needed elsewhere. With
Brigadier General Michel Tumseh in charge and the blockade

broken by our V'Dan allies, the Terran Army stationed here on Dabin is quite capable of cleaning up the planet, both of its Salik infestation and of the not-cats which they so rudely dumped on this beautiful world.

"The V'Dan Fleet has agreed to leave several ships behind to keep your system frogtopus-free," she added with a gesture upward, encompassing the slowly darkening sky, "as per their joint military contract with this world. With their arrival and support, both groups have things well covered on the ground and in the sky. Our only regret as your joint protectors is that the heavy press of the war in other star systems forced us to leave the system blockade in place until now."

"General . . . there have been recent, widespread rumors of Feyori involvement in this whole matter. Is that the reason why you came to Dabin?" de Marco asked perceptively.

Ia was very grateful the question had been phrased in a way where she could answer truthfully.

"No, meioa," she said with a slight, quick shake of her head. "I came here to ensure the Salik entrenchment was dug out in time for a majority of them to be chased off-world by the Fleet's arrival. There were too many things that could go wrong, and many which did, requiring me to be present and on hand for numerous quick alterations to the Army's various plans—I should say that *no* plan survives completely intact after engaging an enemy, Meioa de Marco, even one that can be foreseen and planned for as mine usually are," Ia added to stave off the next most probable question. "This is a truism as old as any military system, Human or otherwise. A good military will adapt, and can eventually overcome its obstacles. Even under the most trying of circumstances, as you and your fellow colonists have seen."

Switching gears smoothly, the reporter continued her interrogation. Ia patiently endured it, keeping her expression

polite, her replies vague on the more sensitive details, and
her attention on how everything she said might impact the
timestreams. It was just one more battle, though at least in
this one she didn't have to risk losing an eye.

JULY 25, 2498 T.S.
V'DAN IMPERIAL WARSHIP *T'CHU-CHEN VIZETH*
SIC TRANSIT

"Okay, spill," Christine Benjamin ordered her commanding
officer the moment both women were settled on the lower
of the two bunks in their shared cabin. Settled with cups of
V'Dan-style caf', that was, low in caffeine compared to the
hybrid Terran-V'Dan version but without any of the bitter-
ness associated with the original Terran kind.

"Spill what?" Ia asked. She knew the purpose of this
moment in time, but it did have a lot of possible directions
in which it could go. "Spill my caf'?"

The older woman rolled her eyes and stretched out her
leg, nudging Ia in the thigh with one ship-booted toe. "Spill
your emotions and reactions, woman. I did check you over
briefly after you lost your eye, and when you were past the
initial shock of losing our soldiers, but we weren't exactly
private when it happened. Then you took off and left
me with Harper and the Company. The Feyori Meddling,
the unexpected attack, the loss of your eye, the loss of Private
Benjamin and the rest, followed by more shocks from the
Feyori, finding Mattox and everyone in the Army HQ being
overrun by Meddler influences . . . then having to confront
the Meddlers, followed by confronting Mattox, the inquiry
into your accusations, the expulsion of the Salik from Dabin

and the mopping up that needed to be done . . . need I go on? You've had a very rough two months."

Leaning back against the foot of her chaplain's bunk, Ia sighed and looked up at the underside of her own narrow bed. She had been given the equivalent of a private cabin, albeit one shared with her chaplain, but quarters on board the *T'Chu-chen Vizeth* were tight, carrying as it was a full complement of ground and ship forces, plus the members of her Company. The surviving members, that was. The others in her crew were bunking in rotating sleeping shifts.

She didn't want to talk about it but knew that the Department of Innovations and the Command Staff were expecting her to remain stable, which *required* talking about it . . . *Except there is a loophole in that loop.* "I don't want to talk about it."

Bennie lowered her chin, giving Ia a stern look. "As your psychologist, Ia . . ."

"I am still quite Human, Bennie, and it is a *very* Human reaction to want to dig in one's mental and emotional heels and *not* want to talk about a difficult subject. A whole shipload of difficult subjects," she added sardonically. "A ship that blew up in my face *after* I blew up the real one."

"Mm. Anger," Bennie observed, sipping at her caf'. "I know you already went through the shock phase, and the denial . . . although from what Jesselle says, your denial actually took place before the camp was attacked and routed."

Ia pointed a finger at her friend. "I already did all of that, Bennie. All the way through bargaining and acceptance, too. I may have done it out of order, but it's all done and over with."

"But there's still anger in there," her friend and counselor observed.

That made her roll her eyes. "Of *course* there is. They shouldn't have had to die!"

"Your crew members?" Bennie prodded. "Is that what you're most upset about?"

"*All* of them. Soldiers. Civilians. *All* of them." Ia slashed her free hand outward, indicating the whole universe. Or at least Dabin. "All those lives lost, because Mattox refused to accept any other battle plans than his own, refused to see that he couldn't plan his way out of a paper bag, and refused to accept that his *mind* had been compromised. Ginger and Teshwun, for screwing everything up. For hiding the truth of Time itself from me—*me*—and warping Mattox so that he caused the deaths of all those lives. For *their* causing the loss of all those lives."

Bennie accepted that, mulling it over in silence for a bit. After half a minute, she asked shrewdly, "What about your eye?"

"Immaterial." Ia didn't pretend this time not to know where the conversation was going. "Whether I had lost it until it could be vat-grown and replaced on this ship or could—and did—replace it myself, my own suffering is immaterial. In fact, I'm more upset I don't know how to fix everyone *else's* injuries in a similar, Feyori-based way."

"So why not learn?" the redhead offered, tipping up her mug to drain it. She caught Ia's level stare when she lowered the emptied cup. "Ah, right. Your lack of *time* for such things."

"I still have far too many prophecies to readjust thanks to the mess on Dabin. Enough that it'll take me three solid months to get caught up on fixing everything so that the final outcome is still the same, but that doesn't include all the stuff I'll actually have to do over the next three months. And don't say I'll have the time for it here on this ship. This is my opportunity to give the V'Dan the majority of my prophecies for *them*, many of which will also have to be adjusted. What happened on Dabin, all the rifts and ripples and rumplings in the fabric of the timestreams, those won't stay on Dabin alone. I can make allowances for all those hardships, but it still takes time to fix everything.

"Thankfully, since we're almost done, I'll have eighteen minutes to compose a few of them before we'll both have to change into Dress Grays for our first formal dinner in the V'Dan version of an officers' mess," she added.

"Almost done? What makes you think we're 'almost done,' here?" Bennie challenged her, raising one auburn brow.

"Because it's going to conclude with the same answer I've given myself since I turned fifteen, the same answer I've always given you. If it's something I cannot change—and I cannot change any of what happened—then I am not going to burden my soul with worrying over it, regretting it, or even thinking about it," Ia stated. "Which means not *talking* about it. Talking just gets me angry that it happened in the first place, and gets me mad that I cannot do anything to change it anymore. Neither of which are productive emotions. In fact, they're big time-wasters, and Time is a very precious commodity."

She drained her own cup and uncurled from the older woman's bunk. Holding out her hand, she accepted the other mug from her chaplain and carried them to the caf' dispenser in the corner, where the machinery would clean and store the mugs for later use.

"It's not a healthy thing to do," Bennie warned her. "Repressing and denying your emotions, I mean."

"No, but as I said, it's a very *Human* way of dealing with something I cannot change. At least, not any more than I've already tried."

Technically, her words weren't entirely true. Technically, she could order a couple Feyori to go back in time to try to stop her younger self from damaging the timelines, from accidentally exposing and being counterfactioned by

Miklinn, so on and so forth. But that way meant demanding the sacrifice of at least one of the Feyori's lives. Killing Teshwun *had* been a case of her being a vindictive, territorial bitch, and she still could and would kill any that stepped out of line by trying to counterfaction her efforts, but the rest of them didn't deserve to die simply because she ordered them to die. The rest had every right to live . . . and as she *could* still set things up for the salvation of the galaxy, that drastic an option just wasn't an option.

But she couldn't *explain* that to Bennie. Not when this whole conversation was going into her personnel file as an official counseling-session report.

Reaching into her storage locker, she pulled out one of her new workpads and a handful of datachips, both crafted in the V'Dan style. Information-storage technology changed from decade to decade in the modern era, but these were prophecies for the very near future. They didn't need to be transcribed onto long-lasting, acid-free, archive-quality paper. They just needed to be transcribed into current V'Dan technology for the ease of their recipients.

JULY 27, 2498 T.S.

"Congratulations on your promotion, General Ia," Emperor Ki'en-qua allowed, dipping his head slightly in acknowledgment of the new rank. "I see you have finally gained the *practical* authority you need."

There was an eight-second lag delay, four seconds coming and going, but only because the *T'Chu-chen Vizeth* was now quite far from the V'Dan homeworld. Unlike her previous ship, this vessel was a capital ship, more than large enough to carry its own dedicated, vacuum-sealed hyperrelay hub deep within the mass of the ship, permitting them a direct link to the Imperial Palace.

"Thank you, Eternity," Ia returned politely, using the proper honorific for the V'Dan Emperor. She bowed her head a little deeper in return, keeping her eyes on the red-clad figure on the other side of the commscreen. "I'll confess that it wasn't a very high probability on my list. At most, I had figured to earn two stars' worth by the end of the Second Salik War, and most probably less than that. I could have done my job well enough under those conditions, but I am grateful for the rank I have been given—I am the Prophet, yes, but even I can be blindsided by a rare possibility. Thankfully, a positive one this time."

"Indeed. A reminder that you are still mostly Human, and thus liable to fail . . . which most of the Sh'nai faith has overlooked even though it's written at least three times in the High Book," Ki'en-qua allowed.

Ia nodded. "The good news is that I have been instructed by Admiral-General Christine Myang, with the Terran Premiere's permission, to lend my full advice to the V'Dan High Command and the Imperial Forces, both the Fleet and the Army. Contingent that I send a copy of everything I give to your people to the Terrans as well. That's also the bad news," she added with a touch of regret. "The semigood news buried in the bad news is that they mostly want that information for archival and post-battle-analysis purposes. The uncomfortable-for-me news is that they want to make sure I'm not giving your people *more* information than I'm giving the Terrans."

The Shield of Thirty-Seven Worlds was not a stupid man. He shook his head wryly. "The only reason why you'd have to give us more information on what to do is if we were doing so poorly that we *needed* that information—and I'll trust you to keep *that* quote to yourself, General. It was not said as an insult on the ineffectiveness of the Terran military, never mind my own. Indeed, the results you engineered on Dabin, giving your lowest organizational levels free rein to do as *they* saw fit, speaks volumes to the contrary."

"I would not be so tactless if I could help it, Emperor Ki'en-qua," Ia replied smoothly. Her one act of tactlessness, where Miklinn had been concerned, was more than enough warning against fumbling a second time.

"One would hope. As for your orders, we would not object to some of our due prophecies being shared with our Terran kin," Ki'en-qua added, using the plural "we" that meant he spoke for his High Command as well as himself and his Empire. "But I must insist as the Emperor that all precognitive missives that deal with *sensitive* V'Dan information be restricted to V'Dan eyes only. We may both be Human Empires, but we are not the same."

"I regret I do not have the authority to guarantee such an arrangement, though I of course would honor it in a heartbeat if my orders allowed," she returned politely, if dryly. "But if Your Eternal Majesty would care to bend your hyperrelays into diplomatic channels, and confer with the Terran Premiere about your perfectly valid concerns, then perhaps the Commander in Chief of the Terran Space Force would allow what the Admiral-General has not. Until such time, I'm afraid my orders must stand as they have been given to me, and I will carry them out as instructed. I am merely a soldier, not a seasoned diplomat."

Unspoken was the understanding that a copy of this conversation was already being recorded for the Terran military to peruse. Ki'en-qua didn't blame her for it, thankfully. He was a rare leader, one who honestly cared for the betterment of his citizens, yet one who understood the need for political maneuverings and certain expediencies. Ia had long ago felt a deep gratitude that she wouldn't have to work around him and the V'Dan government he presided over to get her many tasks done within his jurisdiction. That was a trouble for a different generation to deal with. As it was, she still had to work around the demands of Terran politics, Dlmvlan, K'Kattan . . .

"The Terrans may not know yet what a rare gem they have in you, meioa, though I suspect your Admiral-General has finally begun to notice a glimmer or two of it," the V'Dan Emperor stated. "If I could, I would give you the rank of a Grand General in my own High Command. That is, presuming you could manage to direct the V'Dan battlegrounds as well as you have directed the Terran ones."

This was the single most important moment in her conversation with him, though the rest of it was important enough to tread carefully. She had to appear as though she were still firmly collared by the Terran leash despite her huge jump in rank and authority. A quick check of the timestreams showed her an even, calm delivery would spark the right idea in his mind.

"If I had that kind of permission from my superiors, I gladly would, Eternity, and I would strive my best not to abuse such faith and trust. I would give an equal level of precognitive service to each of the other members of the Alliance as well," she added carefully, with neither too much nor too little emphasis on her words. "I may have *carte blanche* regarding my work within the Terran military, but only within it, and there are limits."

"I'll keep that in mind," he returned dryly.

Ia didn't want to think about how well things were going. Such hubris would lead to more carelessness on her part. She still had the horror of losing a certain Private N'Keth to

Friendly Fire on her mind despite the intervening time, and the trouble it had taken to patch that break in the temporal universe of What Should Have Happened. She had also needed to take her chief medical officer aside and apologize in private for ignoring Jesselle's advice on what was wrong on Dabin. Ki'en-qua continued, recapturing her attention.

"As it is, what you can share is already far more than we would have without your very timely aid, General," the Emperor of V'Dan was saying. "We are grateful as a nation that you are so willing to share them with non-Terrans."

"The abilities I possess as the Prophet of a Thousand Years should serve the needs of the many. Not just the needs of a few, however important they may be," she stated aloud. "If you can convince my superiors, I will serve the needs of other governments such as your own as surely as I serve the needs of mine. Our fates are all bound together in this particular fight; we should help each other as much as possible. Just as the fate of the people of Dabin required efforts from both the Terrans and the timely assistance of the V'Dan to thwart our common foe, it will continue to require all our efforts until the threat is gone. But I will also not go against the expressed orders of my superiors, the Admiral-General and the Premiere of the Terran United Planets Council."

Emperor Ki'en-qua dipped his head slightly. "We will take your words and thoughts under advisement, General Ia," he replied diplomatically. "In the meantime, I have advised Admiral V'Chech to give you and your soldiers all the assistance they reasonably may. I understand you will be in transit for another seven days before reaching your destination. It is the honor of V'Dan to carry the Prophet of a Thousand Years and the savior of our Joint Colonyworld of Dabin to her next destination. You may ask him for anything reasonable that you or your crew may require."

That last was stated as a reminder that Dabin was one of the many worlds the Empire shielded jointly with the Terrans, but one still under the V'Dan Imperial Shield. Bowing in her seat, Ia gave the only reply she could. "It is my honor to serve and to save, Eternity. I can do no less. My Company and I have been received with full honor and welcoming arms aboard the admiral's ship. He and his crew are a credit to your Empire."

"Then I am well pleased. *V'Daannia'nn sud-dha.*" A gesture ended the transmission on his side.

"As Fate wills it," Ia murmured in Terranglo, ending it on her side. The V'Dan controls for the comm station in the conference room she had been allowed to use weren't configured like Terran ones, but it didn't take her too much effort to figure out how to ship a copy of her interview with the Emperor to the Terran Command Staff before closing the hyperrelay channel.

All this secrecy, with each government fighting to prevent the others from knowing things that honestly wouldn't harm their standing . . . It'll be a relief to be slotted into the command structure for most of the others so I can dispense with disclosure this and discretion that. In the meantime, all I can do is "hurry up and wait." O, the joys of military life.

Without the elevation to General, I'd be forced to continue giving covert assistance to the other governments. But now . . . oh, Christine, you do not know how much easier you have made my job. You know I'll continue to give covert assistance, but if the Emperor of V'Dan can pull enough diplomatic strings, the moment I can assist the others openly, this war will leap *toward victory, not just crawl . . .*

. . . Oh God. She closed her eyes. Her mind leaped from Christine Myang to Christine Benjamin to Philadelphia

Benjamin. To the others lost on Dabin. *Inyul Svarson, Helen Nabouleh . . . Helenne Franke. I liked Nabouleh. Damn fine pilot, and a damn fine cook, just like Philly . . . She made those little bite-sized puff-pastry things with the spices and the cheese . . .*

Helenne Franke did knitting in her spare time. She was making all the officers and noncoms gloves for Chanukah gifts. I was planning on wearing mine, too. And Inyul Svarson . . . he kept threatening to turn off the heat in one of the cargo bays and open up a water pipe to make a skating rink for some winter-style recreation, or maybe reconfigure a misting machine to create a snowfield . . .

Good people, who didn't have to die. Who should not have died . . . but did. She could still hear Mishka in her head, pointing out that the "patient" of the Army Brigade was sick with some internal disease, and herself blithely brushing off the idea that Mattox wouldn't cooperate. *It's my fault. My arrogance. My blind faith.*

I am an officer. I know that soldiers die. Hellfire, I know that civilians die! And I know, I know, that no matter how carefully I husband my resources, how carefully I plot and plan and contrive . . . some will die.

But it still hurts.

This was the corollary to her plans to save the galaxy. The hellfire and the hardship and the damnation of it. No matter what she did, people were going to die. More people if she *didn't* act than if she did, a lot more people. But even if the mess on Dabin hadn't happened, a lot of people, good sentients both Human and otherwise, were still going to die. Tears stung at her eyes.

A *lot* of people.

Wiping at her eyes, she let her head droop against the edge of the padded backrest. But only for a few moments. A leftenant of the V'Dan Fleet was on his way to ask for advice from the Prophet. Not for himself, but for his son, to ensure his son lived a good and long life. Ia didn't dare refuse. For the entire time that she was on board the *T'Chu-chen Vizeth*, she had to present herself as the Prophet of a Thousand Years as well as a Terran officer, a woman whose coming was long predicted by the holy writings of the Sh'nai, the premier faith of V'Dan. The Prophet was supposed to be a beacon of strength and stability in a galaxy where the tides of war threatened to tear away the foundations of civilized life.

She had to be strong because morale was just as important to their Human cousins of the First Empire as it was to her fellow Terrans of the Second; what she had done so far and what she did on board this ship for the next seven days would be discussed all across the Imperial Fleet within a month. It was not an easy balance, because she had to be strong and persuasive, but not aggressive or forceful. She had to be confident and compassionate even when she needed to improvise on the fly. And she didn't dare show any signs of weakness at this juncture. Not when nearly every moment she spent on board in transit was being recorded by the V'Dan ship's internal sensors.

Taking a deep breath, she straightened in her seat, surreptitiously rubbed off one last tear, and squared her shoulders. The V'Dan analysts might see her momentary slouch in the recordings, her brief show of vulnerability . . . but they would not discuss it openly. The crew members on this ship would be left with the memory of a competent Terran officer as well as a living religious figure. Human, with a few flaws and weaknesses, but otherwise strong.

On such tiny things are great mountains built; great faith raised from a seemingly infinitesimal piece of sand, built grain by grain through hard labor, however tedious at times, she reminded herself. Then smiled wryly, forcing herself to cheer up somehow. *Okay, I did want the adulation of the crowds in a great arena, listening to me perform my own songs, cheering me on as I sang. Even if I got the arenas of the battlefield and songs made of prophecy and projectile trajectories, instead of the performance kind, I'm sure it still counts.*

At least Myang has given me permission to conduct the rest of my movements as I see fit in ongoing carte blanche. *Even if I have to report in to her on a regular basis about it.* Tugging her jacket straight, she rose and crossed to the door, touching the controls that slid the panel out of the way.

"Leftenant Shung'ha, please come in," she stated, even as the man on the other side lifted his hand to the control panel to announce his arrival. "I know why you are here, and I am willing to give you a few words of temporal advice."

He blinked at her in surprise, then bowed deeply. "Anything at all from the lips of the Prophet would be a deep blessing."

She stifled a humorless laugh, confining it to a slight twist of her lips. "I'll try to make it a good one, but I can only See; I cannot change what may or may not be. It will be up to your child to live his own life for himself, by himself. Not even a beloved parent can lead it for him, never mind me. Your son is an individual with all the free will implied, and you can only guide him by suggesting and encouraging, not by dragging or demanding. You must keep that in mind as he grows, the same as for your daughter, who will come along in four more years."

"Of course." He stepped inside, giving Ia the room to shut the door in his wake. "And thank you for letting me know I'll have a girl . . . but I'd still like to know, so I can hopefully help guide him. Both of them."

"Of course. Please, have a seat."

AUTHOR'S NOTE

Originally, this was planned to be a four-book series. However, despite being carefully trimmed down, the original manuscript for the fourth novel ended up being too big. Rather than butcher it or publish a book too large and ungainly to hold, the publisher and I have chosen to split it into two books: *Hardship* and *Damnation* (the latter being the original title for the fourth book in the series).

Because of time constraints, I did not rework the ending of this section of the original story nor the start of the next section so that they could stand more on their own—technically this entire series has been written as one story, though the previous three were written to be a little bit more independent than flat-out continuous. With *Hardship* and *Damnation*, this intentional continuity is even more apparent: the story literally flows from one chapter to the next, one book straight to the next. The story has been split at the junction between its two main story arcs, so thankfully this book does have some sense of closure and the next section has its own sense of beginning.

When I posted the news of the manuscript split online,

most of my readers stated their open acceptance of the plan to produce five books in this series, not just four. For those of you who might be less pleased, I extend my apologies. My publisher, editor, and I all simply want to bring you the best story we can produce.

Thank you for your patience in waiting for the second half to reach you, and thank you for your understanding.

Jean

TURN THE PAGE FOR A SPECIAL PREVIEW
OF THE CONCLUSION OF THE EPIC SERIES:

THEIRS NOT TO REASON WHY

DAMNATION

BY JEAN JOHNSON

AVAILABLE IN DECEMBER 2014 FROM ACE BOOKS!

What did it feel like to step for the first time onto the Damnation, *back in August of '98? That's an unfair question—unfair to you, I mean. I "first stepped" onto the* Damnation *when I was fifteen. I knew every pipeline, every cabin, every cannon and every corridor on her before I was old enough to legally drive. And I knew the* Hellfire *just as well, and just as early on, long before my military career began. I have known every single ship I ever boarded long before I touched foot to deck-plate, just as I have known nearly every single person I have ever worked with in advance of that first day, Harper excepted.*

But I will admit I did enjoy that new-ship smell. You don't get that many smells in the timestreams, oddly enough, unless it's temporally important somehow. It almost never is, though. As for the Damnation *itself . . . it was longer, better laid out, and equipped with certain amenities that some would call luxuries, but which have kept my crew sane. It's hard to relax when you fly from one battle to the next with rarely a pause for anything else.*

Beyond that . . . it's just like being back on board the Hellfire. *This ship is our home. In a way, it always has been. In a way, it always will be.*

~Ia

AUGUST 14, 2498 T.S.
TUPSF *LEO MAJOR*
SCADIA, AQAT-15 SYSTEM

The *Leo Major* did not smell like the *Damnation*. Where Ia's ship still smelled of fresh paint, carpeting, newly installed aquaponics, and various kinds of plexi, this larger but heavily battered starship smelled of internal fires, sweat, and dried blood. It also bore the odd odor of hard vacuum, not quite metallic and not quite like dust, the smell of cold frost mingled with the scents of chilled solder and other sealants.

From the swirled bits of debris on the deckplates, they might have gotten the hangar bay functionally airtight, but it was clear there had been far more important repairs on their mind than merely sweeping up. The *Leo Major* wasn't ready even for insystem maneuvers, or those bits of metal and plexi would have been vacuumed up by now, for fear of their being turned into lethal projectiles during a sudden vector change. The civilian spacedock orbiting the third planet from the local sun wasn't quite prepared to service a ship of the *Leo*'s size, but they were doing their best. With the bay sealed and capable of accepting larger deliveries, the work could go a lot faster now.

Saluting the bandaged ensign who had granted her permission to board, Ia waved off the young man's offer to guide her with a murmured, "No need to bother, Ensign; I already know the way. Please fetch a three-ton hoversled for Private Runde, and prepare to board live cargo for the life-support bays."

"Uhh . . . aye aye, sir," the ensign stammered, eyeing Ia as she headed into the damaged ship.

She did know the way, though she had never stepped foot aboard a battlecruiser of the Talon Class before. Three levels up to Deck 25, five cross-corridors aft to Lima, and one side trip toward the port brought her to the boardroom for the Marines Company stationed aboard. Here, the visible damage to the ship was considerably less, though the damage to the brown-clad men and women inside was quite evident.

One of the women, sporting a blue regen pack strapped over one ear, caught the movement of Ia's approach out of the corner of her eye. She turned to see who had entered, caught sight of Ia's Dress Blacks with its two-tone stripes of green and gray, the four stars pinned to her collar points and shoulder boards, and stiffened. "General on Deck!"

"At Ease, meioas," Ia quickly ordered, since there was more than one soldier with an injured arm in the room. "I'm not here for your salutes. You earned my respect when you donned the Brown of the Marines, and earned it again with how well you fought today."

Some of them relaxed at her speech. Others stood a little taller with the pride her words invoked. Most of them parted to either side a little, opening up an aisle between her and their current commander. Standing in front of the officer's desk, on the dais in front of the sloped tiers of seats, was a man she had not seen in over eight years. He stared at her, squinted . . . and then sagged back against the table, resting his hips against the edge.

"Well, double-dip me," Brad Arstoll muttered slowly, staring at Ia as she closed the distance between them. "It *is* you! I'd heard some wild-asteroid tales about someone with your name pulling all sorts of *shova* out there, but . . . it really *is* you, isn't it? And a *shakking* general—look at you!"

Ia gave him a half smile and spread her hands slightly. "In

the four-star flesh. I'm here on the *Leo* for two reasons. Three, if you count the shakedown flight out here to help you and the Scadian Army fight off the Salik invaders earlier today."

"Well, we appreciated that," he agreed.

"No thanks are needed. First off," she stated, digging a hand into her Dress Black jacket, pulling out a small black box, "I am authorized by the DoI to confirm your field promotion, *Captain* Brad Arstoll. Effective immediately, you are now officially in charge of D Company, 3rd Legion, and not just the Acting Captain for D Company, 3rd Legion, 3rd Battalion, 4th Brigade, 4th Division, 2nd Cordon Marine Corps. This box holds a data file with the pertinent DoI paperwork . . . plus your silver tracks, of course. You've earned them."

"Thank you, sir," Arstoll murmured, accepting the package. "I wish I hadn't."

"I know," Ia murmured back, knowing he meant he wished he hadn't earned it at the expense of the loss of his CO. "Captain Ling-Bradley was a good leader. But so are you." She tapped the box now in his hand. "There's a second datachip in here with a few precognitive directives you might find useful. Beyond that, I know the Corps trained you well. You have my confidence, and that of the Command Staff."

"Huh," he grunted, a humorless laugh. "Of *course* they'd be confident. The Prophet of a Thousand Years told them so. If this is just a favor to an old Basic Squadmate . . ."

"You've *earned* it, so step up to the job and suffer, soldier," Ia corrected him firmly, pushing the box against his chest. He winced a little; his ribs were taped, waiting for the bone-set serum to finish healing the fractures earned in combat. She didn't push hard, though, and removed her hand once he got the point. "Second . . . I lost five good men and women on Dabin. Lives I shouldn't have had to lose," Ia admitted, jaw tightening for a moment. "I may be a massive precog, but I can't control everything. Because of it, I need replacements. I have two already in transit to meet up with my ship in the Tilfa System, but I'm here for the other three.

"If you don't mind, I'd like to take one of your Marines," she added, glancing over her shoulder at the men and women listening with various levels of interest and boredom as the two of them had caught up with old news. Her words piqued interest even in the most bored of the soldiers. "The last two I need are serving in the Scadian Army in the Orbital Fleet. I convinced the Admiral-General to help with some pre-maneuverings on getting them transferred, so I have a writ from the Scadian military leadership allowing me to recruit whoever I like. I'll still have to do a little diplomatic dancing once I get down to the surface, but it'll be worth it."

"*Shakk . . .* I wonder what strings you had to pull to get *that* done," Arstoll muttered, eyeing her. "These colonists are proud as hell about serving their planet. They wouldn't even have accepted *our* help if they'd had enough ships to cover all vectors. They don't lack the fighting skill or the tactical smarts, and they don't lack any bravery; they just lack the equipment to get the job done."

"I know. That's why I need two of them. They're the best shot I have at filling the gaping holes the Salik blew in the best crew of the Space Force. As for the Marine . . . I'll need your Private Second Class Julia Garcia."

"*Garcia?*" Arstoll exclaimed, eyes wide with disbelief. Other voices joined him in their confusion.

"Wrong-Way Garcia?"

"*That* piece of *skut*?"

"Sir, if you think *Garcia* is going to . . . er . . ." The speaker, the woman with the missing ear, trailed off as Ia turned to face Arstoll's soldiers. Her hard stare silenced all of them.

"Private Garcia," Ia enunciated carefully, with just enough

volume to fill the boardroom as she shifted her gaze from face to face, "is a far better soldier, and a far better Marine, than all of you combined. In my hands, within one year, she will be the hero of a hundred fights and the savior of more than a million lives . . . and that is *not* hyperbole, meioas. I have foreseen it—speaking of which," she added, lightening her tone as she shifted her gaze to one of the taller, redheaded men. "Private McCraery, remember to hit the deck flat out instead of just duck on the sixteenth of September, at about two o'clock local. You'll know when. I'd rather you didn't get your head blown off because you overestimated the height of the incoming attack. Captain Arstoll will still need you afterward, so keep yourself alive."

"Uh . . . yes, sir," he agreed hesitantly.

"Private Sangwan, since you were trying to be so *generous* with praise for Private Garcia," Ia added, turning back to the woman with the regenerating ear, "you can go help her pack her things. We leave in thirty-three minutes from Docking Bay B. Dismissed. Corporal Vance, you were about to ask your CO for a priority list of mechsuit repairs, on behalf of the *Leo Major*'s manufactory bays. You will need A through C Squad functional in the 1st Platoon, followed by B through E in the 2nd. The rest in those two Platoons have minor repairs they can manage on their own. The 3rd and the 4th Platoons will just have to wait their turn on the things they cannot fix themselves—Private Sangwan, you have been *dismissed*."

"Beg pardon, sir?" she asked, glancing between Ia and Arstoll, then at Ia's green-and-gray stripes . . . which were on the sleeves and pant legs of an otherwise all-black uniform. "Aren't you like Special Forces, or Army, or something?"

Ia pointed at the stars on her shoulder board, speaking slowly and clearly. "I am Command Staff, soldier. *Everybody* in the Space Force is under my chain of command, save only for my peers on the Staff, the Admiral-General, Secondaire, and Premiere of the Council. You have your orders. Dismissed."

"Sir, yes, sir," she muttered, face flushed with embarrassment. Turning crisply, Sangwan headed for the doors out of the Company boardroom.

"Captain Arstoll, when you have a few minutes later on today, please remind your troops how the Space Force chain of command works," Ia stated dryly, watching the other woman retreat.

"Sir, yes, sir," he agreed, giving the departing, flinching Sangwan a hard look. "I'll have her checked for a lingering concussion, too. I *thought* my Marines could count four stars on their own."

A few of the others carefully looked anywhere but at their CO and the visiting, white-haired brass in front of him.

Nodding, Ia closed her eyes for a moment, focusing, then opened them. "Sergeant Yangley, the Navy order forms for what you need to requisition materials for the life-support bays are now appearing on your workstation screens back in the clerk's office. I've already filled in the authorization codes for everything but the fish stock. Scadia doesn't have enough of the right kind of fish just yet for your shipboard aquaculture needs.

"Being aware of that, I have brought over a tank of tilapia from the *Damnation*, along with enough feed to last them until you get the cycle balanced in the second bay and it becomes self-sufficient. Private Runde will already be loading them onto the hoversled fetched for her from the ensign on duty. Make sure to sign for them. Get to it."

"General, yes, sir," the sergeant replied crisply, turning to leave on his appointed task.

"Good meioa. The rest of you already know what you need to do. Since I am aware of those needs, and that when you put your minds to it, you are a competent crew, you don't have to ask your captain anything right now; you have *my* permission for the tasks at hand. Go do them," Ia directed the men and women before her. "That means *dismissed*."

They scattered. When the last of them had left the room, Ia moved over to lean back against the table next to her old Basic Training Squadmate. It felt good to slouch a little, good to rest for a moment.

"Rank hath its privileges," she murmured, glancing at him. "I hope you don't mind me sending them off like that, but they honestly can handle everything, and this is literally the only time off I'll have from my duties for months to come, waiting for Garcia to pack. It's not much of a Leave, but I'll take whatever I can get. So . . . How are you doing, Brad? I mean, *really* doing?"

Brad shook his head. "Between you, me, and the bulkheads?" he asked in a bare murmur, not nearly as sure as she was that there weren't any listeners still nearby. "Like fresh, steaming shit. I had the Captain on the commscreen when the hull breach hit our docking bay. I *saw* him get sucked outside. He was not in a pressure-suit. This is *not* how I wanted my next command."

Ia clasped his shoulder, giving him a brief moment of comfort. "I know. I wish I could've helped prevent it . . . and I know you'll hate me for saying this, but . . . you're going to be the right person in the right place at the right time because of this. Not just today, but multiple times in the next few years. The universe needs Captain Brad Arstoll to take full command of D Company. Do good things with it. Save lots of lives. Make as good a career for yourself and the meioas under you as you can."

"How do you live with yourself?" Arstoll asked her, frowning at his former Squadmate. "Seeing what you do. Knowing what you do. *Doing* what you do, and *not* doing. If even half the rumors running around the Space Force in the last few weeks are true . . . how is it that you've stayed *sane*?"

"I have too much work to do to go mad and not enough time to dwell on my mistakes. Or to keep track of old comrades, other than snatches here and there. You ever heard what happened to Sung, and Crosp, and the others from Basic?" Ia asked. "Spyder's with me, and Sergeant Tae's the uncle of my first officer, of all things, but I've been too busy with other concerns to check on the rest."

"Uhh . . . Crosp got called back home to take up the reins of the family business. That was before the war started," Brad dredged up out of his memory. "Sung . . . hell if I know. The one thing I knew, she was being shipped off from Basic to stand guard at some embassy among the Gatsugi. She's probably still doing that. Sergeant Linley always praised her hand-to-hand and her observational skills, said she'd be great for guard work. Oh, and ZeeZee made it to Sergeant First Class last year. Wait, you said Spyder's with you?"

Ia nodded. "Lieutenant Second Class—Field Honor, like you and me—and he's in charge of my 2nd Platoon, plus serves as the tactical coordinator for all mass troop movements. That got put to the test on Dabin just recently, which is why I need replacements. He does say 'hi,' by the way. Sorry, I almost forgot to mention that. I've had a lot on my mind lately."

"I can only imagine what you have to keep track of. Can you, ah . . . you know, see them right now?" Brad asked her. "I mean, see the others in our old Squad since you say you've got a few minutes?"

Ia lifted her brows at the suggestion, then shrugged. "I suppose I can check."

Closing her eyes, she flipped herself onto the timeplains and searched. It didn't take long to find the old threads from her Basic days, nor to follow them down through to the current day. Sobered, she opened her eyes again.

"I'm sorry to report that Sung died during the initial invasion of the Gatsugi homeworld. She was taken out while defending the Terran Embassy from a clutch of Salik robots," Ia stated quietly. "She took more than a few with her, but they still took her out."

"Damn," Arstoll whispered, hanging his head. "I liked her."

Another brief glimpse—since she had the time to spare for it—gave Ia another view on their old Squadmates. "I can see ZeeZee's still a Sergeant First Class. He'll live for at least three more years, but I cannot guarantee beyond that point. The second war front will evoke too many shifting possibilities for his sector of space—if he goes, it won't be by war, but by little butterfly-wing effects. Crosp . . . has two kids, twins, and looks like he acquired a thriving munitions business with military contracts, so he's still supporting the war effort in his own way.

"The rest are . . . still enlisted in the Corps in various duty posts around the war front, except for Kumanei. She opted for pilot training in the Navy, and is flying drop ships as a Chief Yeoman out of . . . Battle Platform *Anna Yesarova*," Ia concluded, double-checking the name. "I can't tell you where, though; that's classified above your pay grade."

"What's this second war front you mentioned?" Arstoll asked, distracting himself from the grim news of Sung's death.

"The Greys are coming back. Don't share it with your troops just yet," Ia added, ignoring his sharp, worried look. "They don't need to fret themselves to death over it."

"*Shakk* . . . Ia, *can* anything be done against them?" he asked. "I don't think our tech's progressed nearly enough to even sneeze on them, but . . . well, we beat them back with psis last time, so we do have enough of 'em this time, right?"

She shook her head. "They're a dying race, and they're growing more and more desperate. It's even odds they'll get their hands on the Salik anti-psi machinery, and if they do, it'll be a very hard-fought war. But we *will* stop them.

"I have foreseen it."